THE WINDER

THE
WINDER

JOHN HUNTER

Matador
9 Priory Business Park,
Wistow Road, Kibworth Beauchamp,
Leicestershire. LE8 0RX
Tel: 0116 279 2299
Email: books@troubador.co.uk
Web: www.troubador.co.uk/matador
Twitter: @matadorbooks

ISBN 978 1800460 584

British Library Cataloguing in Publication Data.
A catalogue record for this book is available from the British Library.

Printed and bound in Great Britain by 4edge Limited
Typeset in 11pt Adobe Garamond Pro by Troubador Publishing Ltd, Leicester, UK

Matador is an imprint of Troubador Publishing Ltd

In fond memory of Lyra McKee (1990–2019) for her enthusiasm and support in what I was trying to achieve

CHAPTER 1

Jacko stood glumly at the side of a field while a mechanical excavator stripped away the turf and weeds between two carefully positioned lines of red marker poles. He knew there'd be nothing there. Murderers didn't bury their victims in open spaces, even if they were in a hurry. Next to the hedge there wasn't much in the way of concealment either. Still, it had to be investigated. The police officer in charge knew they'd find nothing too but had to go through the motions, seeing as a statement had landed on his plate. The witness had told the desk sergeant that he'd seen a body being buried in that very spot, he couldn't remember quite when of course. Probably about twenty years ago. He didn't know who it was either. Very helpful. They were always the same, these walk-ins, they alleged some murder had happened years ago, but there was never a missing person to go with it. Not that the witness was a liar or anything, he obviously believed what he was saying, but there had be some other explanation. Jacko had worked on several of them, just like this one. It wasn't a matter of finding a body, more like showing there wasn't one there in the first place.

The machine bucket slid under the topsoil exposing a smooth, almost sensuous red surface, nothing whatsoever indicating the ground had been disturbed since the last Ice Age. Another no brainer, another wild goose chase, another allegation refuted. Having waved the driver to stop he walked across to report back to the officer in the unmarked police vehicle.

'Nothing, Dunc. It's home time. I'll write the usual statement and email it over. You'll need some scene photos for the record.'

Detective Sergeant Duncan MacBrayne was enjoying a cushy number sitting in his car talking into his mobile. He switched it off having made some hasty farewell comments in a soft tone that suggested he'd not been talking to either his boss or his bank manager, and wound down the window. 'Well, we had to make sure,' he said, looking out rather sheepishly, and then shouted across to the photographer who was also recumbent in a small white van marked 'CRIME SCENE SUPPORT' parked nearby.

Jacko climbed into MacBrayne's passenger seat, slightly out of breath through being a little overweight, and gratefully accepted a cup of coffee from a flask. It was sunny outside, but not warm. Standing about in the cold, either waiting for someone to arrive, waiting for something to finish, or waiting for something to happen was the essence of scene of crime work as far as he could tell. He'd come to expect it. The hot coffee slid down inside. He shut his eyes as its warmth did its work and he could have happily fallen asleep with the sun filtering through the windscreen, the gentle hissing of MacBrayne's car heating system and the barely audible music playing through the radio. All he needed was a ginger biscuit to dunk in the coffee.

'Any other police jobs afoot?' MacBrayne asked, looking across from writing down some notes.

Jacko stretched as well as he could in the confines of the passenger seat and stared blankly at the dashboard. 'A couple of searches for Thames Valley – both lost causes like this one. Otherwise just civilian jobs. Usual stuff, council advice, assessing the archaeology ahead of housing developments, planning enquiries. Not very exciting.' He looked mindlessly out of the window as he watched the scene photographer climb up a pair of step ladders, take a shot, check the image in the back screen, then move the steps to another position.

'I've been asked to see the coroner tomorrow, though. Not sure why. Seems a bit odd. Something to do with a pensioner found dead up the church tower in Middle Belford. Can't for the life of me see what he wants to talk to me for.'

MacBrayne looked at him suspiciously, 'You sure that's what it's about?'

'That's what I was told on the phone. Some issue, is there?'

MacBrayne's face took on a slightly puzzled expression, 'Better let the coroner tell you. I thought the Middle Belford job had been sorted, but presumably it hasn't. The boss won't like that.'

'Won't like what?'

'DCI Flett's signed it off, so he won't like it if the coroner's cranking it up again, stirring things when he's already put them to bed.'

'Bit of a hot potato is it then?'

'Well it wasn't, but it looks like it might be a warm potato right now. You ever met DCI Flett?' Jacko shook his head. MacBrayne breathed a loud sigh and looked at him with an expression that managed to combine both exasperation and pity. 'Huh. I expect you will soon then.'

* * *

'What? You mean the old man was decapitated?' Jacko said loudly, sitting upright so quickly that the beer slopped out of his glass. 'That part wasn't in the newspaper.' He'd felt uncomfortable even before that snippet of gory news, not relishing this meeting with Her Majesty's Coroner in the first place. They sat opposite each other in the Red Horse, the only surviving hostelry in Middle Belford, now filling up with lunchtime drinkers from the local farms. What was all this cloak and dagger stuff, anyway? More to the point, what did it have to do with him?

'Do please keep your voice down,' this thin-faced, serious-looking man whispered across the table. 'I've formally opened an inquest, but adjourned it for the time being until the specific circumstances of death are clearer.' He glanced nervously out of the window, watching a group of middle-aged cyclists dismounting in the road. With his grubby dark suit which emphasised a bad case of dandruff, greasy black hair and piercing little eyes he looked emphatically out of place in a bar usually frequented by dungaree-clad farm hands. More suited to a dingy office in a Dickens novel, Jacko thought.

'Turns out the deceased was the local clock winder,' the man went on. 'He was up the clock tower when one of the sets of weights that he'd just wound up came down on his neck, a bit like a guillotine I suppose – had the same effect, unfortunately. No-one seems to have any idea why, or how.'

He stopped again as the cyclists appeared through the bar door. They looked hesitantly around, then dumped their helmets on one of the tables and tugged at their lycra crotches before sitting down. He waited until they'd ordered and were engrossed in bicycle talk.

'His torso was only discovered when the bell ringers went up for their weekly practice and noticed a bad whiff. One of the women climbed up to the clock chamber to see what it was, then fell over the body while she looked for the light switch. Turns out it was an old chap called Tommy Johnson, a local octogenarian who'd been winding up the clock for years. He usually wound it on Mondays, then went off to play bowls with his mates, regular as clockwork, if you pardon the pun.' He smiled weakly. 'Last Monday, the fifteenth, he never turned up for his bowls.' He paused to take a sip of his orange juice and brush some dandruff off his shoulders.

'Of course the woman who found the body the following Thursday was hysterical. Terrible sight, by all accounts. We thought it must be some industrial accident. The health and safety people crawled all over the place looking for non-compliance on fire hazards, unstable access ladders, unguarded machinery, pigeon vermin – the usual stuff – but couldn't find anything amiss.'

'And the police?' Jacko asked, somewhat indifferently, still wondering why he was being told all this.

'Not very helpful. Initially they designated it as a crime scene to be on the safe side, kept the details out of the press, then decided it wasn't a crime scene. All a bit of a mess. The tower keys were in the old boy's pocket so he must have locked himself in for some reason, goodness knows why. The only other set hangs on a hook in the vicarage and the housekeeper swears no-one's touched it.' He took another sip of orange juice while Jacko shuffled, still with no idea where this was all going.

'You may be wondering,' the coroner continued, noting Jacko's defensive body language, 'why I wanted to talk to you.' He paused while one of the cyclists wandered past looking for the toilet. 'My problem is that I'm faced with a fatality that doesn't seem to be either an industrial accident or a crime, and for the life of me I can't see it as suicide either. It's not a problem I can resolve myself, and the police have shut the door on it. I need a bit of help.' He smiled benignly. Jacko, not knowing what else to do, smiled back equally benignly.

'It's not someone with a specific expertise I need. It's someone with an inquisitive mind to work out what goes on up a church tower – I need a better picture, how all these old bells and clock workings function, someone with a bit of an historical background, someone fairly practical.' So that was it, Jacko thought. That's what this is all about, sounds like a lot of work and angst if what Duncan said was true. Not on your life, mate. Decision made, now how to get out of it.

'I've been making enquiries,' the coroner continued, 'I been asking around for someone who can think outside the box a bit and pull it all together.' His voice took on a pleading tone. 'It's a bit of an uphill struggle, I know, but your name came up as someone who might relish the challenge?' He leaned across the table with a questioning look. Jacko was on the point of politely declining on the grounds of workload but found himself thwarted by the coroner's trump card.

'And naturally there'll be a daily fee up to the maximum court rate for professional witnesses.'

That changed things completely. The man must be desperate. This was good money. A day on those rates wasn't far off what he could earn in a week doing his usual stuff.

'If you were to take it on, of course we'd give you all the assistance you need – the post-mortem report when it's done and the crime scene manager's report too, and the various statements. That goes without saying. You'll have full access, but I'd need a report within the month.' There was yet another pause as two more cyclists made their way to the toilet and another one returned.

'Well?' It was almost a whisper.

This wasn't Jacko's scene at all. He knew nothing about clocks or bells and the whole idea of getting caught up in a coroner's inquest made him shudder. On the other hand those fee rates weren't to be sneezed at. The decision was made somewhat reluctantly.

'I'll see what I can come up with.'

'Excellent!' the Dickens character seemed pleased. 'My secretary will be in touch. You'll need to come to the village again, of course. When you do, the vicar's given a set of tower keys to a pensioner who works as a handyman up at the manor – an old chap called Seth Hetherington. He did the clock winding if old Tommy was away for any reason, and the vicar's nobbled him to take it on again. He's the Rev Rogers – a bit of a frosty character, by the way.'

The coroner slid himself out of the narrow gap between the bench and the table seat, squeezed himself against the wall to allow more cyclists to pass in each direction, then adjusted his suit and vanished out into the sunshine with a nervous wave. Wondering what he'd let himself in for, Jacko went to the bar for another beer.

CHAPTER 2

Jacko's immediate thoughts were to have a quick look at the church while he was in the village. Middle Belford was fairly small and the church dominated the landscape in a subtle rather than overbearing way. It was a comforting, maternal sort of landmark, one which had stood for over a thousand years while cottages and farms clustered in its shadow.

He left the pub and walked down the main street using the tower as a guide. It was hot and deserted, like siesta time in a Spanish village. But this wasn't Spain. An uneven path led off the narrow pavement to the lychgate where he paused to look at the parish notice board, edged with cracked black paint. It told him that the vicar, the Reverend R Rogers MA (Cantab), took communion every Sunday at 10.30 am precisely. Marriages, baptisms and funerals were by arrangement. St John's was the sort of church he liked – old and slightly battered with nooks, overgrown trees and lengths of ruined walls scattered among its headstones. It was idyllic, particularly in the late afternoon sunshine, quintessentially

English, soothingly leafy and almost timeless. In the nearby lanes, countless generations of workers and their families had been born, lived and died without ever losing sight of its tall yellow tower. The clock chimed high above him, a reminder of time passing.

A few wooden benches intended for the elderly, but now more often occupied by passing cyclists eating their sandwiches, had been set along the flagged paths, each bearing a small brass plaque commemorating some loving husband or wife. Rather pointless, Jacko thought, seeing as the names were now illegible. Like most of the churches nearby, or at least those that had avoided being bombed in the 1940s, St John's was a mixture of architectures, rather like a dog with an interesting and varied pedigree. The Normans had started it off and the medieval masons had added aisles and created ornate stonework in its friezes and gargoyles. It would have survived as such, even despite the carnage of the reformation and the occasional direct hit by civil war cannonballs from nearby Edge Hill, but the Victorians had finally put the boot in, well intentioned no doubt as a restoration, to make it what it was today. Jacko could sense its history, could still read its biography in the altered stonework.

As he stood there in the sunshine, slightly elated by that second beer, he decided it was as good a time as any to find this Seth Hetherington. He'd driven past the manor on his way in, and it was easy walking distance from the church. It was Monday too, the day the old boy was supposed to wind up the clock. He could go up with him. Save another visit.

Decision made, it took him little more than ten minutes on foot to reach the manor's tall, intimidating stone gateposts. Even then, at a little after four-thirty, the air was still sultry without even the hint of a breeze, and his T-shirt was sticking unpleasantly to his back.

Once through the gates the manor grounds provided a welcome canopy of beech trees to keep the sun at bay. He stopped to enjoy the shade, sat himself down on one of the low stone walls that ran along either side of the driveway, and pulled away some branches to get a better view of the building. He couldn't see much, just a large oak door fronted by a metal grill, with roses and a buddleia growing up the ironstone walling. Foxgloves and hollyhocks stood in clumps around the doorposts then fanned out to border a flagged path which led to a manicured lawn. It had that subtle blend of formality and the *laissez faire* that seemed to stereotype the English country house and garden – it was somehow disordered, but in an orderly way.

Jacko remembered the place reasonably well. Because it was a Listed Building he'd worked there several years earlier on behalf of the council ahead of some alterations. The job had been to carry out basic historical research and survey work. It was bog-standard but unusually interesting, not least because of discovering that the manor was once surrounded by a moat, although all that was left of it now was a duck pond on one side. Like the church, bits of the building had been added to or changed over the centuries, all duly spotted and described by Pevsner in his *Buildings of England*. It was that important. Latterly, though, it had been the long-standing home of the Wainwright family, purchased in the 1890s on the profits of an expanding cutlery business. The family was responsible for adding a hideous wing at one end, the mock-Tudor design of which was now thankfully obscured by an uncontrolled Virginia creeper.

The Wainwrights were universally unpopular in the village and were the subject of considerable gossip. The current alpha male, Charles Wainwright, had emerged from an expensive public school which had seen his father, grandfather and great-grandfather all knocked into socially acceptable shape. He was sent to work in the family business, a knife and fork factory in Birmingham, where he was able to exercise his leadership skills, and in due course he took over the company, but only part-time. This had allowed him to ride, hunt and shoot on the estate and become schooled in the family political dynasty. His grandfather had been an MP, and his father, Sir James Wainwright, had been a minor Shadow Minister in the 1990s before eventually retiring from the constituency. The old boy was now well past debating ability, but maintained a public image as president of the local hunt and the golf club, as well as sitting on various boards, committees and trusts of whose purpose he was never entirely clear. Many local people still revered him because they thought he stood for traditional values and standards; many people despised him because he was so out of touch, and many more simply tolerated him because he was just an old fart.

The school tie had worked well for Charles and it was not long before he'd been dispatched to Tory party HQ as a potential successor to Sir James. He networked well and was predictably adopted as Tory candidate in his father's constituency, eventually winning the seat. Such was the socio-economics of the region that even a ferret wearing a blue rosette would have been elected.

On the basis of what he'd heard about Charles Wainwright, Jacko had no wish to meet him.

Suitably rested, he carried on scrunching up the gravel drive towards the manor when he heard a hammering from an adjacent stable block built of timber and brick. He made his way across and discovered the noise belonged to an athletic but grey-haired individual who was half-heartedly knocking down a stone boundary wall. Jacko guessed he must have been well into his eighties, his weathered leathery skin indicating a lifetime of outdoor labour. Even so, it didn't seem right that a man of his age should be doing such heavy work, especially in this heat. The wall stood to about waist height, with some of it now reduced to a heap of yellow rubble and cement. The elderly man was trying to secure the head of a sledgehammer back on its shaft.

Jacko called out across the drive, 'Mr Hetherington?'

The old man raised his head suspiciously before nodding.

'Why don't I hold the shaft while you bang a wedge in?' Jacko suggested. The partnership succeeded, the implement was returned to working order, and the old man muttered his gratitude before sitting down and mopping his brow with a filthy handkerchief.

The two of them sat on a bench against the stable wall chatting politely about the village until the old boy discovered Jacko's interest in all things historical. At that point he became unexpectedly talkative, regaling a stream of snippets of local history and anecdotes. The church, the manor, the pub and the surrounding fields all featured in a convoluted and mostly improbable narrative. History, fiction and folklore became threaded together in an impossible tapestry that made Jacko smile. When the old man heard that Jacko wanted to see up the tower, he insisted on taking him there personally. It would be a pleasure. Normally he'd wait until he heard the clock strike six before he went, but they might as well go up sooner.

In preparation the old man slowly packed away his tools, locked up, and the pair set off down the drive towards the main gate. They'd barely passed the end of the building when they encountered a well-dressed figure riding a tall chestnut mare advancing up the drive. The rider was having some difficulty in holding down the horse's head. Jacko heard Seth mutter something under his breath and the two of them moved to one side to give the mount space. They stood, waiting for the horse to pass, Jacko pretending to check out some messages on his mobile phone. He hoped the horse might move by, but it drew up directly alongside them, snorting impatiently.

'Who are you and what are you doing here?' the rider asked rudely in a public school accent, glaring at Jacko, looking him up and down, scanning him like a machine. 'These are private grounds.' He was tall, well-built, and impeccably dressed in riding gear. This was a man who liked exercising authority, not one interested in discussing the weather or the test match score. Being high up on horseback gave him a significant physical superiority which he played to his advantage. The horse shied and he reined back its head.

'I set the dogs on gypsies last week,' he added threateningly. 'I'll do it again if I find anyone trespassing.'

'As a matter of fact it's Mr Hetherington here that I've come to see,' Jacko responded cheerily with an ingratiating smile. 'My name's Jackson, I'm a landscape historian. He's kindly helping me out with some research into local history.'

'Nonetheless, you're trespassing, Mr Jackson. I did not invite you on my property and I'll ask you to leave. I've learned to distrust uninvited strangers – travellers, gypsies, immigrants – call them what you will, in any shape or colour, mostly criminals and liars in my book. There are far too many undesirables around these days, whites as well as blacks, trying to change things, out for themselves. No we don't need them. Now show me some credentials please Jackson, or I'll take further action.'

The horse started to rear and the rider calmed it down by letting it circle, crunching its way through the gravel, before siding up to Jacko once more.

Jacko, quietly horrified at what he'd just heard, fumbled in his pocket and pulled out a grubby business card which he passed up. He could feel the heat radiating from the horse as he did so. The card was duly studied and returned dismissively.

'You'll appreciate,' came the rider's response as he wrestled with the horse's head again, 'that Hetherington has work to do as my employee. I don't pay him to waste his time on hobbies and irrelevances such as history, Mr Jackson.' He turned towards the old man who had already backed away in the deference expected of him. 'Hetherington,' he said sharply, 'I assume you will be making up this time tomorrow and will complete the demolition of this wall that I'm paying you for? History will still be there afterwards. I had expected it finished by this evening.'

The despicable way the old man was being treated made a normally tolerant Jacko justifiably angry. 'Just a minute,' he interrupted, trying hard to restrain himself. He lowered his voice, moving closer to the horse and out of earshot from the old man. 'Don't you think it's rather hot for an elderly person like him be doing this sort of heavy work? And he doesn't seem to have any basic facilities, does he?'

'That's none of your business, Mr Jackson. The arrangement I have is one between employer and employee. And what's more,' he said as he lowered his own voice and moved his head nearer to Jacko, 'who else would pay some useless old fool like him a proper wage? I'm doing him a favour. As far as I'm concerned, anyone over the age of seventy's a waste of space and should be put down. You do-gooders are all the same – socialists, conservationists, environmentalists, whatever you call yourselves. Why don't you just mind your own business and bugger off?'

He glanced across at the old man, straightened himself up, sneered, and was about to ride away having assumed the last word, when Jacko decided to play a different card.

'I take it you've listed building consent to demolish that wall?'

It was very much a bluff, but it had the desired effect of wiping the sneer off his face. He turned, visibly redder, and lowered his head again to Jacko.

'Listen, Jackson. You're annoying me. This family's lived here a long time. I think I have a better understanding of these things than those arseholes in the County Planning Department. They're just paper pushers. I wouldn't trust a local authority worker to tie my shoelaces.'

'I'll take that as a "no" then,' Jacko said, but before any further exchanges could be made the horse and rider had galloped off smartly up to the manor, leaving Jacko and Seth covered in gravel and dust. There was a pause as they looked at each other.

'Charles Wainwright MP', said the old man quietly as the dust settled.

'Wanker,' added Jacko less quietly, and they made their way down the drive and out of the gates.

CHAPTER 3

The old boy walked irritatingly slowly and by the time they reached the church porch the sun was already going down. Jacko opened the heavy oak door and they stepped inside. A large weight on a pulley slammed it shut behind them, making them feel like animals caught in a trap. They were stranded in a void of gloom and silence, surrounded by the silhouette of tall nave arches whose shapes had become lost in semi-darkness. Once his eyes had acclimatised, he could see how the sunshine splayed weak colours through the painted glass, spreading bands of light across the dark wooden pews. It was a captivating image but might have been more alluring without the stale smell of furniture polish, damp stone and old flowers.

Seth beckoned him along, opened the tower door and led him up several flights of rickety wooden steps. They stopped briefly in the ringing chamber where Jacko noticed, hanging on the wall, a list of former tower captains written in gold lettering on a polished wooden board. He pointed to it, at which the old man made an unpleasant guttural noise and spat on the floor. Must have touched a nerve, Jacko thought, and followed him as he disappeared up a wooden ladder into the darkness of the clock chamber itself. Seth groped his way across to the far wall and switched on the light.

'Always need the lights on in here,' he said grudgingly. 'Even in summer it's too bloody dark to see what you're doing.'

Hardly surprising, Jacko thought to himself as he looked up at two narrow windows above head height, both heavily encrusted with cobwebs, and a chink of light that came from an ill-fitting wooden door that led outside to a ladder down to the roof. In a way, the murkiness of the place made the physical beauty of the brass clock engineering all the more stunning. It was the shining assemblage of cogs, levers and ratchets that did it. Some moved quickly, some slowly, but all were driven by the swing of a huge pendulum with an audible ticking heartbeat. Simple and effective, he thought. But the real work of genius was the way the different sized cogs had been designed to create harmony with the passage of time, expressing it through moving fingers on the four tower faces and through the quarterly chimes. Josiah Smith of Brosley (1848) was emblazoned on the clock's steel casing, and Josiah should have been justifiably proud of what his company had produced. It was testimony to precision craftsmanship, skill and patience, with not a microchip in sight.

Jacko supposed that men from the village had taken pride in nurturing that clock, or its predecessor, for decades, if not centuries, climbing the tower steps to keep the mechanisms oiled, caring for its wellbeing, attending to its needs. It was a pity that the bells that once measured out the routines of life in the field and farm – milking times, meal times, sleeping, waking, the complete schedule of rural living – were no longer needed. The chimes still continued, but now only as a forgotten echo of history.

His nostalgia was broken by the old man calling him across and pointing to the open glass door of the clock housing. On the inside was a series of scribbled signatures and dates, partly in ink, partly in pencil, of those from the village who had served their time clock-winding over the previous one hundred and fifty years. It was a simple, informal testimony to their service. There were maybe fifteen names there, and the record was neither brash nor pompous, quite different from the golden lettering in the ringing chamber below. It was personal and sincere, and a treasure for any local historian who understood the sentiment lying behind it. Jacko photographed the winders' names, several being barely legible. Old Tommy's was the last, with the end-date scrawled as '2019'.

'That's odd. When was that final date of 2019 put on?'

'Not sure,' the old man muttered. 'Maybe the vicar wrote it, but I don't know when. Rogers can't wait to get the new motorised winding system installed this year. It's been paid for, now it's just a matter of fixing the date'.

Jacko drew a breath in surprise, 'New winding system? I didn't know about that.'

'No, nor did most people here. Just the chosen few. It's one of those things that Rogers wanted to do. Didn't tell anyone, just went ahead with it. Tommy found out only by chance when he bumped into the engineer one day. Crying shame really.'

Having checked the time, Seth wiped his hands on his shirt, took down the winding handle from its hook, slotted it into place and started winding up the first set of weights from where they hung near the base of the tower. After a while he stopped, allowed the gravity catch to lock into the spindle ratchet, then peeked over the parapet in the corner to see how far up they'd come. Jacko's heart leapt. Was that what Tommy Johnson was doing when the weights fell and killed him? Christ, how did the weights get released? The old man carried on winding until the weights appeared above the parapet, stopping only when they reached the ceiling above him. The gravity catch locked in once more and the weights remained hanging, still swinging slightly. He pulled out the winding lever, repositioned it, then hauled up the two sets of weights in the other corner in exactly the same way.

Jacko became absorbed in watching the cog actions, mesmerised by the different speeds and the light reflecting off the brass movements. There seemed to be no obvious way it could malfunction, at least not without human interference. 'What do you do if it jams?' he asked in a way that he hoped might sound casual. 'Is there a way of releasing the weights?'

'Dunno,' Seth shook his head. 'I've never needed to do it. Never had a problem in the few times I've done the winding. Tommy never spoke of it.'

Jacko wandered over to the old wooden door that led outside to the roof. He tried it. It was unlocked, secured by a sandbag propped against the bottom.

Seth was watching him. 'I don't think there ever was a key for that. Not as far as I can remember. There's a few empty hooks here and there, but I've never seen no key. Sandbag does the job well enough.'

Jacko dragged it away and pulled the door inwards leaving them both momentarily stunned by the blast of fresh air and natural light that followed. He peeked out, there was a small metal ladder leading a short distance down to the nave roof and to the base of the flagpole. The roof had only a slight pitch and was lead-covered, and around the perimeter was an ornate low parapet of yellow latticed ironstone interspaced with a few ugly gargoyles. Below those, on the two long sides of the nave were the roofs of the north and south aisles. There was more lead there, and another latticed parapet on each, suitably gargoyled, with a sheer drop down to the ground. When he'd seen enough, he pushed the door shut and the chamber returned to its gloomy state.

'Just before we go, did you or Tommy ever need to go up into the belfry?'

'Nah.'

'Why not?'

'Bats.'

Jacko was about to reply when they were both silenced by a deafening clatter from the belfry above them. The noise was monumental and the whole fabric of the tower seemed to be swaying with the vibrations of the huge bronze bells. It was six o'clock and the entire roof of the chamber above their heads became alive with moving pulleys and clicking ratchets joined together by bits of wood, angle brackets and beams with holes that allowed the cables to be fed into the necessary positions. Glorious clockwork in the true sense of the word.

'I usually try and leave before that happens,' the old man said apologetically when it finished.

The two of them climbed carefully down the stairways into the base of the tower, locked the door behind them and went outside into the evening sunlight. Standing in the entrance to the porch they looked out across to the vicarage, a vast white painted edifice which lay sprawled out opposite in nineteenth century upper class splendour, now the home of the formidable Rev Rogers.

The vicarage may have been fit for purpose in Jane Austen's time, but it certainly wasn't now. According to old Seth, the Rev Rogers wasn't fit for purpose either. He chortled away as he described Rogers' sermons as being so long that the diminishing Sunday flock preferred to pass away and be eaten by worms in the ground rather than listen. It seemed that the only positive elements of Rogers' incumbency were his twin daughters, Suzie and Linda, whose libidos had been a constant source of village gossip throughout their teenage years. Didn't know who they got it from, mind, the old man grunted. Not Rogers, that's for sure. Must have been Mrs Rogers. He gave a dirty laugh as he told the story. For reasons no-one knew about it seems, Mrs Rogers had chosen not to accompany her husband to the parish. He lived alone in the vicarage, apart that was from Mrs Jefferson, the lady who came and 'did' a couple of times a week. The two daughters were finishing their degrees, one in Newcastle or somewhere, the other in London.

Jacko knew more about the building itself, but only because, ironically, he was due to work on a development project there shortly. The vicarage had become too old, too big and too expensive to maintain for just a single parson. Everyone knew that, especially the church commissioners, who had soon cottoned on to the fact that they could knock it down, build a smaller vicarage and make a fortune by flogging off the remaining grounds for new housing.

The commissioners' initial planning application had gone down like a ton of bricks in the village – posters, village meetings, the lot. Not to mention a two-fingered wave from the planning committee too. Jacko had provided some of the historical evidence that had helped the rejection, mainly the likely existence of Viking graves from the original churchyard which now partly lay under the vicarage grounds. And so it was back to the drawing board for the commissioners. But they returned with a clever plan – a small ghetto of 'affordable homes' and a change of use for the current vicarage itself into a care home. That did the trick and was generally much more acceptable, but not to the Rev Rogers. His cage had been well and truly rattled by the whole business. He'd taken a rigorous stand against any development whatsoever, and his village brownie points increased exponentially overnight. People muttered that maybe they had been wrong about him after all. But despite the fuss he'd made, the planning application eventually went through, subject to the archaeological recording of the grounds for which the council had hired in Jacko as project manager. Unlike the vicar, he was quite looking forward to it.

* * *

The pair of them left the church and, during their slow walk back, Seth persuaded Jacko to try his hand at bowls. He'd be welcome. Why not, Jacko thought. Nothing else to do that evening but chat to his girl friend on the phone, but that could wait. Bowling might be interesting anyway.

When they arrived at the village hall he counted about a dozen men of similar age to Seth, in various sizes and proportions, and in various states of mobility. They were milling about, rolling out the mats and unpacking bowls from their bags. The hall was a strange place, not unlike an aircraft hangar, built entirely of wood and painted white. It had a colonial feel to it, more appropriate to a consular outpost in some African republic just without the union flag. According to Seth the hall had come into its own during the war when the parish offered to run dances there for the airmen billeted at a nearby US base. It was a successful venture which allowed the airmen to take advantage of many of the women who weren't yet spoken for, and indeed many who already were. Now, on Mondays, the old boys rolled out the mats and spent an evening bowling from one end to the other. As Jacko soon discovered, it was more an occasion for reminiscence than competition, and for nostalgia and story-telling rather than sporting ability. Odd to think that the history of the village was played out and regularly rewritten on a bowling mat.

He joined in, albeit hesitantly. Local rules stated that each player had their own set of named score cards kept in folders in a cupboard. At the end of the year each player's scores were totted up and the annual champion declared. Jacko was dispatched to get himself a clean card, to learn how to fill it in.

He went over to open the cupboard door and then had a thought. Inside were a series of folders bearing the names of the individual players. He flicked through them until he found one with old Tommy's name on it and, when he was sure no-one was looking, quickly opened it, took out one of the completed cards, folded it, and slid it neatly into his pocket. He then picked up a clean card from a pile on the top shelf and closed the cupboard door. No-one had noticed.

After about an hour he made his excuses and walked back to his car. Thinking about it, having two jobs, one in the vicarage grounds managing the archaeology, the other next door in the church with this clock and bells business, was really quite convenient. Given the fuss over the planning, the obstinacy of the vicar and now the decapitation of the old clock winder, he wondered if they might somehow be related. Too much of a coincidence, surely?

Once well out of earshot of the others, he pulled out his mobile phone. He needed to know a bit more, so he rang his son Alex who was a DS in the county fraud squad and a useful, if reluctant, source of police information for him. There was no reply. Jacko swore mildly under his breath but decided not to leave a message. It could wait.

CHAPTER 4

The next morning, Jacko rang up his old friend Alison in the county planning department. He'd spent over a decade working there himself, but finally became so cheesed off with the internal politics and with banging his head on the wall of public accountability that he threw in the towel. His purpose was to check on the status of the wall that Charles Wainwright was having demolished. He had a suspicion that it had protected status and couldn't be pulled down, at least not without a load of bureaucracy. Alison would know. There was a time when he would have felt guilty for dobbing up someone like that, but it had quickly got personal with Wainwright and he didn't care. Alison politely promised to look into it and inform the enforcement officer if there was a problem. Feeling pleased with himself, he then looked up the address of the nearest bat preservation office, finding to his surprise that there was one in Warwick. He jotted down the details, had a quick coffee then drove over. He had an idea that it might be useful to find out a bit more about bats.

The bat premises were located in a pair of temporary offices in the yard of the council buildings. He climbed a short flight of wooden steps into what looked like a static caravan and entered a cramped office, not dissimilar to his own front living room. Sitting behind a cluttered desk was a tall, geeky-looking man as badly dressed as he was, eating what looked like a falafel sandwich from a paper bag. Jacko felt immediately at home. The man introduced himself as Robin and Jacko gave the excuse that he was on a courtesy call, keeping local environmental groups in the picture ahead of the vicarage excavations in Middle Belford. It seemed a rather pathetic ruse but the man swallowed it whole. His visitor was perceived as a kindred spirit and was subjected to a diatribe on bats' breeding habits, feeding characteristics, preferred environments and modern vulnerability. Jacko was wondering how he might get St John's church into this one-way conversation when it was conveniently done for him.

'The reason we'd be interested in what you're doing at the vicarage,' Robin explained, 'is because it's close to one of the study areas where we monitor bat behaviour very carefully. There's an important colony that roosts in the belfry at St John's next door, but we tend to keep quiet about it. Bats have rather a bad press. Is there anything else I can help you with?'

'Hmm, really? In the belfry at St John's?'

'Yes, they fly in through the gaps in the tower's louvres. Clever little creatures aren't they?'

Jacko tried not to sound too interested. 'Must be difficult to monitor them. All those stairs too. How often do you have to go up there?'

'Never,' was the immediate smug answer, as though he'd been itching to tell someone. 'They get disturbed too easily. Odd isn't it? They don't get phased by bells chiming away every fifteen minutes but even an occasional visit by a human can knock them right off their routines. No, no, we do it all remotely now with a small static camera positioned up in the belfry itself.'

'A camera?' The words came out squeakier than he intended. He sat up in surprise.

Robin dropped his tone and looked suspiciously at him. 'Keep it to yourself, won't you? I don't think we've even told the vicar'.

'But doesn't that need wires, wouldn't it create a lot of disturbance?'

'Not at all. There's a small black box connected to the main wiring system that runs through the belfry. It sends images via a wireless link down to another small box located at the back of the nave next to the tower. It looks a bit like something that measures humidity, in fact that's what the vicar thinks it does. We can collect the data from it as and when. The camera's triggered by a special sensor. It only switches on when it detects movement, ultra sonics or something, and that's basically all we're interested in for this research project. I can show you some footage if you like? It's not terribly interesting. We keep it for about six months before we wipe it.' He tapped away at his computer, waited, tapped some more, then finally turned the screen towards Jacko.

The image was a bit grainy, but clear enough. The camera must have been fixed high up in the far corner of

29

the belfry, its main focus being on the rafters where the bats were roosting, but it also covered the top of the steps leading up from the clock chamber below. A small digital clock at the bottom of the screen showed the exact time any bat movement occurred.

'Yes, I see,' Jacko said slowly, trying to suppress his interest. 'So you can calculate how long they leave the tower for, can't you, then see where the returnees roost?'

'Absolutely, absolutely, that what it's all about.' It was now Robin's turn to get excited 'There's a territorial aspect to it. Our next stage is to tag individual bats and look at their social hierarchies when they return to the roost. This is just the pilot part of the research. Absorbing, isn't it? Would you like a copy of this to look at? It's no bother.'

No-one in their right mind, apart from Jacko whose pulse was racing, would consider watching a video of bats flying out, then flying in again, hour after hour. What Jacko really needed though was the most recent footage that covered the period around Tommy's death, and a plausible excuse for asking for it. After a few moments of watching Robin typing away on the computer, the light bulb moment arrived.

'I don't suppose you've got the last few weeks there? That'll be nice and close to the forthcoming excavations at the vicarage next door. We can compare a "before" and "after" can't we? See what disturbance the earth-moving machines have on the bats' activities?'

Robin turned from the computer and looked at him with a sense of admiration, 'Hmm, good thinking. That'll give us another dimension.' He did some more rapid typing and waited for the computer to respond. 'Ah, here it is. The latest download we have is for July ending last week, so that'll take us up to, let's see…' he turned to his wall diary. 'The data was collected quite recently, in fact only four days ago. I've a spare data stick I can let you have. I've only flicked through the images, but I don't think you'll find them very interesting.'

'Oh, I'm sure I will,' Jacko replied, smiling.

* * *

Jacko drove back to his small house in Compton-on-Stour, travelling on air with the data stick burning a hole in his pocket. Compton was a small town, usefully central for most of the south midlands. It had everything a middle-aged bachelor needed: several pubs, a supermarket, a hardware store, two butchers, cafes, and those essential components of independent living – take-away restaurants and a chip shop. His house was just outside the market square, a single-fronted terrace in a line of period houses in Cattle Street. It was probably the smallest house in the terrace, certainly the least pretentious and the one needing most repair work.

He made himself a coffee and nibbled on some oatcakes before putting the data stick in his laptop. It took a while before the data morphed itself into a recognisable image on the screen, still grainy but clear enough to see the bats roosting, the open floor area by the bells and the top of the steps leading up from the clock chamber. The date and time were at the bottom of the screen. Old Tommy's last winding session was supposed to have been on a Monday, almost certainly July the fifteenth. Jacko let the recorder move on at its own speed from the first day of recording. It was like watching paint dry. The camera only jolted into action with movement, which was mostly at night when the bats moved in or out through the tower louvres to feast on gnats, midges and whatever else they could find. They seemed to go out in sporadic convoys, then back in again several hours later in much the same way.

Fast-forwarding the life of a bat seemed to make little difference until, well into the middle of July according to the date on the screen, something happened. He almost missed it, and by the time he'd clocked it, jumped up and rushed to the screen, the camera had moved on. He fast-rewound the data a few days and watched it again. There it was – a figure, a shadowy figure at that. Bugger the grainy monochrome image. The figure appeared from the stairs and entered the belfry. It was too jerky and pixelated to see whether it was male or female, large or small. He or she seemed to be wearing jeans, a dark top and some form of hat or cap. Even when the face turned to the camera it was impossible to make anything out. The digital clock showed Monday July fifteenth, the same day the old boy may have met his end. Christ, maybe he wasn't alone up there?.

The figure remained in the belfry, just off camera to the right with the time showing as 17.31, shortly after the half-past chimes. Jacko let the tape move on at its own speed. It picked up movement again at 17.43 when the shadowy figure began to walk back across the floor. It stopped at the top of the stairwell momentarily then crouched, looking down into the clock chamber. It paused there for a time and then moved quickly down the stairs. That was at 17.45 exactly. The image became temporarily blurred, presumably because the bells were chiming. The figure never reappeared. Jacko wound and rewound, played and replayed, but there was nothing else.

The next two days of tedious bat activity were unproductive until, on Thursday July the eighteenth, three days later at 18.42, the head of a figure appeared at the top of the stairs. It looked around, shone a torch, paused, but went no further and vanished down the stairs again. Its face was partly concealed by a white hood.

CHAPTER 5

Jacko drove to police HQ to see Barty Webb the crime scene manager. He parked in the visitor car park, checked in at security and was directed towards reception. Once he was away from the surrounding buildings he stopped and rang up his reluctant son Alex, who worked at the same complex. He had a ploy in mind, although it was a bit of a long shot.

'What is it this time, Dad?' was Alex's distrusting response, having recognised the number on his screen. 'I'd a missed call from you the other day. Is this some underhand half-baked fishing expedition of yours?'

'Melvyn Cleaver,' said Jacko.

'Who?'

'Melvyn Cleaver. Dr Melvyn Cleaver. You know, the bloke who does your document authentication? Signatures on cheques, handwriting comparisons… all that fraud stuff.'

'Yes. What about him?

'Do you still use him? Is he still on contract to your unit?

'Yes, but what's that got to do with anything?

'Does he do loads of comparisons for you? I mean, could we slip another handwriting comparison into his caseload without anybody noticing?'

'We? We?' came the incredulous reply. 'No, *we* can't. Forget it.'

'Okay, just a thought, thanks, Alex. Sorry to have bothered you.' He rang off.

Police HQ was one of the old ones, located in a converted stately home that was no longer fit for purpose. It probably gave the force a bit of a boost when it was first taken over, particularly the Chief Constable at the time who liked to swan about with the airs and graces of the landed gentry. But the rooms were now all the wrong size for meetings and offices, for training purposes or as operational centres. As the force became bigger, as policing became more varied, and as the technological world moved on the stately home could only respond by sprouting Portacabins, incongruous new wings and antennae, with bands of cables running along the ground and up the walls. There was nowhere decent to eat, the toilets were antiquated and essential facilities had to be squeezed into existing spaces. And when the Disability Discrimination Act came in, a whole plethora of ramps, lifts and handrails had to be factored in as well.

He waited at reception until Barty Webb appeared to escort him up to the CSI offices. Barty was a stocky, athletic-looking person with a thick neck and virtually no hair. Many people said he looked like an alien. He and Jacko were both practical, hands-on people, they'd worked together before and respected each other's talents. He led Jacko through a labyrinth of passageways until they reached his offices, which were dingy and cramped but as well equipped as space would allow.

'I've got all the St John's stuff here ready for you,' Barty said as he dumped various piles of papers on the table and brought up a set of images on the computer screen. 'I'm not sure what you'll make of it, or what the coroner's interest is. We did our usual bog-standard recording – photos, plan, exhibits and reports – on the basis that it might have been a suspicious death, but DCI Flett, the investigating officer finally stood us down on the basis that there was nothing untoward. I have to say, I pretty much agree with him. Looks like a sad accident brought about by mechanical failure – a job for the HSE. Poor old sod. Help yourself. Let me know if you want anything else. I'll be around pushing paper and catching up. Have fun.'

Jacko flicked through what there was – a list of exhibits, some scene reports and statements, all of which were very descriptive, and some sketches and measurements.

'Is there an instrument survey plan?'

'Nope, too small an area.' Barty said. 'Much easier to do it manually using the method you showed us. There's a sketch here,' and he pulled out a measured drawing on graph paper from one of the folders. 'It assumes that the four tower corners are exact right-angles, which they're probably not, but it's accurate enough for our purposes'.

'Out of interest, was the door to the roof open or shut when you were up there?'

Barty thought for a moment, then looked through some notes. 'Yes,' he said finally, 'it was open. I remember now, it was flapping a bit and the pigeons had got in. We shoved an old sandbag against it to keep it closed.'

'One other question. Did anyone go up to the belfry on the floor above?'

'Not exactly. I went up the steps and popped my head in but it was full of pigeon shit and feathers. Didn't seem much point in going further seeing as all the action was on the floor below. Flett wasn't interested in it either.'

Jacko started to work his way through the images on screen, flicking through some quickly, others slowly, until he came to those of the torso.

'Jesus, what a mess,' was all he could say. It didn't seem worth trying to be more descriptive.

He went through them all, one after the other, taken from every angle, distant and close-up. The torso was covered in dried blood and heaving with maggots, lying part-slumped against the wooden parapet and part splayed out on the floor. The arms were raised but the hands had slid down from their grip on the wooden rail.

'Mercifully it was a quickie by the looks of it,' was Barty's response, glancing up from his paperwork. 'At least the old chap wasn't put through any pain. And if you think that's a mess, you should see what happened to his head when the weights made a sixty mile an hour sandwich of it with the tower floor.'

'Nothing was moved before you got there was it?'

'Not as far as we know. The only person up there was the bell-ringing lady who found him and she came down straightaway with the screaming heebie-jeebies. The bell-ringing captain, an arrogant sod called Toller, poked his head up after that to see what the fuss was about, and then we were called.'

'What's that for?' Jacko asked, pointing to one of the images. 'The long stick thing lying on the floor?'

'Don't know. Probably for opening windows or louvres or something.' He shuffled through some papers, 'Look, it's here on the plan too,' and pointed to the graph paper. 'Think it's relevant?'

'Dunno. Just a thought.'

Jacko skimmed through the rest of the photographs, but there was nothing there he thought might be important. He asked Barty if he could copy a few of the images for his report to the coroner and he left a little later with yet another data stick to his name.

* * *

Strictly speaking, Barty, or one of his colleagues, should have escorted Jacko back to reception to be relieved of his visitor pass and set back into the outside world. But everyone was busy and Jacko volunteered to make his own way back. His ploy was to make his way through the labyrinthine building to his son's outfit in another part of the complex. It was an entirely illicit manoeuvre which succeeded through a combination of blag and confident swagger. He'd deliberately worn a suit to make him look eminent and that helped too. Someone his age, freshly shaved, neatly dressed in a dark suit and tie and striding purposefully was bound to be important. Eventually he strutted into the fraud unit's reception and announced that DS Jackson was expecting him, which he wasn't. He put on all the airs of a senior officer from another force, or at least from a different part of this one, and marched into his son's operational briefing room. The receptionist was completely taken in by the bravado. 'Yes, sir,' was her immediate response, without thinking it necessary to ask for clearance.

Alex saw the besuited figure out of the corner of his eye but was occupied with a colleague and a computer screen. The penny didn't drop, but it did on the second take. He looked up, mouth open momentarily, then bore down on his father with a glare in his eyes.

'What the hell are you doing here, Dad?' he asked through clenched teeth. 'How the hell did you get in? This is a secure area.'

'Apparently not,' Jacko said jovially. 'Consider me a test for your security system, Alex. Just as well I don't have a Kalashnikov down my pants, isn't it? Could have taken the lot of you out by now.'

One by one, heads in the room began to turn from their computer screens to see what was going on.

'Father,' Alex hissed, moving up to him, 'God help me if I don't clock you one here and now. What the hell are you after? Tell me before I throttle you in front of all these witnesses.'

All eyes in the room were now looking in their direction. Alex moved back a little and Jacko put on an artificial smile to reassure any anxious faces.

'Whooah,' he said in a hushed voice. 'No need for this, I'll be off in a tick, but I just need a little favour first. Now if you could see your way to sliding this handwriting comparison into Dr Cleaver's case load, I'll leave straight away.' There was a pause in which he waved some papers in his hand. 'I promise,' he added, followed by a patronising smile.

'Watch my lips, father,' was the exasperated reply. 'I have no intention of supporting any of your hair-brained ventures. You've conned your way in here, now for Christ's sake get lost before I have to call security and have you arrested.'

'Come on, Alex, why can't you just slip a simple extra handwriting comparison into the pile? Who'll notice?'

'For God's sake, don't you realise every single case is accounted for, processed and monitored? Any discrepancy between the specified list and the actual list might mean losing a case on a technicality and causing an internal investigation. Have you any idea what you're trying to drop me into?'

'Look, it's simple. All I need is your expert chappie, that Dr Cleaver, to tell me, quite independently, whether the hand-writing on this,' he waved aloft Tommy's bowls card, 'and this,' he waved his photo of the signatures from the clock glass casing in the other hand, 'are the same or not. Anyway, the coroner's asked me to look into it, so it's quite legit.'

That was the moment, almost by divine intervention, that Dr Mervyn Cleaver himself, handwriting guru, expert in forgeries and document fraud with a reputation of being bomb-proof in court, decided to enter the room.

'Another one for me?' was Cleaver's immediate bombastic question, impervious to the atmosphere and seeing Jacko holding papers aloft. Alex tried to intervene, but Cleaver was having none of it. He strode over and gleefully snatched the two documents from Jacko's raised arms with a hand of enormous fingers.

Cleaver was a man on the portly side of normal, dressed in a light brown cord suit that had seen better days, with a blue silk handkerchief stuffed into the breast pocket. He wore suede shoes and a blue linen shirt open at the neck. Oddly, his head seemed larger than it should have been in relation to the rest of him, and the thick black hair that curled over his ears hadn't seen a comb for months. Every other part of him that protruded out of the cord suit – hands, ears, nose and probably his feet too if he took his shoes off – also seemed too large for his body. In a strange way he was grotesquely interesting to look at.

'Well,' he said, scanning the papers quickly. 'This is a bit more interesting than the usual disfigured cheques and forged wills you put my way, Alex.'

'It can really wait, Mervyn,' Alex interjected. 'It's low priority and it's not even in the budget yet.' It was a desperate last effort to pull it out of the system, but Cleaver was having none of it.

'Do you know?' he said, turning to Alex. 'I could do with a change – something different, something more exciting than the half-baked, idiot-generated forgeries that I get to deal with here. Have you any idea how monumentally boring the usual crap you put my way is? I've reached the point that I positively look forward to a criminal mind that challenges me. In fact, I have the utmost respect for a sophisticated forger who wants to take me on. This job isn't about the criminal justice system any more, it's about the education system. Half the forgeries you give me are by people who can't even spell.' He pointed to the pile on his desk, 'This lot's less to do with crime and more to do with the sad state of literacy in society.'

Diatribe over, he studied Jacko's documents while people quietly returned to their chairs to avoid further confrontation.

'I like a change,' he said, leaning towards Jacko and whispering in his ear. 'You're not part of this shower are you? They're an anal lot. No interest in their work. It's all process-driven as far as they're concerned. Might as well get them counting sticks of rhubarb. Now, what is this? A signature list with dates on the back of a door, and a score card from a bowls game? What do you want me to do?'

By now Alex had given up. Jacko took the opportunity to seize the initiative.

'Just a provisional comparison if you could, sir,' he said politely. 'It would give us an idea as to whether further enquiries were necessary or not. We'd like to know whether the last date on the list of signatures – that's the "2019" – was by the same hand as the person who filled in the score card.'

'Bowls, bowls. My goodness. "Ay, there's the rub" – that one's from Hamlet,' Cleaver chuckled to himself. 'Not many people know just how many bowling metaphors turn up in Shakespeare's dramas. This is more like it. Much more interesting. Yes, I think we can have a crack at that. Pity there are only four numbers, and it's on a photo, but let's have a look. Seems Shakespeare knew a fair bit about bowls.

Probably played it when he wasn't writing plays. Let's try the microscope. And did you know that the jack bowl – that's the one you're supposed to bowl nearest to – was sometimes called the "mistress" in Elizabethan England? So when old Shakers writes about "kissing the jack" there's a whole new level of *double entendres* to play on. Fine stuff. Yup, the inflexions and angles all seem to be the same. Nope, I can't see any obvious differences, although we are working with only four digits. The fact we have a "2" and a "9" is helpful. They're usually quite distinctive, graphologically speaking. If there were differences I'd expect to see them there. From a preliminary point of view I'd say they were by the same hand. Hope I've got it right, otherwise,' he chuckled, '"My fortune runs against the bias," another fine bowling metaphor. Richard the Second, that one. Would you like a formal report?'

This time Alex managed to get in first. 'No, no, that's fine, Mervyn. Just your preliminary observations are fine. Very helpful. Many thanks to you.' He was trying hard to show he was still in charge. Jacko took back his documents and Cleaver resigned himself to the pile of folders in front of him.

Alex engineered his father to the door and moved to within an inch of his face. 'This is unforgivable,' he hissed. 'He thinks you're a police officer. You've conned your way in here, and you've conned him.' He was red in the face with fury. 'I'm taking you to reception and seeing you off the premises personally before anyone finds out. This is so unprofessional I could kick you down the stairs.'

* * *

You had to hand it to Charles Wainwright MP for being such a slick bastard. When the next issue of the weekly local newspaper, the *South Warwickshire Herald*, came out he featured in a fine photograph on the front inside page. Under the header of 'Wainwright Saves the Day' was the following text:

Charles Wainwright, the MP and owner of Belford Manor, saved the day last week in arranging to demolish a wall in the manor grounds. The wall was next to the place where a visiting school party was due to enjoy their picnic. It was seen to be in danger of collapse, and, forsaking affairs of state in Westminster, our MP rushed back and personally supervised its demolition.

The wall was part of a Grade II listed building, but a county spokesperson said that in emergencies safety issues normally took priority. The MP had since sought retrospective listed building consent which would normally be granted under these circumstances.

The photograph shows Mr Wainwright standing next to the rubble congratulating a smiling Mr Seth Hetherington, one of the village pensioners, whom he employed to assist in the demolition. 'I think it's very important to help boost the income of pensioners like Seth,' he said. 'They can still play a very valuable role in our society and we have much to learn from them and from their experiences'.

Jacko wondered how high up the political ladder this issue had climbed, but you had to admire the way they'd turned the whole thing around. And Jacko had no hard feelings for Seth, whose palm had undoubtedly been greased by Wainwright to keep him quiet. As for Jacko, well his card was now well and truly marked. He rang up Alison in County Records to find out what had been going on. She apologised. It had been taken out of her hands by "someone upstairs" and decisions were made by those well above her pay grade. Yes, Wainwright had demolished a wall which was within the curtilage of listed building and therefore required formal consent which was given retrospectively. As for the part about the school children, she'd taken the liberty of trying to find out which school it was, but had been reprimanded by her line manager two levels up and told to mind her own business. Her view, unsurprisingly, was that the whole thing stank.

CHAPTER 6

Jacko had been for a long walk in the Cotswolds to clear his head. Back at home some three hours later, fully recharged and with the junk in his brain flushed out by the fresh air, he'd decided a night in front of the TV was in order – just some mindless crap that required no concentration, something intellectually moribund that made no demands on him whatsoever. He poured himself a beer and flopped into a chair by the TV. Maybe he ought to ring Lucy too. He'd not spoken to her for almost a week and felt a bit guilty. They'd not managed to get together for the best part of a month now either, other commitments seemed to have conspired to get in the way. Both were in their mid-fifties, divorced and with their own lives to lead. They lived about two hours drive from each other, not the sort of distance to easily nip across and meet up. Jacko dialled her number, half expecting she'd be out at some function, or conscientiously helping a postgraduate string a thesis together at the university where she worked. Her home phone was tuned to ring seven times before it reverted to answer mode. On the sixth ring he was about to replace the receiver when there was a clatter at the other end.

'Well well, I thought you'd given up on me!' came the sarcastic greeting. 'Am I the lucky girl then! What have I done to deserve this accolade of attention? Is it my birthday? No. Is it the anniversary of my divorce? No. Is it Christmas? Ooh. Better check in my diary because I haven't ordered a Christmas tree yet...'

'Just thought I'd give you a quick call to see how you were,' Jacko said patiently, 'seeing as we hadn't been in touch for a while. Thought we might meet up somewhere for dinner?'

'Missing me already, are you?'

'Apart from that, I need a decent meal and I can't afford one. Where have you been? I tried you about a week ago but got nowhere.'

'Cambridge, running a course for rich foreigners – a programme which possessed no academic credibility whatsoever. It could have been delivered by a gerbil, but it generated thousands in funds for the university, hence by my boss's definition it was a major success. My view is it's a waste of time and a prostitution of intellectual standards. And while we're on the subject of intellectual standards, what have you been up to? Apart, that is, from not answering my text messages.'

'Sorry, I've been side-tracked. I just haven't looked at them of late. Anything urgent?'

'Nope, only my suggestion we meet up in London the week after next for a couple of nights of good food, wine and some theatre. I've already got the theatre tickets booked. I've a conference there and it would give us a chance to catch up, chill out and have a weekend together. You game for that, or will it interfere with you playing Sherlock Holmes? I assume that's why you've been so quiet?'

'Sorry about that. I'll tell you about it when we meet up. Apart from a police job there's a big excavation coming up. Text me the dates and I'll book a hotel. Meanwhile, I could do with a teeny-weeny favour?' He paused, noting a suspicious silence at the other end. 'Um, I wondered if you'd be going back to Cambridge in the near future?'

'As it happens, I just might be.' She sounded wary, 'There's another bloody day course there next week. I wasn't planning to stop long. What is it you want me to do?'

'I could do with some information from the alumni office there. It's about a Rev Rogers. I'll email you the details later.'

* * *

The Rev Rogers was busy in the vicarage, packing. He'd made a policy decision to get out of town before the development of the vicarage and its grounds became fully under way. Having booked himself into a retreat called St Aidan's somewhere on the Northumberland coast, he was looking forward to guaranteed peace, quiet, the opportunity to worship in an environment unencumbered by members of the public, and the chance to make a personal pilgrimage out to the monastery on the island of Lindisfarne. He admired those early monks with their reliance on piety, austerity and devotion to prayer. His previous incumbency had been in an urban parish in Cheshire, just outside the Welsh border not far from Chester, where his adherence to traditional values of spiritual discipline and his insistence on maintaining the old theologies had not endeared him to either his parish or his elders. His move to Middle Belford in the Coventry Diocese had been choreographed by the church authorities: there was no doubt the Diocese of Chester did not agree with the nature of his ministry, and coincidentally there was a gap which was difficult to fill in Middle Belford. He'd been put out to graze, and he knew it.

He'd tried to bring up his twin daughters, Suzie and Linda, as a single parent, but he knew he'd failed dismally. He also knew that most of the village talked about it. They were young women these days, with their interests and ambitions, and had all but left home for good. What he now needed was a new focus, and his sojourn to Northumberland to immerse himself in the Age of Saints was his means to achieving it.

Mrs Jefferson, the lady who cleaned the vicarage, had been given three weeks off from cooking and housework. She failed to see much point in cleaning the place anyway if it was going to be gutted, but it meant being deprived of income while he was away. She made a fuss about it and he'd reluctantly agreed to pay her a small retainer to keep her quiet.

He hadn't been away anywhere for years and had no idea what to pack. Both daughters were in London at the moment but they'd agreed to travel the relatively short distance north to help him out. It gave them the opportunity to make a final visit to the old house and gardens where they'd spent their teenage years. It had been a wonderful old house to grow up in, with passages and staircases to be explored, creaking floors to frighten them at night, a mysterious cellar, and a garden full of trees, bushes and secret paths to play around.

The girls had been adopted by the Rogers soon after birth, but neither remembered much about their family life in Cheshire before they moved. He'd been strict with them, but he'd always been sympathetic to them as they grew up, always gave them time when they wanted it, and always made sure that he attended any school event in which they were involved. Mrs Rogers, however, seemed to despise the time and attention he afforded them; she performed her motherly duties clinically and without fuss, but organised them to fit around her own social interests. The twins thus grew up in a household largely devoid of emotion.

He was happy to be sent anywhere the church thought his ministry might be best suited. In that respect his environment was irrelevant – urban, suburban, rural or overseas made no difference. Mrs Rogers, on the other hand, was a townie. She thrived on a busy life – shops, people, cinemas, meetings and dinner parties – in fact all the things that he loathed. He'd attempted, in the early years of their marriage, to mould her into the role of the stereotypical vicar's wife by asking her to back him up with minor church tasks such as making teas and accompanying him at social events. She immediately told him what he could do with that idea. Over the years their relationship deteriorated badly, although they tried not to let it affect the girls.

When he was offered the move to Middle Belford she saw it as the final straw. She was appalled by the remoteness of the place, the lack of transport, the dearth of any shops other than a small general store and a post office, and the fact that there was no signal on her mobile phone. A visit to the vicarage did little to help. It was too big and draughty, had no central heating, the kitchen facilities were medieval and the garden impossible. She gave him the ultimatum: it was either Middle Belford or her. He'd chosen the former.

* * *

The twins, both extremely attractive, shapely and with shoulder-length fair hair emerged from the car at the vicarage smartly dressed. Anyone meeting them that day would have encountered two thoughtful, courteous, mild-mannered daughters – a far cry from their wild, party-going alter egos that bore the same names in the student scenes of London and Newcastle. Most people found them visually indistinguishable, but their father had always been able to tell one from the other, although he could never actually put his finger on how he did it. It was just something that he knew. Both were entering their final year at university, their study programmes having been interrupted on several occasions by time abroad learning new languages, travelling, and some modelling.

He was delighted to see them and had arranged for a reluctant Mrs Jefferson to prepare some lunch. It was an enjoyable occasion with memories exchanged across the table. Polite questions about their studies and their friends were diplomatically answered. Both daughters were involved with putting their mind to their final year dissertations, Suzie on a project involving modern languages and Linda on one dealing with local history. It occurred to him that Linda might usefully get in touch with the man who was managing the excavations, Jackson. He had a doctorate, so he must have a modicum of academic credibility, and he presumably knew about local history. Jacko's business card was on the mantelpiece with all the other information the council had sent and he handed it across. To the great relief of the twins this brought them around to the topic of the building development and his impending visit to Northumberland. He wasn't sure what to take and for the first time in his life he allowed his daughters to go through his wardrobe. Their reaction, having started this exercise, was one of measured horror. His clothes, including his underwear, were either grey or black, irrespective of their original colour, and mostly threadbare; it was an embarrassment to them that he should be wearing any of it.

The outcome of this wardrobe audit brought out the best in the twins. He was led into the driving seat of his Jaguar and together they drove into Banbury, where they made a bee-line for Marks and Spencer's. Once there the twins took over the men's department, lifting items off shelves, checking on colours and size, holding jumpers up to the natural light, discussing their father's style suitability, piling clothes up for him to try on, making demands on the assistants, and generally providing authoritative opinion on their father's sartorial makeover. Their effort even extended, without embarrassment, to the underwear section, where they loudly discussed the relative merits of the different styles, giggling quietly to each other over the underwear of recent males of their acquaintance before deciding on the choice of boxer shorts for their father. He had no say in these purchases whatsoever but seemed content to acquiesce, not to mention being just that little bit proud of his daughters' control of the situation. They persuaded him to subscribe to a store card, and they left the shop armed with bags of clothes that their father would proudly try on again and pack in the evening. Back at Middle Belford they shared a pot of tea and some scones that Mrs Jefferson had prepared, then, job done, they drove away down the drive with their father waving wistfully from the vicarage window.

* * *

Archaeological work started at the vicarage the following Monday and Jacko was duly on hand to supervise arrangements. Firstly, the two temporary huts and the toilet facilities arrived on the back of a truck. Jacko oversaw their positioning, arranged the electricity supply for the lighting, heating, computers and the essential facilities of kettle and microwave oven, then waited for the plumbers to connect up a temporary water supply. Chairs, tables and storage shelving were installed. It started to become quite cosy. He reminisced a little about how he began life on digs, usually without any facilities other than a camping stove and some dirty mugs, sitting out in the open on upturned buckets, carting all the tools backwards and forwards every morning and every evening. Now it was all respectable, all written into the planning process and costed properly with everything adhering to health and safety requirements. By the time the professional archaeologists showed up, a mechanical excavator was being driven off a low-loader ready for the work to start.

The excavator driver was a friendly little man called Ditmar with bright blue eyes set in a round head, not unlike a balloon, who proudly sported a brand new set of green overalls supplied by the excavator hire company. Jacko had hired the machine to skim off the topsoil to allow the archaeologists to work more efficiently. In fairness the company hadn't exactly recommended Ditmar, just pointed out that, being new, he could do the job but maybe not as quickly as an experienced driver, hence the reduced cost.

Jacko had tried to explain to Ditmar that the gardens had been earmarked for building and he needed the machine to strip away the surface soil in specific places so that he could check for any archaeology underneath. It was bread and butter to Jacko but a completely novel concept to Ditmar, who nodded vigorously nevertheless. Jacko had also noted, disturbingly, that English was not his native language.

'Gut machine, Meester Jaaksin, yes?' the diminutive man had said as he climbed into the cab. 'Ditmar, ver gut deeging, yes?' and he experimented with knobs and levers while Jacko and the others tactfully retreated to a place of safety. Jacko sat in his car making notes and mulling over the plans sent by the developer, periodically walking over to monitor Ditmar's progress. It was erratic. The skimming wasn't how he wanted it and he asked Ditmar to do it again, and then a third time as the excavator bucket lurched from side to side, periodically crashing to the ground with a noisy metallic bang or with the bucket arm barging into trees. Jacko regretted his cost-savings and tried to avoid the concerned looks of his archaeological colleagues. However, the outcome was eventually tolerable and Jacko waved to Ditmar through clouds of diesel fumes to move to the next section.

Elsewhere in the grounds there was the whirr of chainsaws, blue smoke and a flash of red helmets as contractors roped themselves into the trees. Branches came crashing down, followed by the trunks in segments before the roots were dragged out by a machine. By lunchtime almost a century of elm, mountain ash, birch and a rogue monkey tree had been decimated, chopped into fire-sized logs for seasoning, or turned into chippings. Three chestnuts were left. They were protected by preservation orders, taped off to keep the machines away, and were sacrosanct. By that time the entire argument as to whether development should have taken place at all had been forgotten and replaced by a discussion on names. Various opinions suggested the new care home should be called 'The Chestnuts'; others suggested the new road should be called 'Conker Lane' rather than 'Vicarage Drive'. And so the arguments continued, diluted and trite.

CHAPTER 7

The initial work involved stripping off the plants and shrubs at the back of the grounds as well as clearing the walled vegetable garden. The second of these locations was where Jacko suspected the Viking graves were. Once the topsoil had been clawed away by Ditmar's clumsy efforts and heaped up elsewhere, the archaeologists moved in and unearthed areas of stone flagging, lines of plant bedding and hard earthen pathways. He insisted that all the flags should be planned and recorded in the usual way before they were removed, despite the fact they were quite modern. Eyebrows were raised, but nobody openly questioned it. The slabs were crude, mostly cracked and barely worth selling on by the builder for crazy paving. Underneath them was a mish-mash of different soils full of centuries of domestic rubbish that the archaeologists were obliged to work their way through. As it slowly began to be cleared Jacko's hunch was proved right. In the smooth grey surface of the natural subsoil underneath lay the dark outlines of graves. About half a dozen of them were exposed at first, each orientated roughly east/west like long macabre shadows.

Quietly satisfied and feeling particularly smug, Jacko hung around for a while watching the clearing work progress, then left the site. He went across to the church and spent a while mooching around the graveyard trying to piece together in his head the bits of information about the bats, the shadowy figure in the belfry and how on earth someone could get up the tower if the door was locked. The only other point of access would be from the roof, then up the short iron ladder attached to the tower and in through the rickety door into the clock chamber. But it would entail getting on the roof in the first place, and that would require a proper builder's ladder, not a domestic one like the thing he'd bought at B&Q in Banbury. The door at the top of the tower was only held shut by a sandbag pushed against it and could probably be opened with a bit of a heave from the outside. But why all that bother? His imagination was beginning to run away with him. Foul play? Surely not? That was ridiculous. Why would anyone go to all that trouble to bump off a octogenarian clock winder, and what could the motive possibly have been? There had to be a more logical solution somewhere.

Still mulling it over, he sat on one of the benches in the churchyard absorbing the symmetry of the church's architecture. The proportions were perfect. Somewhere lost in history was a skilled architect who probably spent several years of his life working out the design of the church and supervising its construction. Eight centuries later his building but not his name survived. Jacko wondered who he was and what he would have thought about the village now, and the landscape around it. He visualised this medieval craftsman with his scrolls of drawings laying out the footprint with ropes, choosing the materials from the local quarry and supervising its construction. How long did it take, where did the labour force come from, how were they paid and how often did the patron visit to check on progress?

This exercise in imaginary time travel was brought to a sudden halt when he noticed a grey van parked at the church gate. The sign on the side, 'Midlands Clocks Ltd', slowly sank into his consciousness – it had to have something to do with motorising the clock winding mechanism. The engineers were probably working up the tower right now. Grabbing his camera from his car parked nearby he made his way inside the church, through the unlocked tower door and up the stairs, eventually emerging slightly out of breath into the clock chamber to the astonishment of two serious-looking clock engineers.

'Sorry,' he muttered. He waved his camera aloft. 'I've just come to take a few photos for the local history group before the new motor gets installed. Hope you don't mind, I won't get in the way.' It was a very plausible excuse and the two engineers nodded. Both looked like they'd been in the business a long time. They knew their clocks and how to maintain them. Between them on the floor was a piece of sacking on which had been carefully positioned lines of specialist-looking brass tools, all beautifully cared for and cleaned. Jacko took a few photos to make his visit look plausible and chatted enthusiastically about the mechanism in the pretence of being some nerdy clock buff. He couldn't help notice that they kept smiling at each other. During the conversation it transpired that one of them had given both Tommy and Seth some form of induction on the winding procedure years ago, although he couldn't remember when.

After a while, he thanked them for their time, moved the sandbag away from the outer door and told them he'd be going out on the roof to photograph the gargoyles while he was up here. They winced when the cold blast of air from the open door hit them. 'Sorry,' he muttered, then quickly went out, bracing himself against the wind and pulling the door behind him as well as he could. He clung to the iron ladder and climbed the short way down to the apex of the nave roof. Despite the sunny weather it was cold up there with a strong wind gusting and the rope around the flag pole strumming like a drum beat. It was quite an experience. He felt utterly uncomfortable and wholly exposed to various parts of the village but, happily, not to the vicarage. The lead-covered nave roof sloped gently down to a stone lattice parapet, and his eye was caught by the savage iconography of the gargoyles which drained surface water away. Perhaps it wasn't such a bad idea to have a look at those after all, but if he went any further round to the south there was the risk of being seen from the vicarage. He crept back a little and peeked around the other corner of the tower to the north where he felt more comfortable. It was quieter in the lee of the wind, and he made his way slowly down the gentle slope of the roof crab-like on his hands and feet to the parapet, then peeked over the edge. The houses on that side were hidden by tall trees at the edge of the graveyard. It occurred to him that this was probably the only place on the whole roof where someone could move around and not be seen. He went cold thinking about it.

Feeling slightly uneasy, he crept slowly back up the roof, keeping as low as possible until he reached the base of the iron ladder which led back up the outside of the tower, and back into view from the village. Making his way hesitantly up rung by rung he wished he was fitter and less overweight, then finally managed to cling to the top rung, balancing against the gusts. He was out of any shelter, the wind howled around his ears and he pushed against the wooden door to get back to safety and out of sight again. Strangely, the door failed to budge. He pushed again, but it seemed to be stuck. That was odd. Perhaps it had jammed and just needed lifting up a little, or a wiggle to the handle. That failed to work either. Hell, maybe the engineers had forgotten about him, locked it and gone away for the day. Shit! No, no, there was no key, was there? What the fuck was going on? Maybe they had just moved the sandbag back to keep out the draught, in which case a good shove should move it. He put his whole weight against it, or as much as he could without falling off the ladder, but it made no difference. The sun went behind a cloud and it became colder, and darker. A wave of fear came over him and a cold nausea. Did someone think he was getting too close to finding out what really happened to the old man, and now it was his turn? Shit. He pushed harder and banged the door at the top and then again at the bottom in case it was jammed. He pushed again, this time as hard as he could, and in desperation, but there was still no way it would open. By now the wind was blowing straight through his clothes. Shit, shit, shit. Panic began to set in and he broke out in a cold sweat, his hands became clammy and his pulse became faster. Then, all of a sudden and without warning, the door flew open with his next push and Jacko fell on his face inside to be greeted by two engineers bent double with laughter, barely able to stand up.

'Hoo, hoo, hoo! Got you, got you,' roared one of them, 'Should see your face, hoo, hoo, hoo!'

Jacko was on his hands and knees on the floor. 'Bastards, bastards,' he shouted back, red with anger, and they howled even more.

One of them managed to get a sentence out, 'Sorry, son, couldn't help it. It was too good an opportunity. Hoo, hoo, hoo. You should have seen yourself! What a picture! Hoo, hoo, hoo. Sounded like you were going to wet yourself!' He was wiping the tears from his eyes. 'Made my day, that has!' Jacko gathered that they'd heard him coming up the iron ladder, taken the long pole that looked like it was there for opening windows and just held the door shut with it from a distance for a bit of a laugh. It was a long time before he saw the funny side of it.

He left the church feeling humiliated and made his way across to the vicarage where the archaeologists were packing up ready for home. The tall figure of Mark, the dig supervisor, was standing looking at the site while in conversation with the vicar, who was curiously smart and trendy. The dismal stained grey suit that characterised his persona was no longer evident, instead he sported a natty checked jacket, dark blue trousers, a matching blue shirt and shiny brown shoes. Apart from the statutory clerical collar, he could have emerged from the shop window of a gentleman's outfitter. Mark saw Jacko coming and shouted over to him.

'Looks like we've got them all now, Jacko. I reckon fifteen graves in all. Most of them are clear enough, but the ones closest to the vicarage look a bit disturbed.'

'Disturbed?' the vicar asked, clearly concerned. 'You mean someone's dug into them?'

'In a sense, yes,' Jacko replied as he joined them. 'When they started using the graveyard they probably had some idea of how the graves were going to be organised.' He pointed across to the dark discolouring in the ground, 'If you look at the graves over there, they're in neat rows and probably the earliest. As time passed and more bodies needed burial, they probably ran out of space and buried them on top of earlier ones, like at this end. That's all we mean by "disturbed", there's nothing sinister about it. It happens today in the present churchyard too.'

'But how do you know there are fifteen graves? It just looks like one messy stain in the ground to me. Fifteen's pushing it, isn't it?'

'I grant you,' Mark said, taken aback by what he saw as a criticism of his professional competence, 'it's a bit difficult to see now, especially since the soils have dried out, but when they were still damp you could see the outline of each individual grave. I better show you.' He vanished poker-faced into one of the huts and returned with a scale plan fastened to a drawing board. The vicar took it and studied it intensely. 'I see, I see,' he glanced from the site to the plan, then from the plan back to the site again. 'Still looks like guesswork to me,' was his considered judgement as he handed it back.

'Well, let me tell you how the system works,' Jacko interrupted quickly, realising that Mark had taken serious exception to the man. 'These grave outlines on the plan will have been drawn and checked by different people and each grave numbered. It's a sort of quality control. We need to know what order they were buried in this particular "messy stain" as you call it so that we can work out a sequence when we excavate. As it stands it looks like grave 13 – this one here,' he pointed to the plan, 'is the latest in this particular group.' He held the planning board under the vicar's nose and circled the grave with a pencil.

The Rev Rogers seemed disinclined to discuss the matter further and looked around what was once a fine vicarage garden in a rather detached way. He hunched his shoulders a few times, as though uncomfortable in his new clothes, before turning to Jacko and changing the subject.

'I plan to travel tomorrow. To me this whole business of digging up bodies is getting to me,' he snorted, then scribbled on a piece of paper and passed it over to Jacko. 'This is my mobile phone number. Perhaps you would be good enough to call me when this is all over? And the sooner the better as far as I'm concerned.'

'Of course, we wouldn't want to disturb your holiday,' Jacko said agreeably, smiling as best he could.

'Holiday? Who said anything about a holiday? I certainly didn't. I'm away to a retreat for as long as it takes to avoid this morbidity.' He looked directly at Mark, 'Have you any idea how long it will take? Presumably you can tell me that without resorting to guesswork?'

Mark, it has to be said, showed remarkable restraint. 'Well, excavating graves is specialist work,' he said in a calm, professional way through gritted teeth. 'We have two staff here trained to do it. It takes roughly a full working day, weather permitting, for one person to excavate a single grave.' He scratched his chin. 'I suppose, given holiday time, contingencies, and so on, a couple of weeks? I can't be more accurate than that.'

'Will there be flesh on them?'

The question came out of the blue. Jacko and Mark looked at each other in surprise.

'Er, well...' Mark said, somewhat thrown. 'The soil here isn't particularly acidic but given the bodies are likely to have been in the ground for well over a thousand years – it'll just be the hard tissue, the skeleton, that's left. That's our assumption anyway.'

The Rev Rogers snarled back, 'Ah, assumption rather than guesswork this time? Well there's a change!' He glowered at the two of them like a schoolteacher admonishing eleven-year olds. 'So if I asked you how long it takes for flesh to decay in the ground, you couldn't give me an accurate answer to that either, could you?'

The two eleven-year olds weren't expecting that one. Jacko, sensing Mark's increasing anger, thought it better to step in, 'It depends on a host of different things – climate, depth, and soil bacteria to name a few. It's not an exact science but here, as a calculated guess, not more than a few years.' Mark nodded in agreement, his eyes focused firmly on the vicar, his fists clenched in his pockets.

'Ah, a *calculated* guess this time. Well, things are looking up even more,' Rogers commented sarcastically. 'I've also had it on good authority that the bones will be mixed up by roots from the chestnut trees. I suppose you can't give me a definitive answer on that one either, can you? Will they or won't they?'

Jacko and Mark looked at each other again. What the hell was the man driving at? Were there fumes coming out of his new clothes that were addling his brain? Was he just being difficult, or did he have some agenda they didn't know about?

'Well, that's always a potential problem,' Mark tried to explain, 'but our guys are skilled enough to sort that out when they're excavating. They've done this many times before.'

The vicar wasn't to be derailed. 'And at the end of the day, how will you know if the bodies are Vikings or not?' It was almost as though there was a list of questions the man was working through. Jacko explained as best he could about how when the Vikings were pagan the bodies were all buried with grave goods – weapons with the males, or jewellery with the females. Recognising those was easy. But when they became Christianised, sometimes they had no grave goods at all, other times they put a single item or two in with the burial – sort of hedging their bets – or sometimes they symbolically broke an object, often a prized sword and laid it with the body.

'And if there aren't any bent swords or goods, what then?' the vicar asked impatiently. 'You can't tell, can you?' he said smugly. 'Bit of a waste of time and money really – money that could be spent much better elsewhere. Why bother? Why don't you use machines to dig them up instead of these labourers?' he said dismissively, pointing to the archaeologists. 'Wouldn't they be better off working in Tesco?'

Jacko did his best to control himself. Mark, on the other hand, had seen the red mist and was up for a fight. He moved towards the Rev Rogers, raised himself up straight and towered over him. Jacko moved to intervene but Mark waved him aside.

'Let me give you a simple explanation Mr Rogers,' he said patronisingly. 'One that you might understand. The first thing to remember is that the development of this churchyard results from a decision of the church commissioners – your lords and master, not ours – to sell this land for profit. It's not our doing. So let's get that straight to start with, shall we? It's because the commissioners want to develop that we've been asked to recover the bodies. That's what we're trained to do.' The Rev Rogers was now looking astonished and a little sheepish. 'Secondly,' Mark continued, 'these "labourers" as you call them, are all highly skilled. Do you know how many bones there are in an adult human skeleton?' He paused, waiting for an answer that never came. 'No, I thought not. Well there are over two hundred, more in a child, and these so-called "labourers" can recognise all of them, identify the proximal from the distal ends – that's the tops from the bottoms to you – recognise which ribs lie in which order, the arrangement of the twenty-four bones in the spinal column, and which teeth fit where in the upper and lower jaw. Three of them, including myself, have doctorates which, incidentally, I note you don't have. The others all have masters degrees, which of course you do have, but unless I'm mistaken, it just involved paying ten quid for the privilege. My "labourers" took a full year out of their lives, at their own cost, to study for theirs.' The vicar was noticeably getting paler by the minute. 'Thirdly,' Mark went on, clearly on a roll, and even more menacing than before, 'we afford dignity to each individual both in recovery and in reburial. I would have thought that you, as a spiritual leader following a Christian code, might have understood that. But clearly you don't. And finally, given that the commissioners are destroying their graves, we have an opportunity to discover a little more about past societies by studying their bodies. Let me emphasise it. And please watch my lips – we're undertaking this whole exercise professionally.' He stooped and lowered his face to within inches of the vicar. 'If you don't fucking like it, I suggest you complain to your bosses, the church commissioners who instigated it, the local authority who approved it, and the Chartered Institute for Archaeologists that governs our professional standards.' And with that he walked off.

Jacko and the vicar stood in stunned silence, Jacko thoroughly impressed by Mark's uncharacteristic diatribe. It wasn't like him at all. He and the vicar looked at each other for a moment.

'Yup, that's about the gist of it,' Jacko added cheerily, and walked off too.

* * *

Jacko met up with Mark in one of the huts. Mark was sitting in a chair in the corner having an illicit cigarette, elbow resting on table. 'Sorry,' he said. 'Lost my rag there. The twat wound me up. Thought I was going to clock him one. Sorry, shouldn't have said what I did. Stupid of me.'

'Nah, forget it,' said Jacko. 'He had it coming. What the hell was he driving at? It was like he was deliberately saying things to get us wound up. Anyway, I'm sure he won't take it any further. All you did was a bit of plain speaking.'

Mark drew on his cigarette then flicked the stub out through the open door. 'Come on,' he said, let's get out of here. I better leave the door open for a few minutes to get the smell of fags out.'

Pondering on the behaviour of the Rev Rogers, Jacko had a worrying thought that he'd kept to himself. 'While we're waiting,' he said, trying to think it through, 'can I have a quick look at the grave plan you showed him, and also the plans of the later stone flagging on top of them? Just an idea I've got.'

Mark pulled them out. They were on transparent drafting film so they could be overlain on each other. Jacko shuffled them around, looked at them hard, and made various humming noises. 'Do you mind,' he said at last, 'if I take these home tonight? I'd like to have copies made.'

'Fine by me, but I'll need them back in the morning when we start excavating the graves.'

'And out of interest, who have you got lined up for that? Is Christine still on the books? She's the best one you've got for a job like this, and I'd really like her involved.'

'Christine? She's the one you use for your forensic work, isn't she?' Mark asked, clearly curious. 'I can arrange to have her here if you really want. She's on another job in

Gloucestershire, but I can move folk around. Trouble is that would mean waiting a day or so.'

'Tell you what, start tomorrow as planned, but kick off with the clear-cut graves at the far end. When Christine comes, can you put her in the messy lot at this end where there's more obvious disturbance? It'll need someone really good like her to sort out commingled bones. Have you got her number?' Mark looked it up on his phone and Jacko wrote it down. They both packed their bags and Jacko strode off to his car, leaving Mark to turn out and lock up.

CHAPTER 8

'Tommy, you're just going to have to accept it sooner or later, it's inevitable.' The Rev Rogers looked at him hard. They sat together on a bench in St John's churchyard on a chilly spring morning.

Tommy stared down at his feet, tapping them on the flagstones. His voice was slow, almost pathetic in tone, 'I just don't see the point, I don't. Twice a week for over ten year I've been winding her. I done all that's expected.'

'We've always been grateful for everything you've done, and that's not the point, Tommy.' The vicar had dreaded this moment, telling the old boy that the one thing he cherished most in his life was being taken from him.

'It's traditional, that winding,' the old man complained, his eyes still fixed on his feet. 'It's been done for generations. That clock was built for this church in 1848. Craftsmanship it is, a one-off. Been there for over a hundred and fifty years. Still works a treat after all this time. No need for changin' it that I can see.'

'Best look at it differently,' said the vicar sympathetically. 'By electrifying it we're keeping it going for another hundred and fifty years. If we don't do something now the chances are the clock workings will have worn out in their present state even before you and I are worn out. And it's not just that, there are a host of reasons I could go into.'

'And I can give you a host of reasons why you shouldn't,' was the frosty reply. 'I thought a man of the cloth would value tradition, like, but you're like every other incomer, full of smart arse ideas, trying to change stuff that don't need changin'. What's next then, eh, stoppin' the fifteen minute chimes 'cause some dinky new folk can't sleep well? Then we'll have the cattle silenced will we, 'cause their mooing wakes folk up too soon, then have them banned altogether because of the smell they make? And then maybe flog off the bells and have tape recorded chimes instead? Thin end of the wedge this is.'

The Rev Rogers sighed and looked away, 'Tommy, you've got it all wrong. It's no job for an old man like you, nor Seth, when he does the winding for you. And who's going to take the mantle when you two leave this world? The stairs aren't safe, the mechanism needs attention, it's not guarded properly, and the open weight chutes make it draughty for the bell ringers. The ladies who do the ringing aren't getting any younger, and other folk just don't seem interested in taking over. Congregations are down, it's a struggle to keep the spirit of Christ alive.' There was a sound of frustration in his voice. 'I'm doing everything I can.'

Tommy looked at him, 'Have you tried making them sermons more interesting?' he said with a sneer.

'If it's fire and brimstone you're after, Tommy, then go and become a radical evangelist. It's not what we do here. We're concerned with helping the needy, comforting the bereaved and providing guidance through life's course. And when did you last listen to one of my sermons?'

Tommy pulled out his pipe and fiddled with it before answering. 'Sometime last century.' He paused and looked up, 'And when did you last visit the needy? Drove round in your Jag did you?'

'I follow Christ's calling in many different ways. Not everyone understands them.'

'No I bet they fucking don't.'

'Tommy, there's no need for abuse. I used to think you and I got on well, we have our agreements as well as our little differences, don't we?'

Tommy fell silent.

'All I'm trying to do,' the vicar continued, 'is to follow Christ's example, make this a better world to live in and to follow the scriptures. When did you last read the bible?'

'School, and that was enough. Talk about movin' with the times. How can you believe all that stuff – miracles, walking on water, feeding thousands of folk with a bit of bread and fish, like, the sea opening up and letting Moses through, an' all that?'

The vicar was on a loser and he knew it, 'It's mostly figurative, Tommy,' he said, 'it's not supposed to be real, it's to do with the power of faith, and we…'

'Like 'ere, is it?' the old man interrupted, pointing to the graveyard and struggling to his feet. 'All these folk lying heads at the west, feet at the east. Why's that then? Bible tells us that on judgement day all them dead, here and everywhere else, they'll rise up facing east yelling "Hallelujah!" That's it, in't it? All facing the Good Lord?'

The Rev Rogers attempted a reply but didn't get very far.

'Well the Good Lord didn't know much about yew trees, did 'e, then?' Tommy interrupted. He went over to a nearby headstone next to an overgrown yew. 'Look here then, read it then, vicar.'

The vicar knew what was coming, but read it out nonetheless. '*Joseph Randolph Cooper. Blacksmith. Laid to rest in the care of the Lord, August 4th 1859 aged 64 years. Dorothy Isobelle Cooper. Fell asleep February 21st 1865, his much beloved wife aged 67 years.*'

'And this un,' he pointed to the adjacent headstone.

'*Agnes Maud Graham, married to God and taken in peace, July 17th 1872 aged 41 years.*'

'Just look at these 'ere headstones,' said Tommy. 'All of 'em twisted, lopsided and undermined by the yew roots. So what does that do to the bones, roots pushing everywhere, mixing 'em all up? Old Mr and Mrs Cooper all a-jumbled up then, maybe bits of Mr Cooper bein' a-pushed into spinster Agnes Graham. "Taken in peace", was she? More like "taken in pieces", I'd say, after this,' he chuckled at his own joke. 'What's it to be on judgement day, then, vicar? Bit of a mess, eh?' He went on triumphantly without waiting for reply. 'So what 'appens then when the big trumpet blows? Old Mr and Mrs Cooper leap out with the wrong heads on and bits of Agnes caught up with them?'

'Yes, yes, yes,' The Rev Rogers finally managed to butt in. 'I know what you're saying, but it's just a figurative way

73

of expressing it. It's the souls that rise, not the physical parts. It was written like that so that people in earlier times who didn't have any education might understand the theology behind it better. The souls of the dead rise and are taken their separate ways, the good to heaven and the evil given time to repent.'

Tommy made his way back to the bench and thought for a while. 'How does that affect other events you and I know of, then?' he asked slowly.

The vicar turned and looked at him angrily, 'I thought we'd agreed that there were some things no longer up for discussion, Tommy. That was part of our bargain. That was why I agreed to pay you to take on the winding.'

'Bet that payment don't appear in the parish accounts, do it?' Tommy smirked again.

The vicar moved his head inches from Tommy's, 'Don't go down that road,' he said, glaring at him. 'You know full well it comes out of my own pocket. It's a personal arrangement.'

Tommy stood his ground, 'So what happens when the clock's got a motor, then? What happens to my monthly payoff if there's no clock to wind?'

'I'll have to think of something else, maybe a bit of tidying up in the churchyard, or cleaning inside, something like that we can pay you for.'

'Or maybe just nothing,' added Tommy, 'like, just leave me the notes once a month in the usual place'. It was spoken almost threateningly. 'I mean, like, I'm a bit old now for doing a lot of bending and moving stuff. Windin' the clock's one thing, that's a skill, but a man of my years has to think about his body now. Tidying up and cleaning, well that takes a while longer, involves stooping and carrying. No, that's not for me at my age. I ain't a tidier or a cleaner, I'm a winder, and if there's no clock to wind, well I'll just take the money instead. Ain't my decision to motorise it, is it?'

The vicar glared at him. The suggestion was not unexpected. The next one was.

'And while we're on the topic,' the old man said with renewed boldness, 'maybe you could see your way to leaving me a bit more. Price of things these days, and you've never upped it since we started, have you? Consider it a rise in insurance premiums, if you like.' It was followed by another smirk.

The Rev Rogers got to his feet and stood over him, looking round to see if anyone was in earshot. 'That's preposterous. I just don't have the money, and I certainly won't have it when I retire. For heaven's sake, be reasonable.' He lowered his tone while a woman with a child in a pushchair ambled past. 'All right,' he muttered, 'we'll forget the work part and make it a purely financial arrangement.'

Tommy looked up at him quizzically. 'No,' he said firmly. 'Not enough. I need more, say two hundred a month will do me fine. Think of it as helping an old soldier.'

'Two hundred! Two hundred! I can't afford that. What we had was an amicable arrangement. This is nothing more than blackmail.'

'Cost of livin' increase, I'd prefer to call it. Man of your standing should be careful, I'd have thought. Wouldn't want the wrong thing getting out about you, would we now?'

'May I remind you,' came the hushed tone through gritted teeth, 'of your own implication in this and what might happen to you.'

'Thought of that,' said Tommy. 'Being an ole bugger, a bit simple like, I'd say I was made to do what I did. Just simply didn't know better. Just helping out a man of the cloth, a respected man in the community.' There was a pause. 'Two hundred's not a lot to ask, is it? Helping the needy, I'd say.' With that he got up and shuffled away, leaving a shocked and red-faced Rev Rogers standing by the bench.

Tommy shouted back to him, 'We can start the new arrangement when the windin's all put in. So the longer it takes to install her, the less it'll cost you in the long run. Fair deal, eh? Wouldn't want you sellin' the Jag just yet, would we?' With that he made his way out of the churchyard and down the road, leaving the vicar locked in thought. Tommy was right, of course. Who would blame an old pensioner like him? No, he'd just have to find the money somehow. Unless he could find an alternative solution, that is.

CHAPTER 9

Jacko was fast asleep in bed when, at about 1.30 am, he was awoken by the phone ringing. He groaned. Who on earth would want him at that time of night? He groped for the receiver, still with his eyes shut.

'Sorry to bother you, Dr Jackson,' said a formal voice at the other end, but there's been a serious fire in the grounds of the vicarage in Middle Belford.' There was an expectant pause. 'Hello?' the voice said again, this time louder. 'Can you hear me, sir?' Jacko made a mumbling noise and the message was repeated. He was half asleep and too stunned to say anything. The voice continued. 'A temporary site hut that you use there has been destroyed by fire, sir. We'd appreciate it if you could visit the scene as soon as possible.' The voice paused again. 'Are you able to confirm that, sir?'

'Yes, yes, sorry, hell,' were the first comprehensible words he managed to get out as he found himself caught up in the duvet. 'The vicarage – the site hut, hell, when?'

'One other question, sir. We're assuming that no-one was likely to have been in the building. Are you able to confirm that too?'

'Yes, yes,' he answered hurriedly, hunting for his clothes. 'It's just a temporary site office used during the working day.' Christ, he suddenly thought, the hut had all the records in it. 'I'll come as soon as I can,' he said, pulling on his socks. 'Is the fire brigade there?'

'Just damping it down, sir. They're about finished.'

What the hell was going on? A fire? Burnt down? How had the fire started? Must have been some electrical malfunction. Shit. Everything was switched off, wasn't it? Mark always checked things like that. He tried to remember what was kept in the hut that was at risk. Just about everything. All the records – site logs, excavation notes and context sheets. And all the plans. Fuck, the plans, they constituted the main record made so far. They were on plastic film. They'd be the first to go, melted. Shit! Then he remembered, thank God, he'd brought the important ones home with him to look at last night. They were safely tucked up downstairs in his office.

It was all still a blur when he climbed into his VW and, partly dressed, arrived in Middle Belford some twenty minutes later. His stomach filled with nausea when he saw two fire tenders and a police car parked up the vicarage drive. The whole place was flooded by the light from arc lamps. A pall of smoke hung in the air. He climbed slowly out of the car and was met by a uniformed officer who led him through a taped cordon. There were still a couple of onlookers hanging around, but the main show was over.

It must have been one hell of a bonfire, he thought. The chestnuts were badly scorched, the ground was baked hard, and all that was left of the main site office was a rectangular pile of smoking debris unrecognisable as anything other than a mixture of burnt timber, melted plastic and twisted metal.

The fire fighters were beginning to clear up their gear, hoses were being rolled up and cups of tea were being made available by the unusually benign Mrs Jefferson, who'd opened up the vicarage kitchen. She, it seemed, had been the first to see the blaze from her terraced cottage across the road. By that time the hut was well ablaze and when the fire brigade turned up some twenty minutes later it was too late to do anything other than ensure that nothing else caught fire.

He was led to the more senior of the two police officers at the scene, who seemed to want further confirmation that no-one was inside the building.

'No, no,' Jacko assured him, 'the office is only used in the working day. There are only two keys to it, I have one and my colleague has the other. We both left together last night. I can't see that he'd come back in the middle of the night. I'll ring him anyway to be on the safe side.'

He pulled out his mobile phone and called Mark's landline. There was no answer. 'He's probably still asleep or couldn't get to the phone in time – it's a downstairs one,' he said with slight concern. The officer was looking at him intently. 'I'll try him again'. There was still no answer. He gave him a couple of minutes then called him once more. Still no answer. He was beginning to become concerned.

'Did you actually see him leave, sir?' the officer asked.

Jacko thought a little. Shit. He'd left before Mark had. 'Um, no, I suppose I didn't…' he said, trying to remember. 'Thinking about it, I must have left just before him, but he was packing his bag, turning out and preparing to lock up. I assumed he'd left just after me. He certainly didn't give the impression of staying on.' Then a thought struck him. 'Just a minute, we leave our cars round the back behind the walled garden, so if his car isn't there he'll have gone. If he isn't at home maybe he's at his girlfriend's or somewhere. I'll try his mobile.' He tried twice. Each time it went straight to voicemail.

The officer fetched a torch and the two of them walked through the grounds. Away from the glare of the lights it was difficult to see anything. The outline of the walled garden was barely visible, bushes seemed to jump out in front of them, the grass was wet and he was beginning to feel apprehensive. 'It's a short wheelbase Land Rover,' he said to break the uneasy silence, 'old style.' The officer remained silent. They reached the wall and found the small iron gate that led through into the flat area now designated as a car park. The officer shone his torch around. On one side the beam picked up piles of logs, mounds of soil, building machinery and excavation junk. In the dark they looked eerie, the shadows moving and changing shape as the beam lit them up. He shone it on the other side, moving the arc of light slowly around. Suddenly the beam reflected off something shiny. 'Christ, shit,' was all Jacko could say as the officer focused the light on a Land Rover parked out on its own at the far end. They hurried over.

The doors were locked and the officer shone the torch inside. It was empty.

'Can you confirm this is his car?' asked the officer grimly.

'Pretty sure,' he answered quietly. 'It was the only Land Rover here.'

'Right,' was the officer's response as he took control of the situation. 'We better get back and make further enquiries.'

They made their way back. It seemed to take longer. His nerves were now on edge, not helped by the smell of burning that became stronger as they neared the scene. When they reached the light of the lamps around the smouldering remains, the officer made some phone calls and took a colleague to one side. They spoke earnestly. Jacko stood mesmerised next to the burnt out mess, staring, completely shattered by the strong possibility that Mark had been burnt to death inside the site hut. The senior fire fighter came over to him solemnly. Once the remains had cooled down further, they'd need to sieve through them. Maybe it would be best if he left the scene for the time being. Perhaps he might like to walk up to the vicarage and have some tea? It might make him feel better? He was about to respond when his mobile rang, its jingly tone a complete contradiction to the gravity of the situation. Apologising profusely, he wrestled it out of his pocket and looked at the screen. It was Mark.

'Christ!' he yelled, 'Where the hell are you?'

The voice at the other end sounded surprised. 'In bed, where do you think I am? I've a load of missed calls from you in the middle of the night. What the hell's the problem?'

'Why didn't you answer the fucking phone?'

'For Christ's sake I was in bed. Thought it was some of

those cold calls on automated rotas, you know, insurance protection refunds, stuff like that. Then I saw it was you, so I called you back.'

'Sorry. It's a relief to know you're alive.'

'What?'

'The site hut burnt down in the night. We thought you were inside it.'

'Why the hell would I be inside the site hut in the middle of the night?' It was his turn to get irate. Then the situation began to dawn on him, 'What's going on?'

'Mark, what's your car still doing at the vicarage?'

'What? My car? What's that got to do with it? Oh, I see. It wouldn't bloody start, would it? Had to borrow a bike to get home. Took me over an hour. But for Christ's sake, what's all this about the site office?'

Jacko explained as best he could. Mark wanted to come out to the site there and then, but Jacko told him there was no point, not until morning anyway. They'd meet up and assess the position then. He rang off, leaving Mark disgruntled but Jacko and the police officer somewhat happier.

'Do we have any idea how it started?' Jacko asked him.

'The vicar, the Rev Rogers, says that he saw two people smoking in the doorway of the hut last night, sir. He was very clear about it. If he's right it was possibly a cigarette end then. That's what we're working on for the time being anyway.'

How the hell could a cigarette end have caused this mess? Yes, Mark had been smoking, but he himself had seen him flip the butt out of the door on to the gravel. It couldn't possibly have been the cause. Must have been an electrical issue, surely? He started to wander towards the burnt shell of the office but was immediately called back by the officer.

'Sorry, sir. I'll have to ask you to keep away. No-one's allowed there until the fire investigator has been. He's due sometime later in the morning.'

He stared glumly at the remains for a moment, then went back to his car and home for some coffee.

* * *

Jacko and Mark, both tired out, met the next morning at 8 am. Mark had a lift in from his girlfriend. The two men – crumpled, dejected figures, neither quite sure what to do – stood and looked at the pile of black debris. One by one the rest of the team showed up and formed a slowly growing group of huddled figures in the car park.

Eventually Jacko and Mark went to examine the burnt remains, having first assured the uniformed officer at the scene that they wouldn't step inside the blue and white taped cordon and wouldn't touch anything. The officer seemed more interested in talking to the female archaeologists than watching them, so they moved as close as they dared to the debris and leaned over the tape. The outline of the hut was clear enough. It seemed to have collapsed inwards.

'How the hell did it start?' Mark muttered yet again as he paced around it, occasionally bending down or crouching, looking carefully at this and that. He must have circled it at least half a dozen times, continually muttering and making comments to himself in a way that made Jacko increasingly irritated. Then he went back to the surviving site office, found a piece of paper and drew from memory a rough plan of the office before it went up in smoke. He called Jacko across and between them they added in from memory the positions of the chairs, tables, filing systems, plan store, electrical sockets and wiring, windows and door. Then he went outside again, this time holding the sketch, and walked round the debris a couple more times. He kept muttering, making comments to himself, irritating Jacko even more. Finally he seemed happy with his findings.

'Right,' he said. 'Look at this. Look at the window at the far end of the hut – the glass has shattered and then twisted and melted with the heat.' He moved round to the other side. 'Now look at this window, the one by the door. The glass's just cracked or broken, and it's not twisted or melted. What does that say to you?'

Jacko thought a bit. His brain wasn't on full power yet. 'Erm, something about different levels of heat, maybe?'

Mark was getting absorbed. 'Must be,' he said. 'Doesn't that mean that the seat of the fire was at the back rather than the front of the hut?'

'I suppose it could, but couldn't that also mean the materials there were more combustible and therefore it was hotter?'

'Materials like what?' said Mark, pushing their sketch plan in front of his nose. 'There was fuck all at the back. Everything's here at the front, or at the door end. Even the electrics are at the door end. The fire started where there was nothing to start it.'

Jacko looked hard at him, 'What are you saying? That it wasn't an accident?'

Mark shrugged. 'Dunno, but it doesn't make sense to me. Can't really get near enough to see anything though.'

By now Jacko was getting curious, straining to see over the cordon. The young police officer had moved away slightly and could be seen in earnest conversation with Trudi, one of the diggers. He had his back to them and for the time being was oblivious to anything else. Jacko and Mark looked at each other with a common idea in mind. Then, like two naughty boys, they quickly pulled up the metal rods that held the cordon tape then ran around and planted them nearer the debris, tightening up the tape as they went. When the officer finally glanced back he was reassured to find them still standing outside the tape, but failed to notice that the cordon was significantly smaller than before.

'You know, I could be wrong,' said Jacko, 'but it looks to me like most of the twisted melted glass at the back is *under* the collapsed wall panel.'

They looked at each other in silence as the realisation dawned on each of them independently. Mark was first to speak, 'Doesn't that mean that the window was broken *before* the heat melted it then?' They both stared down at the remains. 'Christ, if that's the case then it wasn't an accident, was it? Someone smashed the window and then set fire to the hut. Who on earth would want to do that, or why for that matter? '

At that moment there was the sound of a car on the gravel drive. They turned to see a dark Jaguar make its way out of the gate and accelerate down the road. They didn't expect a wave or a friendly toot on the horn, and they didn't get one.

* * *

Jacko was in the process of getting the excavation back on track when the duty police officer wandered over with a message. It seemed now that his bosses and the fire fighters saw no need to send a fire investigator out. No-one had been injured, and the fact that the vicar had seen people smoking there gave a good enough reason for the fire. Jacko looked at him in astonishment. The decision just didn't make sense when the whole thing was so suspicious. The officer shrugged his shoulders in a sort of 'sorry, mate' fashion. As far as he was concerned they could remove the cordon and do what they wanted. He just had to sit in his car, fill in the necessary paperwork, then he'd be off.

'We'll have to do it ourselves then,' he said slowly to the policeman, trying to think on his feet. 'We can excavate the fire remains forensically just in case anything shows up. You never know, do you?'

'Fine by us,' was the unenthusiastic response. 'You can do what you like here now, sir.'

'But if something did turn up,' Jacko insisted, 'wouldn't it be better if you were here to witness it? What we have in mind won't take more than about an hour or so…' he paused, 'Look, we've drawn up a rough plan of what was where in the hut when it burnt down.' He waved it in front of him.

The officer shook his head in a disinterested way. 'Not really my job, sir, I'm afraid. I'll be needed back at HQ, we're always short-staffed.' He moved back towards his car. Deflated, Jacko waited until he was part way there then, in a moment of inspiration, called across to one of the archaeologists standing by the site office.

'Trudi,' he shouted. 'We've got clearance to get in here now. Could you bring your kit and do a job on the debris, please?

The police officer's pace faltered and he diverted his route slightly to meet Trudi as she trudged her way across. They exchanged a few words and the officer accompanied her back to the debris.

'I'll just hang on a bit to see what you're doing,' he said agreeably, and he trotted off happily to get his coat from the car.

While he was out of earshot, Jacko quickly explained to Trudi what was required and whispered a few words in her ear.

'You want me to do *what?*' she said defiantly.

'Just this once, please,' Jacko mumbled, putting on his pathetic persona.

She looked at him suspiciously then, with some reluctance, set about disentangling the collapsed window at the back of the hut, removing the debris in layers and recording it all carefully. In the process she gave a verbal blow-by-blow account of what she was doing as the officer stood by, pointing out how the broken glass had melted underneath the collapsed panel. The young officer nodded happily in agreement at everything she said. Then she did the same with the window at the door end, pointing out the differences, and how they might be interpreted. He nodded and smiled again. At Jacko's suggestion she took samples of burning at various points using a clean pair of rubber gloves for each one and bagged them separately. Each one was numbered and its position plotted on the plan. Jacko then put them together in a box which he sealed up and handed to the officer.

'What's that for?' he asked, surprised.

'Hadn't you better take them with you?' Jacko said. 'If we ever need to look for an accelerant used to start the fire, then those samples are essential. We'll have to ensure a proper chain of custody won't we?'

The officer was looking uncomfortable with this responsibility. 'You know, sir,' he said falteringly, 'this is really for CSIs. I'm not quite sure of the protocols here.'

'I don't think that's a problem,' was Jacko's advice. 'But if we don't follow the continuity process then the evidence, should we ever want to use it, would be inadmissible. Pity to waste all Trudi's efforts, eh?'

That seemed to do the trick, and Trudi played her part by looking forlornly at the officer with large wide eyes. She glared at Jacko when the officer's back was turned.

'The easiest way,' said Jacko, 'would be if we signed this box over to you, then you take it to HQ and lock it in the store under whatever log number this incident's been given. Then you can forget about it.' The officer seemed slightly more comfortable with this notion and signed a document that Mark had quickly prepared. Pretty straightforward, he thought. Can't be any harm in that. He also had Trudi's phone number scrawled in biro on the back of his hand.

* * *

The excavations of the graves took the anticipated two weeks. Every night, at the risk of appearing paranoid, Jacko insisted that each day's records were taken off site and brought back again the next day. As arranged, the individual graves at one end were excavated first, then Christine arrived and started work at the other end where the graves seemed to have been disturbed. She had more experience at excavating skeletons than anyone Jacko knew, having served her time in the commingled mass graves of the Balkan conflict. He'd known her for years. Like Jacko, her mind worked forensically. She was a natural choice for this job.

The hope of all concerned was that there should be some grave goods to prove that Vikings were buried there. They were not to be disappointed. Of the fifteen graves excavated five of them contained bent swords which had been positioned next to the body at burial. The iron blades were all badly corroded, but some of them showed traces of decorated silver hilts. Jacko was no expert, but he knew enough from the silver decoration to realise that they were of genuine Viking workmanship. A conservator was brought in and the swords, or what was left of them, were taken away to be stabilised and studied in more detail. As far as anyone could tell the graves with the swords were male skeletons, as were most of the others. A few had features specific to females, but the anthropologists would be sorting that out in the laboratory.

One of the graves, grave 13, proved to be especially interesting. Not only was the skeleton that of a female who appeared to have lost most of her teeth, but it also contained a large bronze brooch that lay on her chest. For some reason it attracted the largest crowd of on-lookers as Christine exposed the remains little by little. No formal visitor tours had been arranged but folk kept arriving, curious to see what was going on. Jacko had to set up hastily arranged cordons and a staff rota for giving brief guided tours. Middle Belford was a busy little village and the excavations created a novel social experience. Huddles of people stood chatting away, gossip was exchanged, young mothers came with pushchairs swapping baby notes, and the old men waved their walking sticks in greeting and made nostalgic noises about Middle Belford's history. It had occurred to Jacko that if he'd been more commercially minded, he could have made a small fortune in selling tea, coffee and burgers.

The archaeologists excavating the skeletons were asked to give a running commentary as they worked, showing which bone was which, and explaining what they were doing as they went along. Questions were fired in as to how the skeleton was lying, what tests they could do on it, how they could tell whether it was male or female. Jacko stood back and watched it all with growing amazement. Fair enough that people had a natural morbid interest in skeletons, but there was surely more than that evident here. It was a type of theatre, a sort of performing art with a single actor in centre stage. It was compulsive to watch, even though it progressed at a snail's pace. In some respects it was theatre-in-the-round. Shakespeare himself might have felt quite at home. The finale was the uncovering of the bronze brooch, which was greeted with predictable 'oohs' and 'aahs' as Christine slowly exposed a bright green object, keeping the crowd spellbound with a description of the animals she could see depicted on the brooch surface.

Jacko slid away to do some quick homework. He had a pretty good idea what the brooch signified but needed to check it on his laptop. It turned out he was right – it was known as a tortoise brooch, probably because it looked a bit like a tortoise. It was oval, convex and about four inches long showing a decoration of animals with claws, tails and heads. It was instantly recognisable and some of the best possible evidence for the presence of a Viking population. He made his way back on site, voiced his findings to the crowd, and was surprised to find himself being applauded. The brooch was duly lifted and the crowds drifted away. The show was over.

CHAPTER 10

DCI Flett was old school and a loner – grey, haggard and already past retirement age. He'd learned his trade on the streets of Glasgow, knowing that to catch criminals he'd need to think like one. He worked on hunches, feelings and bent the rules without qualms. He'd stayed in the job partly because he liked policing, partly to fund his hobby, and partly to pay off his ex-wife. He had no family he'd ever want to contact and his wife had walked out on him years ago because of his obsession with trains and model railways, which had taken over the attic, the garage and part of the downstairs of their 1920s villa.

Flett's boss, Superintendent Roberts, could not have been more different. His only hobby was in police management. He was fast-track, new school, half Flett's age, immersed in management-speak, and a great believer in sending his staff on courses. The two didn't see eye to eye, and never would. Flett couldn't for the life of him understand how a twelve-year-old who sat in a chair and spent all day in meetings could know anything at all about policing. For his part, Roberts saw Flett as a loose cannon, unreconstructed, politically incorrect, unable to fill in necessary paperwork and a procedural corner-cutter.

Flett's office was two floors up in the police HQ. It was an open plan arrangement, totally incompatible with an old building, and gave Flett minimal privacy other than with a three-quarter height glass partition on three sides. The rest of the open plan was taken up by desks, filing systems and computers manned by his team of eight junior officers led by senior side-kick DS Duncan MacBrayne. There were cables and wires across the floor, shelves top-heavy with redundant paperwork, and waste bins overflowing with sandwich wrappers, empty milk cartons and torn up papers.

On the same day that Jacko and Mark stood in the vicarage gardens staring at the burnt detritus of their site office, DCI Flett was sorting through his paperwork to see what was ongoing, and what had just kicked off. There was a set of emails from the superintendent regarding adherence to protocols, procurement compliance and attendance on courses.

He called over MacBrayne then sat back and waited for him to get settled. 'Now then, laddie,' he said, gesturing to papers on his desk, 'what's new?'

'A fire last night, sir.'

'Where?'

'In the grounds of a vicarage in Middle Belford.'

'So what got burnt, some pews and hymn books?'

'No, a site hut, boss,'

'A site hut! Are you wasting my time, Dunc?'

'No, boss, but the fire chief needs to know if we want to deploy a fire investigation officer.'

'Why in God's name should we want to do that on a garden shed?'

'Site hut, sir.'

Flett ignored him. 'Did someone get cremated alive in it? Did it involve burning an effigy of the Archbishop of Canterbury?

'Er, no, none of those, boss,' MacBrayne muttered. 'It was just a site hut used by some archaeologists.'

'Ha! Destroyed some little brushes and spoons, did it? Dear Lord, Dunc,' he said, putting his head in his hands with dramatic aplomb, 'what's becoming of us? Are we expected to pump our hard-earned budget into this sort of nonsense?'

'How shall I answer him, boss?'

Flett looked at him in surprise. 'Tell him to bugger off,' adding, 'diplomatically, of course.' He sat back in his chair. 'That's that sorted. What else have we got?'

MacBrayne pushed an open file across the desk, 'It seems the decapitation up the church tower has come back to bite us.'

'I thought we'd given that the thumbs down?'

'Well we had, but the coroner still hasn't released the body. Seems to think there's more to it. Wants some more information before he feels able to reconvene the inquest.'

'Fair enough, our hands are clean on this one, we've done the scene work, written the report, it's the coroner's predicament, not ours. So what's the problem?' He stared at MacBrayne expectantly.

MacBrayne hesitated. 'Um, the coroner's hired in someone to look into it for him.'

'Oh, has he just? Who?'

'Dr Jackson.'

'What?'

'Dr Jackson, boss.'

'I heard you the first time.' He glared at MacBrayne, 'The history man, is it? Come to poke around, has he? What the hell's the coroner want to bring him in for?'

'To be fair, boss,' MacBrayne said, 'Jacko's been helpful in the past, on quite a few jobs. He has his advantages. He knows about things we don't. He can do things we can't get away with without filling in forms, and this time he's coming out of the coroner's budget, not ours.'

'Jesus, he's still a loose cannon. He's not accountable. More to the point, he gets on my tits.'

'Come on boss, that's only because he's a bit of an academic, and you don't like academics – especially since the super started talking about "intellectualising" the units. Jacko, for all his faults, is on our side and he usually does a good job. If he comes up with anything, it's got to come back to us to investigate further, so he can't be too much of a maverick.'

Flett snorted, 'Maybe you're right. Let him work his arse off on the coroner's budget.' He snapped shut the file and pushed it to one side, 'But let me know what the bugger's up to. Right, what's next then?'

MacBrayne bent down and lifted a box file off the floor and deposited it on the desk with a thud. 'Human trafficking, I'm afraid. We don't seem to be getting anywhere very fast on this one, and Superintendent Roberts has issued more instructions.'

'Has he?' Flett muttered sarcastically.

'The immigration people have been telling us for a long time they've intelligence that groups of illegal immigrants, mostly women, are being smuggled into the UK from eastern Europe and/or Africa. They're not organised by gang-masters for picking strawberries, runner beans or any of that stuff, they're here on the promise of well-paid work, which then dumps them into the sex trade, mostly in the London area.'

'So why does that even remotely affect us? We must be the farthest police force from any coastal port of entry. And we're nowhere near London. Is this one of Roberts' jokes?'

'No, boss, but the intel's saying that it may all be organised from somewhere in the Midlands.'

'Somewhere in the Midlands?' Flett moved forward in his chair. 'Well, that narrows it down doesn't it?

'I think, boss,' MacBrayne said tactfully, 'that the idea is that we should be alert to the issue. The super's keen on being proactive. He wants us to keep our eyes open, be aware of anything that might be suspicious – no more than that at this stage, sir.'

'Very wise of him,' came another sarcastic response. 'Tell me, laddie, how many illegal women are being trafficked?'

'They don't know.'

'Where are they entering the country?'

'They're not sure of that.'

'How are they being transported?'

'That hasn't been looked into yet, boss, I don't think.'

'Where are they being kept?'

'They don't know that either, sir.'

Flett nodded. 'I see. Not a lot to go on, is there? Other than the fact, of course, that the big cheese of the whole exercise may be "somewhere in the Midlands". Well, well, excuse me if I don't get over-excited about this one, won't you. What about the source of the intelligence?'

'All we're told is that it's probably quite reliable,' MacBrayne smiled in a sickly way.

'Well, "probably quite reliable" doesn't quite tick the box for me either. Still, we better do what we're told, hadn't we? Round everyone up please, we'll have a quick scrum-down.'

MacBrayne left the glass office and shouted for everyone's attention. There was reluctant moving of chairs, some muttering and the assembled masses of the general crime unit gathered together by the window to be addressed by their leader. Flett bided his time by shuffling some papers. After a suitable interval he strode into the main office.

'Okay, everyone,' he looked around at a sea of bored expressions. 'We've had a missive from on high. We need to be alert for women, probably of east European or African origin, being imported illegally for the sex trade. We don't know much about the offences, but Superintendent Roberts has it on reliable authority that the business is being organised from somewhere in the Midlands.' He paused, 'The women appear to be based in London.' He paused again and moved to one side. 'Detective Sergeant MacBrayne will now give you further details. Please pay attention.'

MacBrayne stood up, 'There are no further details.'

'Thank you, Detective Sergeant MacBrayne. Now, are there any questions?' There was some yawning and shuffling from foot to foot.

'Just exactly what should we be on the alert for, boss?' was the first hesitant enquiry. Flett waved at MacBrayne to answer.

'We need to take particular note of vehicle movements at night, especially minibuses or large vans, unusual quantities of food and drink being purchased by strangers, complaints about noise, actions that don't seem to fit into the rural ways of life in these parts, and so on. In fact, anything unusual at all. The chances are that the whole business is London-based, but we can't take any chances, especially given the intel about the Midlands.'

'Exactly, MacBrayne,' Flett barged in. 'I couldn't have put it better myself. Admittedly, there's not much to go on, but it just shows you all how lucky we are to have a superintendent the calibre of Mr Roberts picking up the ball and running with it like this.' He paused until the suppressed giggling had stopped. 'I want you to put a gentle word out with uniform, with the community policing lot, and with traffic. Anything that comes back, no matter how minor, channel it direct to Duncan here, who'll report to me. If something's running on our patch it'll be a big one. Any questions?'

People began drifting back to their computers.

'Ah, before you all go back to work – we've another little problem,' he added. 'You'll probably remember the old boy whose head came off in a church tower. Well, that job isn't as dead as he is. The coroner's brought in a certain Dr Jackson to snoop about. Clearly doesn't trust us to have done our job properly. I want Duncan to go and see him, find out what he's up to and see what rubbish he's raking through. I need someone to go with him.' There was no response. 'Someone maybe who hasn't met him before. Good training.' There was still no response. 'Might even learn a bit about history.' There was absolute silence and all eye contact with Flett was broken as heads quietly turned to piles of paperwork and computer screens. 'How about you, Jennie?' he asked to the back of a woman's head at the far end of the room. Jennie scowled into her screen. 'Good, that's fine then, Jennie Braithwaite it is. Well done, lass.'

Jennie grimaced and whispered across to MacBrayne, 'What's this Jackson bloke like?

'I suppose he's a bit different from your usual forensic – he's obsessed with historical things, but pretty genuine. Likes to get it right rather than think about how much he's getting paid. If you speak to the CSIs they hold him in pretty high regard. Tends to be hands on.'

'Is he young, dashing and handsome?'

'Er, no, that's not a description I'd use.'

'Pity, I could do with a bit of that.'

'Try middle-aged and intellectual.'

'When you've all finished chattering,' Flett boomed, 'perhaps we can all get back to work.' He was about to return to his desk when the phone went in his office. He let it ring. As it seemed to have no intention of stopping he felt obliged to pick it up. It was Superintendent Roberts' secretary. Would he mind coming over for a few minutes? Now would be fine. Only if he was free, of course. Yes, in about ten minutes, that would be splendid.

He strode off, wondering what was afoot. It took about five minutes to weave his way through the building to Roberts' mini-suite located in a rather fine wood-panelled part of the old hall, one yet to be subdivided into smaller unworkable offices. He announced himself to the secretary and then went to use Roberts' private toilet knowing that he'd be made to wait, just for the sake of it. By the time he'd used as much soap and as many paper towels as was practical he emerged to find that Roberts was ready to see him. The secretary, Janet, led him in formally. They crossed from lino to a thick pile carpet and Flett was confronted by a twelve year old boy sitting behind a large wooden desk.

'Alastair, how good of you to spare the time,' said the child. 'Do sit down. Can I get you a coffee?'

Flett nodded, 'Thank you, sir.' Traditionally the coffee was good, as were the biscuits that accompanied it.

Roberts duly instructed Janet and settled back in his plush chair. His legs were too short to reach the ground and he was able to swing them back and forwards. He flicked inanely through some papers on his desk, his mind elsewhere. 'I've just a couple of things I need to fly past you, Alastair,' he said casually. 'Things I'd welcome your advice on. I think you've a much better feel for these things than I have.'

Flett recognised the flattery element. It normally preceded either increased work-load, admonishment, or both. 'Only too happy to help, if I can, sir.'

'Well the first thing is this business about illegal trafficking, these women, you know. The source we have for this is a very reliable one. Of course, it wouldn't be proper of me to go into any detail. You'll have to take my word that it comes from the very highest authority, very high. We may be in the middle of something very big indeed.'

'All in hand, sir,' Flett breezed. 'The staff have been briefed and tasked. It has an operational status direct to me via DS MacBrayne. We've given it high priority.'

Roberts' expression suggested this was an unexpected response. 'Oh, splendid. I, er... knew I could rely on you to run with this.' He said slightly abashed, 'As it's so important, I'd like a daily update from you, please, Alastair. Better send it with a worksheet, you know, all the usual – who's been tasked to do what, where, observations made, implications, priority levels, and so forth. Keeps the ACC and the filing johnnies happy.'

Flett's heart sank. Bugger the ACC, he thought. The ACC didn't have to do the paperwork, didn't have to coerce plods on the street to fill in forms, didn't have to collate it all, then spend the time getting it typed out so it could sit in a file that no-one would ever read.

'Absolutely fine, sir. Will more staff be available for this?' It was a long shot, but worth a try.

'No, I'm afraid not. These are austere times, Alastair.' There was a knock at the door and Janet arrived bearing a tray of coffee. 'Ah, the coffee, excellent! You prefer yours black, I seem to remember, Alastair?' Flett nodded.

'No biscuits today, I'm afraid. We're on a diet at the moment,' Roberts said chirpily, patting his stomach. Janet smiled sympathetically. 'Trying to lose a little bit of excess here. No fatty foods and a spot of jogging's the order of the day!' Flett's heart sank for the second time.

'Now, the other thing,' Roberts continued. 'This business about the old chap who got himself decapitated up a church tower.' He paused. 'I'm a bit concerned about this man Jackson who the coroner's brought in to help out. I looked at the file and we've effectively closed the case. Is there something I should know? This Jackson's causing a bit of a problem.'

'News to me, sir. What sort of a problem?' It sounded interesting.

'Seems he's upset Charles Wainwright MP by accusing him of this and that. A complaint came in to the chief constable. They both sit on some committees together, golf too, that sort of thing. The CC asked me to sort it out, seeing as you were responsible for the case,' he said pointedly, staring hard at Flett.

'What exactly did the man do to upset the MP, as a matter of interest, sir? Nothing untoward, I hope?'

'It seems he accused our parliamentary representative of not treating his servants properly, and then criticised him for knocking a wall down or something.'

'Servants? A wall? I can't honestly see how that relates to us, sir. What's the connection?'

'Rather a tenuous one, I'm afraid. Wainwright has seen Jackson's business card, which has the word "forensic" on it, so he naturally assumed it had something to do with us. I suppose in a way it does.'

'Well, I would have seen that as the coroner's issue and prerogative, sir. If he wants to employ him, that's his business, not ours, surely?'

'Indeed so, but it's also a case on which we, by which I mean you, Alastair, closed the file. We don't want to be in a position where this man Jackson's coming up with evidence that we, by which I mean you, missed, do we? And upsetting the MP, by which I mean the CC, into the bargain?'

Being patronised by a twelve-year old was hard to take but Flett, quietly seething, tried not to let it show.

'Already on the job, sir,' he said breezily. 'MacBrayne and a DC have been tasked to see what it's about.' Again Roberts looked surprised. 'I should add, sir, that we've worked with Jackson in the past. He functions as a consultant when we've needed to find and excavate buried murder victims. He has a doctorate and is highly regarded.' His strategy was an optimistic one. Making Jackson kosher would put him onside rather than offside and Roberts was likely to be impressed by the doctorate. Indeed he was.

'A doctorate, you say? Well, it's good to have some more academic brains on the case, I should think. Wait a minute. I may have already come across him. That name rings a distant bell.' He opened a desk drawer, pulled out a file labelled 'Conferences' and flicked through it, eventually pulling out a particular programme. 'Yes. Yes, here it is. I heard him give a lecture on finding missing persons. Very impressive, I remember. All hi-tech stuff now. Well, we're lucky to have him on board.' He became thoughtful for a moment. 'I take it you can control this Jackson and make sure that if he comes up with anything new we can act on it without looking complete Charlies?'

'Absolutely, sir,' Flett lied.

'And can you keep him off Wainwright's back?'

'Not a problem, sir. I'll have a word with him myself.' Another lie.

* * *

At the same time as Flett was telling porkies to the superintendent, MacBrayne and Jennie Braithwaite were on their way to Jacko's home in Compton-on-Stour, where they spent half an hour with him over coffee. They made their way back red-faced and defensive. It was bad enough that Jacko had worked out the likely time of the old boy's death when they hadn't, but the fact he had evidence of someone else being up the tower was an unmitigated disaster. This decapitation now had all the trappings of a murder – one they had collectively missed and signed off. Flett predictably exploded when they stood in his office and gave him the news.

'Not alone up there? Are you telling me this is a possible murder?' he shouted. 'And how the fuck did Jackson know there was someone else in the tower?' he demanded, pounding the floor while MacBrayne and Jennie sat nervously at the front of his desk. 'The CSIs took the place to pieces, for Christ's sake. I've read through all the statements, I've even been up there myself. The whole job was thoroughly handled. All done by the book. So what the hell's the problem?'

MacBrayne patiently explained about the bat tape and the shadowy figure in the belfry. Flett sank into his chair and closed his eyes in anguish. 'For God's sake, how did we miss that? Didn't anybody see it? Bloody Jackson of all people. Shit.'

'It was in the belfry, boss. We had no reason to go up there, did we? It's pure luck that Jacko came across it, he admits as much. Um… but the light in the clock chamber might be something we should have spotted.'

'The light?'

'Apparently it's always gloomy up there. You have to put the light on even in midsummer to be able to see the clock workings. When the bell ringing lady went up she was trying to find the light switch when she fell over the body.' He paused to let Flett think it through. 'In other words the light was off. Tommy couldn't work in the dark, so whoever else was up there must have turned the light off before doing a runner.'

Flett groaned, 'Why the hell didn't any of us notice the light? Christ, what a mess. Get me Jackson on the phone, someone please,' he shouted. 'Get him before Roberts finds out and we're all in the shit. Much though I dislike the man we may need him onside to get out of this one.'

* * *

The next day an email from Dr Zanbar, the forensic pathologist, pinged its way through to Jacko's inbox. While not exactly old friends, they knew each other from conferences and had once worked together on a memorable case involving a woman buried in a back garden. Jacko remembered him as an exceptionally tall, long-legged individual who wore green wellingtons on site and maintained a fairly gung-ho attitude towards his profession. Even in crime scenes where everyone was dressed in white hooded clothing and became an anonymous white blob, Zanbar was recognisable as the figure standing head and shoulders above the others with the elastic bottoms of his protective suit halfway up his legs. Unlike some forensic pathologists who loathed interference, he was open to ideas and was happy to work with archaeologists and anthropologists if he thought they'd something to offer, and provided they weren't going to throw up or talk to newspapers.

The gist of the email was simple. Would Jacko like to come over and discuss the report with him as the coroner had asked? For security reasons it wasn't possible to email it or send a hard copy in the post, but he was happy to run through it with him and discuss the findings, such as they were. The phrase "such as they were" indicated that he didn't think there was much to discuss. Jacko met up with him in his office where Zanbar passed him a box file to look through while he busied himself with other paperwork.

After several minutes, during which time Jacko browsed three bundles of photographs, Zanbar voiced his summary findings. 'Not much to say is there really? Fairly straightforward, in fact. As you might expect?' He looked directly at Jacko, awaiting a reaction. There wasn't one, so he went on. 'Cause of death, predictably, by decapitation, by some heavy object dropping guillotine-like from on high. Charlie there,' he pointed through a glass partition to a white-coated assistant, 'did a great job in pulling together all the bits of the fractured skull after it was shattered on the tower floor. The cause of death was very straightforward and Charlie carried out the main post-mortem.'

He paused, slightly concerned, 'I assume you know the head was on the ground floor of the tower, and the body on the second floor?' Jacko nodded and Zanbar continued.

'Charlie established that the impact was at the back of the head. The old boy must have been peeping over the edge, God knows what for, when the weights came down. But it doesn't really matter now, his head was ripped clean off, and that was the end of him, poor sod.' There was a further pause during which time Jacko remained in thought. Zanbar stared at him intently. 'Something on your mind?

'Well, just a thought really. I was wondering whether there were any marks on the body itself?'

Zanbar sighed impatiently, took a bundle of images taken by the scene of crime photographer, shuffled through them, found the one he wanted of the naked torso, and pushed it in front of Jacko, 'Not pleasant is it? Bear in mind that the flies and pigeons had been at him. This next one is after Charlie had cleaned him up a bit.' He pushed another photo across the table, this one showing Tommy's torso front down on the mortuary slab. 'He scrubbed up quite nicely, didn't he?'

'What's this?' Jacko asked, pointing to some apparent bruising in the central upper part of the back.

Zanbar pulled the photo across, delved into the bundle again and produced an enlargement. 'Yes, we noted that. Only minor contusions, bit of bruising, nothing more than a knock really. Could have been peri-mortem or a bit earlier perhaps, not possible to tell which.'

'How about the front of the torso?'

Zanbar looked at him with a half smile that suggested his finite patience might soon be running out, and delved into the folder for a third time. He flicked through the pages and pulled out another photo that seemed to satisfy him,

'How about this one?' The body showed a very faint line of bruising running across the front of the chest.

'Is that the same sort of cause?'

'Pretty much, but this looks like he banged into something like a table-top with a long flat edge, again peri-mortem or not much earlier. These marks certainly weren't the *cause* of death, so I've merely done what I normally do: identify them and record them, but not pass opinion unless asked if they might be indicative of the *manner* of death.'

'I just wondered if this horizontal bruising could have been caused by the wooden ledge on the parapet when he was leaning over?'

Zanbar stared hard at the image, 'Hmm. I think my opinion would be that the weights must have come down so quickly to take his head off as cleanly as that, there would have been no pressure exerted there.'

'What if he was held there and was struggling against it?'

'I suppose it's possible,' he said thoughtfully, 'but then there might be bruising where pressure was exerted to keep him in that position.'

'Like on his back?' was Jacko's helpful response, pointing to the photo where the bruising on the back was clearly visible.

Zanbar looked hard at him, 'Just what are you trying to say? That this isn't an industrial accident?'

'It just seemed a possibility to me, under the circumstances. It's not impossible, is it? I mean, if this came to court and you were asked...'

'Wait a minute, wait a minute, one step at a time, here, Jacko. At the moment I've been required to establish a cause of death and undertake the usual examination of the deceased, recording everything from tattoos and bruises to prostheses and dentures. This report then goes off to the coroner, and he takes it from there. It's not for me to speculate. If I'm asked I can give opinions and, if you really want to know, and this is off the record,' he continued staring hard at Jacko as he said it, 'it is possible that the bruising is commensurate with what you were thinking, but it's also commensurate with a host of other eventualities. On its own it wouldn't stand up in court. You'd need more.

'Finger nails?' asked Jacko brightly.

'What about them?'

'Anything underneath them?'

Zanbar leaned forward again and grabbed the folder. 'Let's see what Charlie says, shall we?' He skimmed through some pages of text, found what he was looking for and ran his finger down the relevant page. His eyebrows narrowed as he read it, then he looked up, but before he could say anything Jacko jumped in.

'How about nothing but dirt under the finger nails on the left hand, but mineral grains and mortar under the finger nails of the right? Am I getting close?'

'How in God's name did you know that? It's virtually what it says here,' he pointed to the open page. 'Almost word for word.'

'Just a theory I had,' said Jacko, finding it hard not to sound smarmy. 'I get the impression there's a bit more to all this than meets the eye.'

Zanbar was courteous enough to agree, albeit reluctantly, that he might have a point, 'I'll check through it all and look for anything else before I send it on to the coroner' he said. 'Seeing as you can't take the report away, you better sit here with it for a while and make notes. I have to go out. Ask Sarah in reception if you want a coffee.' He stood up, took down a white coat from a hook and gawkily heaved himself into it. 'Oh yes, Jacko,' he said, 'I should remind you, of course, that you're not allowed to photograph it either.' He winked. 'I'll leave you to get on with it for about half an hour.' He left the room. Jacko took the cue and pulled out his phone.

CHAPTER 11

Jacko took the train down to London, travelling on the cheapest route which took him to Marylebone where he managed to get a decent coffee and a sandwich from the M&S platform food store. He was feeling particularly pleased with himself for having managed to organise the day so efficiently. He'd been in touch with Benedict, an old friend who worked at the British Museum. Benedict was generally considered a bit nerdy but he knew more than anyone else about Viking objects. Jacko had arranged to drop off some photos of the swords and brooch they'd found before meeting up with Lucy. Rather tiresomely though, he'd had a call from Linda, one of the daughters of the Rev Rogers who had suggested to her that he might be able to offer some help on her dissertation. The cheek of the old bugger expecting him to give up his time after all the hassle he'd given them. Presumably he'd be back in his vicarage soon. Jacko had rung him twice to tell him that the graves were finished, but the phone had gone over to voicemail each time and so he'd left messages. If the miserable sod didn't answer the phone or bother to listen to messages, then that was his lookout.

On the plus side, Linda lived in London and he'd managed to organise a meeting with her at his hotel that afternoon. He'd booked in at the Westminster Gardens which was a bit more upmarket than his usual haunts, but he got it cheap on a late booking internet site. It was supposed to be a bit classy, the sort of place Lucy would appreciate. He emerged from the underground into hazy sunlight at Tottenham Court Road, made his way to the British Museum where he left the photos at reception, then took the tube to Westminster.

* * *

The Westminster Gardens was very grand with an impressive portico and a uniformed doorman. It was decorated inside with thick carpets, dark wooden furniture and large mirrors, the sort of place that oozed anonymity and was well suited to anyone just wanting to eat, drink and sleep without much interruption. The staff were all dressed immaculately, the men with neat slicked-back hair and the women impressively made-up, all in dark suits. The reception desk was busy with a group of Japanese tourists and he decided to sink himself in to a plush chair to wait. At least the air-conditioning made it pleasantly cool. He waved across to a waiter and ordered an Earl Grey tea with lemon and a slice of carrot cake to keep him going until dinner. The fare eventually arrived beautifully presented, but delivered by a waiter who gave the impression of being robotic. Predictably, there was very little change out of a ten pound note, so little in fact that the waiter never returned with it.

After the best part of ten minutes he began to get up to make his way towards reception but his attention was caught by a young woman dressed in a bright yellow top and dark blue jeans coming through the door. She had soft but very defined features, shoulder-length fair hair and a beautifully proportioned body. Various male heads pretended not to turn. She looked around, fixed her gaze on Jacko who was struggling to get out of the low plush chair, and went over to him.

'You're Dr Jackson, aren't you?' she said. 'I recognised you from the photo on your web site. I'm Linda. You said we could meet up here, but I'm a bit early.' She looked apologetically at him through large brown eyes.

He stared at her in astonishment and wished he was thirty years younger. 'Of course,' he said, regaining his composure, 'call me Jacko, everybody else does. And let me get you a drink. I've just had a tea but I was thinking about something stronger now.'

'Thanks, Jacko, good of you to see me. I was worried you might be some frosty old academic who wouldn't even answer my emails. Do you drink prosecco? It's my favourite.'

Jacko beckoned over the waiter and asked for a wine list. It was the same robot as before and Jacko gave him the cold stare for not bringing him his change. He looked through the list. God, the drinks were expensive, he thought, but seeing as they'd each probably have a couple of glasses it was worth getting a bottle. He chose a mid-range one that was listed at £24.95, knowing that among the notes in his wallet he had a twenty and a fiver. Some nibbles appeared followed by the ice bucket. The prosecco was duly uncorked, the robot ungraciously filled two glasses, placed the chitty in front of Jacko and stood erect next to him motionless as though his battery had run out. Jacko pulled the two notes out of his wallet and handed them over, 'Please do keep the change,' he said in a loud voice.

They clinked glasses with a buoyant 'Cheers' and Jacko began to feel rather relaxed.

'Isn't this naughty,' she said sweetly. 'I'm so grateful you could see me at short notice like this.'

Introductions complete and glasses charged, she began to talk about Middle Belford, what a weird place it was, how she was never going back if she could help it, and what it was like being a vicar's daughter in the middle of nowhere. Jacko tried some subtle questioning about her father and the church, but the seed fell on stony ground. She either knew absolutely nothing of interest to him or was feigning ignorance. It was just then that she seemed to have caught sight of someone. 'Excuse me, just a minute. I've an idea!' She went over to reception where she was greeted by one of the suited flunkies. They clearly knew each other, she pointed out Jacko to him, then there followed an animated exchange of conversation. The flunkie consulted a computer screen behind reception, then there was some nodding. He got a peck on the cheek for his troubles and she came back smiling.

'At least I can do something in return now,' she said. 'That was the assistant manager, or one of them. I met him here before when I was doing some part-time work. Didn't realise he was still here. Anyway, I know how the room allocation system works at the desk, so I've managed to get your room upgraded at no extra cost. I told him you were very important,' she winked and smiled at him. 'Unfortunately, they didn't have any junior suites left, but you're now in a superior executive double instead of the standard double, which is the next best thing.' She leaned over and topped up the prosecco, 'Here's to a more superior night's sleep!' she toasted. And they raised their glasses again.

Jacko was delighted. He was on top of the world. Today, for once, everything was going right. Linda told him about her twin, Suzie, how they were identical and tended to wear similar clothes. Only close family could tell them apart and they each had t-shirts made with 'Suzie' or 'Linda' printed on the front. But then they used to swap them over, so no one really knew who was who. They used to take on each other's roles and commitments if one of them didn't feel up to it or couldn't be bothered. She admitted coyly that they'd both passed their driving test, although only one of them took it, and that they messed up each other's private lives with hilarious effect. Jacko was already getting them both muddled up, even though he'd only met one. Eventually he thought he better find out why she wanted to meet him before the prosecco sent him to sleep.

'Right,' he said eventually, trying to raise himself up in the chair. 'What is it you want to talk to me about? You said something about a dissertation. Local history or something, wasn't it? Hadn't we better sort it out?'

'Yes, I'd almost forgotten. I'm supposed to be doing a dissertation on local history as part of my finals. My tutor's useless, but Dad suggested you might be able to help locate the right sources. He says you're the person in charge of messing up the vicarage grounds?'

'No, I'm not in charge,' was Jacko's rather annoyed reply. 'My job's to co-ordinate the groups that do the work. The decision to build was made by the church commissioners – they're the ones messing it up.' Linda looked abashed. 'Sorry,' he apologised quickly, 'that came out a bit stroppy, it wasn't supposed to.'

'No offence taken,' she said brightly. 'I didn't mean to sound critical, but the whole business is putting Dad through an awful lot of angst and he's got no-one to help him out since Mum left. She wasn't our real Mum, of course,' she added, 'We never found out who our real Mum was. We were adopted by the Rogers family, but Mum Rogers walked out on us when we moved to the Belfords about twelve years ago. We weren't that particularly close to her. Dad was better. In some ways we were pleased to see her go. The house was always full of arguments, she hated the country and she said if Dad ever moved there, she'd walk out. And that's what she did.' She thought for a moment and dabbed at her eyes with one of the serviettes that came with the nibbles, 'She's never even bothered to come and see us since. All we've to remember her by are a few photographs and a lock of hair that she kept from when she was a little girl. We kept it in our bedroom in the vicarage and took it out from time to time to look at. Silly really, but girls do that sort of stuff. Come on,' she added quickly, 'let's finish off this prosecco before we get too maudlin.'

They drained their glasses. 'Right, it's your turn now, Jacko. You haven't told me a thing about yourself, have you?'

she asked. 'What interests you apart from digging holes, then? Dad said you were involved in forensics. What's that all about?'

She sat fascinated as he told her about his work with police forces and in mass graves, how he helped locate clandestine burials and then excavate murder victims.

'That must be awful. How do you cope with it? Is that why you're involved at Dad's church? He told me there's something to do with the pensioner that died up the tower there, isn't it?'

Jacko shrugged, 'I'm just helping out the coroner on that one. It's not really up my street. I'm happier with archaeology and old buildings.'

'Do you know the manor in the village then? Dad said it was as old as the church. We used to go to fetes there when we were younger. It's such a lovely old building and grounds, but the people who live there were awful...' she stopped suddenly. 'Oh, gosh, I'm sorry – maybe they're friends of yours. I shouldn't have said that.'

'Don't worry. I can't stand them either, in fact I had an altercation with the MP, Charles Wainwright, last time I was there. I'm afraid he and I don't get on at all.'

'It seems a big lonely house for just a few people, doesn't it? You'd think they might welcome a visitor or two. Wonder what they get up to in there? Someone said they had a few foreign people living in too – probably servants. Did you ever bump into them?'

Jacko shook his head. It was an odd question for her to ask and he wondered why she seemed so interested in the place.

'Mind you,' she went on 'if I owned it, I'd turn it into a hotel or club or something useful with lots of flunkies everywhere, low lights and lots of antique furniture. Could even turn the cellars into bars.' She giggled.

That was the point at which Jacko supposed it was time they got down to the business of the dissertation. This was a road he'd been down many times before in helping students. He knew if he wasn't careful he'd end up writing the thing for her, so he found out what she was interested in, suggested a structure for it, then dictated a list of sources that she'd need to consult. It took them about half an hour to sort out what she should do before she finally finished making notes and packed her bag.

After she'd gone he felt quite elated, his ego boosted by a combination of prosecco and the lingering kiss she left on his cheek as she stood up to leave. He went over to reception, collected the key to his superior executive double and vanished in the lift thinking what a pleasant afternoon it had been.

* * *

He enjoyed a long and frothy shower using as many hotel freebies as the en-suite provided at executive level, walked out into the bedroom clad only in a towel wrapped loosely around his waist, and switched on the TV, finally settling on a Eurosport option showing live Spanish football. He sat on the bedside chair which seemed unusually comfortable, put his feet up on the bed and stared at the screen, trying desperately hard to keep his eyes open. It was only when he looked down that he noticed with horror the extent to which his stomach appeared to hang out over the towelling. He stood up and looked at himself in the mirror, moving this way and that and altering his pose, occasionally drawing his stomach in to see which angle looked least offensive. He was in the middle of this narcissus exercise when the door opened and the stylishly elegant figure of Lucy floated into the room. She was slender and wore a thin blue cotton dress, sandals and had her hair up – her smooth neck emphasised by a pair of long silver ear-rings.

'I'm early!' she announced with a smile. She threw her bag into the corner, came over to him, wound her arms around his neck, and pressed her lips into his, drawing her hands slowly down his back.

'Oooh,' she said after a few seconds, 'you're as good as naked. Not often a girl gets a treat like this in the afternoons. I think I rather like it.'

Jacko, embarrassed, did his best to draw in his stomach and mumbled something about the over-heated tube service and the need for a shower.

'No matter,' she said, stroking his front, 'and don't try and hide it.' She giggled, 'It's maturity. I'll take you as you come.'

She pulled herself away, giving him a tweak in the groin in the process and moved across the room. Jacko began to make his way to the bathroom to get dressed as she sank into a chair and became engrossed on her mobile phone, giving him the opportunity to manoeuvre more effectively.

'The conference finished early,' she muttered, still fiddling with the phone, 'so I thought I'd come straight here. I like this room,' she added, looking round. 'Very chic.' There was a pause. 'Right. This is what I think we should do. There are a couple of sales I want to go to in the Euston Road. Why don't we meet up at the brasserie across from here in about an hour and a half. Then you can buy me some dinner?' She looked up expectantly for the response. He nodded happily.

She made her way to the door. 'Oh, by the way,' she said, 'you know that favour you asked me to do in Cambridge? You were right about that vicar of yours, that Rev Rogers. He graduated in the early 1970s. You got the college right too, he was at Jesus. And there's more you might like to know.'

Right then Jacko wasn't interested, his mind was on covering himself up. 'Oh, thanks,' he said, peeping out through the half open door. 'Tell me later.'

From then on the rest of the day went smoothly. They had a good dinner with a reasonable amount of wine and chatted away as they always did, both at ease with each other.

Back at the hotel Jacko crawled into bed while Lucy was in the bathroom. He often wondered what a smart high-powered university figure like her saw in a scruffy reprobate like him. It can't have been his brains, and he certainly didn't come under the category of 'a bit of rough'. She eventually emerged in a new white nightdress in which she looked superb. It gave her a sensual maturity that he found difficult to describe. They lay together, his arm around her, her head on his shoulder, and did what they could of the *Guardian* crossword. It was one of those strange things that people do, a sort of convention, but it let them both unwind mentally.

After several minutes of anagrams and clues she snuggled up closer to him, leant over, put the pen on the bedside table and let the newspaper fall to the floor. Jacko reached over and turned off the light.

CHAPTER 12

Invigorated by rest, good food, wine, and not forgetting a couple of nights under the sheets with Lucy, Jacko returned to put the final touches on his report to the coroner before sending it off. The main thrust had been written earlier, but he usually tried to let these things lie for a few days then look at them afresh. The content was dynamite. He knew that. He also knew the coroner would have no option but hand it over to Flett and all hell would be let loose.

He was right. Two days later the report landed on Flett's desk. He quickly digested its contents, cursed Jacko for being such a smart-arse, and quickly devised a damage-limitation strategy before sending it upstairs to Superintendent Roberts. As expected, Roberts wasted no time in requesting a meeting.

'I am very concerned about this report, Alastair,' he said, once Flett had appeared through the door and had been waved dismissively to a seat. He was about to amplify his concerns when Flett interrupted him.

'As indeed am I, sir.' Roberts looked up, surprised. Flett continued with feigned anger, 'None of my staff have been on a roof safety course, sir. I suppose it's just as well the coroner brought in Dr Jackson. He doesn't have the good fortune of being supported by our health and safety directives. Without him risking life and limb on the church roof we'd never know about the likely entry and exit route.'

'Um, well… in a way I suppose you're right,' was all that Roberts could think of saying in reply. 'Why haven't we had staff on roof safety courses, I wonder?'

'A management oversight perhaps, sir?'

Roberts glared at him, 'On the topic of oversights, Alastair, how on earth did your team miss the camera in the belfry? Goodness me! A critical piece of evidence missed through sloppy investigation… I'm afraid the buck has to stop with you on this one, Alastair.'

'Beg pardon, sir,' Flett said, trying to sound offended, 'You can hardly cast blame on the team for that one. We had no evidence whatsoever to suggest that this might be anything other than an industrial accident. Nor did we have any cause to look up in the belfry. Even the vicar didn't know there was a camera there.' Roberts began to take on a pained look as Flett continued his prepared excuses.

'You must appreciate too, sir, that there's a real risk of Weil's disease from the pigeon and bat droppings up there. Cutbacks have meant that neither the team nor the CSIs are equipped with personal breathing equipment any more. We do what we can,' he said, waving his hands in the air with theatrical exasperation, 'but it would be irresponsible of us to otherwise risk our staff, wouldn't it?'

'Um, in a sense I suppose you're right, Alastair. These are points of resource I shall pass on to the ACC. I agree they're significant, although I have to say the circumstances are rather unusual – church roofs, belfries and such like. Nevertheless, it's clear from what I've seen of Dr Jackson's report that we have no option but to pursue enquiries and upgrade this to a potential murder. That means preparing a press release and keeping the tabloids at bay. It's a mess, Alastair, a real mess and I hold you responsible. On the positive side we can request increased central funding from the Home Office, of course. You might give thought to using some of it to bring Dr Jackson on board as a temporary consultant. He seems to be one step ahead of you, and we don't want any loose cannons on this one do we, Alastair?' He gave Flett a sarcastic smile. Flett winced, but being stuck with Jackson was a relatively small price to pay.

* * *

Later that day Flett called MacBrayne into his office to discuss how the enquiry might proceed, seeing as there was neither a suspect nor an obvious motive. Barty Webb was dragged in from the CSI unit, and DC Jennie Braithwaite was brought into the inner sanctum because she had more experience than the other DCs. The four of them sat round the desk looking far from happy. Superintendent Roberts, in his infinite wisdom, had strongly advised setting up an incident room and asking HQ's command centre to allocate them an operations name. According to a course he'd been on, this would be beneficial for ensuring management focus, morale stimulus, and intra-unit bonding. In the absence of anything better at that early stage, Flett rang up the command centre for advice. Personally, he would have been happy to call it *Operation Bell Tower* or similar, but this was a name instantly rejected as being too pertinent to the case. Apparently it needed to be a name that was more distant and, to be consistent, had to be in an alphabetical sequence from the name of the previously allocated operations – *Operation Courage* and *Operation Dreadnought*. It needed to start with an 'E'. Flett asked the operations manager to request a new name and was allocated *Operation Eric*.

'*Operation Eric*? Eric? Who the hell's Eric?' asked Flett disgustedly down the phone. No-one seemed to know. 'It's a bit of a comedown after the others, isn't it?'

'We don't choose the names ourselves, sir,' said the voice at the other end. 'The names are generated randomly by computer in order to avoid any personal associations. We just allocate them when requested.'

'Could we possibly have a different E-word?' asked Flett. 'Eric just doesn't have quite the right gravitas for our purposes.'

'Sorry, sir. If we let people choose names, it wouldn't be random then would it?'

'So could we perhaps go directly to the next letter in the alphabet?' Flett asked in a tired way.

'Er, well, I suppose there's no real reason why we can't, sir. I suppose that's perfectly possible. Would you like me to see what it is?'

'Please do.'

There was some audible tapping of a keyboard down the phone. 'Let's see now,' said the voice. 'Ah, here we are. That'll be *Operation Fanny* then. Is that more appropriate?'

'Fanny? *Operation Fanny?* Are you having me on, laddie?'

'Sorry, not at all, sir. That's what the computer's given us, sir.'

Flett and MacBrayne looked at each other. Barty Webb and Jennie Braithwaite stared hard at the floor to avoid eye contact. 'I think we'll stick with *Operation Eric*, thank you very much,' said Flett, trying hard to restrain himself. He slammed down the phone.

* * *

Under the banner of *Operation Eric* officers were subsequently dispatched to various tasks. These included examining old Tommy's personal life and banking details, investigating the movements of relevant personnel – the vicar, Captain Henry Toller and the bell-ringing ladies – talking to the old boys who played bowls, and making house-to-house enquiries. Jacko was drawn in on a weekly contract as soon as the increased funding was confirmed.

DC Jennie Braithwaite had been tasked to look into Tommy's routines. She started by talking to the old boys at the Red Horse and the Bowling Club and found he'd been a handyman, joiner and farmhand all his working life and never left the village. He'd always been paid in cash at the end of the working week and never had a bank account. Even his pension was collected in cash from the Post Office every Thursday. To a man they all agreed how generous he was when it came to buying drinks or if they went out anywhere. He was always the first to put his hands in his pocket, or if anyone was short he'd always help out. Nice old chap, really.

She made a visit to his small council house which had been made secure since his death. Inside it was basic and unremarkable. Apart from a TV, a radio, a telephone and some antiquated kitchen appliances there was little to suggest that the bungalow belonged to the twenty-first century. It had a coal fire, rugs on a lino floor and an ancient three-piece suite with the arms virtually worn through. It lacked anything in the way of luxury: there were no nick-knacks and almost nothing in the way of memorabilia. The only items of note were two photographs on the mantelpiece, one of his wedding day, of him and his wife, and another later one probably taken on his retirement at a farm down the road. She took the latter to get it copied.

His wife had died a few years before and, as far as anyone knew, there were no living relatives. He was the last of the line. She looked in the kitchen, opening the cupboard doors and drawers. A few tins of this and that were inside, but only bare essentials. There were no racks of spices, half-used packets of pasta, or even a bottle of ketchup – in fact nothing to indicate he cooked, or even ate regularly. Perhaps that was just because he was an old man, a widower, and never bothered much with food. The only evidence of recent life was a half-filled ashtray of pipe waste, a couple of empty Golden Virginia tins and a box of Swan Vestas full of dead matches. The place made her shudder. It was bare, cold and uncompromising. It smelled musty and unloved.

Having pulled on a pair of crime scene gloves she opened the drawers in the bedroom one by one, casually sifting through the contents, mostly to get a feel of the man and his lifestyle. It didn't take her very far. Everything about the place, from clothes to furnishings and décor, spoke of simplicity. The only surprise came in the form of a square tobacco tin shoved at the back of one of his clothes drawers. She opened it and found it contained seventy pounds in new ten pound notes. She closed the lid again and put the tin in her bag. Presumably, in the absence of a bank account, that was his way of saving to pay service bills or for any emergencies. She went through the pockets of his coat and trousers. There was nothing apart from bits of grass, some screwed up paper and loose change. In one pocket was a small business card from the Pear Tree in Loxton, a pub about five miles away, advertising a new menu. That at least was out of context and she put it in her pocket to follow up later.

Outside was slightly more inspiring. Tommy's bike was in the unlocked shed together with a selection of tools of various functions and ages. There was a work bench that had clearly been used regularly and a set of garden implements. She was wandering through the tall weeds at the back when she was accosted over the fence by the woman next door. Once Jennie explained that she was part of the enquiry team the woman became very forthcoming, but she seemed to know nothing more than Jennie had already worked out that morning. He was just an old man, he pottered around, always very polite, but kept himself to himself – that was his generation. She wouldn't hear a word against him. Once, she told Jennie, when her husband was off work with a bad back and they didn't have much money, Tommy lent them the rail fares so they could visit their daughter's new baby in London. He wouldn't take the money back, even though they'd tried. He said that he had no family and he was glad to be able to help folk who had.

She locked the house up and was about to drive away when a thought struck her. She left the car, went back into the house, wandered around it again, and then went to the shed before returning to the car. She was right. Nowhere in the house was there a book, a magazine, a newspaper, a letter or even a biro. Not even a TV guide. She sat in the car thinking for a while, then looked at her watch and drove to the Pear Tree in Loxton where, conveniently, it was lunchtime.

Originally a large old country house, the Pear Tree was now a hotel and restaurant with a huge extension at the back. It was the sort of posh place where she'd quite like to be taken out to dinner. The restaurant part looked a bit formal for lunch, but there was a bar round the side with several nooks and crannies which looked less intimidating. She chose a place by the window, wondering how much she could justify on expenses, but once she saw the price list she decided just to have the soup of the day.

A smiling young woman came over to take her order. Jennie asked for the soup, then showed her warrant card and asked if she might speak to the manager. At the sight of the warrant card the woman seemed visibly jumpy and when the soup came it was brought by a tall, worried-looking manager dressed in an impeccable pin-stripe suit.

'I'm sorry to bother you,' Jennie said, 'but we're making enquiries about an elderly gentleman who died a few weeks ago. We just need to clear up a few loose ends.'

The manager looked relieved, 'Yes, of course. How can I help?'

Jennie pulled out old Tommy's photograph, 'I wondered if you recognise this person from the restaurant or bar?' she asked. 'He had one of your cards in his pocket. He probably just picked it up somewhere, but we need to find out as much as we can.'

'Recognise him? Of course I recognise him,' he said to Jennie's great surprise, and he sat himself down next to her with a sigh. 'This is Mr Johnson. He's quite a regular here. Or rather he was, until his accident. We read about it in the paper, and now I gather his death might be suspicious. It's a terrible shame.'

Jennie was stunned into momentary silence, 'A regular? You mean he used to drink here at the bar?'

'No, no, he used to take dinner here, probably about a couple of times a month on average. Not in the restaurant, which I think he found a little formal.' He nodded in an understanding sort of way. 'Here in the bar. He always liked the table hidden away in the far corner by the window. I think it was the quietness and the view he was fond of. He came in on the early evening bus. The table was normally free at that time.'

Jennie was still trying to get her head round it. She'd just seen the prices for the lunchtime menu. How could he possibly have afforded dinner here?

'Did he just have one course and a drink?'

'Goodness me, no!' The manager sounded shocked. 'It was normally a full three course dinner. He particularly liked his steaks, did Mr Johnson.' He added, 'And his wine of course.' He went quiet for a moment. 'I'm so sorry,' he said again. 'It's so, so sad and we'll all miss him. He was a very generous man, you know – always gave large tips to the girls.'

'May I enquire how he paid for his meals? Was it by credit card?' 'No, no, always cash. And any change he gave straight to the girls.'

'Do you think I'd learn anything more about him from the girls?' Jennie asked, noting the manager's worried expression return as she did so.

'Er... I don't really think so. To be honest, I don't think their English is up to it yet. Most of them are from the eastern Baltic. All official and above board of course,' he added hastily, weaving his fingers together in a nervous reaction.

'Thank you, you've been most helpful. There's just one final question, if I may. Did Mr Johnson order from the menu?'

'Interesting you should ask that. No, he always asked me to recommend what I thought was best that night, and if it didn't suit him, he went for the steak,' he paused. 'Always medium-rare,' he added, smiling sadly at Jennie.

CHAPTER 13

The first debriefing took place the following day. Flett's senior team, including Jacko, were crammed into his office.

'Right, are we all here?'

'Apart from DC Lazenby, boss,' MacBrayne said. He went to get the bat film and some statements from the bat trust people. He should be back soon though.'

'Okay, you first, Dunc,' said Flett, leaning back in his swivel chair and putting his hands behind his head. 'Tell us where we're at.'

'Not very productive so far, boss. In fact bugger all from the house-to-house enquiries. Most of the recent incomers to Middle Belford didn't even know Tommy existed until the newspapers got wind. The longer standing folk knew of him though, or at least they knew he did the winding. It was only the old boys who played bowls who had much of an idea, and then only because sometimes on Mondays he was late at the village hall because of a winding problem.

'They're a funny lot when it came to interviewing them, not very forthcoming. Turns out one of them had been interviewed by the police before. That was old Seth Hetherington several years back. Jacko's met him, he works up at the manor and was a mate of old Tommy. Someone answering his description was seen near a possible crime scene at a village miles away, but at the time he was trimming hedges in Middle Belford. The joke was that there must be someone else as ugly as him in the neighbourhood. In short, boss, the enquiries got us nowhere, although one thing did stand out like a sore thumb – namely that very little goes on in a small village like that without somebody knowing about it. If there *had* been anything unusual the evening of the old boy's death, someone would have noticed.'

'Maybe that's exactly the point,' Jacko suggested. They all looked at him, then at each other, waiting for an explanation.

'Come on then, laddie,' Flett said, 'spit it out.'

'Um, well…' Jacko began hesitantly, 'the point is that maybe they did see something important, but it wasn't unusual, so it just didn't register.'

'Like what?'

'Well, I can't really say because I wasn't there. But we've asked them if they saw anything unusual, haven't we? We've not asked anyone what actually occurred between, say, four and seven o'clock? Like builders working in the village, sheep being moved from one field to the next, groups of cyclists passing through, or the fish van arriving. You know, ordinary stuff like that.'

'Good point, Jacko,' MacBrayne conceded. Flett snorted quietly and tasked Jennie to look into it.

'Okay. My turn now,' Jennie pulled out her notes. 'It's a bit odd, boss. The old boy was an eighty-something year-old, widower, no known family, lived alone. Farm worker most of his life. Lived on a pension in a council house. A miserable place – cold, sparsely furnished and nothing of any value there. Never had a bank account either.'

'So, what's odd about it?' Flett commented, 'Just an old bloke trying to make do on a pension like thousands of other poor blokes.'

'Well that's the funny bit. I don't think he was that poor. He was getting money from somewhere. All his mates said how generous he was, the neighbour said he'd lent them money when they'd needed it and didn't want repaying, and there was a baccy tin containing seventy quid hidden in his sock drawer.'

'Could be he was just thrifty and saved up?'

'No boss, there's more. A couple of times a month he took the bus to Loxton and had dinner at the Pear Tree. He had a large meal, with wine, and tipped the waitresses heavily. They recognised him there from his photo. He may have been to other restaurants too. I only found out about that one from a card in his pocket.'

Flett sat up, 'The Pear Tree? It's only people like Roberts that can afford to go there. Where the hell was this money coming from? Did he pay cash there too?'

'Yes, boss, every time. The manager remembers him well. Even remembers how he liked his steak cooked. Odd isn't it? And I took the liberty of tracking the tenners from his baccy tin. They were all new. Five of them were originally drawn from the Post Office in Middle Belford, the other two were drawn by the Rev Rogers – he's the local vicar, sir – from the Nat West in Banbury. I thought we might be on to something there, but according to his bowling mates it seems the vicar used to slip him a few quid now and again for winding up the clock.'

'That's not going to make him rich is it?' muttered Flett. 'Dunc, have a look at Rogers' bank details, just to be on the safe side. And out of interest, where *is* our man of the cloth? Shouldn't he be back from his jollies by now?'

'I've tried ringing him,' Jacko chipped in. 'He gave me his mobile number but it goes straight to voicemail each time. He's not responding to messages either. All I know is that he was supposed to be at St Aidan's retreat somewhere on the Northumberland coast.' He pushed a piece of paper containing a scribbled phone number across the table.

Flett turned his attention back to MacBrayne, 'Dunc, the sooner you find this bloody vicar the better. Use Northumbria police if necessary. I'll clear it with Roberts. Now let's get back to where we were,' he flicked through his notes. 'Right, so in short it looks like our friend Tommy's getting access to fairly large amounts of cash from an unknown source. He's not spending it flamboyantly, he's not altering his visible lifestyle and he's having expensive meals out in a place no-one can see him. That suggests to me that although the money source may or may not be illegal, it's not a source he wants anyone to know about.'

'How about the horses, boss?'

'Don't think so, Dunc,' Jennie pointed out. 'I took his photo round all the local bookies. They'd never seen him. Can't have been the lottery or premium bonds either – any decent-sized payout there would need a bank account. I think you're right, boss. I think someone's paying him, and it's not for work done. Hush money, maybe?'

'Hush money? Keeping quiet about what exactly?' Flett snapped. 'What on earth could happen in that God-forsaken little village that might need hushing up? Do mucky things take place behind closed doors that we don't know about? Old ladies running a brothel, séances during lock-ins at the tea shop, cannabis being grown in the school's *Blue Peter* garden, or maybe sheep buggering on Tuesday nights in the barn?'

'I did wonder,' Jennie said rather hesitantly, once Flett had finished his rant, 'whether the Pear Tree itself was involved somehow. What if it was used for employing or trafficking illegals? Could that be what's going on? Maybe Tommy saw something there once?'

'What makes you think that?

'Just a feeling about the way the staff at the restaurant reacted to me, and what I saw behind the window dressing, but nothing I can really put my finger on. Just the sort of vibes you get when you've been in this job for a while.'

'Well, the super wanted us to keep our eyes open on the illegals front, so we better pass it on. It's probably nothing to do with our case at all, but we'll keep an open mind. Anything else?'

'Just one other thing, sir,' Jennie said, feeling uncomfortably centre stage, 'I don't know if it's relevant or not, but I think Tommy was illiterate.'

'What?'

'He couldn't read or write, sir.'

'Yes, I know what illiterate means, thank you,' he glanced at Jacko, who was visibly stunned by this revelation.

'Illiterate?' Jacko said in a loud voice, 'Christ, he can't be...' the others all looked at him.

Jennie thought she better explain, 'It's just a feeling, but there was no reading material in his house, no books, mags, not even a newspaper, and nothing to write with. He never used the menu at the Pear Tree, he always asked the waiter what he'd recommend.'

'If he's illiterate then we have a problem, lassie, a big problem. Jacko's good friend Dr Cleaver, the handwriting guru, thinks both his bowling card and the end date scribbled inside the clock workings were written by the same person. If it wasn't the old boy, then who the hell was it?'

At that moment MacBrayne's phone burst into song. He answered it quickly, 'Sorry, boss, it's DC Lazenby.' He stood up and moved to the side of the room away from the hubbub in the outer office. There was a momentary pause during which he looked alarmed. 'Christ,' he said, holding his phone close to his ear, followed by a longer pause, then, 'Christ,' again.

'What the hell is it now?' demanded Flett.

'It's the bat trust, boss.'

'What about it?'

'It was burnt down last night.'

* * *

MacBrayne drove Flett to the fire scene. It was a grey, drizzly morning and the windscreen wipers clicked away as slow streams of traffic hissed along through rain. Flett, who didn't believe in coincidences, sat morosely in the car. Arriving at the scene they met a rather disconsolate DS Lazenby, hands in pockets, glumly surveying the charred remains from outside the cordon. The whole atmosphere was wet and depressing. What had survived of the offices was a complete mess, unrecognisable as a set of temporary buildings and more like something out of a war zone. Everyone had been accounted for and the veritable Robin and his colleagues stood bemoaning the loss of all their research and records to anyone who would listen. A fire investigation officer had already arrived – a balding man in a white protection suit – who was sifting through the remains, taking samples, photographs, and making copious notes.

'Pretty convincingly arson, is my contention,' he said when Flett came up to the tapes. 'Can't be positive yet, of course, but I should imagine the seat of the fire was over there,' he waved in the general direction of where the back of the building had been. It was a black congealed mess that looked no different from the black congealed mess where the front of the building had been. 'Almost certainly an accelerant, but I'll have a better idea of what it was and where it started when I've looked at the samples in the lab. Can't think of a reason to burn down a bat office, though.' He chuckled quietly to himself as though enjoying some private joke.

He continued probing through the remains with a rod in silence, turning over pieces of debris and putting numbered markers in the ground. His attitude to police officers was based on the premise that they'd no understanding whatsoever of what his job involved, and in his experience it wasn't worthwhile trying to explain. After a few minutes, noticing they were still there, collars turned up against the rain, he called them over, 'There's nothing you can do, you know, unless you're just keen on getting wet. You might as well bugger off back to HQ. I'll email you the provisional findings as soon as I have them.' He gave them a patronising farewell smile.

Just as they were turning to go he shouted after them, 'Do you think it's related to the fire at the vicarage in Middle Belford? Funny we should have two fires out here such a short time apart, isn't it? Suppose it's just coincidence…'

'What the hell's he on about,' Flett asked MacBrayne as they returned to the car and shook the rain off their coats.

'Well, boss, that was the fire that burnt down the archaeologist's mobile office – you know, Jackson's office – a couple of weeks back.'

'For Christ's sake, why wasn't I told of it?'

'With respect, you were, boss. You said we didn't have the resources to bother about a few little brushes and spoons being torched and we weren't to arrange an investigation. If it helps,' he added hastily, noting Flett's increasingly reddening face, 'Jackson's people did some of the work that fire investigation bods normally do. Maybe we can get something out of that?'

Flett sat and glared out of the window. The man in the white coat was right – it was all too much of a coincidence, and he'd cocked up. He let MacBrayne drive back and sat hunched up in the passenger seat cursing periodically at anything that took his fancy. It was otherwise a journey spent in silence until they reached the office where they were informed that Superintendent Roberts had requested an urgent meeting with Flett's team.

'Bugger,' was all that Flett was able to mutter, 'he just wants to rub my nose in it. I hate the little sod.'

* * *

The team was rounded up and made its way to Roberts' office like a group of recalcitrant school children summoned to the head teacher.

'What the hell is going on?' was Roberts' no-nonsense opening gambit. 'I'm told there have been two suspicious fires. Is there a connection, Alastair? Are they both to do with this damn pensioner up the church tower? How far have you got in sorting this mess out?' He waved his hand across some papers on the desk in frustration. 'And I gather one of the fires wasn't investigated properly. Good God, am I dealing with a bunch of amateurs?'

'Steady on, sir,' Flett explained. 'As you'll realise, it's early days yet on the bat trust fire, but the investigator's of the opinion that arson is likely. If it is, then it may have been done specifically to destroy the camera data from the church tower. We don't know that yet.'

'You realise that, if this is arson Alastair, we may have a maniac loose in the area.' Roberts was playing the public concern card. 'We can't just sit around waiting for him to burn another property. So far no-one's been hurt, but there's already public distress and the local reporters are starting to poke about.' He held up his hands in frustration. 'And why wasn't the vicarage fire investigated?'

'We had no reason to think it was started deliberately, it was no more than a site hut. There was no obvious purpose behind it, and in all fairness there still doesn't seem to be one. It could just have been kids, or even a cigarette end.'

'As it happens, Mr Roberts,' Jacko interrupted politely, 'it was a strategic decision not to use valuable resources in deploying an investigator there. It was my suggestion. You see, some of my staff on site were already cross-trained in basic fire investigation principles.' Roberts looked surprised, but not as much as Flett.

'We made a full photographic and planned record of the burning and collapse processes, and also took a series of samples in case they were ever needed to test for accelerants.' Roberts was now looking at him suspiciously, sitting up straight in his chair and occasionally doodling with his pen on the top of a folder. Jacko was feeling unusually confident. The other three were looking bemused.

'Very commendable,' Roberts said eventually, 'but I'm afraid it would all lack police verification, not to mention proper chain of custody. If the evidence was ever needed, I'm afraid it just wouldn't be admissible – it would look a bit amateur, you see.' He gave a smile so patronising that Jacko felt like leaping across the table and punching him.

'With respect, I don't think it would be at all amateur, Mr Roberts. I don't know whether you're aware of the relevance of archaeological techniques in fire investigations? They've been widely developed and used in the aftermath of fires at places like Windsor Castle and the Mackintosh-designed

School of Art in Glasgow. I wonder, have you attended any of the new fire investigation awareness courses designed for senior management?' There was a blank look from Roberts so Jacko continued. 'Well, I've had an input into some of them and the methodology's now well accepted.' Roberts shifted uncomfortably and made a note of the course, while Flett was beginning to see the light at the end of the tunnel.

'Over the years of working on crime scenes,' Jacko continued, 'one of the things I've learned is to cover my back. I made sure that our entire procedure was carried out under the watchful eye of your duty officer. You'll find it in his log – PC 1739.' Roberts looked up at Flett who beamed back at him. 'You'll also find that all the records and all the samples were signed over to him in a sealed box and made secure in the HQ archive store catalogued under the incident number. The custody chain has been followed to the letter.' Roberts was looking slightly stunned, while Flett nodded happily.

'You might call it amateur,' Jacko went on, 'but I think you'll find it all perfectly admissible. I'm no expert of course, but in my view it was arson. Your fire investigator will be able to make up his own mind from our records.'

'Thank you, Dr Jackson,' Flett chirped. 'So that's the picture for you, sir.' He agonised as to why Jacko had got him off the hook. Favours probably, he thought suspiciously.

Roberts composed himself. 'Right, it seems I've been underestimating your team once again, Alastair. 'Naturally I shall recommend analysis of the samples. Let me know immediately of any results, won't you?' He began folding up his papers to signal the meeting was over. 'Oh yes, I've been looking through the records,' he added casually, 'we've only ever had one bad fire in the division since records were started – two elderly folk died when their house burned down in Little Frampton. It was a while back. Ironically, there was a chap in Middle Belford who was questioned about it.' He looked up, 'You know about this one I take it?'

The uneasy silence at the other side of his desk was broken by MacBrayne. 'Oh yes, sir,' he said cheerily. It was only part-lie, well concealed under a confident smile. 'We've already come across that in our enquiries.' He didn't know for sure, but guessed it must have been old Seth Hetherington who was once interviewed. He'd assumed it was for burglary, but until now it hadn't occurred to him that it might have been for arson.

'Good, well unless there's anything else,' said Roberts, 'I shall let you get back to the office.' He smiled in his inimitable greasy way.

'Just one thing, sir.' This time it was Jennie's turn. 'This business about the illegals. We may have something,'

'Good, good, excellent, go on,' he re-adjusted his back cushion, sat down again, and stared expectantly at her.

'Well it's just a feeling, sir, but I had cause to make enquiries about this decapitation case at the Pear Tree in Loxton – where the decapitated pensioner used to eat quite regularly. It just seemed that the staff reaction to me was, well, unusually twitchy. There were a lot of foreign workers there – that's hardly unusual, I know – but I just sensed something wasn't quite right.'

'The Pear Tree? Out of the question. No, no, impossible,' Roberts became agitated. 'The owner's a great friend of the

CC. He dines there regularly. We can't respond to undefined hunches in a place like that.'

'You did ask us to keep our eyes open, sir,' Flett argued. 'After all, sir, this is a major crime we're supposed to be looking into. We can't just ignore the place because important people may visit it. I can't run an enquiry around people's egos, sir.' Roberts was looking out of the window into the woodland patiently waiting for Flett to finish. 'My suggestion, sir, with respect,' Flett continued, 'would be for the unit to make an unexpected visit and check the credentials of the staff, or alternatively to put some covert observation on the place for a few days.'

'With respect, absolutely not,' came the categorical response. 'We'll do no such thing. Good heavens, Alastair, what are you thinking of? We've already had the CC complaining about Dr Jackson's treatment of the MP, now you want to upset the applecart again by raiding the premises of his important social colleagues? No, I absolutely forbid anyone from your unit to do such a thing.'

There was an uneasy silence during which Flett decided it would be prudent to make their departure. 'Well, thank you for your time, sir,' he said as they lifted themselves from their chairs. 'Naturally we'll keep you in the loop regarding the fire investigation work.'

They left the room together and went out through the fresh air to their own building.

Jennie was upset. Her face was flushed and her heart was pounding. She wasn't a big woman, more compact in a very athletic, fit sort of way, and definitely not the sort of person to pick a fight with when she was irate. 'Jumped up fucking twat,' she muttered, 'all I did was what he asked us to do. And then he goes and rubbishes it in front of everyone. Makes me feel like a piece of low life from the gutter.'

'That,' said Flett, 'is because he's a manager not a policeman. He doesn't understand hunches. If he can't give things numbers, put them in boxes, ascribe them names, count them or send them on courses, then he can't cope with them. You know, Jennie,' he whispered to her, putting his arm round her in a rare exhibition of affection, 'you should feel sorry for the bumptious little shite.'

CHAPTER 14

They met up again in the afternoon. Flett had made sure there was plenty of coffee on tap and even bought a packet of biscuits from the canteen. MacBrayne and Jennie looked at each other in amazement – the offer of biscuits in Flett's office was unprecedented. Perhaps here was a lonely soul, they thought, finally recognising that the only few friends he had on the entire planet were those he worked closely with. Could biscuits, albeit plain digestives, be his way of a new bonding process, a tentative effort to demonstrate partnership and camaraderie?

'Contributions for the biscuits would be appreciated,' he said gruffly as they trooped in and took their seats. They settled down, Jennie and MacBrayne appearing slightly apprehensive, Jacko by contrast bright and enthusiastic.

'Right. Down to business.' Flett leaned across the desk to them, 'This is off the record. Not a word outside these four walls. And this conversation never took place. Got it?' Heads nodded. 'It's the Pear Tree. It needs to be observed covertly. Roberts has a bee in his social bonnet as to why we should leave it alone, but sadly he doesn't understand policing. As far as I'm concerned it's essential to further our enquiries. No question about it. Do you all agree?'

Jacko nodded enthusiastically. MacBrayne closed his eyes, he knew what was coming.

'But as you will remember,' Flett continued, 'Superintendent Roberts' exact words were, "I absolutely forbid anyone from your unit to do such a thing." That's a shame, but of course, strictly speaking, Jacko here isn't part of the unit so he doesn't count.' He paused and three heads turned towards Jacko, who sat there in all innocence. Suddenly the penny dropped.

'Me? You must be joking. I can't do covert stuff.'

'Nothing like learning new skills,' Flett said brightly after a short pause, adding less tactfully, 'Even at your age. Dunc and Jennie here will teach you the basics. And as a special treat, here's a present for you.' He pushed a package across the table. 'It's a new phone, compliments of the force. It's a pay-as-you-go jobbie, but you'll have to buy your own top-ups. To be on the safe side use it whenever you're talking to one of the team instead of your own mobile. And we want it back afterwards.'

MacBrayne pulled out a large scale map of the area and laid it across Flett's desk, pointing out the Pear Tree. It was surrounded by fields and hills on one side and at the back, by houses and buildings on another, and by the road at the front. 'We're planning a three stage approach for you, Jacko: firstly you'll be doing a relatively brief assessment from the outside pretending to be a rambler; secondly a longer observation from nearby, probably from inside a parked car, and finally we'll book you into the hotel as a guest for a couple of nights. It's all very straightforward.'

'Well it doesn't sound very straightforward to me. I'm not trained for this sort of underhand stuff.'

'Jacko, it's a piece of cake,' Jennie added. 'We'll get you a new aerial photograph to help you understand the lie of the land better. For the first part, all you have to do is go walkies using the public footpath in the hills at the back of the pub, get a better idea of the layout, then go up further and find a quiet lookout spot to stay in. The route's used by ramblers, so you'll need to blend in. Take a backpack so that you look like a walker, a pair of binoculars, and wear a woolly hat. The path runs along the back of the premises, then winds up through the hills, in and out through the trees. It should give you a chance to have a close look at the place without it being obvious.'

'So I just take a walk, make my way up the hill, hang around for a while and then come down again?' he asked suspiciously.

'That's it in essence,' Jennie added. 'You just need to blend in. The important point is not to get yourself noticed. It doesn't matter if you're seen, but it does matter if you're noticed. There's a difference. The worst thing is if you're *recognised*, in which case we abort the whole operation.'

'And how long do I stay up there for? I wasn't planning on doing an Arctic survival course.'

Jennie pointed on the map to woodland near the top of the hill. 'You need to find a comfortable spot up here for a few hours where you can see all the comings and goings. We need you to find out about the positions of outside doors, types of deliveries, general busy times, quiet times and so on. You'll get a basic feel for it if you're up there for a day, then we can firm it up with a couple of longer sessions observing in a car at street level. Look, there's a pond up there. If you meet anyone, you can always pretend you're into newts or something.'

'Now for the second part,' she pointed to the map again. 'There's a church car park nearby where you can stay in the car overnight. It's not ideally situated, but it'll do. It's a long stay car park, so you won't look out of place. Whatever you do, don't use the pub car park itself. I clocked an armoury of CCTV cameras when I went there. We'll get you into position as soon as it's dark, somewhere you can get a good view but without a streetlamp shining on you. Stay there until about seven in the morning, after the cleaners have arrived, then stand down.'

'What if I want a pee?'

'Use your initiative,' was MacBrayne's unsympathetic advice.

'Thanks a lot. Very helpful of you. And what happens when I finally get to stay at the hotel, assuming I survive all this, won't I be a bit obvious snooping around on my own?'

'Far from it, we'll give you a good cover,' Jennie assured him, then smiled knowingly at MacBrayne. 'You're going on your honeymoon there, you and your new wife.'

Jacko's face went white, 'My what?'

'Wife, Jacko. That's the plan. We'll book you both in under false names. It'll be a quiet room at the back where you can look out over the secluded access points. Your wife's called Judy by the way.'

'Well thank you for telling me.'

'Don't worry, she used to be a DC in Flett's unit,' MacBrayne reassured him. 'She left to set up a private security company. She's good. Sometimes the boss hires her in for particular jobs.'

'We chose her specially,' Jennie continued. 'You know, someone appropriate to your age, not some floozy you might have picked up at a night club. Can't have you looking like a Mr and Mrs Smith, there for a naughty night with your secretary, can we? It has to look genuine, so you're a nice mature middle-aged couple, probably second time round. And don't be concerned about the sleeping arrangements, you'll be taking it in turns to keep watch, so there won't be any opportunity for hanky-panky. Judy's done this before, she'll keep you in line.'

'What's this Judy like, then?' Jacko asked tentatively. 'You seem to know a lot about her. Will I get on with her okay?

Jennie and MacBrayne looked at each other. 'Oh, yes,' they said in unison, trying not to smile, at which point Flett decided it would be a useful time to stop for tea.

* * *

Jacko wandered outside in the fresh air, enjoying the smell of the woodland on the edge of the grounds. There were a couple of men out there managing the estate, more like groundsmen than gardeners he supposed. Not a bad job really. He envied them – they had minimal responsibility, they weren't required to show initiative. They turned up at work at half past eight and left again at five. The times of their breaks were predictable, before and after work their time was their own. They could read books, watch TV, go to the pub, cook the dinner, play with the kids, sit in the bath and fantasise, or generally mind their own business. They didn't have to get paperwork ready for the next day, stay up half the night trying to meet deadlines, worry about what to say to people, think three weeks ahead, or plot political schemes. That sort of nonsense went on upstairs, on a higher pay grade where ambition rather than satisfaction ruled the day, where everyone looked over their shoulder, and where conversations were analysed word for word in the reflective solitude of the toilet cubicle. Instead their achievement was simple, rewarded by watching things grow and seeing the seasons change. Okay, so they may not get paid that much, but it was a job with few worries and work that allowed them to switch off at the end of the day. Even if no-one else noticed that the leaves had been cleared away, how effective last year's pruning of the shrubs had been, or the cuttings that had rooted in the greenhouse, it didn't matter. It was a relationship of harmony, not one of competition.

He could see the growing advantages of that sort of work, especially since he was now committed to a venture of unprecedented challenge at the Pear Tree and had no idea what to expect. His enthusiasm for forensics was strangely ambivalent – it came in bursts with great spurts of adrenaline, but then dissipated quickly once the reality set in. But he couldn't wimp out now, he was up to his neck in it.

He stood looking at the woodland, listening to the jackdaws cackling, his mind miles away in some fantasy of a quiet life reading a book on a sofa, when an arm crept inside his and gently tugged him.

'Come on, 007,' said Jennie, 'the boss wants you back.' She gave him a little peck on the cheek.

* * *

'Right, Dunc, what did you get for us on this other fire? Where was it, Little Frampton or somewhere?'

MacBrayne pulled a large cardboard file out from an orange plastic Sainsbury's bag under the table. 'Well boss, it seems that eight years ago a small farmhouse in Little Frampton got burnt down with an elderly couple inside it.' He looked up, 'That's about five miles from here, boss.' He shuffled through the papers. 'Cause of fire was never determined, but there were lots of rumours at the time about arson. The old couple weren't very popular, kept themselves to themselves. Other than the fact that everyone who knew them said they were unpleasant, there wouldn't have been much of a motive. Oh, and there doesn't seem to have been any family to inherit, not even a dog's home. Could have been a fag end that started it – they were both smokers – or a loose coal from the fire. It was a thatched place. Would have gone up in no time. That's about all there is to it, boss. The local newspaper, the *Herald*, made a meal of it. In fact there's more in the paper than there is in the file, although it's mostly supposition. The only point of vague interest is the fact that someone saw a person near the scene just before it caught fire. Seems it was an oldish bloke, medium height wearing a light blue shirt. Not a lot to go on in the half-light, but the police checked out likely candidates in the social clubs, bowls clubs and so on from the villages round about. A few old boys were interviewed here and there, one of whom was a chap called Seth Hetherington in Middle Belford. He had a cast iron alibi. Can't put much weight on it really – quite a few folk were interviewed and the description was a tad on the general side to say the least.'

Flett's antennae began to twitch. 'Wait a minute. Three possible arsons in the same area? This Hetherington, the chap Jacko met at the manor and an old chum of the deceased, was around for all three fires and interviewed about one of them. I don't like coincidences. Jennie, see if you can dig up anything else on Little Frampton. And Dunc, can you quietly look into Hetherington's background a bit more? Preferably without him finding out.' Flett began to gather together papers from his desk, a sure sign that the meeting was coming to an end. The others got up, ready to leave.

'Oh, by the way,' Flett asked, attempting to remove a rogue paperclip caught up in his files, 'before we split, do we know anything about Hetherington's alibi at the time of the Little Frampton fire – cast iron, you said, Dunc?'

'Yup, got it here boss,' MacBrayne rummaged in his Sainsbury's bag and fumbled through some papers. 'Here we are, yes. He was seen cutting hedges in Middle Belford at the time. He didn't have a car and anyway he can't drive, so it puts him squarely out of the frame.'

'Who was it that saw him and gave him the alibi, then? Presumably several folk?'

'I don't think so, sir. Let me check. Just one I think.' There was an uncomfortable pause while he scanned the page. 'Oh God.' He looked up aghast. The others stared at him. 'Just the one alibi, boss. It was the vicar, that Rev Rogers.'

* * *

'Is this really so difficult?' boomed Flett, staring hard at a subdued MacBrayne sitting in his office two days later. 'He's a vicar, he looks like a vicar, he talks like a vicar, he wears a bloody dog collar that makes him stand out like a vicar, and we know the registration of his motor. Why the hell can't we find him?'

'Agreed, boss, but we keep going up dead ends,' MacBrayne squirmed slightly on his seat, nervously rubbing his hands back and forth along his jeans. 'So far we've traced him to that retreat in Northumberland, the one Jacko mentioned. He was there for a couple of weeks and they've got him on their residency records, then they said he'd gone over to Lindisfarne for some spiritual replenishment.'

'Some what?'

'Spiritual replenishment, boss. Lindisfarne's an old monastic centre where the monks lived a life of austerity and piety. He'll have gone on a pilgrimage, you know the sort of thing, in this case probably to soak up the vibes and recharge.'

Flett folded his arms and sighed. This wasn't getting any better. He swung his chair round to look out of the window at the grey drizzly morning. All very depressing. The concepts of austerity and piety reminded him of his boyhood in Scotland, growing up in the shadow of a disciplinarian father under a strict God-fearing regime. Austerity had been something he wanted to forget, not deliberately seek out. They'd lived in a small fishing village on the west coast, him and his two older brothers. One had joined the church, the other became a fisherman like his father and, like his father, had drowned at sea. He couldn't remember much that was good about family life. 'Go on,' he sighed.

'The trouble is,' MacBrayne continued, 'we don't know exactly how long he was in Lindisfarne for. There are only a few standard tourist places to stay in, but he wasn't at any of those. I'm still trying to find where he might have stopped. Anyway, I asked the local boys there to see if anyone remembers the Jag, and it seems they do. Apparently some old biddy complained about it being parked in front of her house rather than in the main car park. It was seen for a few days, but exactly when, no-one can remember. It certainly isn't there now. No luck on the alerts either, boss. I think if it was on the road it would have been clocked by now. We've even looked at airport and ferry terminal car parks. My guess is it's in a garage or lock-up somewhere, out of view deliberately or otherwise.

'I've also been in touch with Mrs Jefferson, you know, she's the cleaning lady at the vicarage. When he left he gave her a retainer for three week's work – she hasn't heard from him now for three weeks and she doesn't see much point in starting to clean a place that's going to be gutted anyway. She's a bit pissed off with the whole thing. Oh, yes,' he added, 'his bank account's clean – no unusual income or expenditure – it's all consistent month after month. He takes out roughly the same fixed sum in cash every month, usually several hundred quid. Not quite sure what his expenditure's on though.'

'Well, presumably he's alive and kicking then,' was Flett's frustrated response. 'And we can't even take out a warrant for him because he hasn't done anything. I'll report all this to Roberts. Unless we can find something solid against him, we'll just have to be patient.'

'I'm glad you're feeling patient, boss,' MacBrayne said rather sheepishly, 'because I'm afraid I haven't managed to find old Seth Hetherington either.'

'Dear God, Dunc…' Flett shut his eyes and scratched the back of his head. 'This is an old bloke in his eighties. He can't drive, can barely ride a bike and probably hasn't been out of Middle Belford much since he was born. He can't be that difficult to track down, for goodness' sake?'

'We've looked in all the usual places, boss. His neighbours haven't seen him for a while – of course, helpfully, they can't remember when. The old boys he played bowls and drank with at the Red Horse were wondering where he'd got to. Seems he had family somewhere, but no-one knew who or where, and anyway he sometimes vanished for a few days. Seems he was a fairly private bloke. He's a cunning old bugger, and like our deceased friend Tommy he works on a cash basis only. No bank account as far as anybody knew. Sorry if I'm sounding a bit peed off here, boss, but it's like being in a time warp investigating this lot. Even in his house it was like being in the 1950s. When I went back there, he'd helpfully left the door key under the mat, but inside it was Spartan, all basic stuff, nothing unusual, everything left as though he was coming back. The milk in the fridge had gone off, but he could have forgotten about it when he went away. He's in his eighties after all.'

At that moment the door opened. 'Found old Seth yet, Duncan?' came Jennie's cheery voice as she walked into the office with the most impeccable bad timing. They both glared at her.

'Sorry, have I said something wrong? Er… it's just that the old boy seems to have done a runner. It looks like we're not the only one hunting him. We had the posh folk from the manor enquiring of his whereabouts. Would you believe it, they want him arrested. Seems they'd paid him cash up front for some garden clearance work and he hadn't finished it. Now they want him locking up.'

'Let's suppose it's all innocent,' said Flett philosophically. 'We'll just have to assume for the time being that he's gone off to see his great cousin or whoever. All we can do is wait, just like with the bloody vicar.'

'With respect, boss,' said MacBrayne with some hesitation, 'I don't think it is all that innocent.' As the words came out he felt Flett's stare burn through him like a laser. 'Um, there are two things that worry me, boss. First, I took the liberty of going to the Post Office. It was hard work getting information out of the old biddy who works there, but it seems that Seth didn't draw his pension last week. That's the first time either she or the other staff there remember him missing his entitlement. Even when he went away, he always told them when he'd be coming back to claim it.'

Flett rested his elbows on the desk and put his head in his hands. 'And the second?'

'Our friend the church clock.'

'What about it?'

'It's stopped.'

Flett immediately looked up.

'It ran down last Tuesday. It should have been wound up by Seth on the Monday, but can't have been.'

Dear God,' Flett murmured. 'What have I done to deserve this? We're missing a trick somewhere, something staring us in the face that we haven't noticed. We've a suspected murder up the tower, a vicar that's done a runner, three fires which may or may not be connected, and an octogenarian that's missing. And now the bloody clock's stopped.'

He walked across to the window, stayed to watch a grey squirrel scamper across the lawn before vanishing up a tree, then turned to a rather embarrassed Jennie who was standing waiting patiently. 'Well lass, now you're here, have you brought us any news on the Little Frampton fire?'

Jennie glanced across at MacBrayne wondering how best to respond, but a decision was avoided by a knock on the door followed by the appearance of DC Lazenby's smiling face.

'Wait,' shouted Flett, immediately erasing Lazenby's smile. He beckoned to Jennie to continue.

'The Little Frampton case hasn't any legs, boss. There's just no evidence for anything. But there is something else. Do you remember you tasked me to find out what normal things were happening at Middle Belford the day old Tommy died? Jacko suggested that folk might not have bothered to mention ordinary events, thinking they weren't important.'

'Yes, yes, go on. What was afoot that no-one bothered to tell us about?'

'The window cleaner.'

'The window cleaner?'

'Yes, the window cleaner,' she repeated excitedly. 'He visits the village every few weeks, always on a Monday, and does his round of customers. Not only was he in town on the day old Tommy died, but he cleaned the vicarage windows too. What's more he has a special ladder for the vicarage because it's on three floors.'

'What time?' asked Flett, immediately alerted.

'No-one can remember exactly, but the window cleaner says that he and his mate went in for a cup of tea at the vicarage courtesy of Mrs Jefferson there. They always have a good gossip with her and she bakes them scones. She confirms they were in there for about forty-five minutes or so, which was fairly usual, and it was around five or six-ish in the evening when they'd finished their round. They worked it so the vicarage was the last call. Pretty well everyone knew their rota and timing, which is probably why nobody mentioned it to us. Interesting thing is though boss, the vicar joined them this time. Kept chattering on apparently.'

'Did he just? Well, well. Any idea where they parked during this delightful tiffin session?'

'Yes, boss, where they usually did – in the car park area immediately next to the church and out of sight of the vicarage.' Jennie sat back feeling very pleased with herself, and Flett heaved an audible sigh of relief.

'Thank God. At last! At last we're beginning to get somewhere…' his gaze landed on Lazenby still motionless by the door, fearful of movement or speech.

'I can't take much more today, laddie,' he said, 'but seeing as you're here, what is it?'

'The fire reports, boss,' he said hesitantly. 'You asked me to let you know when they were finished. The fire investigator's just signed them off, sir.'

'And?'

'Both the fire in the vicarage grounds and at the bat trust were arson, sir.'

CHAPTER 15

MacBrayne and a reluctant Jacko were off to the manor at Flett's behest, the excuse being to respond to Wainwright's complaint that the old boy had done a runner from an unfinished job. No-one else would get that sort of police response and Flett hoped they'd feel privileged and hence forthcoming. The manor's gravel drive took them in a wide arc around the old stable block where Seth worked, but there was no sign of any activity. There was an autumn feel around, the leaves were beginning to turn, some had already fallen and many of the plants had started to seed. A yellow-brown tinge was beginning to show across the long grasses in the paddock. This was the time of year when the landscape would need a gardener to cut back all the mellowing growth, turn the soil, and prepare the ground for winter. If Seth didn't show for a while, Jacko thought, Wainwright would have to pay someone a proper wage to do the job. Serve him bloody well right.

They drove up to the front of the house where the main oak door was protected by an openwork wrought iron grill.

Its purpose was for both security and decoration, and it worked well on both counts. It clearly said 'bugger off', but politely, to anyone who might want to ring the bell-pull. Jacko couldn't help finding it reminiscent of a portcullis, no matter how fine its artistic achievement.

They carried on around the side to what might be described as the back door in the nineteenth century wing of the house, half hidden by a dense Virginia creeper which was in the process of turning from dark green to purple and showering a flutter of leaves with each light gust of wind.

MacBrayne drew the car to a noisy halt on the gravel and got out. Jacko, by agreement, stayed slumped in the passenger seat, trying not to be noticed. Two horses stared out arrogantly at the visitors from an adjacent stable and observed MacBrayne with some scepticism as he made his way around a stone mounting block to the porch. It was stone built with a wide entrance filled with clutter – a few garden implements, buckets that appeared not to have been used for decades, some mechanical parts lying on the ground belonging to an unknown device, and a black electric bicycle propped up against one wall. Leading from it was a small chamber with a broken wooden door housing an antiquated toilet with overhead flushing system, complete with hanging chain and a cracked wooden seat covered in cobwebs. In fact, cobwebs were a major feature of the porch interior. He rang a bell high up on the wall, heard nothing and so rang it again. He was about to return to the car defeated when footsteps could be heard approaching from inside, followed by the mechanical sounds of locks being turned and bolts slid. The door opened inwards with some gusto and a small woman, wiry, wrinkled and wearing a housecoat, framed the lower half of the huge opening. She had one arm against each doorpost barring entry. Even from where Jacko was sitting she looked ferocious, certainly as daunting as the portcullis at the front.

'Yes?' she barked at MacBrayne. She had pursed lips and a crumpled face like a squeezed lemon. Everything about her was thin and wizened in a way that reminded MacBrayne of an evil witch from a fairy tale.

'Police, DS MacBrayne, ma'am,' he said, opening his warrant in front of her. She ignored it.

'What do you want? I'm busy.' Her accent was foreign with an irksome tone to it.

'We're following up a complaint, ma'am. A complaint from the manor this morning, a complaint regarding a Mr Seth Hetherington.'

'Nothing to do with me. I'm the housekeeper,' she made to close the door.

'Is there anyone else who could help us, ma'am?' MacBrayne asked quickly. 'A formal complaint's been made and we're obliged to follow it up, otherwise we'll have to assume the complaint's been dropped.' She looked sourly at him without comment. 'I'd be grateful if you could give Mr Wainwright my details, ma'am,' and he handed her his card. She took it disdainfully, as though it were diseased.

'One last thing, ma'am,' he added before she finally closed the door. 'Do you know where we can find Mr Hetherington?' The witch pointed down towards the old stables.

'Is it possible for us to have a quick look down there? I'm sure Mr Wainwright would want us to investigate his complaint as thoroughly as possible.' He gave her an ingratiating smile.

'As you wish,' she said. The door closed, the key was turned and the bolts slid back.

'Miserable old bag,' he muttered as he returned to the car. They drove back down the drive until they reached the old stable block again.

The whole place was exactly how Jacko had seen it before – Seth's tools were lined up against the wall, sheltered from the elements by the overhanging slate roof, his bench was there in the courtyard, now with some browned, seedy-looking hollyhocks and foxgloves threatening to fall across it, and the door into the stables was slightly ajar. The only difference was the presence of a battered yellow skip containing rubble from the demolished wall together with some other junk and garden rubbish.

They pushed open the stable door and accustomed themselves to the gloom inside. There was no electricity there, or at least none that was connected, and the only light came through the open door or was filtered through the film of cobwebs that decorated the small windows. There were a couple of inner rooms, presumably for tack or other horsey purposes, both equally gloomy, everywhere coated in dust, grime, or both. They opened cupboards, poked around on shelves among various jars and bottles of congealed liquids, tins of solidified paint and rusty tools. Neither really knew what they were looking for other than anything unusual, or something that might have a bearing on Seth's whereabouts.

'What's this?' MacBrayne asked, picking up a plastic box that lay in a corner on the floor, partially hidden by some racks of sacking. He was in the front room of the block and the box was lying at the far end in the semi-darkness.

'Looks like a lunch box to me,' Jacko commented, taking it out to the light. Inside was a crumpled polythene bag and a chocolate bar wrapper. 'I wonder if this was Seth's? I can't think who else it might belong to. It's not the sort of thing he'd leave behind – he'd need it for the following day.'

'Unless he wasn't coming back,' MacBrayne pointed out pessimistically. 'I'll go and get the torch from the car.' He returned a couple of minutes later with a powerful torch that lit up the room like a set of floodlights. They both saw what a shambles the place really was. It was filthy from floor to ceiling, unused and unloved, but built with a beautiful hardwood framework crafted by someone who knew all about working timber.

'What a shame,' Jacko moved his hand across a joint by the door, feeling how smooth it was and how tightly the pieces of cut timber had been fitted together.

'What a dump,' was MacBrayne's only response. 'Did the old boy ever use it?'

'He probably came in here for his lunch or for a break when it was raining, otherwise he'd sit on the bench outside.' Jacko pointed to an upturned wooden box that may have acted as a table, and a smaller box next to it covered with old sacking that could have been used as a chair.

'Not my first choice of dining area,' grunted MacBrayne and shuffled off. 'Must be potty to even consider eating in this hovel.'

'I think that's the only facility our friendly MP allowed him. You'll notice there's no toilet either.'

'Yes, thank you, I'd already clocked that from the smell of piss out around the back.'

'Dunc...' said Jacko slowly with the sandwich box still in his hand, 'When did it last rain?' MacBrayne stopped for a moment and pushed away a cobweb from his face.

'You mean, when might he have last used the hovel? Good thinking. From memory, not for a few days at least. Let's check.' He pulled out his mobile phone, tapped a few keys, waited, tapped in a few more, muttered about trying to get a signal in the middle of nowhere, waited again and swore mildly. 'Gottit!' he shouted finally.

'And?'

'Would you Adam and Eve it? Only been two wet days recently – eight days ago and last Monday. Well, Seth's been seen since eight days ago, but no-one's seen him since last Monday – that was the day he never turned up to his bowling evening, and the day the clock was never wound up either.'

'So,' said Jacko, 'we could suppose he was here last Monday having his lunch inside because of the weather, but never came back on the Tuesday.'

'Steady on. That's pushing it a bit, and it's all based on a lunch box. Can't see Flett swallowing that one. Anyway, given it's possible, maybe we ought to look in the back room.' He walked across and shone the flashlight around the walls. Their eyes both followed the beam as it lit up the corners, shelves and heaps of rubbish casting eerie shadows across the floor.

'Hold on,' Jacko said, stooping to look at the floorboards. 'You didn't sweep the floor or anything did you?'

MacBrayne look at him in mild amusement. 'Sweep the floor? You must be joking. It needs more than a yard brush to clean this place up.'

'Well, someone's swept it, haven't they?' Jacko said pointedly. 'Look. It's completely clean, apart from around the edges.' He took the torch from MacBrayne and shone it at the floor, not directly, but at a low angle which showed up a series of small sweep lines of grime across an otherwise clean floor. 'Compare it to the one we're standing on,' he said, and did the same with the torch across the floor of the front room. It showed a thick layer of disturbed dirt from where they'd been pottering around. 'What d'you reckon to that, then?' he asked.

MacBrayne looked in detail at the floor in the back room as he shone the torch back and forth. 'I see what you mean,' he said thoughtfully, kicking himself for not spotting it first. 'Better keep out of here for the time being, just in case. Maybe we should have a scout around outside instead.'

There was little to see there either. The whole of the surroundings were overgrown with hogweed, in some places up to head height. A cursory search showed nothing and they abandoned it.

'Waste of time,' said MacBrayne, pulling sticky burrs off his fleece. 'It needs looking at properly. Trouble is, there's nothing to justify bringing in a search team, just a lunch box and a clean floor – hardly conclusive of anything, is it? Flett would think we were off our trolleys, and bloody Wainwright would have a field day with the chief constable if we implemented a formal search on that basis.'

Jacko began wandering around the courtyard while MacBrayne busied himself in the car making a few notes, before flicking his notebook shut and starting up the engine.

'Come on, there's nothing more we can do. Let's make a move,'

'I don't like this,' Jacko said as he got to the car.

'What don't you like?'

'The skip.'

MacBrayne turned off the car engine, 'What about the skip?'

'It's not got much in it. In fact there's barely a layer of rubble covering the bottom. I had a quick poke inside it to see.'

'Sorry, I'm not with you here. Am I missing something?'

'Again, it's probably nothing, but if you look at the pile of rubble that's left, and the surviving foundations of the wall, a good deal of rubble must have already been disposed of.'

'And?'

'Well this isn't the first skip that's been here then, is it?' Jacko pointed out. 'I mean, I'm not saying anything, but a skip must have been here and then been emptied at the tip, and Seth Hetherington's gone missing. Just an observation of events and a coincidence, that's all.'

MacBrayne lifted himself out of the car and pulled out his mobile phone. He walked over to the skip and rang the skip company's office number, barely legible on its side. Jacko could make out a female voice at the other end. There was a pause while she collected some information. MacBrayne thanked her, looked at Jacko, and dialled another number.

Then followed an animated conversation just out of earshot, during which MacBrayne walked backwards and forwards, occasionally waving his arm about, his voice varying in pitch.

'What the hell was all that about?' Jacko asked him when he returned to the car.

'Your suspicions were right. This isn't the first skip. One was taken away last Monday afternoon, the same day we think the old boy may have gone missing. And it was full. It seems the manor people asked specifically for it to be changed for an empty one that day, although I've yet to find out exactly who rang the company.' He settled himself back in his car seat. 'I've just spoken to the boss, who isn't the happiest bunny in the world right now. I've finally managed to persuade him that we have to take this one seriously on the basis of a missing person enquiry. He's agreed to instigate a full crime scene search of the stable block here, and to track the disposal route of the skip. He's off to talk to Roberts right now. Good luck to him, I wouldn't mind being a fly on that wall.'

'All a bit of a long shot, given the evidence. I'm surprised he's taking the risk, putting his head on the block like that.'

'It's not his head that's on the block.'

'Whose is it then, if it's not his?'

'As a matter of fact it's yours, Jacko. The boss will tell Roberts that it's your idea, and as Roberts thinks the sun comes shining out of your intellectual arse, the rest of us are in the clear.' He gave him a hearty slap on the back. 'Come on, stop worrying and get in the car, the cold's getting to me.'

CHAPTER 16

Jacko had prepared himself carefully for his first undercover role. Walking in the hills was something he did frequently and he already had the necessary clothing and paraphernalia. His kit – decent boots, fleece, waterproofs, binoculars, digital camera, GPS and a small hiking rucksack – were well seasoned, and his fleece even had some grubby badges signifying successful completion of the West Highland Way, the Millennium Way and other hiking achievements. Either from a distance or close up he looked the part. He needed no new gear that might flag him up as a fake, or make him stand out like some designer-clad idiot. Better still, the colours were all dark and subdued, black, browns and dark greens, including a woolly hat, and made for good camouflage. The hat was a present from Lucy after one of her East European conference jaunts. She preferred to buy gifts with a story to them, although he'd forgotten the precise narrative belonging to this one – it was probably alpaca wool, hand-knitted by some aged crone in the back end of Estonia using natural dyes only found near a secret mountain stream. Lucy had told him jokingly it had magic properties. Of course he didn't believe her, but he was still a teeny bit superstitious about it, and carried it every time he went hiking. He also took with him a notebook and pen, a small Dictaphone and, as a fail-safe, a book on newts.

On the appointed day and with the weather forecast unusually accurate he drove, fully prepared, into the car park. He eventually found a space with the best view of the Pear Tree for the subsequent night's watch. The little heaps of mud across the car park from people scraping their boots confirmed the place was popular with walkers. He sat in the car and took out a copy of Flett's aerial photo to make sure he was familiar with the hotel buildings. It was a good image, taken from a fairly low altitude but showing the whole of the main building, extension and outbuildings in an L-shaped configuration. The car parking area was towards the rear, guarded by three tall security pylons bearing CCTV cameras, and interspersed with grassy banks and shrubs. Behind it, at the back, against the open hillside, stood a line of storage sheds and units, part-timbered by the looks of it, with a single pitched roof. The entire circumference of the complex was fenced and seemed to have patches of creeper-like plants growing over it.

Having folded up his map and changed into his boots, he hoisted his backpack on to his shoulders and made his way nonchalantly down the road feeling good inside. It was a bright crisp morning with a hint of autumn in the air, and the leaves were beginning to turn in the line of beeches bordering the hotel. He sauntered along and turned out into open country, the fresh breeze on his face. As the path rose upwards the hotel complex came into view again to his left, its layout becoming clearer the higher up he went. From the map contours he'd calculated the best position for viewing it, balancing distance and optimum view carefully, and logged it as a way-mark into his GPS. It bleeped as he reached it, at which point he knelt down pretending to tie his bootlace, taking the opportunity to give the whole place a casual once-over from the rear. There were no surprises. The car park was beginning to empty as last night's guests started to disperse, and there were metallic clatters and some shouting from the kitchen as a youth wearing a blue and white checked apron came out to empty the rubbish, bringing with him through the open door the seductive whiff of frying bacon. The rear of the storage sheds was visible and he made a mental note that there were no doors or access points at the back. He also noticed that the fence between him and the sheds was in dire need of repair and was accessible in several places.

With his bootlaces suitably fiddled with, he stood up, hunched his backpack up on his shoulders and plodded onwards. It was mostly hill pasture, but the grass was still lush and green for late summer and the sheep were making the most of it. Ramblers were a facet of daily life for the sheep, who continued their munching as he walked past, showing any displeasure by urinating rather than moving out of the way. He reached the path's highest point slightly out of breath, stopped to admire the view and consulted the map again, leaning against a newly installed kissing gate. A group of organised ramblers moved up the hill behind him in a long string, characterised by their grey hair, Nordic walking poles, bulging backpacks and incessant chatter. Jacko stood to one side, leaning over his open map, to let them through. Almost without exception they all spoke to him with a greeting or a comment, one old biddy poking him with her pole, 'Nice bum,' she commented before trotting off giggling down the other side of the hill.

His plan was to follow the path further on, out of sight of the hotel, then double-back behind the hill and take a position high up in the small patch of woodland to monitor any comings and goings through binoculars. He had a quick look around. The rambling pensioners were well ahead into the distance and there were no other walkers or farm vehicles in sight. After staying on the path for a good five minutes he veered off along the line of a field wall in an arc that took him round to the wood at the top of the hill. It took him about fifteen minutes in all. The landscape became rockier and he was forced to scramble over rough ground until he reached the seclusion of the wood, panting from the climb.

It was barely fifty metres across and about half that in width. The trees hadn't been managed for years and the undergrowth had taken over to provide a thick belt of heavy bramble. He forced his way around it as best he could to find a half-decent observation spot where the chances of being scratched were lowest. There wasn't much choice. To make matters worse, the pond shown on the map had dried up in the hot weather and transpired to be little more than a low-lying area of boggy ground with a few open pools and clumps of reeds. Any newt worth its salt would have packed up and left.

He established a reasonable lookout point in the brambles on the edge of the wood. From there he could look down at the hotel in the distance and spot anyone coming up the hill. If anyone came over the horizon from behind him, rapid calculations suggested it would take at least twenty minutes for them to reach him. So if he scuttled back to the other side of the wood periodically to check, then he'd have reasonable warning.

What he hadn't bargained for was the fact that there was someone else already in the wood. As he stumbled his way through the undergrowth trying to find the most convenient route around the brambles he almost tripped over a man sitting cross-legged on a green Barbour jacket spread out on the ground. The man's pose was leprechaun-like, and he appeared engrossed in writing notes in a small book. It wasn't clear who was more surprised. They both looked at each other in astonishment. The man was bearded, quite stocky and wore a flat cap, a dark green fleece and gaiters over the legs of his jeans.

'Hello,' Jacko said in the absence of anything else that came to mind, aware only that the whole strategy for the day had instantly flown out of the window and his clever plan was now completely screwed.

'Hello,' was all the bearded man seemed able to utter. 'What brings you here?' he added eventually, at a loss as to what to say. Successful small talk during an unexpected encounter in the supermarket was taxing enough for most people, but on the top of a hill in the middle of nowhere it required a special skill which neither of them possessed. 'Ah, you must have come up very quietly,' the man muttered next. 'Never heard you.'

'No,' Jacko replied, pushing his social skills to the limit, 'I mean, yes, just arrived here. Doing some newt work at the pond over there,' he pointed vaguely in the direction of the dried bog. 'Mind you, not much pond left since I was here last time.' He hoped reference to the regularity of visiting might improve his legitimacy, and prayed the man knew nothing about newts either. 'Any vibrations in the ground tend to frighten them off. I have to be as quiet as I can.' There was a note of academic seriousness in his voice.

The man nodded understandingly and rose to his feet. As he did so Jacko glimpsed a pair of binoculars and a lens case in his open rucksack before it was hoisted out of sight.

'You?' asked Jacko politely, 'Out for a walk? Good weather for it.'

'Well, not really,' came the slow reply. 'I'm interested in ancient monuments, you know, Romans and things like that.'

'Not much up here though, is there?' Jacko enquired innocently.

'Oh, you'd be surprised. I'm looking into Iron Age hill fort positions.' Then he carefully added, 'That's why I walk the hill tops like this one.'

'That'll keep you fit,' Jacko replied with a patronising smile, noticing the size of the man's stomach as he struggled to get his arms into the Barbour jacket. 'Are there many hill forts around here?' he asked, knowing full well there weren't any.

'Oh yes, you'd be surprised how many there are. I'm trying to do them all systematically, hence the early start on this one!' He gave a cheery grin and made himself ready for departure. 'How are we doing for time, I wonder?' He pulled out his phone and held it at various angles trying to see the face. 'Bugger,' he muttered as he pressed the keypad. 'Battery's flat. Sorry, do you have the right time?'

Jacko patted his pockets to see which one contained his phone, eventually found it and pulled it out. He noticed the man was now leaning against a tree adjusting the straps on his rucksack. For reasons of instinct rather than logic, Jacko opened up his phone and took a photo of the man whilst telling him it was around quarter to ten.

'Thanks. I'm in good time for the next one.' He gave Jacko a big smile, 'Hope I've not disturbed your newts too much. Good hunting!' And with that he moved through the wood and walked down the back of the hill. Jacko watched him from the cover of the brambles until he'd rejoined the path and disappeared over the brow of the next hill.

After this unexpected incident, his enthusiasm took something of a nosedive and he spent much of his time in constant sorties backwards and forwards to see if the man was coming back. His observation on the hotel, meanwhile, showed little other than visitors coming for lunch, delivery vans bringing provisions, and a dray supplying the beer. There were a couple of different firms making the deliveries, either from normal transit vans or chiller vans like the ones that Sainsbury's or Tesco use for home deliveries. Apart from the beer kegs which were sent down chutes into the beer cellar, all the other boxes, and all the crates of vegetables and fruit, were stored in the sheds at the back. One of the sheds must have had a large walk-in fridge judging from the quantity of meats and ice-packed material delivered. He could just make out the names of the delivery firms on the sides of the vans, photographed them when he could, or wrote them down and texted them to MacBrayne with the delivery times, as instructed. He also sent him the photo of the bearded man in case anyone recognised him, and explained why.

Six o'clock was the agreed end point, by which time he was cold and pissed off. Nothing much had happened, he'd drunk all his coffee, eaten his sandwiches and he needed a bath and a beer. Making his way down the back of the hill he joined the path, meeting up with a few other walkers on their way back to the car park. Passing the rear of the hotel as part of a group he felt comfortingly invisible. Then, having reached the church car park, he finally heaved himself into his car, not bothering about scraping the mud off his boots, and drove off with the heater on full blast. His phone began to find signals and then celebrated by pinging all the way home with incoming messages from Flett, MacBrayne and Jennie. But the most important message was from Lucy.

* * *

The next day they all sat round Flett's desk for a debriefing. Jacko related the events as fully as he could and wrote up an unofficial report, seeing as it was an unofficial exercise. 'Good work,' Flett said begrudgingly. 'It seems we're not the only ones interested in the Pear Tree. That chap you met up there, do you think you convinced him you were a *bona fide* newt boffin?'

'Pretty sure I got away with it. He didn't quiz me or anything like that, and I must have looked the part. He certainly wasn't an archaeologist though, unless he was some form of fringe loony.'

'No, he wasn't an archaeologist,' Flett sounded unusually positive. 'He's a spook.'

'A spook? What's a spook? Are you telling me I've seen a ghost?'

'I suppose, in a sense, yes. They do like to think of themselves as phantoms. That photo you took, we circulated it to a few of our old friends in special branch, and they recognised him. He's an ex-DC who used to work for SO15 – that's the Met's counter-terrorist outfit – so he'll be skilled in various techniques of observation and covert work. He officially left SO15 a few years back. He's still in a job apparently, but no-one's prepared to tell us what he's doing or where he is. We'll just have to assume he's working in intelligence somewhere.'

'You mean like MI5?' Jacko asked, the colour draining from his face as the full reality of his experience on the hilltop slowly dawned.

'It's nothing to worry about,' Jennie said in a comforting sort of way. 'These people are on our side.' She paused for a moment, adding, 'Or they're supposed to be.'

'What's interesting,' Flett went on, 'is that we're not the only people interested in the Pear Tree. It confirms there must be something going on there. And if Roberts found out that the MI5 lot are working on his patch without him knowing, he'd blow a gasket. But of course I can't tell him because we haven't been up there, have we?'

'Jacko, is there any way he could have photographed you while you were talking to him?' MacBrayne asked, 'Maybe when you were distracted or something, like you did with him?'

'Not a chance. We were only together for less than five minutes and I would have noticed.'

'They've all sorts of tricks up their sleeves, you know. Are you sure he didn't have his phone or camera out at all?'

'Only once,' Jacko answered cheerily, 'but his battery was flat.'

'Ah.' He went quiet. 'You fell for that one, did you?'

'What do you mean?'

'Is this what he did?' MacBrayne pulled out his phone, held it out in front of him pretending to see the time then said, 'Bugger, the battery's flat. Do you have the time, Jacko?' Jacko looked at him pathetically, suddenly realising what had happened. 'What did you do then?' MacBrayne asked. Jacko glumly looked down to pull his phone from his pocket. 'Click,' said MacBrayne, 'I've just taken your photo.'

'What's your thinking then now, boss?' Jennie asked. 'Is the Pear Tree being used to hide illegals? Bit public isn't it?'

'Agreed, but there's got to be something running otherwise the spooks wouldn't be interested. Could be that the hotel, or more precisely the catering element of it, might be used as a source of food destined for the illegals. Maybe part of a bigger racket. Let's poke it about a bit. Why don't you find out when their main deliveries are, and the quantities of food and produce delivered using the names on the vans that Jacko recorded? You'll need to see the purchase orders and possibly get some inside information too. Dunc, use the financial brains that Roberts thinks you've got and find out about the Pear Tree's ownership. See if its management's involved in supplying any other hotels or bars. We need to find out if foodstuffs are going *out* from the hotel, as well as going in.'

'So what's all this got to do with Tommy, or Seth for that matter?' Jacko asked, feeling rather confused

'Christ knows, but here's a little something you might like to mull over in the meantime. Duncan's found out that Jennie was right, old Tommy *was* illiterate. He couldn't even scrawl his signature. His mates in the Red Horse confirmed it, and it turns out that his bowls card was always filled in for him by our now absent friend Seth Hetherington. Suck on that one for a bit.'

Jacko was stunned. 'Christ, that means that if Seth filled in the bowls card, then he wrote the date in the clock casing too?' He was trying to pull it together in his head. 'But when I asked Seth who'd written it, he claimed he didn't know, said it was probably the vicar. That means that he knew more about all this than he let on. Why would he have written the date up and then denied it? I mean, there was justification for it with the clock about to be motorised, wasn't there? Or did he know something was going to happen to Tommy?'

CHAPTER 17

The following day Jacko found himself sitting in his trusty VW in the church car park, gazing out at the impressive stone frontage of the Pear Tree. He'd already tried to call Lucy to follow up her text message from the day before but wasn't able to contact her. He was now apprehensive on two counts: firstly he was badly shaken up from his encounter with the spook, and secondly MacBrayne had arranged for him to meet Judy that evening. She was the woman, his newly-wedded wife, of unknown age, appearance and character, with whom he was to share a bridal suite in a few days time. He'd decided not to mention this to Lucy for the time being. The plan tonight was that Judy would keep him company in the car for a while, arriving about 11 pm. That way they'd at least know what each other looked like.

Once at the car park, he'd followed MacBrayne's instructions to the letter. He'd parked in the optimum place for observation away from streetlamps, removed the interior car light bulb and had a pile of sandwiches and a flask of coffee at the ready for the long wait. He was surprised how dark it was in the car. The streetlamps were quite a distance away, there was virtually no neon glow, and he found himself groping around to find things that he'd left on the passenger seat.

Up until about 10.30 pm it was fairly quiet; just a few comings and goings in the bar and restaurant. The main activity had been a family celebration of some kind, by the looks of it a sixty-fifth birthday dinner, complete with balloons and attended by several generations of the same family – or at least through the binoculars they all seemed to have similar facial characteristics. Needs a wider gene pool, he thought. He must have seen about thirty of them go in, all dressed to the nines and looking uncomfortable. When they emerged again soon after 10 pm, it was a different scene altogether. Maybe a few bottles of wine washing down the fine cuisine had helped. They were all clutching each other, kissing, and in some instances, propping themselves up. Whatever feuds had existed before dinner had been anaesthetised, albeit temporarily. The celebrity of the day appeared to be a tall man with thinning grey hair dressed in a smart suit, always centre stage, with family focused around him. He was being treated with obvious deference by the hotel staff, but was holding a balloon which did little for his image. Eventually and with much noise they shuffled themselves into cars and a couple of waiting taxis, then vanished away into the darkness.

Other diners departed in twos or small groups, and the few solitary drinkers made their way out down the steps and back to their homes. By 11.30 Judy still hadn't shown up. She hadn't turned up by midnight either, by which time the bar attendants were clearing up and the lights were being turned off. A couple of taxis rolled by to take some staff away, and the place finally became dormant apart from a few lights in some of the bedrooms. The occasional car droned past and a couple of pedestrians walked quickly along the end of the car park. Each time he heard footsteps approach he expected to see the mysterious Judy turn in his direction. One of us must have got the date wrong, he thought, and looked at his watch again. One o'clock. The temperature was beginning to drop. Jesus, it was going to be a long night. A few moments later, just as he felt himself dozing, and without any warning, the passenger door opened and a dark shape positioned itself in the passenger seat, shutting the door silently behind. Without the interior light coming on Jacko had no idea what creature it was, only that it seemed large and had affected the car's suspension.

'You shouldn't have left the door unlocked,' it whispered in a husky female voice. 'Bloody daft thing to do. Anyone could have got in'.

'Are you Judy?' Jacko whispered back rather stupidly, anticipating the answer would be in the affirmative.

'Just as well, isn't it?'

'I'm Jacko,' he said, rather more pathetically than he'd intended. The cold was getting to him.

'Thank you, I'd already worked that out.' They both fell silent. It was not a good start to their marriage.

'I'm afraid I didn't hear you walk into the car park,' Jacko said apologetically. 'You must have been very quiet.'

The shape shuffled itself into a more comfortable position. 'I've been sitting in a car two spaces away for the last three hours.'

'Christ, I never noticed you.'

'That's because you weren't looking for me.' There was another awkward silence.

'Want a coffee, Judy?'

'Got any food?'

'I've a couple of sandwiches left and a few biscuits. Any good?'

The creature became more amenable. Perhaps it just needed feeding. 'Thanks,' it said, cramming a Waitrose Essentials cheese and tomato sandwich into a hole in the upper part of its amorphous shape. 'I forgot to bring mine in the rush to get here.' There was the noise of hearty chewing and swallowing. 'Sorry if I sounded a bit sharp. It must have been the hunger.'

'It's okay. Not much been happening out here has there?' he whispered. 'All very quiet.'

'That's usually the way of it,' she said, wiping some crumbs down into the footwell. 'Did you see the old man's birthday party?'

'Yeah, wonder who he was?'

'Didn't you recognise him?' she asked, surprised. 'I thought everyone knew who he was. He's the chief constable. Didn't he look a prat holding a balloon? Pity I didn't have my camera. Could have made a bit of money selling a photo to one of the tabloids.'

Jacko was about to comment when the sound of footsteps from the road came into earshot. They both fell silent, expecting the person to walk past the end of the car park and away down the road again. But the steps were unusually slow and measured and were accompanied by flashes of light from a torch. Instead of walking past, the person turned into the car park, stopping here and there, and shining the torch this way and that, into each car in turn.

'Shit,' said Judy. 'Quick, snog me.'

'What?'

'For Christ's sake, snog me.' There was urgency in her voice.

Jacko, confused, remained motionless. Judy grabbed him by the collar, pulled him on to her, trapping pieces of fallen sandwich between them both, and pressed her mouth into his.

'For God's sake, it's like snogging a corpse,' she hissed. 'Give the impression you're enjoying it. Move and wriggle a bit.' Jacko did his best to oblige. Out of one eye she saw the torch coming nearer, the footsteps slowing down.

'Put your hand up my jumper, quickly,' she said. 'Make it look real.'

'What?'

'Put your hand up my fucking jumper now for heaven's sake!'

Jacko hesitantly obliged, his mouth still pressed dryly against hers, and wriggled his hand tentatively up somewhere just north of her navel. Suddenly his elbow was grabbed and jerked up so that his hand shot up under her jumper and landed on her left breast. The torchlight was flashing around the next car.

'For fuck's sake show some passion,' she said, and to his horror Jacko felt her hand rubbing up and down his groin, not in any subtle romantic way, but reminiscent of how his mother used to knead dough on the wooden kitchen table when she was making bread. The torch beam landed on them and moved around.

'Dirty bastards!' shouted an excited male voice behind the torch. 'I know your sort.' The torch shone for far longer than was necessary on their moving parts. 'Dirty bastards,' he shouted again, 'Doing it in a car. And in the church car park.' The pair of them patiently carried on until he'd had his fill of voyeurism and moved away, the torchlight flashing elsewhere.

They gradually ceased and Judy stopped making dramatic moaning noises and wriggling sensuously. 'Just some old pervert getting off on watching other people,' she commented casually, as though it happened to her all the time. 'Dirty old git. And don't get any funny ideas about this,' she hissed, 'I'm gay.'

Having finished the sandwiches and coffee they settled down and chatted in hushed tones until about 5.30 am, when she slipped back to her own car and drove away in the dark, leaving a spread of crumbs and empty sandwich wrappers behind. He still had little idea what she looked like. At about 6 am, just as he himself was preparing to leave, an unmarked white transit van appeared, turned off its headlights as it entered the hotel car park and drove around to the back, reversing against the sheds. The driver got out and was met by another man who seemed to appear from nowhere. The van's rear doors were opened and one of the sheds unlocked. From where he was sitting Jacko couldn't tell whether they were loading or unloading. He used his binoculars to try and see the registration plate, but it was still too dark. There seemed to be just the two men working there, then the doors were shut and the van drove out of the car park, headlights still off until it reached the road. He'd been waiting patiently and recorded the number plate as best he could in the half-light as the van accelerated past. He waited a little longer then drove back towards Compton, stopping only in a lay-by for a long-awaited pee and to text the van's registration to MacBrayne. By the time he reached home MacBrayne had already replied, *'If that van comes again, check the registration number will you? It doesn't match the vehicle.'*

He flung his phone disgustedly on the sofa and took himself to bed, falling into a deep sleep almost instantly.

* * *

The next night, still bleary from day and night being reversed, he took up his now familiar position in the car park by the church and prepared himself for another long night of covert observation. This time he felt slightly more confident as he settled down to watch the comings and goings at the hotel. It was a Sunday night, business was brisk but not heavy, and the restaurant was far from full. Most of the diners were couples having a meal out and leaving early. It was one of those bars where it was table service only with free nibbles arranged decorously; orders were taken and served by a flunky in a suit. Looking through the binoculars, the only folk there were probably businessmen obliged to stay the night ahead of meetings in the morning. No-one else in their right mind would pay those prices unless they were trying to impress somebody.

By midnight the place had effectively shut down, the bar and restaurant had closed and there were only a few lights on in the bedroom windows. It was colder than yesterday and Jacko was wearing extra clothes in anticipation. He glanced around the car park. It was less busy than the night before, there were just a few cars with heavy dew beginning to form on the windscreens. Autumn seemed closer and he could sense the sounds and neon glow being blanketed as a mist started to form. He watched the streetlamps become blurred, saw water droplets form on the car, and the hotel slowly begin to vanish from sight. It was half past midnight.

He sat tight until about 5 am, by which time the mist had thickened even more. He was bored silly. Not even a pervert with a torch had provided a diversion. He just wanted to be back at home and in bed, preferably with Lucy. Despite his extra clothing he was cold and shivering, his coffee was exhausted and his bladder was swollen. He had to get out and relieve himself, blaming a combination of the cold and advancing years for the urgency. There was no option. MacBrayne had recommended keeping a bottle in the car to avoid this, but after a half-hearted attempt to unzip himself and get into an appropriate position through the various layers of clothing, he abandoned the idea. Having carefully opened the door, he slid himself out of his seat before creeping around the back of the car where he relieved himself with immeasurable delight against the churchyard wall. He propped himself up with one hand, breathing deeply with unfettered joy for what seemed an eternity. Turning back to get into the car it struck him that trying to see the number plate of the van in the mist would be impossible unless he was almost next to it. But maybe the mist, or fog as it was by now, would let him get close to the back of the hotel without him being seen. If he got a move on there was still time, and if he got caught he could just say he'd been walking home from a piss-up and got lost. It seemed perfectly plausible.

Without thinking further, he locked the car, heaved his excess clothes around him giving the inadvertent impression of a down-and-out, and moved out of the dark towards the street. He needed to get to the rear of the sheds where the fence was broken. A direct approach through the hotel car park was a no-go route because of the security cameras. It had to be around one of the two sides. One side had private houses there and, from memory, they were fenced and gated. God knows why people did that. What on earth was the need for huge black iron fences with gold points on top and electric iron gates? Ostentatious displays of wealth, like Iron Age hill forts, probably. He would have liked to explore this ethnographic analogy of social dynamics further, but 5 am in a church car park and in thick fog was neither the time nor the place.

The only viable route to reach the rear of the hotel was down the side and through a field. There was no traffic and he walked brazenly down the road into the cushion of fog, looking for all the world like some form of itinerant. He wore an overcoat over a series of fleeces, baggy tracksuit bottoms over long-johns and a woolly hat that covered his ears and tied under his chin. There was a gap in the hedge, and he turned swiftly into the field then stopped briefly out of sight of the road.

Before long his face and clothes were dripping with moisture. The field was slippery under foot. Happily the hotel was barely visible through the gloom, and he slithered his way through an emerging crop of sugar beet while keeping a hedge between himself and the hotel grounds. Straggly brambles hung out below knee level and clumps of hawthorn had sprouted where he least expected. This was becoming a bad idea. Worse, and to his personal annoyance, he felt the need to have another pee. It hadn't been long since the last one but there was a similar urgency and he had to stop again, this time waving the flow around to try and minimise the noise of splashing. By the time he reached the corner of the hotel complex his trainers were caked in mud and he was barely able to keep his feet. He stopped to re-orientate himself. The rear of the sheds lay off to his right behind the broken fence. He could just about make them out and tried to find a way through the openings where the posts had broken. Lifting his leg over the collapsed woodwork, normally a simple physical exercise, now became an unusually cumbersome procedure, and his entire body seemed to be held down by invisible weights. His left leg finally made it across, but his trailing leg became caught and he fell flat on his face in the wet undergrowth. He lay there for a moment while he tried to gain his wits. Everything was dark, wet and miserable, his clothes were soaked from the fog, and he was out of breath, desperately unfit. There was a dampened glow of neon from the hotel car park which lit up the silhouette of the sheds. On the plus side, he was in the right place. On the minus side he hadn't brought a torch and he hadn't really got a clue what to do next, other than he needed to pee again.

By the time he'd struggled to his feet, mostly by clawing himself up the rear wall of the sheds, the decision was made for him with the sound of a vehicle entering the car park. The engine noise became louder as it neared the sheds, changed gear and reversed. He could vaguely make out the reversing light as a white glow within the neon. It backed up to the sheds and stopped, then there was the noise of doors opening and shutting. He carefully felt his way along the wall to the end of the sheds, his legs so thick and heavy with clothes and mud that he could barely move one in front of the other. He wished he'd never left his car. Still, all he had to do was get the van's registration number then he could go home. He dragged his way slowly around the end of the sheds, carefully avoiding a pile of what looked like empty gin bottles, and tentatively peeked into the car park, his chest pounding with fear. No going back now. Just get the number and bugger off. Job done. Yes, it was a white van. Thank God for that. Now, where was the number? Bugger, bugger. It must be on the left hand rear door which was open and facing the other way. He'd have to wait until it was shut to see it. Shit. And the damp had got to his bladder again. He was desperate for another pee. He moved back out of sight, automatically touching his woolly hat for inspiration. He reckoned there were just two people there, the driver and another man who looked like he'd come out of the sheds.

Was the place important enough to have a watchman? By the time he peeked around the corner again they'd finished whatever it was they'd been doing. The driver shut the van doors, but just at the point when the number would have been visible, the other man walked and stood in front of it, chatting to the driver. Jacko cursed to himself. Nothing was going right. The two men were in heated conversation, both seeming jumpy, but he couldn't hear what they were talking about. Then, as the driver began to walk towards the van the other man went with him and, in answer to Jacko's prayers, moved away from the number plate. Jacko frantically memorised it, moved away out of sight and scribbled it on the palm of his hand with a biro, breathing a huge sigh of relief as he did so.

Then, in his hurry to return to the rear of the sheds and back to the relative safety of the sugar beet field, he stumbled into the pile of gin bottles that he'd so carefully avoided earlier. There was a crash and a clatter. The two men stopped in their tracks and turned around.

'Jesus, what the fuck's that?'

'Dunno. Probably just an animal.'

'What sort of fucking animal makes that sort of noise?'

'Dunno. Fox maybe?' One of the men went to the corner and looked around. It was pitch black.

'Go get the torch.'

The driver opened the van door and took a flash-lamp from the side pocket. As he returned a strange low wailing sound started. Both men stopped and looked at each other. The driver went back to the van again and hauled out a crowbar from under the seat.

'Foxes don't make that sort of noise,' the other man said, and together they moved gingerly towards the side of the shed, one shining the torch, the other wielding the crowbar. The fog was as bad as ever, despite it being past sunrise. It was difficult to make anything out, but as they got nearer the torch picked out a large dark eerie shape.

'Jesus.' They both stopped.

'*Flower of Sco'and, when see ye agaaain,*' it wailed, '*th'a fought'n died fur wee bita heels a' glen.*' The voice rose with crescendo in the wrong places and with the words slurred.

It was a tramp-like creature, wet and filthy, leaning with his head buried in a woolly hat against the wall. He was singing away, probably *Flower of Scotland*, one hand holding a gin bottle, the other directing a flow of urine casually in any direction.

They moved nearer to see him more clearly, but retreated as an arc of piss came towards them.

'*Stoood 'gainst him, fuck'n Edwuuds army,*' it continued unmelodiously as the two men wondered what to do next.

'Should we tell the boss?'

'Nah. That'll drop me in the shit for not noticing him earlier. Let's just forget about him.'

'*Hameward 'e sent um, fuckun English cunts,*' continued the song, with modification.

'Think he saw anything?'

'Come on, what d'you think? He can't even see his own dick.'

'*Tee think ageen.*' An empty gin bottle was lobbed in their direction and the shape shuffled off through the broken fence.

'*Thouwer of Sco'and, when see ye agaaain,*' it wailed once more, the voice becoming lost in the fog as the figure disappeared from view.

Jacko kept moving, hoping to hell he'd got away with it, stumbling and sliding among the sugar beets. The sun was doing its best to break through the fog, but there was still enough cover to avoid being seen. When he reached the road he turned and walked as fast as he could in the opposite direction until the hotel was out of sight. When the road was clear he stripped off his outer clothes, hid them behind a hedge and walked back briskly towards the hotel, woolly hat in hand and hair slicked back. He looked almost normal. By the time he reached his car the sun had finally broken through. He hopped in and drove away like any other commuter off to work, stopping only to collect a pile of clothes hidden behind the hedge.

CHAPTER 18

Barty Webb and his team of CSIs had ensconced themselves in the old stable block at the manor while Flett sat uncomfortably in his car. He'd managed to get a search warrant from the magistrate without too much bother, but hadn't been able to find Superintendent Roberts to give him the heads up. He was away at some meeting or other. He'd emailed him instead. It wasn't an ideal situation, knowing how touchy Roberts was about upsetting the local big-wigs. Roberts still didn't know they'd been watching the Pear Tree either. He now had two opportunities to blow his top.

The warrant to search the old stables had been served up at the manor. Flett had been looking forward to seeing the reaction on the smug Wainwright faces, but sadly for him none of the Wainwrights were at home. Instead he was faced with the abrupt treatment metered out by the weasel housekeeper.

'Do as you please', she'd snorted through the half-open door, and blankly refused to give him any contact details for the Wainwrights who were in London and not to be disturbed. Then she'd shut the door in his face.

'Suit your fucking self then,' Flett had muttered under his breath, wondering what on earth went on in this enormous mansion which only seemed to contain this niggardly little witch. He drove back down the drive to the blue-taped area, made a few notes, spoke briefly to MacBrayne and then sat in his car flicking through the pages of the latest *Model Railways and Locomotives* magazine. He expected the old bag to ring up one of the Wainwrights who would contact the chief constable at the first opportunity who then, in turn, would be on the phone to Roberts whose little brown nose would be pulled out of someone's arse and made to give an explanation. Given the severity of this social discourtesy it wasn't likely to be much more than a couple of hours or so before Roberts would be tracking him down to pass the buck accordingly. He looked at his watch. Any time from now on, he thought, and turned off his mobile phone accordingly.

About thirty minutes later MacBrayne appeared in his whites, still inside the blue tape, with his mobile phone pressed against his ear. Flett smiled. MacBrayne seemed to be on the defensive.

'The boss, sir? I'll see if I can find him. It'll take me a minute, sir, I'm inside the crime scene cordon.' There were some agitated noises at the other end of the phone.

MacBrayne went on, 'Er, yes, sir, we've categorised it as a crime scene for the time being,' This didn't seem to have a calming effect and the person at the other end was becoming animated.

'It's designated as a missing person's case, sir,' MacBrayne said in answer to a question. There was a further pause during which the chattering became louder.

'I'll see if he's still here,' MacBrayne said, and looked questioningly at Flett who shook his head.

'Just missed him, sir, sorry,' he said after a suitable interval. The noise at the other end continued.

'Well if his phone's off,' MacBrayne said politely, 'it's because he's driving, sir. No, none of the cars have Bluetooth any more, sir, budget cuts, you know.' The conversation eventually ceased and Flett gave him a thumbs up.

As the two of them were debating the best way of handling Roberts, Barty Webb called them over. His bald head protruded straight out of his whites without any obvious space for a neck. He blinked in the sunlight like a mole emerging from underground.

'Got something for you boys. Let me show you.' He threw a set of whites at Flett who struggled to get them on.

'That's an XXL size,' Barty said helpfully. 'Nothing personal, you understand, Mr Flett. The big size makes it easier so you don't have to half-undress first.'

By the time he'd finally got it on, Flett looked like something from outer space. The legs were too baggy, the arms carried on down well past his hands and the top of the hood stood about a foot above his head. They signed in with a grumpy-looking uniformed officer at the door and ducked under the tape. Barty led them in, firstly through the outer room where he said they'd found nothing, then into what was probably the tack room. He made them wait at the entrance and called out to the two white-suited figures inside to move to one side.

'Someone's had a damn good go at cleaning the whole place out. Done a pretty good job too. Apart from brushing out all the grime, a whole load of disinfectant's been used, probably bleach, but they've missed bits, like they usually do.' He called over to an anonymous white shape, 'Ted, show 'em where the blood is.'

Ted obliged, pointing out at least half a dozen points flagged up by little markers. They were low on the walls, at the floor edges and on the legs of some wooden trestle arrangement. All had escaped the rigours of cleaning.

'There's been a fair bit of blood flying around here,' Barty went on. 'Look up there,' he gestured to the ceiling where a further set of markers had been tacked. 'You can barely see them, they're no more than dark brown stains, all dried up. A lot of blood's become saturated in the timbers.' He waited while the two officers took it all in.

'We should manage to sample most of them. The DNA can be turned around in about a week, but it'll have to be a private lab, and that'll cost you. Do we have a DNA reference set for your old boy?'

'Not yet. Dunc, get Jennie to go back to his house and see what she can find – tooth brush, hair brush, anything that's likely to be useful.'

'Okay, but according to Jacko he didn't have much hair to brush, boss, and from the smell of his breath Jacko didn't think he brushed his teeth much either. I'll tell her to see what she can find.' He was moving towards the door when his phone rang.

'Sorry, boss,' he said to Flett as he pulled it out, then, 'Yes, of course, sir,' to the person down the phone. It was a short conversation. 'Superintendent Roberts is on his way, boss. Wants to see what's going on. Sounds a bit frantic to me.'

'Anything else before he comes, Barty?' Flett asked. 'I know it's early days but I need every straw there is to clutch at. Roberts has this peculiar belief that the upper levels of society and the landed gentry never get involved in crime.'

'Huh,' was Barty's opinion. 'In my book, it's mostly through crime that they got where they are.'

'Precisely, but Roberts is too busy looking up his own backside to have worked that out yet. I need anything you've got, no matter how insignificant, that I can use to delay things.'

'Okay, right, well we've got the brush that was probably used to sweep the place out. It'd been stuffed up in the rafters which makes it look suspicious. Can't see any blood on it, but we can send it off for testing and possible prints. And we're still working on the outside of the building. It's badly overgrown, so it's taking a while. At least another day, I should think. Uniform can keep it secure tonight, so that gives you all of tomorrow to play with.'

'What about cleaning rags, disinfectant bottles or prints?'

'Not a dickie so far, unless there's something we still haven't come across outside. Other than possibly the brush, not a single print in here, mostly the wrong sort of surfaces. Maybe all the rags and stuff went off in the skip? We'll keep looking anyway.'

About fifteen minutes later Superintendent Roberts' metallic red Range Rover Evoque, gleaming from a weekend polishing, slid serenely up the drive. Flett and MacBrayne had remained inside the stables, mulling over various possibilities and options with Barty. Roberts, his hair recently trimmed and wearing a smart dark blue suit with an immaculately tailored shirt and tie, climbed out of the car, slammed the door in a demonstration of authority and frustration, and strode across to the tape where he was confronted by the grumpy-looking officer holding a clipboard who'd moved swiftly to block his access.

'Can I help you, sir?' he asked politely, to Roberts' obvious anger.

'Don't you know who I am?' he spat.

'No sir, and with respect, sir, it doesn't matter who you are. No-one enters without authority and without signing in.'

'I'm Superintendent Roberts, now let me through,'

'Sorry sir, I'll need identification.' The grumpy officer was enjoying this. It had been a long boring shift with nothing much to do other than stand about.

Roberts flashed his warrant card which the officer looked at thoroughly.

'That's fine, we have to do things by the book, don't we sir?' he said patronisingly. 'Now if you could just sign in, please?'

Roberts grudgingly signed the sheet while the officer looked at him.

'Well, aren't you going to log my time of entry to the scene? I'm about to enter.'

'With respect, I'm afraid you're not about to enter, sir. Sorry, but you have to be in whites. It's a crime scene.'

'Dear God, just get me DCI Flett from in there before we waste any more time. I can't be kept waiting like this.'

The officer called through into the block and Flett eventually appeared, yeti-like in his oversized white suit.

'Ah, good of you to make it sir, we were hoping to see you here.'

'What the hell is going on?' Roberts blurted before Flett could continue, 'Good God, Alastair, how could you? How could you embarrass the MP like this? The CC's horrified. What on earth's got into you? You must pull the plug on this instantly. This is insane. What in God's name are the grounds for doing this? You'll get a formal reprimand you know, at least.'

'Just doing my job, sir,' Flett said cheerily. 'I think you should come in and see. I'll get you some whites. What are you, large or medium, sir?'

'Medium,' he barked impatiently, mindful of his jogging and exercise regime of late.

Flett went back inside. 'Get Superintendent Roberts a medium,' he shouted to Barty, who chucked him one over from the box. 'No, wait a minute,' Flett said more quietly with a smirk on his face, 'get me a small too.' He took them both out and placed the small in the medium packet, carefully sealing it up again.

'Here you are, sir, a medium,' he said going outside and giving a packet to Roberts, 'This should do the trick, sir. We'll hang on inside until you're ready.'

Flett, MacBrayne and Barty watched discreetly from the window. The grumpy officer watched at closer hand and with muffled amusement as Roberts struggled to get into a protective suit that was manifestly too small. He'd got his legs in but the crotch wouldn't fit, and no matter how much he struggled there was no way his arms were going to be mobile once he'd zipped up the front. When he tried to walk he wobbled from side to side like a duck. Flett casually went out to see how he was getting on.

'Looks a bit tight that, sir, if you don't mind me saying so.'

'Can't understand it, the mediums never used to be this tight.'

'Ah, that'll be Mrs Roberts' cooking, sir. I've heard she's very nifty in the kitchen. Never mind. I'm told a little porkiness around the mid-rift is considered healthy in the middle-aged these days. Maybe we should get you a large.' He went back inside chuckling happily to himself and returned with a medium which Roberts dutifully changed into, sadly believing it to be a large.

'That looks much better, sir.' Flett commented. 'More comfortable too, I should think. Well, we'll know now for next time, won't we?'

A dispirited Superintendent Roberts duly entered the scene, the grumpy uniformed officer logged in the time of entry, and Flett ran through the whole issue of Seth Hetherington's disappearance, the skip and his potential involvement in three fires. As Barty showed him the bloodstains and the brush Roberts became increasingly miserable, wondering how best to relate these embarrassing events to the CC.

'We need a favour from you, sir,' Flett asked eventually, noting Roberts' distraction. 'There are some CCTV cameras located around the manor further up the drive. We need the recent footage in case they show anything.'

'So how can I help?' Roberts asked innocently.

'Well, we can serve another warrant on the Wainwrights, but I thought it might be prudent to ask them personally to relinquish the footage before we went down that road. Would save a lot of bother and any more embarrassment for the CC, wouldn't it?'

'Absolutely, excellent idea, Alastair, and a lot less heavy-handed.'

'I was wondering whether you'd feel able to drive up and simply ask for the footage, sir? It would come much better from you as a senior officer, and of course you're more familiar with the social levels involved. Would you mind?'

'Ah, well, I think you may possibly be right there, Alastair. I'm more than happy to do that. Give me the footage dates involved and I'll go up there now,'

Flett looked at MacBrayne and raised his eyebrows, gave Roberts the necessary information, and went outside to help him out of his whites.

'I'm sure you'll feel quite at home up there, sir,' said Flett, seeing him into his Evoque.

'Well thank you, Alastair, very kind of you to say so. One always aspires, you know.' With that Roberts shut the car door and slid quietly away up the drive. Flett watched him until he was out of sight.

'Good luck,' he mumbled sarcastically and turned to the uniformed officer. 'Constable,' he asked. 'Do you know the difference between a hedgehog and a Range Rover?'

'Er, no sir, I don't.'

'Well remember this then, the difference is that the hedgehog has the pricks on the outside,' and with that he went back into the crime scene, chuckling away to himself.

* * *

Perhaps Roberts was expecting to be entertained in the manor's drawing room with a friendly glass of port, or invited to be seated in a studded leather chesterfield overlooking the grounds while being offered refreshments by one of the servants. At the very least he would be expecting a hospitable welcome and admittance to some ante-chamber where one of the Wainwrights would listen with concern to this whole dreadful business, and maybe put in a good word for him higher up. But the poor man was to be sorely disappointed. He returned to the stable block, somewhat flustered, less than ten minutes later.

'Any luck on that one, sir?' asked Flett cheerily.

'Er, not quite what I expected really. Not successful at all, in fact. An extraordinarily obstinate woman seems to live there. Calls herself a housekeeper. Completely off her head. Couldn't make her understand a word I said. Probably foreign I should think.'

'Oh dear,' Flett said sympathetically. 'Can't be the same one we met then. We were invited in for tea and crumpets, weren't we Dunc?'

'Yes boss, home baking,' he lied.

'In that case, sir,' Flett asked, 'don't you think we should serve a warrant now? We need that footage urgently.'

'Yes, yes, I suppose so,' Roberts' pride had been severely damaged at the manor. 'Perhaps I can soften up the presiding magistrate on my way back. We'll get something signed and with you in the morning.'

'We'll need their contact details too, please, sir, and their London address. Perhaps you can get those from the CC himself? You might tell him it's likely to be a murder case and that there's really no alternative. MacBrayne here'll get in touch with the Met – they'll have the contact details of all MPs for security purposes. The more avenues we can try the better.' He paused for dramatic effect. 'I suppose if we can't get hold of a Wainwright, we'll have no other option than to break the manor door down to get access.'

Roberts looked at him in horror then jumped when MacBrayne's phone suddenly rang. It was Jennie. She'd managed to get some reliable DNA samples from Seth's house. Flett smiled to himself. It had been a very good afternoon.

CHAPTER 19

Jacko and Judy stood by the reception desk at the Pear Tree holding hands, Jacko uneasily fumbling with loose change in his pocket with his other hand and feeling thoroughly uncomfortable in an unusually smart set of clothes. He'd shaved, even had his hair cut, and was wearing a jacket and trousers instead of his more usual fleece and cargo pants. Judy had collected him from his house at Compton in a hired Ford Focus. He'd only half-recognised her by sight, but he'd remembered her husky voice instantly. There was no mistaking her personal charisma either. She was confident, authoritative and exuded an air of independence. Probably in her forties, he guessed, muscular and obviously kept herself fit. She was feeling equally uncomfortable, much preferring jeans or running gear to the mature black suit she felt obliged to don on this marital occasion.

The receptionist handed Jacko the key and asked if they'd like any help with their bags. They politely refused, preferring to carry their honeymoon baggage of well-concealed cameras, lenses, listening equipment and tripods themselves.

'Come on, darling,' Judy said to him loudly, 'let's see what's in the mini-bar,' and they wheeled their baggage down the hallway and to the lift.

'Listen,' she said in a low voice once they were inside and the door had shut, 'as soon as we get to the room I'm going to do an electrical check, just to be on the safe side.'

'Do a what?'

'An electrical check – that's a euphemism for seeing that there aren't any bugs installed, okay? When we get in, stick the telly on or something, and don't talk about anything other than normal things until I've finished.'

'Bit cloak and dagger, isn't it?'

'Better to be on the safe side, husband darling,' she said and, to his embarrassment, gave him a kiss on the cheek. 'Just rely on me, and don't be over-sensitive.'

Jacko pondered ruefully on the significance of that comment as they left the lift and looked for their room. The place was very smart with plush carpets and expensive wallpaper in the corridors. The hushed sound of classical music drifted from concealed speakers. All the rooms had large dark mahogany doors with gold numbers, separated by distinctive features like ice-makers, or alcoves containing cut flowers or bowls of fresh fruit. The room Judy had chosen was at the end of the corridor next to the fire stairs. Jacko pushed the door open and went straight to the window. It was exactly the room he'd hoped for, not the best view for a hotel guest by any means, but a view that overlooked the end of the sheds and the edge of the car park. Looking across he could even see the remnants of the old gin bottles that he'd stumbled into earlier and the broken fence that he'd had to climb through. He was about to say something when Judy put her finger to her lips, tactfully reminding him. He nodded back, made some exclamatory comments about the quality of the room and the stock in the mini-bar, then switched on the huge plasma screen TV and flicked through the channels. Good, it had Sky Sports too. That was a bonus. He might even enjoy this. Judy, meanwhile, was moving systematically around the room with a small handheld device. She lifted up ornaments, looked behind pictures and mirrors, inside vases and light fittings, and under the bed. She spent some time investigating the telephone, then moved into the bathroom.

'Okay, all clear,' she said after a while, leaping on to the bed and lying there with her arms and legs stretched out. 'That's a relief. Now then, let's go through the strategy again and, for God's sake, turn that bloody football off.'

Jacko obliged, pulled two beers from the fridge and passed one over. It had just gone 5 pm so drinking was justifiable. He moved across to one of the leather armchairs, putting his feet up on the bed. MacBrayne had managed to discover that the hotel was under private ownership – there were no other restaurants or boozers under the same management, and it didn't supply any other eateries. They needed to know whether, if the white van came again, it was loading or unloading. If it was loading, then they somehow had to get it tracked by attaching a device. Its number plate was false too. Jacko had been right both times he wrote it down. There was something shifty going on. They rehearsed their plans in detail then, when hunger got the better of them, ordered a room service meal and settled down with the TV.

They'd agreed to take four hour shifts, Judy taking the first until midnight, Jacko midnight until four in the morning, then they'd watch jointly from four until eight when they'd pack the kit away and scuttle into bed to await the arrival of breakfast room service at nine thirty. Judy moved the furniture around a little then set up a tripod not far from the window. The room had two sets of curtains, heavy coloured ones and lace ones behind. They were both drawn shut while she set the camera up. Once it was properly dark outside, and with the room light off, she opened both pairs, adjusted the camera position and height, and sent Jacko off on an imaginary errand to the car which had been parked deliberately in view of their window. He came back shortly after with the news that nothing could be seen from outside. She closed the curtains again, rummaged for a small toolkit in her bag and disappeared out of the room telling Jacko to behave himself while she was away. Ten minutes later she returned.

'Right,' she said. 'I think we're all set.'

'Where've you been?' Jacko asked curiously.

'Think about it, Jacko. At some point I may need to attach a magnetic tracking device to a van out there. How d'you think I'm going to do it? Lob it out of the window and hope it sticks to the roof? I'm going to use the fire stairs next to the bedroom and go through the fire door at the bottom. It'll take me directly outside where I can hide, okay?'

'Bet the fire door's alarmed,' Jacko smirked. 'You'll look pretty bloody silly if you wake the whole hotel up with lights flashing and sirens going off, wandering round in a nightie holding a tracking device.'

'It *was* alarmed a few minutes ago, Jacko,' she said patiently, 'but it's not alarmed any longer. What did you think I was bloody well doing out there with a tool kit?' Jacko went quiet and blushed, not for the first time. 'Now, just one more thing to do,' she added, winking at him as she placed the *Do Not Disturb* sign on the outside of the door. 'We newly-weds don't want to be interrupted, darling, do we?'

* * *

Jacko decided it was time to turn in. He wasn't allowed to watch the TV because the glare from the screen would have silhouetted the camera, so he went into the en-suite, ran a bath and lay soaking in the hot water. He was relaxing quietly, his mind drifting into realms of fantasy when, with no apparent qualms whatsoever, Judy marched in, pulled the shower curtain around the bath and used the toilet.

'Sorry, sunshine,' she said as she flushed it and pulled the shower curtain open again with Jacko lying prone, frantically trying to move bath foam into appropriate places. 'It's all the free coffee they provide here. It was an act of desperation.'

Jacko dried himself off, got partly dressed, and lay on the bed in the dark dozing quietly, vaguely aware of the grey shape next to him leaning on the wall watching intently out of the window. The next thing he remembered was being awoken by a gentle jolting.

'Your turn,' the grey shape said. 'Did you know how much you bloody well snore?'

Jacko grunted and swung his feet off the bed. 'What time is it?'

'About one o'clock. I thought I'd let you sleep in, seeing as you need more beauty sleep than I do. Just get off your arse and do the business. It's your turn.' Then, as far as he could make out in the dark, she stripped down to her underwear and deposited herself on the bed. 'Wake me up if anything happens,' she hissed, 'no matter what it is.' Shortly afterwards, Jacko heard the unmistakable sounds of soft even breathing associated with sleep.

Keeping watch from a warm hotel bedroom was much preferable to sitting in a cold car. Ample supplies of tea and coffee were on hand. Outside it was another autumn night, the temperature had dropped and a slight mist formed, but nothing like the fog of last Sunday. At half past two a fox appeared from behind the sheds, looked around, and then trotted off into the bushes at the other side of the car park. He logged it in the record book for want of anything better to do. Four o'clock came and passed. It was time for Judy's watch and he was wondering how to wake her up in a politically correct way when he heard the sound of a vehicle approaching. He gave her a violent shake and she jolted into life.

'What the fuck…'

'Sorry, but a vehicle's just come in.'

She was on her feet in seconds, still in her underwear, hand on camera, looking out of the window as a yellow and blue checked police patrol car moved slowly into the car park using only its side lights. It looked like a Volvo estate. It made its way to the rear and parked up at the far end of the sheds, then turned its lights off.

'What's going on?' asked a perplexed Jacko.

'God knows. I doubt if it should be here though,' Judy manoeuvred herself behind the camera, altered its angle to capture the new target and clicked away. Jacko stood well back at the other end of the window watching. After a minute the uniformed passenger got out and walked slowly over to the sheds, looking around as he did so. He gently tapped on a double opening door and waited. A few seconds later one half of the door opened and a man clad in a dark tracksuit emerged. Judy continued clicking. The officer went in and returned with a large box which he put on the back seat of the car, then repeated the operation. The man in the tracksuit went back inside and the police car drove off. All the while Judy was clicking.

'Well, well, well,' she chuckled. 'How interesting is that?'

Jacko was completely mystified, 'What the hell's all that about? I don't understand.'

'Not sure I do either. The police, or really one or two officers, seem party to some arrangement. Wonder what's going on? I suppose it could be innocent, but don't underestimate Flett. He's got a mind like a pack of razor blades. It wouldn't surprise me if he didn't have an inkling of this already and we've been set up to get him the evidence he needs. That guy's a hard cookie. Did you see there's a night watchman in those sheds? Interesting isn't it?'

The rest of the night ran smoothly. There were no other visitors to the car park, no white van, and nothing else to report. They both stayed on watch until 8 am at which time they packed the equipment into the wardrobe and crawled under the covers where they fell asleep. At half past nine, as ordered, room service knocked on the door with two hearty cooked breakfasts. Judy donned a dressing gown and opened the door leaving Jacko half comatose in bed. The maid wheeled in a trolley. It was one of those hostess-type devices with a slow bottled gas burner underneath keeping the food warm. She put it by the window and lifted up the wide silver lid to show Jacko the goodies that lay therein – bacon, egg, sausage, black pudding, tomato, mushroom and fresh toast. The smell was seductive.

'I think you'll probably be needing this now, sir,' she said, winking at him. 'Enjoy.'

* * *

'Anything out there?' Jacko asked as he lay on the bed during the early part of the second night's watch. The pair of them had slept for most of the day at his house in Compton, interrupted only by an unduly long debriefing visit from Flett.

'Nope, not even a fox this time, just a bit of mist starting.'

It had all the makings of another quiet night. Jacko probably dozed a little, but not much more. He was wide awake when his turn came but Judy didn't seem bothered about standing down. They both sat there looking blankly out of the window. As 4.30 am approached Judy made them black coffee. They both needed to be on their toes. If the van didn't come yesterday it was more likely to come today, and probably in the next hour or so. They needed to be pre-emptive so they were both fully dressed in dark clothes, trainers on and ready for action. The plan they had was a simple one, but not without potential snags.

At around 4.45 Judy quietly left the room carrying the tracking device. She went down the fire stairs and slipped out along the corner of the car park, out of the line of the security cameras. The fire door to the car park was one with an angled bar, like at cinemas, that couldn't be opened from the outside. She'd taken a beer mat, suitably doubled up, and wedged the door open slightly at the bottom. Jacko didn't envy her, hidden as she was behind the shed in the cold. There were no frosts yet, but they wouldn't be far off. He tested the view through the camera for the thousandth time and made sure that everything was ready.

By 5 am nothing had happened; they'd agreed that if that was still the case at 5.30 they'd abort and Judy would come back in. Minutes before the deadline was reached Jacko heard the noise of a vehicle entering the car park. It was a white transit van driving only on its sidelights. It turned in a wide loop in front of the sheds, then reversed slightly before stopping further away than previously. Shit. He hastily adjusted the angle and field of the camera, checked the automatic focus and kept his finger on the cable, watching as events unfolded while clicking the shutter at regular intervals. So far, so good. There was a man waiting for it. Shit again, he'd been too busy messing with the camera to see where he'd come from. The driver got out. They were both big handy individuals by the looks of it, and he felt concern for Judy out there on her own. He could vaguely make out her shape by the wall and hoped to hell she'd remembered about the pile of gin bottles.

The driver opened up the van's rear doors while the other man removed a large padlock from the end shed and opened it up. Jacko continued clicking as the two of them carried some large boxes out of the shed and into the back of the van. Well, that's one question answered, he thought. There were also some other packages of different sizes. He cast his eye across to see where Judy was, but the dark shape had vanished. Loading completed, the shed door was shut again before being carefully padlocked. The two men then stayed talking behind the van but there was still no sign of her. How was she going to attach the tracking device? The driver closed the van's rear door. She'd have to do it soon. Bugger, he'd have to follow the plan anyway. He continued clicking until the driver heaved himself into the cab and closed the door. At that point he implemented the agreed strategy: he pushed the camera over on to the bed out of sight and flung open the window which he'd already unlatched.

'What's all this bloody noise about!' he shouted, imitating the best posh accent he could. 'Good God man, people are trying to sleep up here. D'you know what time it is?'

The men both looked up. The driver stayed in his cab, not wishing to abandon the other man who began to move forward as Jacko had hoped.

'Sorry, mate,' the man said in a hushed voice, hoping other people wouldn't be woken up, 'had to make an urgent delivery, perishable goods and stuff.'

'At this hour?' Jacko shouted back, doing his best to prolong the man's attention. 'I'll have to make a formal complaint to the management about this. You see if I don't.'

'Fresh fish, straight from the docks,' came the imaginative excuse from the car park, but to the man's horror and to

215

Jacko's delight, another bedroom window opened further along the block.

'I say, what's going on?' shouted a genuinely plummy voice.

'Sorry mate,' the man said again, now even more agitated and concerned that the whole hotel might confront him. 'Didn't mean to cause any upset. Just doin' our job.' The driver gave Jacko a sickly smile of agreement. He wanted to be out of there as soon as possible. 'We'll move off as quietly as we can,' the man continued, adding, 'Sorry again, gents.'

The van drove off, the other man vanished into the dark and the window along the block was closed with some associated muttering. Jacko shut their own window and stared out to see if he could see Judy in the dark. The place was deserted. He sat down and waited. She'd be back in a minute. He checked the camera, unscrewed it from the tripod and flicked through some of the images. They were fine. A further ten minutes passed. Christ, she hadn't climbed into the van had she, and got locked in? That was exactly the sort of stupid risk she might take. No, maybe she was just lying low until she was certain the other man had gone back to his watch in the shed. After another ten minutes he was sufficiently concerned to go out and check for himself. He slipped out of the door with the key card in his pocket and made his way carefully down the fire stairs. Then he saw what had happened. The folded beer mat was still in the door but must have become sodden in the damp and contracted just enough for the door to have clicked shut, leaving Judy stranded outside. He pushed it open and peeked out to be greeted by a soft but angry voice.

'You took your bloody time, you plonker. I'm nearly frozen to death here.' A dark shape squeezed past him, pulled the door quietly behind and gave him a big hug and a kiss.

'We did it,' she said, 'what a team, let's get out of here.'

She gathered up the remnants of the soggy beer mat, carefully removed a wire that was short-circuiting the door alarm and took off her filthy trainers before making her way back up the stairs barefoot. Jacko opened up the room and Judy slipped in after him.

'You're a star Jacko,' she said, hugging him in the half light once they were inside. 'That was some performance. It gave me loads of time to attach the tracker. Think I'll nominate you for an Oscar.'

'Christ, you're soaking wet,' was all Jacko could say.

'Yup, it's bath time,' she agreed, and stripped off her garments one by one in front of him.

'What's up?' she teased him, seeing his embarrassment. 'Never seen a naked woman before?' Then she hopped off into the bathroom.

By the time she'd returned Jacko was fast asleep under the covers. Pity, she thought, and slid in next to him with her wet hair on the pillow. Within minutes she was asleep too.

* * *

They were both woken around 09.30 with a gentle tap on the door and a tantalising aroma of cooked breakfasts. Jacko, still drowsy, stumbled across the room having first donned the white towelling dressing gown supplied by the hotel and greeted the maid who pushed in the breakfast trolley. By this time Judy was stirring and trying to cover herself up so as not to embarrass the maid. The maid left hastily, unusually hastily Jacko thought.

'I don't think she fancied you,' he said.

'Piss off, and throw me a dressing gown,' was her retort as he went towards the en-suite to have a shower. 'And don't take too long or I'll eat all the breakfast.' As Jacko stopped to peek under the lid of the trolley she took her chance to make it to the bathroom first. He sensed the movement and the pair of them raced across the floor and squeezed giggling through the doorway together. 'Dead heat!'

Afterwards, Jacko remembered none of this conversation. He had no recollection of the breakfast trolley nor of going for a shower, but without a doubt it was going to the bathroom that saved their lives. The subsequent police investigation never fully established whether the explosion was caused by a faulty gas canister on the trolley or a clever explosive device triggered on a timer. Flett had his own ideas. The maid who wheeled in the trolley and who seemed in a hurry to leave the room was never found to be interviewed. The explosion that occurred took out the windows, the door and most of the ceiling. It blew in part of the wall of the en-suite, showering them both with plasterboard, timber partitioning and broken glass. They were both found unconscious.

CHAPTER 20

Jacko's first recollection was of being jolted around. He was on his back and a man in green was standing over him. Everything was moving and his head hurt like he had an enormous hangover. Parts of him ached, parts stung and other parts had gone numb. He had a mask over his mouth and, bit by bit, as his eyes focused, he realised he was in an ambulance.

'You're going to be fine,' the man in green said reassuringly, 'just breathe steadily into the mask. Try and relax.'

Jacko had no idea why he might be in an ambulance. Had he been in a road accident, fallen down the stairs or something? He began to panic. Christ, had he suffered a heart attack? He was that sort of age.

'Just try and relax, eh?' the voice said again. 'We're nearly at the hospital. We'll get you sorted there. No need to worry.'

Jacko blacked out and woke up on a hospital trolley

with several people in light blue gowns looking at him. He appeared to be the centre of attention, but couldn't make out their faces. They shone lights in his eyes and moved his limbs carefully. One of them was taking his clothes off, replacing them with some sort of tunic. He said nothing. Then one of them injected him with something and he passed out again.

He came round in a hospital bed. He had no idea how long he'd been there. There seemed to be more colours, and the people weren't in light blue. He recognised two of them: Jennie and Duncan MacBrayne. They stood looking down at him. Jennie put her hand on his shoulder.

'Thought you might like to see some familiar faces, Jacko,' she said reassuringly. 'The docs tell us you're basically okay, just some superficial injuries and concussion from the explosion.'

'Don't remember. What explosion?' he managed to say drowsily.

'You were in the bathroom at the Pear Tree. There was an explosion and you banged your head on the wash basin. It's not serious.'

Things slowly began to reassemble themselves in his mind. The hotel, Judy, and the white transit van. But they were all jumbled up.

'Where's Judy?'

'She's in another room here. She's quite poorly.' There was no point in beating around the bush. 'I'm afraid she's on the critical list.'

It took a while to sink in. Everything was now confused. His head was full of conflicting emotions and feelings.

'Bastards,' was all he could say. 'Bastards.'

'We don't know if it was deliberate,' MacBrayne said. 'It's being looked into by the bomb people.'

The realisation began to bring Jacko to his senses. 'Course it was deliberate,' he muttered in an angry whisper, trying to sit up a little before giving up and sliding back again.

'Listen Jacko, this is important,' MacBrayne said quietly. 'As far as the press and public are concerned what happened was an accident. We want to give the impression to whoever did this that there's no police suspicion, okay?'

Things were now beginning to re-focus in Jacko's mind. 'But what about all the images and notes, all that stuff?' he managed to say, 'It was all in the bedroom.'

'All safe,' said MacBrayne reassuringly. 'You must have packed it all away in the heavy bags. They were at the other side of the room and shielded by the bed.

'Good,' Jacko said drowsily. His head fell back on the pillow and he sank into a deep sedated sleep.

When he awoke again he found a concerned Lucy sitting next to him holding his hand. 'Jacko, it's me. It's Lucy.' She stroked his forehead. 'Came here as soon as I could when they told me. Couldn't bear to think of you on your own in here. How are you feeling?'

The sleep had done him good and the sedatives were wearing off, making his brain less woolly than before. Everything seemed a little clearer. 'Pretty shit,' he admitted, struggling to sit up. 'No bones broken, just a bit sore.' He squeezed her hand. 'Did they tell you what I was doing at the hotel?'

Lucy nodded and gave him a reassuring smile. 'Oddly enough, your half-baked, naïve life-style is one of the things

I find attractive about you. If you weren't so bloody daft, I wouldn't be here.' She turned away for a moment, seemingly to wipe a tear from her eye. Jacko noticed. That wasn't like her at all.

'You've had a close shave,' she said, turning back and moving closer to him. 'Isn't it time to pack in all this melodrama stuff and stick to safer things?' The suggestion had an assertiveness about it.

'Got to see this out now, Luce. Can't stop now.'

'But you could have been blown to bits.'

'I'll be okay.'

'Like hell you will! Jacko, there's an armed policeman outside this door. For Christ's sake, what does that tell you? Hasn't it entered your stubborn brain that someone's trying to kill you?'

He fell silent, 'Look at it from my point of view.'

'No, look at it from mine,' she interrupted. 'I've sat here looking at you for over an hour before you woke up. Why? Because I wanted to be with you. I love you, for fuck's sake. Give it all up, can't you?'

Lucy couldn't believe what she'd just said. She left her chair and went over to the window. It was a grey, misty morning and the view was over people's back gardens. Some were well kept with neat lawns and borders, others totally neglected, a few had swings, climbing frames and trampolines. In their houses people went about their business, working, relaxing, totally oblivious to the dramas, tragedies and pain played out on a daily basis in the hospital at the bottom of their gardens. She turned back to him. He looked pathetic. It made her smile.

222

'I've got a two o'clock lecture,' she said, looking at her watch. 'I ought to be making tracks. The doc thinks you'll be out tomorrow and back to normal, whatever that is.' She gave him a sly grin, a long kiss and a hug. 'You know,' she added, as she stood up, 'you look about seventy in that hospital night shirt. Doesn't do much for your youthful looks – most unattractive.' She winked. 'Ring me tomorrow, and don't forget we have a weekend date coming up.' She stood with her hand on the door handle. 'I want you in full working order by then.'

She blew him a kiss, 'You've another visitor,' she said. 'It's all go here.' And with that she left, pausing briefly to chat with Alex who was on his way in.

Alex stood at the foot of the bed and looked at his father with a mixture of pity, remorse and irritation.

'That was a near miss, Dad,' he said eventually. 'You were nearly killed. What on earth were you doing? I can't believe you were spending a naughty night in a hotel so near home – and under a different name. Dear God, Dad, you're not in your twenties any more. Does Lucy know what you were up to?'

Jacko was feeling better, but not that much better. 'Most hospital visitors bring flowers or grapes,' he said sourly, 'not rampant recrimination. If you must know we were on a covert job, that's why different names were used. And Lucy does know.'

Alex sat down on the end of the bed. 'Sorry, I just assumed you were out having a good time.'

'A good time! Forget it. No need to apologise. At least I'm alive.'

'So who were you working with? Who's the poor woman in intensive care?'

'I only know her as Judy – she used to work for Flett. Runs her own security business. We were there on a hunch, all to do with these murders I got caught up with. It was unofficial because Roberts was against it. I think Flett's got other reasons too. And you needn't tell me I'm too old for it. I've already been told that once today.'

'Yes, you are too old for it, you silly sod. It's a young person's game, you're not even trained, and by all accounts this is serious crime you've blundered into. Look,' he said quietly and feeling unusually emotional, 'the staff here said you'd be out tomorrow. Why don't you come and stay with us for a couple of days until you're fully fit?'

'That's very generous of you Alex, but I couldn't think of anything worse, and I don't think you or your good lady could either.' They both grinned.

CHAPTER 21

MacBrayne and Jacko, the latter suitably patched up but still feeling the worse for wear, sat in an unmarked police car outside the landfill site's office. It was probably the largest tip in the county and certainly the busiest. Wagons and skips were arriving in quick succession, paperwork was checked at a grubby office, loads were dumped, and the empties driven off equally quickly to collect more. It was an odd atmosphere – exposed and barren with blowing paper and flapping shreds of polythene against a background drone of heavy vehicles. The most distinctive factors were the rotting smells and the shrieks of gulls in the air scavenging for whatever might be causing the stench. No-one walked. Human activity was confined to drivers encased in the cabs of various wagons and earthmoving machinery, or in the confines of temporary cabins where contact with the outside world was made through small sliding windows. The car was parked just outside the main office, the windows tightly shut to keep out the smell, awaiting some information from inside.

They sat in silence, watching a tin can rattle across the space in front of them. It seemed to have little direction, rolling this way and that, stopping and starting as the gusts took it before finally clattering to rest in a bed of straggly weeds growing by the mesh fence. There it joined other recaptured escapees – polystyrene, plastic and paper, anything that the wind or the vehicle slipstreams could send there.

A while back, and to Lucy's great amusement, Jacko had done some research into industrial waste disposal, looking at the various EU regulations that governed skip operators, waste carriers, and landfill sites, and the records and logs that had to be kept. He'd done it for precisely this type of eventuality, and his work had come good. Assuming that all the various parties had done their job properly, there should have been a very specific location and a known depth in the landfill where the skip had been emptied. MacBrayne had been in touch with the landfill management, ascertained when the particular skip had arrived, and left them busily working out where exactly the contents ought to be. He and Jacko looked glumly out over the landscape through the car windows. Neither of them could think of anything less pleasant than what probably lay ahead of them – several days of grubbing around in a stinking mess looking for a possible corpse.

Their thoughts were broken by the office door being opened and the appearance of a burly bearded man beckoning them inside. Taking as little time as possible to move from car to office they entered and shut the door behind them quickly. Inside were a few dirty leather chairs, tables covered with log books and a tattered carpet which partly covered a stained lino floor. The whole lot could have been salvaged from the tip outside. It smelled little different too but at least had the benefit of being heated by a noisy convector fan. A line of filthy hi-vis jackets hung on pegs, capped by a row of hard hats. On a shelf next to them was a kettle, a half-empty milk bottle without a top and a set of chipped, tea-stained mugs. Their entrance was watched by two other equally burly individuals, both with shaved heads, whose function seemed unclear.

'Cuppa tea, gents?' came the gruff greeting, but before either could reply there was a loud roaring which shook the entire office. A vast green wagon drew up next to the window high up on one side, causing the whole room to darken. One of the men slid it open and a large hairy arm appeared clutching some papers, which were duly checked off in one of the logs, signed and handed back to the hairy arm together with instructions. The window was shut again and the wagon roared off.

'Not for us, thanks,' said Jacko, having rapidly assessed the hygiene standards. 'Just had one.'

'What you lot looking for?' asked the bearded man. 'Just curious, you know, mate.'

'We've reason to believe,' said MacBrayne, sounding very policeman-like, 'that someone's been tipping stuff they shouldn't. We'd like to know where it might be just in case we have to recover it.' Seeing suspicion rising in their faces, he added, 'We may never have to, of course, but we need to keep our options open.'

'Yeah, we've got all the details necessary,' the bearded man said. 'A lot of folk chuck out stuff they shouldn't.' The other two chortled and grunted quietly. He was about to continue when the office shook again and with a great roar another wagon drew up at the window.

'The skip you're interested in,' he said once the wagon had sorted its paperwork and driven off, 'was emptied in zone four.' He waved at a plan on the wall, pointing out where the zone was. Jacko went across to it, in the process trying to ignore the magazine photos of naked women that were pinned around it. He looked at the scale. Zone four seemed massive.

'How's it marked out?'

'Poles, mate,' the man said, adding, 'Red and white ones stuck in the ground. The drivers are given the zone number and then fill in systematically between the poles.'

'How's that monitored then?' Jacko asked.

The man just shrugged. 'They work from one end to the other,' he said unhelpfully, 'then they start another row. It's checked every so often and numbered on a plan. And when a full layer's been made, we compress it, then start another. They're numbered too. And when it's a certain height we cover it up with topsoil again.'

'Is that accurate enough to find an individual load, then?'

The man shrugged again. 'Best we can do, mate,' he said sourly. 'Not often we have to find loads again.' The two shaven-headed men chuckled once more.

'So where exactly is our tip load then,' MacBrayne asked, 'apart from being somewhere in zone four?'

The bearded man went over to the plan. 'Somewhere here.' His grubby hand scribbled a circle with a pencil on the plan. 'And it's only got one layer on top of it – a layer of plasterboard and broken tiles. Or at least that what it's in the book as being.'

'So we should be able to pinpoint it easily enough, say in a few days time if we needed to?'

'Well, I was planning to topsoil it in the next couple of days,' the man said, 'but I suppose could leave that bit open for a while longer. Makes my life that much harder of course.' He looked across at the other two men who were engaged in cramming box files on to a shelf, then raised his eyebrows and looked at MacBrayne in a questioning sort of way. MacBrayne glanced to check that both men were still engrossed and slipped two twenty pound notes across the table.

'Not a problem, gents,' the man said smiling. 'I'll make sure it's not top-soiled until you've finished.'

Another loud roar and a minor earthquake heralded the arrival of the next truck, at which point MacBrayne thought it an appropriate time to leave. He manoeuvred Jacko past the naked women and back out to the car.

* * *

Four of them, Lazenby included this time, sat around Flett's desk watching him tap his fingers on its veneered oak surface. He had a slight smile on his usually dour face, the first time anyone had seen him smile for a long time.

'Right, let's have some updates. Jennie first.'

'I've made a bit of progress on the deliveries at the Pear Tree, boss. Not sure where it's getting us, but there's something going on that doesn't look right. I've managed to get copies of the delivery orders from two of the companies involved – I don't know how many outfits deliver there, but these were the two that Jacko spotted. The goods seem fairly comprehensive, everything a restaurant would need. I've got them for the last month. Then I went online and looked at the Pear Tree restaurant and bar menus for the same period and compared the two. Most of it matches, you know steaks, chicken breasts, joints for roasting, dessert type things like cheesecake. Some stuff you can't quantify, like potatoes, bread, eggs, milk, veg and things like that. Then there's stuff that's on the menu but wasn't part of those deliveries, like fresh fish and venison, which must come from different suppliers. But,' she paused for a moment and checked her notes, 'there's also stuff that's been delivered but doesn't seem to feature on the menus at all, or at least I can't find it.'

Flett interrupted her. 'Like what?'

'Well, there seems to be a lot of cheap spiced meat, you know like those processed German sausage things you get in big u-shaped lengths, and also a lot of fish bits, not fillets you understand, packs of tail ends, trimmings and stuff like that. Basically the rubbish bits. As I said, none of those appear on the menus in any form that I can make out, not even in soups.'

'Maybe they were for the service staff at the hotel?' suggested Jacko.

'Thought of that, but the volume's too great. You're talking about feeding quite a few people here. What's your view, boss?'

Flett was beginning to wiggle on his seat like a child urgently needing the toilet. 'As we thought, Jennie, thank you. Good work.' A sly smile crossed his normally crabby face. Something was afoot. 'Dunc, any joy on the Wainwrights' London contact details?'

'No mobile numbers, but I've got their address. They've a large house in North London. Posh area. Not short of a bob or two, are they?' Got the address from the Met. Seems they're not supposed to give it out, but the Wainwrights have got up their noses so much they couldn't care who gets their details anymore. All the boys down there think they're a load of tits – seems they're always complaining, always making demands and just being rude. No love lost there by the sound of it. It's 27 Pennsylvania Gardens, NW1, if you want to make a note of it boss.'

Flett's mouth hung open momentarily in surprise. 'You sure that's right, Dunc?'

'Positive, boss.'

'Well, well, well. Now then, listen to what I've found out, then tell me there isn't more to our toady chums the Wainwrights than meets the eye.' He paused for a moment of theatre. It was like watching a small boy about to blurt out a secret. 'Just before we met up this morning, I had a report from the people who've been tracking the white van, thanks to Judy. When it left the Pear Tree, guess where it went?'

Heads shook.

'The manor in Middle Belford. Does that surprise you?'

There was immediate, astonished silence.

'Christ,' said MacBrayne. 'So there is a connection?'

'Looks that way, laddie, doesn't it?' He paused for further dramatic effect. 'And guess where it went next?'

They looked at each other disbelievingly, and Jennie made a calculated guess. 'London?'

'Not just London, Jennie,' he leaned back in his seat, savouring the moment of revelation and watching their expressions, 'but to an address in Pennsylvania Gardens, NW1. Now isn't that a coincidence!' He waited for the information to sink in.

'Jesus,' Jacko stuttered. 'What the hell's going on?

'So if they're loading food, boss,' MacBrayne asked, trying to work it through, 'then where's it going? Apart from the Wainwrights, what's the connection between the manor and London?'

'Well, if you ask me what's happening, I'd say that the Wainwrights have been accessing foodstuffs from official Pear Tree requisitions. The invoices would be hidden in the hotel's accounts as we suspected, and the food that's been bought gets taken to the manor in Middle Belford, maybe for preparation, and then taken on to London for the illegals. There's an off-chance, I suppose, that they might even be keeping some of the girls hidden up here. The place is big enough, but I think it's unlikely – it's too far from a port of entry. No point in smuggling them in through the south coast and bringing them up to Middle Belford, then shunting then down south again. No, my guess is that it's the food element that's important in whatever grubby operation they're up to. Middle Belford's a useful distance from London, but near enough for transport purposes, there's a whopping great kitchen at the manor and, if Jennie's right, then it's probably the processed meats and fish ends that's being used. And who would ever believe that a distinguished MP could be involved? Remember our initial intelligence – that the whole illegals racket was being organised from the Midlands? '

He shuffled in his chair, deliberating for a moment and straightening his tie. 'The problem is, of course, that if we confront the Wainwrights with the evidence we have so far we'll end up with egg on our faces. They'll say they were buying up unused food from the Pear Tree – you know, stuff that had reached its sell-by date but was still okay – and were preparing it at the manor at their own cost to deliver through their contacts to refugees in London. What could be more public-spirited? Buying up food that would otherwise be dumped, processing it at their own cost, and transporting it down to the poor and needy? What philanthropy! Roberts and the CC would soak that excuse up like sponges. You can just see how they'd spin it in the papers – a picture of Charles Wainwright MP decked out with apron and chef's hat stirring a big vat of stew for the unfortunates. Makes your heart bleed, doesn't it?'

'But this is outside our remit, isn't it boss?' Jennie asked. 'Shouldn't we be passing this on to the immigration people?'

'Strictly yes, but somehow there's a tie-in with our Tommy Johnson murder and the disappearance of old Seth Hetherington. I'd like to hang fire until we get the DNA results back and have had a dekko at the Wainwrights' CCTV images. I don't want our end of it being buggered up by moving too soon. And don't forget we're still not supposed to have been at the Pear Tree. The fewer folk who know about this the better. Someone seems to have been wise to our Pear Tree operation, and not just the spooks. There's a leak somewhere. If that really was a bomb that went off in Jacko's room, then this is serious highly organised crime we've stumbled on. They mean business.'

CHAPTER 22

Mrs Jefferson was hanging out the washing in her small cottage garden in Middle Belford, just opposite the church when, on Flett's instructions, MacBrayne and Jennie paid her a visit to enquire further about the Rev Rogers. His disappearance was becoming both suspicious and irritating. They were also curious to have a quiet look around the vicarage, as was Jacko, who joined them in an unofficial capacity.

It was a small walled garden, but Mrs Jefferson was a keen gardener and MacBrayne happily chatted away about plants and the weather. She was a small rotund lady with wispy grey hair, wearing a blue floral house coat. Watching her hang out the washing, moving pots around the garden, dragging an elderly Labrador off the flowerbed and generally clucking about, MacBrayne considered her to be a useful definition of perpetual motion. It turned out she hadn't seen Rogers. Nor had she heard from him, but she still received regular cleaning money from their direct debit agreement. She went off to her daughter's every weekend to help with the grandchildren. Lovely little angels they were. Made a nice change from being on her own at weekends these days. If MacBrayne wanted the keys to look round, why not? No skin off her nose. She supposed she'd some responsibility for the place, but if Rogers couldn't be arsed to show up and the police were concerned about him, then it was only right that she should help. She trotted off inside and came back with the keys, requesting only that they should remove their shoes inside. She'd just cleaned, but didn't know why she'd bothered.

'One final question,' Jennie asked as she ducked under the washing on her way out. 'Are you concerned enough to report him as a missing person?'

'Lord no, the longer he stays missing the better,' she said indignantly. 'As far as I'm concerned he can stay missing as long as he wants. I think you'll find that's the general consensus too. The only people who seem to be concerned about him are you lot.'

* * *

Jacko joined them as they strode up the vicarage drive, or what was left of it, to the front porch, MacBrayne jangling a set of keys in his hand.

'Bit sparse, isn't it?' Jennie commented as they unlocked the large cream-coloured door and she peered down the long empty hallway.

'It's a bachelor pad,' Jacko pointed out. 'I'm sure there'll be a few theological treatises lurking here and there to keep you occupied if you get lonely.'

'Have we all got rubber gloves on?' MacBrayne asked. 'Jennie, you do the downstairs. Jacko you come up with me, and remember you're not supposed to be here.'

They went their separate ways, opening doors, looking inside cupboards and carefully filtering through drawers without disturbing anything. There was no logical plan to the house. Jacko remembered that Linda had told him about the passageways and stairs that made the house so exciting when she was a child. He could see why. MacBrayne was more concerned with lifting carpets, looking under furniture and feeling for loose floorboards.

'Any joy, Dunc?' came Jennie's voice from downstairs after an interval of little more than ten minutes. 'Bugger all down here, unless you're interested in church music and books on liturgy.'

'What's liturgy?' MacBrayne asked Jacko quietly. 'Never heard of that before.'

'Sort of religious processes. How things are organised and done in church services, that sort of thing. Ritual, I suppose is a better definition.'

'Bit specialised, isn't it?'

'Yes,' Jacko replied, for want of any further amplification. 'Wonder where the twins' room was before they left home?'

'Well, this one's the old boy's room,' MacBrayne said, pushing open the door and finding a large double-bed surrounded by heavy wardrobes, a dressing table and uncomfortable looking chairs. 'Christ, do people still use this type of furniture?' He opened each drawer in turn and carefully felt his way around them, did the same in the wardrobe while passing the occasional comment on the vicar's choice of clothing, then looked under the mattress. 'Not even a dirty magazine,' he commented in disgust.

Jennie had finished downstairs and joined them in the bedrooms.

'His passport's still here,' she said, 'and his cheque book. The freezer's stocked. Looks like he had every intention of returning. Odd thing is that last Saturday's newspaper's is down there in the bin. Mrs Jefferson must have put it there.'

'That's odd. She told me she goes away at weekends,' MacBrayne said, sounding slightly puzzled, 'I'd better check on that.' He went downstairs and over to her cottage. Jacko and Jennie were left upstairs.

'Let's find the twins' room,' Jacko said, opening each door in turn. Jennie followed him around carrying out a quick search of drawers and cupboards as they went.

'How about this one?' she said. 'This is a girlie room if ever there was one.' She was right, it had twin beds, floral curtains that matched the bedspreads, and bookshelves containing a selection of languishing dolls and teddy bears. The walls showed traces of blu-tack where posters had been, only one of Elvis still surviving *in situ*. Jacko carefully opened the drawers in the dressing table, finding himself handling female underwear of unknown vintage.

'Are you looking for something in particular, Jacko, or are you just enjoying yourself?'

'Got a camera?' was his token reply as he lifted some silk and lace items to one side, 'Take a couple of these please.'

Jennie duly obliged, eying him suspiciously. 'What is it?' she asked.

'Not telling, but does the camera log time and date?'

'Yes, what are you doing?'

'Good, but please don't tell anyone.' Jennie saw him slip something in his pocket. 'Come on, let's go.'

They met an anxious-looking MacBrayne outside. Mrs Jefferson hadn't been into the vicarage for about a week. No, she hadn't taken a newspaper in there either, and as far as she knew no-one else had access to the house. Not her problem, she said. And she was right. The only realistic deduction was that the Rev Rogers had returned but vanished again.

* * *

The vicar was indirectly on Jacko's agenda for the Friday evening when Lucy arrived to stay for the weekend. Predictably, she turned up late having rushed from somewhere else but still managed to look immaculate. She dropped her bag in the hallway, threw her arms around him and gave him a long hard kiss. 'Lovely to see you again,' she said with genuine affection and without letting go. 'And you look so much better. I don't think these are going to scar,' she stroked the wounds on his face. 'You'll still be as ugly as ever. How are you feeling in yourself?'

'Physically, okay, but mentally a bit numb. Can't sleep much either. The whole thing seems so horrific and unnecessary. Judy's still in an induced coma too.'

She gave him a renewed squeeze, 'I've had a crap week,' she said, 'and I need a chill-out weekend with you, handsome. What's the plan?'

Jacko ran his hands down her back, squeezing his fingers between her shoulder blades then down, pressing against her waist and further around her buttocks, drawing them together. Her whole body sank into him with a sigh like a deflated balloon.

'Later, you naughty boy,' she said with very little conviction. 'Go and get me something to drink, and we can look at those photos together.'

'Photos? What photos?'

'The ones I took from the records in Cambridge. Shit, didn't I tell you about them? Sorry. Anyway, I've printed them out because you said you didn't want anything emailed to your computer. Sounds all very hush-hush. The photos don't look very interesting to me, though, just pictures of student groups. Get the prosecco and we can go through them.'

Jacko untangled himself and disappeared into the kitchen, returning with a chilled bottle, two flutes and a bowl of nibbles. They sat down on the sofa then Lucy pulled the photos out of her briefcase and laid them out on the coffee table. There were a couple of college photos from Cambridge with the students stacked up in rows, all wearing gowns, and a number of other images, typically of students in small sporting groups, a couple with names underneath.

'Must have been the class of 1971,' remarked Jacko, looking at one of the college photos closely. The students all look a bit wooden, don't they? And the photos where they're wearing sports kit look like clips from *Chariots of Fire*. Where's our friend the vicar in all this then?' He ran his finger along the lines of artificially smiling faces on the large photo of students stacked up on a temporary grandstand. There were one or two that might conceivably be the

Rev Rogers over forty years earlier, but it was going to be guesswork to find him.

'Well the alumni office was sure he'd be on it,' Lucy pointed out. 'I didn't know you could get digital versions of all these now. Usually you've to pay for them, but I said it was for a special occasion for a group of college friends, so she let me have them for free. She threw in the sporty ones in case they were any good.'

'You sure he was there at that time?' Jacko asked, still searching the rows of gauche faces for any similarity.

'Absolutely. She showed me the records. Quite honestly, I don't think she'd much else to do. A couple of the sporty photos have got names on. If he's on one of those, see what he looks like, then see if you can find him on the big college photo.'

Jacko flipped through the others. One in particular stood out, a rowing photo showing eight lanky oarsmen and a diminutive cox standing by a boat under the heading *Jesus College 6th VIII*.

'Hardly Olympic standard is it?' he muttered sarcastically, running his finger across the names in small print at the bottom. 'Wait, wait, here he is,' he said with growing excitement. 'Look... R Rogers. That must be him, surely. There's a certain similarity, although I wouldn't have recognised him in his shorts. Arrogant-looking sod, isn't he?'

'Let's try and match him on the main photo then,' Lucy suggested, and they poured over the large image trying to identify him among the rows of gawky individuals wearing gowns, but without result. One of the other smaller group photos also had names on, but not his. Jacko went back to the rowing photo again.

'That's interesting,' he said, looking at it hard, scanning the other names at the bottom. There's an H. Toller here too. That's the same surname as the bloke who rings the church bells at Middle Belford. Probably a coincidence.'

'Come on Jacko,' Lucy urged. 'Enough of this, let's get some food down us. I'm starving. Where's the wine?'

CHAPTER 23

Flett had a bad Monday. The CCTV tapes from the manor were finally handed over thanks to the intervention of an embarrassed CC, who subsequently vented his rage on Roberts who, in turn, immediately threatened Flett with a verbal warning. To make matters worse, the Wainwrights had already wiped the tapes 'as a matter of weekly routine' and were 'so sorry' at being unable to assist. 'Like fuck they are,' was Flett's considered judgement on this. He kept his head down for the rest of the day and on Tuesday morning called the core team together for a briefing and an update. They were in the process of organising some coffee when the phone rang. As usual it was ignored; eventually it stopped. Jennie was on her way to find some biscuits when it rang again and this time MacBrayne reluctantly picked it up.

'It's the DNA lab, boss,' he shouted across the office.

Flett strode back, more quickly than usual, took the phone and walked to the window with his back to them.

Jennie returned with a pack of digestives and was about to say something when she sensed the atmosphere and froze.

'I see. I see,' said Flett. 'Really? Well, thank you.'

There was some intense chatter from the other end.

'No, not at all.' Flett was being unusually polite. 'Very kind of you. Indeed, we hope so too. Yes, sometime this week. Thank you again.'

He walked slowly back to his desk and replaced the receiver in silence. They all looked at him.

'It matches,' he said coldly. 'We were right. The blood in the old stable belongs to poor Seth Hetherington. Looks like we've another murder on our hands.'

This outcome had always been on the cards, but it was still a shock when it came. What must have happened to the old man didn't bear thinking about. After a few minutes of emotive exchanges, arrangements were made to investigate the landfill site as soon as possible.

* * *

At 8 am the next morning Flett led a briefing for all those concerned. Barty Webb's scene team, together with an OSU (Operational Support Unit) would secure the area of the tip defined by MacBrayne and Jacko on the basis of the landfill plan. The OSU consisted of eight hefty officers, usually but not exclusively male, who enjoyed heavy work and were typically deployed in lifting, carrying, moving, engaging rioters, flourishing chain saws, anything that required intense manual application. When they weren't doing any of those things they were either eating or calculating their overtime bonuses. The landfill management for its part had agreed to make available one of their machines and driver for as long as was needed, on the basis that it might speed things up. Jacko's role was to liaise with the excavator driver and to supervise the systematic removal of waste, arranging it to be spread out on one side where the OSU officers would trawl through it manually under MacBrayne's watchful eye. Apart from human remains, expected as body parts in bags, they were instructed to keep their eyes open for anything that might be associated, like disinfectant bottles, cloths, or whatever was sufficiently different from rubble to merit attention.

When Jacko arrived on site he found the machine was huge – an eight tonne tracked monster with a cab that could revolve a full three hundred and sixty degrees and a selection of digging buckets of various widths, some with teeth.

'That machine okay?' asked MacBrayne. 'Looks a bit big to me. Could build a sodding motorway with that thing.'

'It's bigger than we need but should be fine, it's the operator that counts.'

'That reminds me, we had a problem there,' MacBrayne said casually, 'but it's sorted now. Seems none of the in-house drivers wanted to do it, you know, reluctant to dig up a body, I suppose. But they got us an agency driver. He's supposed to be okay.'

Jacko looked over to the machine where the driver was revving it up, blowing clouds of blue exhaust fumes into the air and checking out the hydraulics and the controls. They could see the machine arm lifting, dropping and moving with great clanking noises, and the cab swinging from side to side checking on height and range.

'I'll go and explain how we want it doing,' Jacko said, to try and get things moving. He pulled on his hard hat and made his way towards the machine. The driver saw him coming, cut the engine to tick-over and opened the cab door as Jacko came up to him.

'Meester Jaaksin, Meester Jaaksin! Ver ver gut meeting too. Yoo well, yes? Ditmar gut.'

Jacko's heart stopped and a nauseous void opened up in his stomach. Dear God, dear God, he thought to himself as the little man with a balloon-like head and innocent smile emerged from the cab. What had he done to deserve this? He could barely believe it. Here he was at a critical moment in a case when he needed to demonstrate method, expertise and professionalism, and he gets lumbered with Ditmar again. MacBrayne noticed Jacko had stopped, blood seemingly drained from his face, looking faint.

'You okay?'

'Er, yes. I'd better instruct the driver so that he knows what we want.' He waved sympathetically across to Ditmar who returned the gesture enthusiastically.

'Looks like he knows you, Jacko,' MacBrayne speculated. 'Worked with him before then?'

'His face seems vaguely familiar.'

He climbed wearily into the machine cab and sat next to a delighted Ditmar, who shook his hand vigorously.

'Good to see you again, Ditmar,' Jacko said very slowly and clearly. 'This is what we want you to do.' He pulled out a notepad and proceeded to draw sketches which he thought might be more fruitful than engaging in verbal miscommunication. He outlined the various stages of the work in numbered drawings which Ditmar studied carefully, nodding in apparent understanding. They were going to excavate out the tiles and plasterboard first, dump it in one place, then start work removing the rubble tipped from the skip more carefully, laying it out in another.

He climbed out of the cab and situated himself at the far end of the area so that he could direct Ditmar to position the bucket where he wanted it, and gave the signal to start. The machine revved up and hurtled frighteningly towards him, the bucket arm waving wildly in the air as Ditmar struggled with the controls. At the last moment, as the machine raced forwards, just at the point at which Jacko was convinced the world might end, it slowed down, the bucket arm was gently lowered in front of him, and he was able to gesture where he wanted to start and how deep. With meticulous care and precision, and to Jacko's complete astonishment, the bucket slid horizontally through the tile and plasterboard, clawed it upwards and dumped it cleanly by the topsoil on one side. Jacko moved across and the operation was repeated. It took barely ten minutes to skim the top half away, then the operation was repeated until the outline of the rubble from the manor's skip became visible underneath the residual stain of broken plasterboard and red tiles.

Ditmar continued as instructed, excavating and skimming with infallible skill. Jacko wondered how this level of accomplishment had been reached in such a short space of time, and reminded himself to be more sympathetic to people undergoing learning processes in future. Each bucket full of rubble was tipped out in an open space for the OSU team to sift through, enthusiastically at first, then as successive bucket loads proved negative, with lowering morale. He'd been down this road many times. Odds-on certainties of discovery always started off in high spirits which then diminished as the end neared without result. Searching for concealed bodies was, he'd realised, as much about eliminating sites as finding the body itself. If the old man, or parts of him, proved not to be here, then this was an option that could be crossed off. It just meant that he had to be somewhere else.

After about two hours, and with the bottom of the rubble in sight, there was a brief moment of salvation in the discovery of an empty industrial-sized plastic disinfectant bottle, which Barty's crew carefully bagged and took away. The OSU boys were temporarily cheered, but as the last of the rubble was spread out before them, they'd all become resigned to a non-event. Jacko instructed Ditmar to widen the excavation around where the rubble had been, but this too proved negative. The teams were stood down and Ditmar filled in the hole again while Jacko and MacBrayne sat in the car feeling depressed.

'Really thought we were on to something here,' Jacko muttered.

'Me too. Wonder if the Wainwrights set us up?'

'What d'you mean?'

'Well, it's a good excuse for keeping us out of the way, isn't it? And they did ask for the skip to be removed on a specific day to make it look suspicious.'

'Who made the call and asked for it to be collected, do we know?' Jacko asked.

'Only that it was a male voice.'

'Doesn't the company record calls, you know "for security and training purposes"?'

'Jacko, this is a skip hire company, not customer services at Waitrose.'

Jacko went back to first principles. 'Let's just suppose, say, that the manor people are involved in Seth's disappearance or murder, and let's just suppose again that the skip was a deliberate red herring. Where would they put the body? We didn't look in the grounds, did we?'

'Only in a cursory way. We never did a full search because we had no reason to until there was a DNA match. But it's a bit too obvious a place to try and hide a body. If a body's found in their grounds it points the finger at them, doesn't it? No, he's got to be somewhere else, bugger knows where though. Unless of course he's been boiled up and fed to the house dogs,' he joked.

'Or to these illegals we keep hearing about,' said Jacko quietly. They looked at each other.

'Christ, I suppose it's a possibility, if they were using the manor kitchen the way Flett thinks.'

'Shades of Adolf Luetgert,' muttered Jacko.

'Who?'

'Adolf Luetgert. He was a successful sausage manufacturer in Chicago in the 1890s, or at least he was until the police found a few of his missing wife's bones and some bits of her jewellery at the bottom of one of his sausage vats. I think her name was Louisa.'

'You mean he put her into the sausages?'

Jacko wondered how he might have been more explicit. 'He was rumbled thanks to a pioneering anthropologist, an academic called George Dorsey, who rubbished the defence argument that they were just animal bones. It's a classic historic milestone in forensic anthropology. Why couldn't it be like that at the manor?'

MacBrayne looked aghast. 'I can't believe what you're saying. We're in cosy middle-class Middle Belford, not in gangster-ridden downtown Chicago.'

'But it's credible, isn't it?'

'So if they did chop him up and boil up the bits, what would be left, and where would the residue be? In their bins?'

'We didn't look in their bins, did we? For the same reason we didn't look in the grounds – no reason to.'

MacBrayne rang Flett to brief him on events. It was a short conversation. 'Right,' he said, lobbing his phone on to the back seat, 'he's not a happy bunny.' He left the car and made towards the site office. It was late afternoon and the wagons were queuing up outside to make their last delivery, waiting for the police cordon to be removed. The OSU and CSI teams were getting impatient awaiting their further instructions. He waved to them, asking them to hang on for a couple of minutes, and disappeared inside the site office. He emerged some ten minutes later and spoke to Jacko through the car window.

'Guess what?' he said cheerily. 'The manor end of Middle Belford gets its bins emptied every fortnight. And guess where that rubbish is now?'

Jacko shrugged, 'About ten metres down, somewhere over there?' he waved his hand in the general direction of the tip.

'Wrong. It's somewhere there,' MacBrayne pointed to the line of wagons lining up to make their dump. 'More accurately,' he added, 'it's the third one along in the queue.'

Between them MacBrayne and Jacko made a series of rapid decisions which they realised they'd have to justify later. The OSU and CSI teams were stood down but asked to be available the next day. MacBrayne allowed the tip to open up and resume business but insisted on impounding the wagon in question, making it secure with a uniform watch overnight. Its driver was far from pleased but became less abusive when he was offered a lift home. According to him, the rubbish from the manor would be somewhere in the middle of the load. He remembered having to reverse all the way up the drive just to collect a few black bin bags. The manor was a pain in the arse to access every time. Not only that, but there was a crabby little woman who'd come out and yell if the wheels went on the grass verge. He was certain the bin bags were black, but he may have been wrong. Very helpful, thought Jacko, searching for black bin bags in a bin lorry.

CHAPTER 24

Work sifting through the rubbish started the following morning thanks to Flett's unenthusiastic blessing. Jacko had suggested they divide the contents into three – two ends and a middle part of the load, defined rather arbitrarily. The rubbish had been compressed by the hydraulic crusher and, when released, emerged slowly from the back end of the vehicle like a vast constipated turd. The OSU team, decked out in protective hooded clothing complete with face masks and heavy duty gauntlets, targeted the middle part first. A few bags were still whole, but the majority had split with the contents spilling, or in some cases oozing, in a stinking mess on the ground or over other bags. The smell was revolting, swarms of flies arrived from nowhere and gulls squawked about, becoming braver and more excited as time went on. Each bag in turn was pulled over to an inspection area where two officers went through it one after the other. As each bag was torn open the contents were sifted and anything likely to be significant passed across to Christine, who Flett had been persuaded to hire in at short notice. Jacko had insisted they needed someone who could recognise the difference between animal and human bones.

It was probably one of the most unpleasant jobs that MacBrayne had ever had to deal with. Apart from the smell, which no-one seemed to notice after a while, it was the sight of compressed, decaying domestic waste – anything from disposable nappies and mouldy food to stinking rags and used sanitary towels – and the need to fight for the bag contents against flocks of gulls. Maggot infestations were common, rats appeared now and again for pickings, and flies arrived in clouds. Because the job was so disgusting, the OSU team took to the task like ducks to water. It was right up their street. Nothing in any of those bags escaped their attention, no matter how stinking, filthy or nauseating. There were plenty of butchered animal bones from meals. Christine said it was like looking at an archaeological assemblage – she could identify a twenty-first century Middle Belford society that preferred chicken and pork products to beef or other animals. It was during a discussion as to whether this reflected social class bias or ecological issues that she suddenly went quiet and asked them to stop work while she checked out some small burnt bones under a portable microscope. The OSU team became unusually subdued. She returned shortly with MacBrayne and Jacko and pronounced the bones to be almost certainly human finger bones. The findings were greeted with inappropriate shrieks of delight.

The bag they'd come from was taken to one side and sealed inside a tamper-proof police container for detailed examination under more controlled conditions. The OSU team returned to kneel in the stench of domestic refuse with renewed vigour, despite the number of bags lined up ahead of them still to be processed. Jacko reckoned it would take at least three more days at the current rate. Meanwhile, as they continued dredging through humanity's domestic offal, MacBrayne contacted Flett for authorisation to have DNA samples taken.

* * *

'An interesting development,' Superintendent Roberts said sourly on hearing the news.

Flett sat at the other side of the vast, immaculately tidy desk trying not to look smug. 'Early days, sir, we need a DNA profile, we're still searching the other rubbish bags, and of course there's no way we can necessarily link the bag it came from to the manor at this stage.'

'Or at any other stage, I should imagine? The bin bag could have come from anywhere in Middle Belford, I would say?'

'Oh yes, we realise that sir, but as the missing person's blood is all over the old stables there, it does rather point in the direction of the manor doesn't it?'

Roberts tapped his expensive Parker fountain pen against his equally expensive leather bound blotter which showed no signs of ever having been used for blotting. He looked hard at Flett, twitching his nostrils rather like a rabbit.

'Do you realise the cost of all these DNA analyses?'

'It has to be done, sir. All part of the technology of modern policing.'

'What do you propose to do next, Alastair?' was all Roberts found it prudent to say at this point, trying to feel his way around the situation and wondering how on earth he was going to broach the subject with the CC.

'We'll need to search the manor and its grounds, sir. I thought I'd better warn you, just in case there was any flak from upstairs.' Roberts looked aghast. 'There's really no alternative, sir. We'd do that anywhere else. Can't just pull back because the people who live there think they're a cut above the rest of the population.'

Roberts ignored him and leaned across the desk.

'Let me put it another way and let you into a little secret, Alastair,' he said, lowering his voice and smiling. 'I'm able to tell you that Charles Wainwright is about to become a cabinet minister in the forthcoming reshuffle – strictly in confidence, of course. That could mean great things for us out here, especially in view of his friendship with the CC.'

'With respect, that doesn't put him above the law sir, does it?'

'Goodness, certainly not. What I'm saying is that it would be inappropriate to pursue that line of enquiry at this rather sensitive stage in the reshuffle. Do you see my point, Alastair?'

'No, sir.'

Roberts gave a loud sigh of frustration. 'Take it as an order then, Alastair. The grounds will not be searched until I authorise you to do so. Are you clear on that score?' Roberts glared at him. 'Be rational, for goodness' sake, Alastair. Why on earth would parts of the victim appear in their domestic waste? It's ridiculous.'

Sometimes Flett found that unexpected statements of blinding simplicity were much more effective than long, drawn-out explanations.

'They may have cooked him, sir.'

'Cooked him Alastair? Are you out of your mind?' Roberts sat looking at him in the same way that a goldfish might. 'Are you telling me the Wainwrights – our MP-cabinet-minister-to-be and Sir James – are cannibals? Good God, what nonsense!'

'I'm not saying that at all, sir. But we have reason to believe that the manor is being used to prepare and supply food for illegal immigrants based in London.' There was an uncomfortable silence. 'The intelligence we have, sir,' Flett went on, 'suggests that the spooks are on to this too. We're sitting on the edge of it because somehow it seems to be vaguely connected with the death of the old man up the church tower and the missing pensioner from the manor. It's all very complex.'

Roberts' voice went up an octave, 'This is a preposterous accusation against the Wainwrights – cooking people?' he squeaked. 'I've never heard anything so ludicrous.'

'Beg pardon, sir, but I've not accused the Wainwrights of anything yet, and certainly not of cooking people. I'm merely pointing out that their extensive kitchen facilities may have been adapted for nefarious purposes.' Flett was beginning to enjoy himself. 'In all fairness, sir, you asked us specifically to keep our eyes open for indicators of unusual activity regarding this immigration sex racket. And that's exactly what we've been doing. We're now reporting it to you – as you asked.'

'What's the nature of this intelligence then?'

'Very reliable, sir.'

'I need to know the source.'

'I'm afraid I can't give you that, sir. It's only one small part of what's going on. There's a wider picture.' He stared Roberts straight in the eye. 'It's my belief that there's major criminal activity afoot, possibly involving serving police officers. Until such time as this is shown *not* to be the case, I think it's probably best if I keep this intel under wraps, if you don't mind.' He gave Roberts a sickly smile across the several square metres of oak veneered chipboard desk. 'I propose to serve warrants for searching the manor grounds in the morning, sir. Subsequent to any findings there, I may need to serve a warrant for searching the manor itself. This will be part of an ongoing enquiry into a missing person whom we strongly suspect may have been murdered. If you thought this a bad idea, sir, then my worry would be that intervention on your part might be seen as being obstructive, bringing your own unblemished reputation under the spotlight. We wouldn't want that, would we, sir?'

With that he stood up and made for a team meeting in his office, leaving a speechless Roberts swinging his legs from his high chair.

'Of course I'll keep you up to speed as we go along, sir,' he added as he left the room.

* * *

'Okay, where next then? Any suggestions?' Flett asked the assembled group when they were all seated in his cramped office. 'Jacko, you're supposed to be the one with the brains. Time to earn your pennies, laddie.'

'Dog shit,' said Jacko unexpectedly; an uneasy hush fell over the room.

'Dog shit?' questioned Flett. 'Is this a criticism of my handling of the job, or is it something you might care to expand upon?'

'I once did a job on the other side of the country where an elderly lady had been camping in the hills and walking with her two Labradors.' The others exchanged glances.

'And?' asked an intrigued Flett.

'Well, it was in the middle of nowhere up in the hills in the Lakes and she vanished – no traces of her anywhere, presumably she died but her body was never found. I was involved in the search. All we found was her tent with everything intact inside. No evidence of foul play or anything like that. About four weeks later the two Labradors turned up in a nearby village, starving, and were taken in by the RSPCA. I think they were eventually re-homed. I seem to remember one was called Chocolate, the other Sweetie, or something.'

'Beg pardon, Jacko,' Flett interjected. 'This is a touching bedtime story, but we're not fully clear as to its relevance.'

'Dog shit. Don't you see? The CSIs went back to the tent area and collected all the dog shit – buckets of it – took it back to the lab, re-hydrated it and sieved it – and guess what was in it – small fragments of human bone, traces of fabric clothing and some teeth, all of which were indigestible. The old lady must have died, the dogs loyally stayed with her like dogs do, then out of sheer hunger, systematically chewed their way through her corpse. What was left would have been scavenged off by other forms of wildlife.'

'Are you suggesting we do that at the manor?' Jennie asked, appalled.

'Jacko's got a point,' said MacBrayne, enthusiastically. 'They could be giving the dogs some of the leftovers. It's a pretty good way of getting rid of the evidence, but we'd have to collect the dog mess specifically from around the kennel area to prove it. I should imagine that the Wainwright lackies just shovel the stuff over the kennel fence every so often. All we'd need to do would be to get the OSU boys to collect it as part of a general search of the grounds.'

Jennie scowled in disgust.

* * *

The following day the OSU team, suitably briefed and finding the instructions hilarious, started their quasi-covert collection process. To anyone else the exercise of collecting volumes of dog excrement in buckets would have been unmentionably disgusting, but they went at it with the enthusiasm and levity of a family setting out to pick blackberries on a Sunday morning, popping them one by one into a Tupperware box in order to make a crumble for lunch. The object was to collect as much as possible from outside the immediate perimeter of the kennels without making it too obvious. Fortunately the Wainwrights were still in London and the wizened old lady seemed to have gone shopping. Within a couple of hours of barely stifled OSU mirth several bucket loads of excrement had been collected and deposited into plastic bins. Jacko kept himself in the background, MacBrayne supervised at a distance, and Jennie discovered she had a dental appointment.

The two large plastic bins were each half-filled – more than that made the weight unmanageable – sealed and designated as exhibits. Jacko and Christine had organised a wet sieving facility in the grounds of HQ where the contents would be spaded out, spread on a meshed sieve, poked about, then sprayed with water to dissolve away the soft parts and allow any insoluble elements to be caught by the sieve. It was standard archaeological wet sieving, apart from the smell. In normal archaeological circumstances the fine tilth that formed the waste from sieving was prized and would be collected and carried to be used in people's vegetable gardens. But these were different circumstances. It was not so much a nutritious tilth as a stinking sludge which, after much discussion, was quietly deposited on the flower beds directly under Superintendent Roberts' first floor office window. The residue was rinsed with clean water, bagged, sealed and taken to Barty Webb's laboratory where Christine went through it under a microscope.

It proved particularly informative. The entire volume of two half dustbins of dog excrement had been reduced to less than a pudding bowl full of bits. Some were fragments of stone, there were pips and seeds as well as small twists of fibres, presumably from clothes that had failed to become dissolved in the digestive tract. There were also some splinters of bone, but too small to identify. But the major discovery, as Jacko had hoped, was the presence of at least half a dozen fragments of teeth, which Christine pronounced as human without any hesitation. Teeth were good for DNA analysis she told them, in fact they were a preferred source because their DNA was protected by the outer core. The teeth were duly sent for profiling and yet another wait commenced.

CHAPTER 25

Privately, Jacko was looking into the life and times of one Henry Toller, Captain of the Tower. He needed to find out if it was the same H. Toller who had been a student at Jesus College and therefore a contemporary of the Rev Rogers. The implications of a common background would be more than interesting. Toller had yet to be interviewed but was now back from holiday and MacBrayne agreed to make him a priority. No-one in the village seemed to know much about him, other than that he was retired, although no-one knew what he had retired from. One of the bell-ringing ladies seemed to think he'd been in the army. His house was at one end of a new development in the village, a detached stone-fronted three-bedroomed dwelling built in the 1980s. Being nosey, Jacko had walked past it a couple of times at night to see if he could see anything through the windows, but the curtains were always drawn. It had a plain fenced garden which exuded an air of simplicity and precision – a neatly cut lawn with trimmed edges, flower beds dotted with regularly-spaced plants and an asphalt driveway which seemed to have been frequently brushed. It gave the impression of an owner who kept things minimalist, tidy and in order, but without much imagination. The car in the drive, a dark blue BMW, was spotlessly clean, even down to its alloy wheels.

MacBrayne rang the doorbell at an agreed time and was invited into a narrow hallway decorated with popular commercial prints of landscapes neatly arranged on the walls and up the stairway. Henry Toller was also neatly arranged, almost dapper in dress, wearing a tight-fitting light blue suit and suede shoes. He was a tall man, skinny in appearance with very neatly clipped hair, the sort of man who was probably insistent about visiting the barbers at regular intervals. Nothing about him was out of place, and his open-necked pink shirt had been carefully ironed with a matching handkerchief meticulously folded in his breast pocket. MacBrayne guessed he was probably in his early sixties. Clean-shaven, he had a long, almost fiddle-shaped head which sported a pair of circular spectacles perched on his nose. It reminded MacBrayne of the faded black and white photos of his grandfather, who had worn a similar pair.

MacBrayne was ushered into the lounge while Toller vanished to make tea; he took the opportunity to have a quick look round unattended. He was hoping to glimpse photos of college days, the odd trophy on the sideboard, some regimental mementos, in fact anything that might give him an excuse to talk about his background. Toller seemed only to have a penchant for popular prints, mostly by Constable, which hung equidistantly spaced on all four walls. He peeked into the kitchen where Toller had his back to him. Like the rest of the house and garden it was immaculately arranged with everything spotlessly clean and in its place. MacBrayne's acute sense of observation picked out two wine glasses and two plates among the pots and pans on the draining board. Maybe he'd been entertaining, but there seemed to be little evidence of a woman's touch in the place.

'You realise that I already gave an extensive interview when Mr Johnson's body was found,' Toller said, returning with a neatly arranged tray of cups, saucers, milk jug and teapot which he set down on a low teak table between them. 'I've told your colleagues as much as I know.' He sounded rather impatient.

'I realise that, sir, and I'm grateful for your time,' was MacBrayne's polite but firm response. 'However, there are a few more questions I'd like to ask you, if I may.' He pulled out his notebook while Toller poured the tea through a sieve into china cups.

MacBrayne began by questioning him about the Thursday when the body was discovered, the events surrounding the discovery, unusual things Toller may have seen on the previous Monday, general talk about bell-ringing and the bells themselves (about which Jacko had given him a quick induction). They then covered old Tommy's background and life in the village in general.

'Well, I think we're nearly there now,' MacBrayne said, after about half an hour of laboured conversation while he pretended to tick off items in his notebook. 'There's just one other thing – the Rev Rogers. You're probably more aware more than most that he hasn't been seen for some time, and there's growing concern about his well-being. You wouldn't have any idea where he might be, I suppose?'

'None whatsoever, I'm afraid. Have you tried contacting his daughters?'

'Yes, no luck there, we've not been able to track them down yet. He doesn't seem to have many close friends. The two of you must have worked quite closely together at the church. We thought perhaps you might know of any little foibles he had, if he was worried about anything, or if he had a bolthole somewhere?'

'I don't think anyone really knows Rogers well. We have a working relationship, that's all. He's certainly never confided in me.'

'Not many folk seem to know him well. Strange for a vicar,' MacBrayne mused. 'Have you known him long, sir?'

'Depends what you mean by "long". I only moved up here about eight years ago, that's when we first met. He and I are both bachelors, you see, neither of us have domestic constraints.' The information was volunteered openly – so there was no Mrs Toller. 'We both have interests in the church, his are spiritual and mine are campanological. It's a symbiotic relationship, works well.' There was a pause as MacBrayne made some notes. 'Is there anything else I can help you with? I really need to get on with some work.'

'No, no, I won't keep you any longer, sir, thank you for your help, and also for the tea.' MacBrayne stood up and moved towards the door. 'I see you like Constable,' he said on his way out, 'I have to say I always find Constable's part of the country, you know East Anglia generally, the fens and so on, rather geographically uneventful, too flat for me, I'm afraid. My girlfriend keeps suggesting we take a holiday there but I'm a bit reluctant. You must like it, clearly?'

'No, I'm a bit like you. I've never been there either, I prefer mountains. It's just that I like the way Constable paints. I enjoy his style and the quaint English atmosphere it represents.'

MacBrayne left the house and returned to his car. He'd done enough interviews in his police career to know when someone was lying. On the passenger seat was the old photo from Cambridge that Jacko had given him, the one showing the oarsmen posing by their boat. He drove around the corner, stopped the car and looked at it hard under the interior light. It had to be him: tall and skinny, and the facial characteristics, although forty years younger, were of the same fiddle-shaped head. He turned out the light and sat thinking about it in the dark with only the neon of the streetlamps for company. Something wasn't quite right about the house and it took him a while to work out what it was. It was the car. It was exactly the sort of house where he'd expect the garage to have tidy shelves of paint pots, tools stacked in trays, everything in order, garden implements hung up in a line. So why was Toller's car still in the drive all shiny and polished, and not in its proper place in the garage? Maybe there was another vehicle in there, the vicar's Jag, perhaps? Certainly worth a punt in having a look.

He climbed out of his car, closing the door quietly, walked the short distance back to Toller's house and peeked around the corner of his hedge. Bugger, there was no window in the garage. He moved a little closer, risking setting off the security lighting, but nothing happened even when he reached the garage door. It was one of the up-and-over types. He pushed it gently and found it locked. Bugger again. Then he noticed a large gap between the bottom of the door and the ground, more than wide enough to poke through a mobile phone on a selfie stick. He didn't have one but he knew Jennie did.

* * *

Flett sat opposite Superintendent Roberts in the latter's office and glared at him. 'It's essential we have a warrant to search the manor, sir. There's just too much pointing in that direction. We'd be neglecting our duty of care if we delay it any further.'

'Out of the question,' was Roberts' consistently firm reply. 'We've no reason to justify it, and we simply cannot afford to upset the Wainwrights any further. We've already embarrassed the CC by searching their grounds. Do I have to remind you that Charles Wainwright is likely to be appointed Minister for Local Affairs in the cabinet reshuffle next week? Just think what that will do for the neighbourhood. We really cannot afford to have any malicious scandal running rampant. It would jeopardise the whole thing. I'm told he'll be giving an inaugural speech broadcast live from the town hall next Wednesday. It's all arranged. The national media will be there and I gather from the CC that he's promised to give our force a special mention. That will give us an immense boost.'

'Frankly,' Flett argued, 'I don't care a toss about the CC's embarrassment or the career niceties of our MP at this stage.

I certainly didn't vote for the slime bag.' Roberts looked up sternly. 'Sir,' Flett added diplomatically.

'That tone's unnecessary, Alastair, and disrespectful.' He paused, 'I'll put it down to stress. Perhaps you need a break. Perhaps this is all getting too much for you. You're not a young man any more, you know.'

'What the hell am I supposed to do? I've a manor worker goes missing, his blood's all over the floor and ceiling, human fingers turn up in the rubbish tip and now we find human teeth in the shit from the manor's dogs.'

'We don't know if they're his fingers or his teeth yet though, do we? Let's not get too carried away on this one, perhaps?'

'Carried away? For God's sake, the dogs are being fed on human remains and you think I'm getting carried away?'

'Look at it another way, it could just be a set of coincidences.'

'Coincidences my arse! Let me tell you what's going on. It's likely that the Pear Tree in Loxton is supplying food to illegal immigrants used for sex work. We believe the food is processed at the manor and then transported south to London. It's my view that the old man's death is somehow connected.'

'Nonsense. Absolute nonsense! What on earth could give you that idea?' Roberts thought for a moment and looked sternly at him. 'You haven't been carrying out covert activity at the Pear Tree, I trust? The place is above reproach.' He stared at Flett. 'If my instructions have been flouted, I can assure you it would be viewed as an internal disciplinary offence.'

Flett ignored the accusation. 'No need to, sir,' he said more quietly. 'The Intelligence Services have already been observing the hotel and that's the information that's coming through.' It was a half-truth, based on supposition, but it had the desired effect.

'What?' Roberts' face went pallid. 'Why wasn't I informed of this? This is my patch. These people are coming in behind my back. Why didn't you tell me this before?'

'As I believe I mentioned to you previously, sir, I believe there to be police involvement, corruption possibly – best investigated internally and quietly, I'm sure you agree.'

Roberts visibly shook as Flett rummaged in his brief case and pulled out two large photographs, pushing them across the table. 'These came my way, sir. I can't give you the source, but as you see, they show a police patrol vehicle collecting boxes of some kind from the Pear Tree in the early hours of the morning – you can see the date and time at the bottom.' Roberts' mouth hung open. 'Not part of the patrol policing I remember from my days, sir, but there again with your fast-tracking you wouldn't have been down that road. Up to no good, I would have thought, sir, wouldn't you say?'

'Well, er, things aren't always what they seem, Alastair,' Roberts mumbled. 'Um, maybe I should make a slight confession here. How do I put it, er, the patrol chaps were doing a little job for me,' he said, clearly embarrassed and not knowing quite where to put himself.

Flett knew damn well they'd been doing a little job for him – he'd already spoken to them and given them hell, now he just wanted to make life uncomfortable for Roberts. He was enjoying it.

'You see,' Roberts said sheepishly, 'I was getting supplies in for the senior officers annual conference, you know there's always a bit of a party at the end. I'm conference secretary this year.' He gave a weak smile. 'The boys were picking up the drinks from the Pear Tree. We get them at cost of course – it's the CC's influence there – and I got the patrol boys to collect them when they were nearby.'

'Ah, I see. Oh, that's alright then, sir,' Flett said brightly. 'Here's me thinking we were seeing an unpleasant example of police corruption. That clears that up – police business, you might say. That's what I assumed anyway. I wasn't sure, just wanted to check it with you.'

'You mean you knew already?'

'Oh yes, sir, but seeing as the photographs came from intelligence sources, I thought you'd want to know that this little episode has a wider circulation than you might have expected.'

'Good heavens, I never realised. Why on earth didn't you contact me earlier?'

'Well for a start,' said Flett, now beginning to enjoy himself even more, 'the intelligence services were watching a property on your patch – a property you directly ordered us not to observe. From memory, I think your words were "I absolutely forbid it", which leaves little room for doubt, and it would have been impudent of us to have proven you wrong so fundamentally, wouldn't it, sir? And anyway, if we'd have told you, you'd have been obliged to tell the CC and that would have put you in a bigger mess with him than you are already.'

Roberts stood up from his desk and wandered to the window, breathing deeply as he went. He needed more oxygen to calm himself down. He stood there for a few moments in total silence, motionless as though he'd been stuffed, giving Flett the thought that he may have had some form of seizure.

'Er, shall I open the window and let some fresh air in, sir?' he suggested.

'Please, yes. Good idea.' Roberts said nodding, his gaze fixed on the woodland outside. 'We need to think this out carefully, you know, Alastair.'

Flett opened the window and they both returned to their chairs.

'I suggest,' said Flett, when Roberts had composed himself a little more, 'that we continue to keep this information to ourselves, for all our sakes. Our direct interests are with the potential murder of a pensioner up a church tower, a case which unfortunately seems to have extended to a possibly related murder in the grounds of the manor. I propose we restrict ourselves to resolving those for the time being rather than getting tangled up in other matters.' He paused, noticing Roberts' apparent physical discomfort. He was shuffling and twitching his nostrils. 'But it would entail two key approvals on your behalf, sir.'

'What's that smell?' was Roberts' unexpected response as he had a careful look under the table, then around the carpet before stooping down and looking at the soles of his shoes.

'What smell? I don't notice anything untoward over here. Polish on the desk perhaps, sir?' he added, bending down to sniff the desktop.

'Are you sure you haven't trodden in something unpleasant, Alastair?'

Flett stood up, checked the soles of his shoes, shook his head and resumed his seat. 'There is a bit of a whiff, isn't there, sir, now you come to mention it. But I wonder if we might return to my requests, sir?'

'It's a new carpet, you know, Alastair,' Roberts said, ignoring him and scouring the floor for the offending source. 'Oh dear, I'll have to get estates in to clean it properly. Yes, yes. What is it you want me to do?'

'Two things, sir, please. Firstly, I'd like you to authorise a search warrant for the manor in Middle Belford. I'll need it in a couple of days time when the DNA results are back. We don't want to give them any warning, and I suggest an early morning raid, sir. As I see it, this is an ongoing part of our murder enquiries, but if it turns up trumps with the immigration racket then we, by which of course I mean you, get all the credit by beating intelligence services to it. A good feather in your cap, I'd say, sir. And of course the CC would be delighted because you've managed to keep his name away from the social spotlight concerned.'

Roberts took a few moments to consider his options. 'I think you're right this time, Alastair. That's a sensible and necessary approach. Agreed. And what is the second request?'

'I want your support in obtaining a warrant for the arrest of the Rev. Rogers on suspicion of murder,' he said bluntly.

Roberts nodded. 'Agreed too,' he said, distracted, still twitching his nostrils.

'Thank you, sir,' said Flett as he stood up to leave. 'Tell you what, sir,' he added, 'I'll just open the window a little more to try and get rid of this smell for you.'

'Thank you, Alastair, that's very kind of you.'

Flett crossed to the window just in time to see another barrow-load of diluted sludge from the dog mess sieving process being deposited directly underneath. 'I'll open it as wide as I can, sir.'

CHAPTER 26

Jacko had been invited to Alex's house for dinner. It was a rare social arrangement, seeing as Jacko and Brenda, Alex's wife, rarely saw eye to eye. She saw Jacko as a prime example of disorganisation and irresponsibility; he was held up as a gold standard of bachelor irresolution and poor taste. 'You'll end up like your father,' was a phrase frequently heard in the Jackson Junior household. Brenda's distilled view of Jacko was that he was simply a bad example; she treated him in much the same way as someone who took in an old smelly dog found wandering in the street. It was an exercise in charity as much as anything else. She tolerated him because it would have been wrong not to.

That evening she was doing something at Guides and anyway was on a new diet, so Jacko and Alex had busied themselves creating a spaghetti bolognese whilst downing a bottle of Australian shiraz. Once consumed, and when Brenda had returned and been engaged in polite conversation before she retired to finish off reading her new crime thriller, the two of them sat around the embers of a log fire still flickering in the hearth of the stone inglenook. Jacko had happily accepted the offer of staying over – an offer made by Alex rather than his wife – and was feeling comfortably relaxed, slumped in an armchair sipping a malt whisky that his son had unexpectedly unearthed from the rear of a kitchen cupboard.

He'd also just had a call from MacBrayne telling him that Judy was now out of the coma; she was still poorly, but the medics expected her to make a full recovery. The news lifted his spirits and gave him new inspiration.

'Maybe we should take a quiet look at what's going on at the manor,' he suggested to his son after much thought, mindful of his covert experiences with Judy, and not a little emboldened by the drink.

'Too risky,' was the immediate response, 'Easier to wait until all the DNA's through then Flett can put the boot in with a formal search warrant. Anyway, there's all that electronic alarm stuff you'd need to negotiate.'

'What if there's a power cut?'

'Back-up batteries.'

'Shit. Well at least we know where the CCTV cameras are. MacBrayne's made a plan of the ones he could find. He reckons there's a narrow band of land through the grounds, at the back, that isn't covered by cameras. He went out specially to check it, pretending to be one of the dog handlers. He's done a load of work on security management so I'm happy to take his word for it.'

Alex was looking at him suspiciously.

'Tell you what we could do,' Jacko suggested. 'The OSU are there again tomorrow along with other search personnel, basically just to finish off a few areas of the grounds. They all look the same in work jackets, no-one counts off how many officers there are, so two more won't make any difference getting out, and two fewer won't be noticed when the vans leave again in the evening, will they?'

'Just a minute, what are you trying to suggest? Are you proposing you and I both travel into the manor anonymously as part of the OSU team, and that they leave us there overnight?'

'Why not? Can you think of a better plan?'

'*We* don't need a plan, because *we're* not going to do it. Are you off your head?'

'Bit of Trojan horse, really, isn't it?' Jacko said ignoring him. 'Don't you see? Their CCTV system is designed to watch for people approaching the manor, not to pick them up once they're there.'

'Dad, this is a completely hair-brained idea. What exactly do you think I'm going to do? I'm a police officer. I can't suddenly jump ship and follow your hunches, especially where there may be organised criminal activity. These aren't nice people you're messing with, you should know that by now.' He passed the bottle across and Jacko topped up his glass.

'Maybe that's why I want to do it.'

'Don't let it get personal. And anyway, what on earth would you plan on doing there all night? Look through the downstairs windows? Just what do you expect to learn?'

'Do give me some credit, won't you? When the building was listed because of its architectural history, a survey plan was made of it, then revised later, and I was part of the team that did the revision. I just happen to have a copy of it back at the house. It shows the layout of the rooms downstairs, the cellarage, and all the entry points. There's a labyrinth of little passages and doorways down there – rooms leading into each other, stuff like that. They used to be used for pantries, wine storage, keeping ice, butlers' hideaways and so on – I remember them quite well.' He was beginning to wave his arms about as memory kicked in. 'I even know about the direction their sewerage system runs, because we did a geophysical survey across the lawns. Come on, with all that information up our sleeves, you've got to agree it's worth a punt.'

'You must be potty. You've seen what these people are capable of at first hand. It's not the Wainwrights themselves you have to worry about, it's their henchmen. The Wainwrights are probably just fronting it, they'll deny knowledge of anything – they'll say they were away most of the time, their housekeeper was in charge. They'll get off scot free and come out of it squeaky clean. Rich influential bastards like them always do. No, Flett's right, we have to do it by the book if we're going to get them.'

'So you're not in with me then?' said Jacko, raising his voice in disappointment.

'Bloody right I'm not,' Alex said, raising his own voice in response and almost shouting. 'Never heard anything so hair-brained – Dad, you're off your trolley.'

'What's going on?' Brenda emerged through the door, reading glasses hanging from a string around her neck. 'How can I relax and read a book with you two hollering? You'll wake the entire village.'

'Sorry love, just a disagreement over professional ethics.' He glared across at Jacko.

'Too much to drink, the pair of you. You ought to know better,' she said fixing her stare on Alex, effectively blaming Jacko's influence. She then turned to Jacko as they both sat there in silence like naughty children being scolded. 'And if it's about another of your mad ideas, Jacko, don't drag Alex into it. His career doesn't need tarring with your mucky brush.' And with that she flounced out of the room, leaving Jacko speechless.

'What's up with her?' he muttered when she'd gone.

Alex shrugged, 'Sorry, she seems a bit uptight at the moment.' He poured them both another scotch by way of an apology.

'Okay, to keep the peace,' he said reluctantly, 'and just to help you out, I'll partly go along with your stupid idea, but only partly. And you'll have to square it with MacBrayne first, understand? I'll get dropped there with you, help set you up, check everything's okay for about half an hour, then leave down the corridor where there's no CCTV. After that you're on your own.' He looked Jacko in the eye waiting for an answer. 'Well?'

* * *

The following day the pair of them turned up for the afternoon shift, suitably attired and looking very much like part of the OSU outfit in their dark blue overalls and black boots. With MacBrayne's hesitant agreement they mingled in with the main group, disappearing into the woods with their search equipment until about half past five, when the light began to fade and the OSU minus two returned to the minibus. Jacko and Alex waited in the shadows at the back of the house, their faces darkened using some facial packing that Alex's wife had discarded. They'd positioned themselves against the rear wall of the manor at the edge of the clearing between the house and the woodland, concealed between two buttresses. It was becoming dark but Jacko had already identified various access points from the plan which was now carefully folded in his pocket. He and Alex had agreed to sit there without moving position until mid-evening, at which point they'd do another part-circuit of the building. Alex would check that Jacko had everything he needed then make his departure back home.

When the time came for Alex to leave both of them were already cold and stiff. Together they'd made a quick reconnaissance of the back of the building, checking to see whether there were any lights or sound of movement. There was nothing, the whole place was quiet and still, not even the dogs seemed interested in making a noise.

'Building must be empty,' Jacko whispered, opening and closing his hands to try and get some feeling back to them. 'Spooky bloody place.'

'Okay, I'll leave you to it now, Dad,' Alex said, anxious to get away. 'Just don't do anything stupid, will you?'

'Let's have one more check along the back before you go,' he whispered back.

'Don't be bloody daft, we tried all the doors and windows, they're all locked and there's no way in. Even if there was, there's no point in gaining entry unless you know what you're going to do inside. I'm off.'

At that moment they both heard a vehicle approaching on the gravel drive at the other side of the house. They immediately crouched down in the overgrown wet grass in one of the old doorways. The vehicle sounded like it had a large diesel engine, probably a van or small lorry. It came to a stop but they could hear voices, at least three of them, indecipherable in what they were saying, but sounding animated. There was the noise of slamming doors, dogs barking, and a sudden bright glare indicated that lights had been turned on at the front of the house. Both of them remained motionless until the lights had been switched off, the voices became lost and the dogs stopped barking.

Alex wished he'd never come and leant back heavily against the door, letting out an audible sigh as he did so. It was followed by a heavy creaking noise behind them, then the sound of splintering wood.

'Shit,' he muttered. 'The door must be rotten.' He fumbled around feeling the woodwork in the dark, discovering that the door post had cracked with his weight and released the lock. 'Christ, I've broken it open,' he said, horrified.

'Best thing you've done all day,' Jacko commented with delight. 'We can sneak in, hide in the small interconnecting chambers and have a good snoop round. Come on, let's go in while we've got the chance.'

'No *we* bloody won't.'

'Come on, we can't *not* take this opportunity. It's been given us on a plate, like divine intervention. We've got this far and...'

Before Jacko could finish his sentence, the entire back of the manor was bathed in light and the sound of voices could be heard approaching from around the corner.

'Christ, it's a security patrol,' Alex yelped. 'Let's get out of here,' He started to get to his feet to make a run for freedom when he felt a sharp tug on his collar, which yanked him backwards through the open door on to the floor of a dark stone-built room. His father was clumsily wedged on top of him, pushing the door shut behind them with his foot.

'They've got dogs out there, Alex – they'll eat you for breakfast, you silly sod.' They untangled themselves and crawled around on the stone floor inside, not daring to put on the torch, and groping for the walls. Jacko felt his way back to the door and ran his hands around the door frame in the dark, gaining a splinter for his efforts. 'Listen,' he whispered, 'I think the door post's only split on the inside, if we push against it with the door shut, it'll straighten the post and the door should seem locked from the outside'. They moved up to it, slithering on the damp flags and put all their weight against it, pushing the post until it was straight. It made an ominously loud creaking noise which they thought all the world must have heard. Jacko closed his eyes in the silence that followed, waiting for the sound of shouting and running feet to investigate it. But there were none. They both remained there, pushing against the door and its jamb in the dark, becoming increasingly uneasy as the sound of talking and the flickering beam of a flashlight came closer. Suddenly, there was barking followed by a rustling noise outside. Two pairs of canine nostrils appeared snuffling intensively in the gap at the bottom of the door.

'Don't make a sound,' Jacko whispered.

'I don't intend to. Just keep pushing.'

The dogs started whimpering.

'What's wrong with those fucking hounds?' said a voice.

'Rabbits or summat. They squeeze in under the door; door's crap anyway,' said another voice. 'Better try it though. Just to be on the safe side.' He went across to the door, reigned in the dogs on a short lead and gave the door a hefty shove. Jacko and Alex were braced ready and the door didn't budge.

'I hate this place,' the first voice said. 'Too spooky for my liking here at the back. Let's finish the round and get back inside.'

Jacko and Alex continued to lean against the door until the voices had died away completely. They both heaved a huge sigh of relief.

'That's it,' Alex said at last. 'I'm off. And if you've any sense, you'll come with me.' He got to his feet and ran his fingers along the door to find the handle. There wasn't one. He felt again, but there wasn't anything to grip with. 'Bugger, switch the torch on, will you, Dad?' They both looked at the door in the torchlight. It didn't have a handle, and there was nothing else to grip. They could see where the post had been splintered and the door pushed inwards, but they'd effectively repaired it and locked themselves in when they pushed it back again. There had once been a handle on the inside but all that was left was a stump of wood and a rusty screw. Now they couldn't get out.

'We're stuck here,' said Alex accusingly at his father. 'Fucking brilliant, just what I needed – breaking, entering, trespassing and causing criminal damage. Please look at the bloody plan and get us out of here.' There were the seeds of panic in his voice.

'This part must be fifteenth century,' Jacko remarked as he shone the torch around the walling. 'Look at the way this wall's been butted up against this one. Floor's probably part of the same build too.'

'There are times, Dad, when you really get on my tits, and this is one of them. Can we look at the plan and see where we are, please?'

'Sorry,' Jacko mumbled and studied the plan in the flickering light of his torch. 'Batteries going,' he said, and switched it off again.

'Jesus, that's all we need,' Alex pulled out his mobile. It didn't have a torch facility, but the screen had sufficient brightness when it was switched on to light up the immediate area with an eerie blue glow.

'This way's best,' Jacko said with unjustified confidence, pointing in front of him, 'it should lead us through another door, along a corridor and to a passageway that leads out to another exit.'

Alex followed his father, both feeling their way along the damp stone walls and becoming increasingly clammy through a combination of fear and stress. The passageway was little more than a metre wide and with a ceiling of uneven height. Alex, taller than his father, had already scraped his head twice and was reduced to stooping, holding one hand up in front of him like an elephant's trunk, feeling for any sudden dip in height. They reached another door, mercifully unlocked, and felt their way through it into a wider chamber. They closed the door behind them and Jacko switched on his torch momentarily and shone it around. It was a simple rectangular part of the cellarage, probably originally designed to store perishable foodstuffs, but in an age of refrigerators and freezers it had been relegated to the storage of junk. There were boxes, cartons, wicker baskets and chests, all covered in grime and not opened for decades. Jacko wondered what delights of past times, what cultural mementos lay hidden therein.

'Christ, look at that,' he said with surprise.

'Look at what?'

'The roof, it's barrel-vaulted. It must be fourteenth century. I'd forgotten all about it. It's remarkable.' He shone his torch on the hand-made bricks and the stone arches that supported the web of brickwork above them. Alex snatched the torch off him and switched it off.

'For Christ's sake, let's concentrate on getting out, shall we? There's a door over there, at the far end. Is that where we go?' He shone the torch on the plan.

Jacko peered at it for a few moments and seemed to agree. 'I think we ought to have a quick look down there first though,' he said, pointing to a small adjunct chamber accessed down a short flight of steps behind the boxes and chests. 'It doesn't go anywhere, but it's where they used to keep dairy produce fresh on marble slabs. Maybe they're still using it for some of their illicit foodstuffs.'

Alex shone the torch across the room to a narrow opening on the left topped by a round arch. 'Let's be quick then,' he said angrily, switching off the torch, and they made their way across with the aid of the light from his mobile.

Alex went in first and down the steps while Jacko waited at the top barely able to see the glow of the mobile as he reached the bottom.

'Eight steps, Dad,' came a voice out of the darkness, and Jacko made his way carefully down to meet Alex at the bottom.

Both had sensed something before they'd even descended the steps, but neither felt it either necessary or appropriate to mention it to the other. They stood together in the dark and the damp without a word, until Jacko finally broke the silence. 'It's that smell,' he said. It was sweet, sickly and became embedded in the nostrils, sitting in the back of the throat destroying the taste of food and drink for hours.

'It's the one smell you never forget, isn't it?' Alex muttered slowly. He switched on the torch.

CHAPTER 27

Jacko and Alex found themselves in a small stone-built room, the flickering torch showing all that they needed to see. It was like a scene from a horror movie. Damp stone walls were covered with mildew, there were patches of frosty white deposit where lime had leeched out from the mortar, and in places the old ceiling had partly collapsed leaving lengths of congealed horse-hair plaster dangling through the cobwebs. Around the walls on three sides were flat marble slabs positioned at waist height. Two of them were empty, but on the third, at the far end, lay the unmistakable form of a human body under loose sacking. They both stood and looked at it for a while then reluctantly moved nearer, slowly becoming immune to the smell. Alex lifted the sack away from its face. It was a bearded male, eyes staring, mouth open, with a gaping bloodied wound at one side of the forehead.

'Christ,' said Jacko, uncovering the man's face a little more.

'Know him?' asked Alex, surprised.

'Yes, I think so. I bumped into him once when I was watching the Pear Tree from up in the hills. I'm sure it's him. Flett reckons he works for the intelligence services.'

Alex carefully turned the man's head to one side and found what he suspected at the back – a small, more precise wound than at the front, and with less congealed blood. 'Projectile entry wound,' he said. 'He's been shot from close range in the back of the head, hence the mess at the front where the bullet exited.'

'Seen those in the Balkans,' Jacko commented dryly. 'Plenty of them. This bloke's been shot like a military execution.' He dug his mobile phone from deep inside one of his pockets and took a series of photographs of both the body and the room. When he'd finished Alex did the same. They'd both fallen silent. For the time being arguments between them had ceased.

'I think we need to get out of here,' Alex said, covering up the man's face again. 'And we may need back-up. I haven't got a mobile signal down here, have you?'

Jacko shook his head, and they made their way back up the stone steps slightly more quickly than when they'd entered. Jacko looked at the map again and pointed to a door opposite.

'Once we're through there, we can either turn left down a passage that takes us into the main part of the house, or we can turn right which leads us to an outside door back into the grounds.'

'We'll turn right,' Alex said firmly in case Jacko had any other ideas, and they made their way carefully through into the next passage. To the left they could hear vague noises of conversation in the distance, and there was a slight glimmer of light visible at that end as the passage turned. Jacko stopped and stared to see where the light was coming from.

'No,' whispered Alex firmly, 'we're not going down there. Not at any cost,' and he pulled his father to the right where they could make out a door a short distance away. It was like the door they'd originally come through, wooden and in need of repair but, like the other one, it was firmly locked. They both felt around, groping for the handle in the dark to see if it could be forced open.

'Switch the torch on, Alex, I can't see a bloody thing.' The torchlight compounded their misery. There was no handle, just a stump of where the handle had been, and there was nothing else to grip on to. They both stood looking at it pathetically, then at each other, before making their way hesitantly back to the room full of boxes and cartons.

'Has it occurred to you,' Jacko said disconsolately as he found a solid box to sit on, 'that the handles have been deliberately taken off, that these external doors have been secured not just to stop people getting in, but also to stop people from getting out? We're bloody well trapped.' He tapped his foot against the box as he tried to think it out. 'Tell you what,' he suggested after a few moment's deliberation, 'why don't you stay here, and I'll see what I can find out if I creep down the passage that leads into the house?'

'Are you completely mad? They'll eat you alive if they find you.'

'Got a better idea, other than just sitting here? If I hear any movement coming in this direction, I'll nip back and we can hide. I've got the layout in my head so I know where I can go, and where I can't.' Before Alex could reply Jacko got up and vanished in the dark, leaving his son sitting alone on a pile of boxes.

The glimmer of light at the end of the curved passageway was still evident, but the voices had now gone. He moved quietly along the stone walls, one step at a time, counting each one in case he had to return to the hiding place in a hurry in the dark. The passage led to yet another door which was slightly ajar. The light was on and he peeked into a dimly lit ante-room, with what seemed to be a kitchen up some more stone steps at the other end. The light was brighter there and he could hear voices coming from it. The ante-room was probably used as a butler's pantry in the days when the well-heeled had butlers as a social norm.

The door creaked a little as he pushed it wider to get a better look. Inside was a table containing a selection of knives; there were some pots and pans soaking in the sink next to him. If he opened the door a little more he could probably squeeze in, even cross the floor perhaps, and maybe peek into the next room where the voices came from. They were male voices engaged in earnest conversation.

He made his move, crept across the room, conscious of his escape route and listened at the bottom of the steps that led into the kitchen. His heart was thumping and he felt strangely light-headed, as though he'd just had a drink on an empty stomach. Steadying himself, he tip-toed up the short flight of steps, in as much as an overweight fifty-something could tip-toe, and positioned himself immediately behind the door. He could only half hear the conversation, but judging from the voices there must have been at least three different people in the room, all male.

The discussion seemed to be about deliveries. Two of the voices spoke English with a distinctive foreign accent, but it was good English, not like Ditmar's. Jacko couldn't work out what the accent was. It certainly wasn't French or Italian, nor was it German. It was harsher than that. The third voice was undeniably English and older, the sort of posh Queen's English that was common among those privileged to attend public schools, the sort expected of BBC presenters in the 1950s. Jacko remembered his encounter with Charles Wainwright MP. It wasn't his voice either. It must be his father, the redoubtable Sir James. As he was wondering what to do next he heard new voices entering the room, one was female and without doubt the crabby old housekeeper who had buffeted MacBrayne at the manor door. The other had an educated voice, not plummy like Sir James, but measured and authoritative, the sort of person who one instinctively felt might be important. He squeezed nearer to the crack by the door hinges to get a better look, only to see to his horror that the housekeeper was making her way towards him.

He backed off rapidly, but the butler's pantry offered no place to hide and he froze there pathetically in the middle of the floor waiting to be accosted, detained, executed and in all probability disembowelled and fed to immigrant sex slaves. But the door to the kitchen never opened.

'No thank you, Olga,' said the new voice loudly. 'I'm driving so I'll just stick to the water that's here in the jug, thank you very much.' The footsteps moved away and the voices became less distinct.

Jacko was glued to the floor, sweating, with his pulse racing and his bowels curiously cramped. The conversation in the kitchen continued and he found himself creeping nearer to try and hear without cutting off a quick escape route. He could only make out half sentences... there was something about 'another ten being moved on Friday.' Another ten what? Then there was 'a regular supply chain' being set up and an 'additional package.' What was all that about? He moved up again to the door to try and hear better, peeking through the gap by the hinge. The figure he supposed was Sir James had his back to him as did the housekeeper, both grey-haired, she half his size. The two foreigners were out of his sightline but he could hear them talking. He was more interested in the new arrival, the owner of the new mature voice who was only drinking water. Each time Sir James shifted from one side to another he could view a little more of the man, but not enough to see his face.

By now the purpose of the meeting seemed to have been achieved and discussions concluded. At the point where scraping of chairs on the flagged floor signalled that they were leaving Jacko beat a hasty retreat back to the darkness of the passageway and hid there, his heart beating faster than usual. He heard the housekeeper come down the steps and deposit the empty glasses on the table before returning back up to the kitchen and turning out the light. There was a loud click as she locked the door behind her. Jacko took a few moments to compose himself and then fumbled his way back through the dark to Alex.

He relayed as much information as he could before sitting down exhausted on the floor, still shaking with nerves. There was something unwholesomely cold-blooded about the whole exercise, and they both needed to get out more than ever. With what little battery life was left in the torch they made their way down the passageway back to the butler's pantry, now locked and in darkness, in the hope of finding something they could use as a jemmy for prising open the outer door. Jacko carefully opened the cupboard doors searching for a suitable implement. 'Bugger all here,' he whispered to Alex, who was engrossed in looking at something else. 'What's up?' he asked his son, noticing his puzzled look.

'Look over there,' Alex pointed to a pile of dishes drying. Jacko had noticed the pans in the sink on his first visit, but not the dishes.

'So, dishes drying. What's the problem?'

'How many soup bowls do you have in your house?' Alex asked.

'Just a couple, in case I entertain. Why?'

'There must be at least fifteen draining here.'

'These people have big dinner parties, Alex, they're in a different social stratum to you and me.'

'Yeah, but they wouldn't serve posh guests with this old cracked white stuff, would they?'

'Suppose not,' then a thought occurred to him. 'Christ, what if the "ten" being moved on Friday are people? These bowls are still wet. D'you think there are people being held somewhere in the cellars right now?' They looked at each other incredulously until Jacko broke the silence.

'Have to get a move on. Give me a hand down under this table.'

'What?'

'The table, under the table, look.'

Alex looked in horror as Jacko pulled a threadbare rug to one side and revealed a rusty drain cover jammed in with grime and dirt.

'This,' Jacko pointed as the torchlight flickered more than ever, 'is how we get out. The Wainwrights once thought they might convert this place into a hotel. There was also talk of a new housing estate in the field next to it, so the water board sank a larger sewage system to cope with the potential. Just as well, eh? I saw it being installed as part of a watching brief, so I know quite a bit about it. It's bigger than the average domestic sewer and wide enough to crawl through.' Seeing Alex's dumbstruck expression, he added, 'And I also know where we can get out of it.'

Between them they cleared away the muck from the edges and began to prise open the cover. It was unexpectedly heavy and, as Alex pointed out, the opening was unexpectedly small.

'It's fairly tight to climb down, but it gets wider once we get into the main sewer,' Jacko said reassuringly, noting Alex's concerns. 'But once we're in, we've to make sure that the lid and the rug over it are left as we found them, that's the tricky bit.'

Once the lid was released and slid to one side, Jacko heaved himself in feet first, found his footing on the metal rungs that led down and disappeared to check it out, returning with a thumbs up. Alex scraped together all the grime from lifting the lid and dropped it down the hole, noting with some discomfort the length of time it took to splash at the bottom. Then he hauled himself in, carefully sliding the lid back on with the rug resting on top and followed Jacko down into the sewer.

After climbing down half a dozen well-spaced rungs he found himself standing at the bottom next to Jacko, who was crawling on his hands and knees halfway into a black hole.

'I'd forgotten,' Jacko apologised, 'that the new wide sewer doesn't start until the outside wall. This is the old one. Can't be more than a few metres long though. Hope you can fit in it.'

It made no difference to Alex who couldn't see anything. He was bigger than his father, his shoulders were wider, but he was considerably more athletic.

'Let me go first,' Jacko said. 'Wait here until I give you a shout.'

Alex stood ankle deep in sewage, in the dark, and waited while Jacko crawled, commando-style, with his stomach, elbows and most of his legs soaked in human waste. The stench was dire, but Jacko was more concerned with reaching the wider sewer than with the urge to retch. There was no light whatsoever, but after little more than the two or three minutes that seemed like an eternity he found more space, the tunnel widened out and he could move more freely on his hands and knees. He called back to Alex, who was having serious concerns about fitting into the smaller hole, receiving a disgruntled mumble in reply. Neither could see anything. Alex was having to drag his shoulders against the sides and struggled to keep his face out of the sewage, while Jacko was tying himself in knots trying to find his mobile phone in his sodden clothing. He could hear splashing and scraping noises behind him as Alex approached, and moved further forward to give him some space. Alex emerged groaning on his stomach behind him, pulled himself up on his hands and knees into the wider space of the new sewer and vomited over Jacko's legs. He took a while to regain his breath, then vomited again. Jacko waited until the retching had stopped.

'You okay now?' he asked. 'Should be relatively plain sailing from here on.'

'This is beyond disgusting, Dad,' he said, slowly getting his breath back. 'The stuff's all over my face. You sure we're going in the right direction?'

'Yup, because we're going downhill, which is why your puke's floating past me and not going the other way.'

'How far to go then?'

'I'm trying to remember. There should be a manhole about fifty metres from the house at the edge of the woodland. The CCTV cameras don't cover it. If it helps, each of these pipe units is two metres long, so you can count the joints.'

They set off, both crawling along through the sewage on their hands and knees, keeping their heads low, their spirits lifting as each successive pipe join was passed.

'Any time now,' said Jacko optimistically as joint number twenty-four was reached and passed, followed by number twenty-five, twenty-six, and then twenty-seven. Joint number twenty-eight proved to be the lucky one. Jacko discovered he was able to stand and felt around until he found the iron rungs. He climbed up and banged his head on the manhole cover, but was too tired even to swear.

He put one hand against its underside but failed to shift it. He tried wrapping his legs around the rungs and using two hands. The cover shifted slightly, but no further. He returned and slid back into the sewer to let Alex have a go. Alex had better luck, the cover shifted and they could feel a welcome cold draught of fresh air. Pushing it to one side was harder. It took both of them crammed into the space to push it away, allowing Alex to poke his head out. Although it was dark they were exactly where Jacko said they'd be. They were in open grassland. On one side he could see the silhouette of the manor, on the other, only a short distance away, the woodland. They both crawled out, keeping as low as possible, pushing the manhole cover back and stuffing grass and anything they could lay their hands on back in the gaps and on its surface. Then they ran crouching into the woods and lay on the ground enjoying the clean air, getting their breath back. Alex's phone pinged with a text message now that he had a signal. He sat up, fumbled with it, read the message, groaned and lay down again in the wet. 'It's from Brenda,' he said dejectedly. 'It says "Where the hell are you, your dinner's ruined".'

CHAPTER 28

Flett sat at his desk feeling particularly dispirited. The office seemed to be more cluttered than usual, it was pouring with rain outside and everything was depressing. Cases were usually much simpler than this. Jacko's discovery of the body in the cellar now added a new dimension, one corroborated by Alex and by the photographs. The issue of the movement of "another ten" on the Friday was a little more problematic – it was only Jacko's interpretation that these were the illegals. He didn't disbelieve him, of course, but Jacko might have got the wrong end of the stick. It was the same with the "supply chain". Did that mean the food? And the "additional package". Was that the corpse? As far as the body was concerned, under normal circumstances he'd have gone in with every blue light he had to investigate it. This was a major crime with major implications, especially since it involved intelligence personnel. He'd told the spooks straight away. As usual they wanted to play it differently, but wouldn't tell him how. Now they were tying themselves up in knots and wanted it hushed – there were bigger fish to fry, they said. He couldn't realistically sit twiddling his thumbs waiting for the DNA results before he went in. Worse, he still couldn't find a connection between Seth's disappearance and whatever was going on up there. It had to be connected. And the bloody vicar still hadn't been found either. Old Tommy's death, which had kick-started the whole damn exercise, was still unsolved. Fuck, what a mess. And he needed to keep Roberts out of the picture too. At the moment he had him over a barrel for misusing police resources, but that was only a temporary convenience.

The final straw came with an email message marked 'urgent' from Superintendent Roberts. Had he seen the news? Well, Charles Wainwright had indeed been appointed Minister for Local Affairs by the PM. Wasn't that splendid? He'd be giving an address in the town hall the following day. There'd be security implications of course, more officers would need to be drafted in, leave cancelled and so on. He and the CC were both sending their congratulations.

'You obsequious little cunt,' Flett said out loud, and pressed the delete button. He sat mulling things over in his mind, the whole unsavoury business of Wainwright's career advancement fuelling him with renewed venom. MacBrayne was summoned and between them they decided on a major search at the manor the coming Friday – the day of supposed activity there according to Jacko – with all vehicles entering and leaving the manor that day being tracked. They spent the rest of the morning deep in organisational strategy and tactics with other units, the OSU team, forensics, and with the Met. Friday's date for the operation was known only to those involved and lay under tight communications lockdown. A false date for the operation, on the Saturday the day after, was fed elsewhere, including to Superintendent Roberts, who he knew would no doubt communicate it to the CC at the first blabbing opportunity.

* * *

Jacko and MacBrayne set off for London in the Ford Focus to butter up Flett's contacts in the Met and to familiarise themselves with the Wainwright premises at 27 Pennsylvania Gardens. Jacko spent most of the journey huddled deep in the passenger seat talking on his phone to various friends and colleagues, and making detailed arrangements about something that MacBrayne couldn't quite make out. It seemed to involve painstaking detail and several different people. Timing seemed to be of the essence too.

'What the hell was all that about?' MacBrayne asked when Jacko had finally finished. 'Sounded like you were organising a conference over the phone.'

'Something like that. Just getting a few folk together for Charles Wainwright's address tomorrow evening. Should be worth attending. Show starts at 6 pm,' he added with a broad smile, 'you should make sure you all come along'.

'You're not organising a demo are you?' MacBrayne asked in a horrified way. 'It would only get his back up.'

'For God's sake, Duncan, do I look like the sort of person who'd stand holding a placard and chanting?'

MacBrayne glanced at him with suspicion but decided not to say anything further.

They eventually reached London and drove slowly down Pennsylvania Gardens until they reached no 27. It was a large detached Victorian building on two floors with some dormer windows set in the roof. Brick-built and in need of some attention, it wasn't particularly inspiring to look at, but it would probably fetch well into seven figures at today's prices. It was the sort of house ripe for conversion into flats or student bedsits like most of the others in the road. MacBrayne pulled up on double yellow lines just out of sight of its windows to get a better feel for the place. They stayed there for about half an hour watching pedestrians of various ages and sizes, cars, comings and goings, deliveries, and a drunk who dragged himself along the wall next to them.

'Interesting sort of place,' MacBrayne commented.

'Can't be many better places to be anonymous, can there?' Jacko pointed out. 'Most of the houses are in flats, there's a transient tenant population – mostly students of all different races and colours – and no-one talks to anyone else.'

The house had a small walled garden that backed up to the rear garden of a similar house on the parallel street behind. The wall was well over six feet tall and the only point of entry to number 27 seemed to be on the road frontage via a pair of large metal gates with gilded spikes on the top, that were locked shut. Jacko suggested they drove down the parallel road behind to see it from the back. As luck would have it, the house immediately behind was being gutted – the inside was being hacked out and dumped in skips, and what was left of the garden was cluttered with builders' vans, piles of sand, palettes of cement bags and a Portaloo. An enclosed plastic chute was attached to the upstairs and there were periodic roars as debris dumped in at the top came crashing down into the skip at the bottom. One or two workmen were meandering about carrying timbers down the steps. MacBrayne parked the car outside.

'Come on,' he said, 'there's fluorescent waistcoats and hard hats in the boot, get kitted up and we'll go in.' Puzzled, Jacko duly obliged while MacBrayne picked up a clipboard and binoculars. Together they marched into the garden.

'Council,' MacBrayne said loudly to the first workman he came across, 'Gaffer here, is he?' The workman mumbled something and pointed up to the house.

'Not to worry,' said MacBrayne, trying to make his voice heard above the din of rubbish sliding through the chute, 'It's not important, we'll see him on the way out, we're round the back.' The man made some vague gesture of acknowledgement, then concentrated on rolling up a cigarette.

'Look,' MacBrayne commented as they went round the rear, 'that's a stroke of luck – all the back windows here are boarded up. None of the builders can see us.'

They went over to the wall that separated them from the Wainwrights' garden, weaving their way through an obstacle course of rubble, rotting wooden sheeting and tall weeds. It was impossible to see over the wall without standing on something. MacBrayne caught sight of an old garden roller lying rusting under a tree, checked its stability, then balanced on it precariously while Jacko kept an eye out. From that relatively elevated position the Wainwrights' garden seemed pretty much unkempt, although some efforts had been made to mow the grass into a semi-presentable lawn. The house had a side door, not a rear door, and a pair of French windows that opened on to a weed-ridden flagged terrace. MacBrayne noted some movement in one of the ground floor windows and pulled out the binoculars. Just then Jacko whistled as a workman appeared down the side of the house. MacBrayne moved down to the ground, turned around and scanned the roof of the gutted house with the binoculars. 'The end ridge tiles look fine,' he shouted to Jacko, 'but make a note of the embossed iron guttering terminals.'

The workman gave a brief wave of acknowledgement then proceeded unashamedly to unzip his overalls and urinate in the flowerbed before returning back round the side.

They waited until he'd gone then Jacko climbed on to the roller, balancing with manifestly less confidence than MacBrayne, steadying himself on the tree trunk with one hand and holding the binoculars with the other.

'Anything to add?' MacBrayne asked, 'Other than sea-sickness that is?'

'Ha ha, very funny. Let's see how much of a mountain goat you are at my age. Anyway, it's got a cellar.'

'Has it? How can you tell?'

'There's a coal chute by the back door. Here, have a look.'

Jacko happily descended to ground level and passed over the binoculars to MacBrayne, who resumed his position on the roller.

'So there is,' he said with some surprise, having finally focused the binoculars. He was about to descend when two women emerged through the door next to the chute.

'There's two people there' he whispered to Jacko, keeping as low as he could on the roller. 'Christ, one of them's the wizened old bag from the manor. That fits, no reason why she shouldn't be here, I suppose. Don't know the other one though, younger. Not difficult that though, is it? They're hanging out washing or something. You take a look.'

They changed places. Jacko didn't need the binoculars to see the women, or to recognise both of them.

CHAPTER 29

The town hall was unusually busy in the lead up to an evening of political speeches. Like many town halls it was a tall, impressive neo-classical building housing a large council chamber which could be readily converted into a meeting hall. For this occasion the seating arrangements had been carefully designed in an arc of individual chairs set in rows to give a capacity of about three hundred. Normally this would have been greater, but such was the public and media interest in Charles Wainwright's appointment that space at the back had been made to accommodate cameras and journalists. All the main newspapers were provided with dedicated seating, and the number of satellite vans parked outside and the thick black cables lining the floor against the walls indicated a high degree of national TV coverage. The arcs of seating focused on a stage more frequently used for local drama and the occasional concert, but today surmounted only by a single oak lectern. Behind the stage was a back-projected screen on which images could be presented.

The evening had been long planned by the local mayor. It was the annual opportunity for the main political parties to voice their local views and policies, and was traditionally a lively event that involved much heckling. Despite objections from the other speakers, Wainwright insisted on speaking last in the programme, although he reluctantly agreed to the same twenty-minute limit as the others. By 5.45 pm the room was already full, standing being permitted at the back and down the side aisles. As 6 pm approached a line of distinguished-looking gentry arrived from a side door and took up a row of reserved seats at the front. It was difficult to make out who they were. There was an elderly man in a grey suit with a stick and a moustache that Jacko took to be Sir James and, among the others, a tall well-dressed man with greying hair that Jacko recognised but couldn't place. It was only later that he remembered it was the same person who'd been having the birthday party at the Pear Tree – the chief constable.

Using what little influence he had, Jacko had arranged reserved seating for Flett, MacBrayne and Jennie at the end of one of the rear rows. The two Scots were sitting looking uncomfortable with the potential boredom, while Jennie scrutinised the guests with interest. Moving across to them, he apologised that he needed to sit somewhere else. MacBrayne looked at him suspiciously but said nothing. Jennie, who was quite enjoying the event, reminded him not to run off after the meeting. They were scheduled to go to Toller's house once it was dark so that she could take a photo with her selfie stick under his garage door. Lazenby was supposed to have gone with her but his wife was in labour and Jacko had been duly volunteered.

Jacko moved away to his seat, the light dimmed insignificantly, and the mayor, weighed down with mayoral chains of office, ascended the podium to half-hearted clapping. His introductory speech was unmemorable – very much a cut-and-paste job, as relevant or irrelevant to this assembly as to a convention of nuns, a rugby club dinner, or the local school's Christmas party. It mentioned the history of the town, a couple of anecdotes about well-known local figures, how important the community was, what his wife had cooked him for dinner, and how much he was looking forward to this evening's speeches. As required, he pointed out the fire exits and the location of the toilets before requesting that each speaker please adhere to the allotted time of twenty minutes plus ten minutes allocated for questions. His exit from the stage was marked by the same feeble applause that greeted his entry.

Jacko sat and fiddled with his phone during the first three speakers: a timid lady from the Green Party who knew her stuff but had no charisma; a bullish UKIP candidate who had plenty of charisma but who didn't seem to know anything, and finally the Labour candidate whose views on hunting abolition and affordable housing in rural areas received only muted support from the audience. It was that sort of constituency.

The most applause was reserved for the Rt. Hon. Charles Wainwright MP, newly appointed Minister for Local Affairs, the final speaker. He took the rostrum with the Tory logo on the screen behind him, arms aloft, smiling, absorbing the warmth of the audience in pure theatrical style, and at ease with the ordeal of public speaking. Jacko was disgusted to see several members of the audience giving him a standing ovation, including the diminutive figure of Superintendent Roberts at the far end of the room.

Wainwright started his speech in traditional fashion, thanking the mayor for inviting him, his Tory agent, his long-suffering wife, and so on, then launched into a series of local anecdotes which Jacko didn't find especially funny but which had the assembly roaring with laughter. Got to hand it to him, Jacko thought, he's a master at massaging an audience, and his comic timing was impeccable. But Wainwright was clearly less competent on the minutiae of the party's dogma – he knew the general elements of policy, but only those which immediately affected him. He was wholly out of touch with anyone who didn't share either his wealth or his lifestyle, disguising his lack of understanding through a combination of showmanship and bravado.

The main elements of his speech had been written for him, and he delivered them with aplomb and oratorical intonation. Standing there immaculate in his pin stripes, in what little limelight the town hall could muster, and with flashbulbs continually lighting him up, he cut the figure he intended to cut – that of a senior political statesman, a man near the very top of the political ladder. His new portfolio gave him a wide remit, including local authority spending, care in the community, and the local settlement of refugee quotas from the Middle East. It was all spoken with conviction and authority, although as Jacko and many others knew, beneath his outer cosmetic crust of sincerity beat the selfish heart of an ignorant self-serving bastard who couldn't care a shit about anyone other than himself.

The speech ended and the attempts of the mayor to conclude the proceedings were drowned out by applause from a large proportion, but certainly not all, of the audience. Jacko saw that Roberts was on his feet again, as was the CC, clapping sycophantically. The noise eventually died away as the mayor held up his hands for silence. But before he could speak, Wainwright whispered in his ear, 'Think I've over-run a little, Alec, not really time for questions, I think.' It was his usual ploy to avoid having to face un-briefed issues that might show him up. But the mayor was wise to it.

'Good heavens, no, Charles. Have to be democratic. The others have faced questions, and so you must.'

'But I really feel…'

His objections fell on deaf ears as the mayor walked to the microphone and asked if anyone had anything they'd like to ask. Several arms were held aloft, some more timidly than others. The mayor picked out one, not entirely at random it seemed later. It was Mark from the excavation. He stood up and asked a simple question about the party's views on immigration. Flett, MacBrayne and Jennie all recognised him from the excavations and looked at each other.

'I had a feeling Jacko was up to something,' MacBrayne whispered, 'he's been very secretive about tonight.'

Wainwright took comfort and relief from the simple question Mark had asked and rattled off the party line about welcoming fellow beings from other cultures, ending with a benign smile.

'But that's significantly different from your own attitude, isn't it, Mr Wainwright?' Mark pointed out.

Wainwright wasn't expecting a follow-up question and paused for thought. Unbeknown to him, the screen behind suddenly filled with an image of the MP himself on horseback talking to the camera. A hush fell across the room. The film was a bit grainy and lopsided, and the sound a bit husky, but there was no doubt who it was on the horse, and there was no doubt what he was saying either. Wainwright turned, curious to see what the audience was looking at, then went noticeably white as he heard his own voice through the speaker system.

'I've learned to distrust uninvited strangers – travellers, gypsies, immigrants – call them what you will – in any shape or colour, mostly criminals and liars in my book. There are far too many undesirables around these days, whites as well as blacks, trying to change things, out for themselves. No we don't need them.'

The room fell completely silent as people looked at each other with a mixture of horror, curiosity and disbelief. At the rear of the hall the media pack was suddenly jerked out of lethargy – cameras were set in motion, reporters stood up to get a better view and mobile phones were pulled out.

Wainwright was horror-struck, 'Good God, where did this come from,' he asked the mayor, and waved to his two aides by the door who were immediately dispatched to turn off the projector. No chance, thought Jacko. Apart from the door being secure, it was guarded by some of Mark's friends from his boxing club. The room began to buzz with excitement. Wainwright was beside himself, desperately attempting to extricate his political career.

'This is just some form of hoax,' he announced unconvincingly and in a quaking voice to the audience. 'There'll be no further questions, thank you.'

'Oh yes there will,' interrupted the mayor, who Jacko was pleased to see had come into his own. 'The other speakers all obliged, and you must too, even if you don't like the questions. It's only fair and proper.'

By this time a distraught CC had caught the eye of Roberts, who was dumbstruck in his seat, and beckoned to him to do something. Roberts in turn had seen Flett and ran up the side aisle to him, crouching as he ran and looking ridiculous in the process.

'Alastair,' he gasped, out of breath from running bent double, 'for goodness' sake you must do something.'

'Like what, sir?' Flett asked. 'If you want me to arrest someone, who do we arrest and on what grounds? No particular offence has been committed, has it? Although I suppose I could arrest the MP for inciting racism…'

Any answer that Roberts might have liked to give was overtaken by the mayor.

'Another question, perhaps?' he asked to the audience, who were now beginning to realise that they were witnessing an historic moment in national politics. Again hands were raised, and again he selected one, not entirely at random. It was Jacko's friend Alison from the planning department.

'Sir,' she said, 'I'm a council employee, and you are now Minister for Local Affairs. Don't you think you should have more faith in people like me who work in local authority matters?'

But before Wainwright could bring himself to reassure her, the screen behind him flared into life. There he was on the horse again spouting his opinions.

'*I think I have a better understanding of these things than those arseholes in the county planning department. They're just paper pushers. I wouldn't trust a local authority worker to tie my shoelaces.*'

'Very interesting,' commented the mayor dryly while Wainwright was frantically signalling to his aides, the chief constable, his aged father, or indeed anyone who might pull him out of this pit. By this time there was intense media activity at the back: newspaper reporters scribbled away simultaneously trying to hold tape recorders aloft; the large TV cameras were whirring on their tripods while their news reporters were phoning London on their mobiles, and shoulder-held cameras, still running, were being carried down the aisles with men trailing cables behind anxious to get closer, all amid incessant salvos of flashlights. The audience was a sea of movement with heads turned in conversation. People were stamping their feet on the ground to a chorus of 'shame, shame'.

'One final question?' the mayor asked of the audience over the din, again selecting a particular attendee, this time an elderly lady wearing a hat who MacBrayne and Jennie immediately recognised as Mrs Jefferson.

'What do you propose to do for the old folk?' she asked loudly to choruses of 'yes, yes, what about the old folk?' from the audience. The room eventually hushed and the cameras focused.

'Er, well, our party policy has always been one of ensuring peace of mind and security in old age,' he said trying to compose himself, 'I am a firm believer in this and...'

'You're a lying bastard,' the old lady shouted back before he could finish as, on cue, the screen lit up again and, once more, Wainwright could be seen arrogantly sitting astride his horse. He lowered his head to the camera and the room suddenly fell silent to hear what further bigotry would be revealed. Mrs Jefferson's question was clearly and unequivocally answered.

'As far as I'm concerned, anyone over the age of seventy's a waste of space and should be put down. You do-gooders are all the same – socialists, conservationists, environmentalists, whatever you call yourselves. Why don't you just mind your own business and bugger off?'

At that point pandemonium broke out: Wainwright made for the door, lashing out at cameramen and reporters who got in his way, the audience stood up shouting and jeering, throwing anything they could at the platform while the mayor vainly attempted to restore calm by waving his arms about. In the melee chairs were knocked over, minor struggles took place between warring political factions, and the VIPs on the front row slipped out through a door behind the platform amid a barrage of missiles. Meanwhile the media coverage continued, the cameras still whirred and at least one news reporter was broadcasting live. MacBrayne and Jennie were stunned. Flett leaned across to them.

'Glad I came. Best entertainment I've had for years.'

CHAPTER 30

After the meeting Jennie and Jacko drove to Middle Belford to take a quiet look at Toller's garage, Jacko flushed with satisfaction, Jennie still curious as to how he'd managed to pull off such a stunt. He explained about his earlier meeting with Wainwright when he was visiting Seth, how he'd managed to set his mobile into video mode without it being noticed, and how he'd just held the mobile in approximately the right direction during their exchanges. The fact that his friends, and indeed Mrs Jefferson who he'd only met recently, were happy to ask the questions, and that the mayor had agreed to choose them, was entirely down to their political leanings and their common hatred of Wainwright himself. The same applied to the running of the film on the screen and the technicians he knew. It was all now on YouTube so that the whole world could see what an arrogant sod the man was.

'I couldn't believe how well the images turned out once I'd taken them,' he said gleefully as they turned off the main road towards the village. 'Thought I'd sit on them for a while in case they ever became useful.'

'Well, I reckon you've done a pretty good hatchet job on his political career. He's now a complete embarrassment to the PM – he'll have to go, no two ways about it.' She switched on the car radio where political correspondents on every station were saying the same – Wainwright's position was untenable.

They neared Toller's house. Jennie pulled up around the corner and turned off the car lights. 'By the way,' she said, 'someone thought Toller had an army background, so Flett's been contacting some of his military chums. If there's anything relevant he'll text us.' She pulled out her selfie-stick and waved it about. 'This should do the trick if what MacBrayne says about the garage door is right. I'll leave my work mobile with you and use my own phone, it's thinner. Wait here until I get back. And don't bloody well move.' With that she slipped out of the car and vanished into the dark.

Jacko sat pondering on the evening's events, periodically checking his watch. Jennie had only been gone a few minutes, but it seemed longer. The security lights hadn't been activated otherwise he'd have seen the glow over the hedge at the far end of the road. He switched on the radio and chuckled to himself as he heard a Tory party spokesperson saying that Mr Wainwright's views were his own and not those of the party. The PM, it seemed, was not making any comment at this stage but would be making a statement in the morning. And Mr Wainwright, unsurprisingly, was unavailable for comment, although the local Conservative branch had called an emergency meeting for tomorrow. He looked at his watch again. Ten minutes had passed, she should be back at any moment. He switched the radio off and stared blankly out of the window.

After she'd been absent for over twenty minutes he decided there was no alternative other than going to see if she'd encountered a problem. He left the car, walked slowly to the corner and saw immediately that Toller's BMW was no longer on the drive. Toller must be out, he thought, his immediate conclusion being that Jennie must have taken the opportunity to investigate further, even get inside the house if she could find a way in. Feeling slightly easier he went back to the car and made himself comfortable. A further twenty minutes passed and she'd still not returned. Something must be wrong. He waited a little longer then left the car, leaving the keys under the foot-mat on the driver's side in case she came back. Not being sure what to do with her work phone, he checked it was on and shoved it under some bags and boxes in the boot, then made his way towards the house. Had he waited another couple of minutes he would have heard the ping of a text message from Flett on Jennie's phone. And had he read it, he would have seen that it said, '*Toller has military background. Electronics and explosives expert. Be careful.*' But Jacko hadn't heard it, hadn't read it, and was instead standing behind the hedge at the top of Toller's driveway.

The house was in darkness, lit only by the glow of a distant lamp-post further down the road. It was enough to make him vaguely visible from the house if he went down the driveway, even if he kept close to the hedge. Was it worth the risk? Jennie must have done exactly that, but where was she? He pulled back. Toller's house was the end of a line of houses with a field on one side which bordered the rear garden as well. He'd have a look there. There might be a less obtrusive way in. He climbed clumsily over a field gate near where the car was parked and walked along inside the hedge line. Whatever had been growing there had been harvested leaving a hard-packed stubble, much easier to walk along than the mud he remembered in the field by the Pear Tree. Toller's house was visible as a silhouette and Jacko followed the hedge looking for a suitable gap. It was of thick hawthorn, far too prickly to venture through, and besides Toller had a low panelled wooden fence erected inside it. He peeked over – there was still no sign of life, nor even a light, from the house, and certainly no sign of Jennie. It was totally quiet.

Worried, he made his way, part-stooping, around to the back where the hedge planting seemed to have been more sporadic, leaving a number of wider spaces near the ground. There was no wooden fence on the inside either. He chose the gap he thought was widest and crawled on his hands and knees through the muddy undergrowth, wincing as the thorns scratched his face and became caught on his clothes, until he found himself in Toller's rear garden. From what he could see it was just like the front garden – lawned, neatly flower-bordered and entirely unimaginative.

By creeping closer to the house he could just make out a thin line of light against the edge of the curtains in one of the downstairs rooms. Keeping to the side of the garden so as not to break open ground, he made his way gingerly to the house wall. He reached the window unhindered, but there was nothing to be seen other than a vertical slice of interior wall, no sounds either. Now what? The best thing to do was to go back to the car, report this all this to Flett or MacBrayne and wait for back-up. Content with his plan he slipped back round the side of the house where a narrow path led between the hedge and the garage and then out to the front drive. He could sidle his way up the drive keeping to the hedge line and be out in the road in no time. He crept to the end of the path and reached the front of the house. It was still completely quiet. Not a whisper. He looked round the front of the garage to check all was clear, and to his utter astonishment saw a car in the driveway. How the hell did that get there? He'd not heard anything. It wasn't Toller's BMW, it was a Focus. Christ, it was their Focus! It was the one they'd driven in, the one they'd parked further down the road – he recognised the number plate. Why had Jennie gone back and driven it down there? He stood desperately trying to sort it out in his mind when he felt a sudden sharp pain at the back of his head. He fell forward, and everything went black.

* * *

It was after ten and Flett was working late in the office. He was worried. Contacting the military had been a long shot and he didn't like what he'd been told. Toller had been an officer, not particularly high profile, but he'd spent fifteen years in Northern Ireland and another five years in North Africa, initially on the ground in de-mining programmes and later in a management capacity. According to his commanding officer, what Henry Toller didn't understand about explosives and bomb-making wasn't worth knowing. He had experience in counter-terrorism, in improvised explosive devices (IEDs), and he knew where to source bomb-making materials and detonators outside the official markets. He was discharged about ten years ago, not entirely dishonourably, but with a sufficiently dark cloud hanging over him to make him unemployable. He was exactly the sort of person Flett didn't want to have to deal with. That said, it put the explosion in the Pear Tree in a new perspective and it added to his growing concerns about Jacko and Jennie making a covert visit to the man's house. Neither of them had phoned in, answered calls or sent texts. They should have been back well before now.

He picked up the phone and rang Superintendent Roberts at home, not something he normally did, but now it was time for Roberts to earn his salary. His wife picked up the phone and did her best to defer any conversation with her husband until the morning but finally, at Flett's insistence, agreed to get him. Flett could hear whispered recriminations and a series of muffled noises in the background resulting from a hand being held over the receiver while a domestic argument took place. Eventually the line cleared.

'I hope this is important, Alastair,' came the voice. 'Do you realise the time? Some of us are about to go to bed.'

'And some of us are still in the office, sir,' Flett retorted. 'I don't want to waste your time, sir, but I need to inform you that I've authorised an armed response unit. I thought you'd want to be kept in the picture.'

'Armed response. Good heavens!' Roberts appeared thoroughly shocked. 'We'll need to discuss the need for this in detail tomorrow morning. There are serious implications, you know.'

'I can't wait until the morning. I need armed officers now,' Flett said, almost barking down the phone. 'I have an officer at a high level of risk. You'll just have to take my word for it.'

'Steady on, Alastair. Do calm down. This is ridiculous.'

'Ridiculous my arse!' Flett bellowed, then gave himself a few moments to compose himself. 'This is important, sir,' he said quietly. 'I think you should be seen to be part of the operation.' He put the phone down.

* * *

Jacko came around. He didn't know when, and he didn't know where he was. All that he knew was that his head throbbed and there was a wet patch, blood, at the base of his skull and down his neck. It was dark and someone was kicking him. It took him a while to realise there was a voice associated with the kicking.

'Wake up. For fuck's sake wake up,' it said. It took him a while to work out it was Jennie's voice. He realised, as his eyes began to focus through the pain, that he was sitting in a chair and that there was another person sitting on a chair next to him. His hands were tied together behind the back of the chair with what felt like cable ties. His feet were fastened the same way, but he could swing them, and it was Jennie's swinging legs from the next chair that were gently kicking him.

'Where are we?' was all he could think to say, his head pounding and the sides of his face still stinging from crawling through the hawthorn hedge.

'Somewhere in Toller's house,' came the whispered reply. 'Dining room, I think. Can't remember. Got hit on the head near the garage door.'

'They must have been waiting for us,' he whispered. The pain from the back of his head seemed to have moved to the front. It hung there like a huge weight thumping from side to side.

'For Christ's sake stay awake. We need to get out of here. Jacko, come on,' she kicked him again.

'Cable ties,' he murmured. 'Can't get free. Hands and feet.'

'Just try Jacko, wiggle your feet, see if you can get a shoe off or something.'

There was the sound of approaching footsteps and two voices, one Jacko thought sounded remarkably like the vicar, the other was presumably Toller. The door opened, the light was switched on and Jacko blinked trying to see where he was. It looked like a small dining room, sparsely furnished with a central table and chairs.

'Dining room,' he muttered before shutting his eyes to keep out the light. Squinting, he saw what he took to be the figure of Toller standing by the open door with a roll of gaffer tape in one hand. In the other he had a handgun held by the barrel. Jacko looked aghast as Toller moved over to Jennie and roughly gagged her, ignoring her shouts and squeals, binding her mouth with the tape, wrapping it around her head until she groaned, spluttered and then went silent. Jacko could see that her eyes were still open wide, burning with anger. Before Toller had finished, she moved her legs slightly to one side, shifted her weight and brought up both feet hard into his stomach as he leaned over her. He gasped, dropped the tape and fell to his knees at which point she kicked him hard in the chin, to the cracking noise of shattering teeth. Toller rolled over, blood seeping from his mouth and shouting obscenities. He pulled himself to his feet and lashed Jennie across the face with the butt of the gun. Blood spattered across the room and dripped down her face.

'Bastard,' yelled Jacko, now fully aware of what was happening. 'Cowardly fucking bastard.'

Toller heaved himself across, cursing loudly, and aimed a kick at Jacko, catching him squarely on his right knee cap. Jacko shrieked in pain, his chair overbalanced and he crashed to the floor on his side. Toller leered at him and kicked him hard in the groin, then again, as Jacko yelled in agony.

'Good God Henry, for goodness' sake stop it,' came the Rev Rogers' barely controlled quaking voice from the door. 'This isn't necessary. There's no need to torture them first. Just gag them and let's get on with it. I really don't want to be party to this.'

Toller picked up the roll of tape and knelt down to gag Jacko, deliberately kneeing him in the face as he did so, binding him as tightly as he could to silence his groans and gasps. He then went over behind Jennie whose head was hanging to one side, eyes shut, blood streaming from her nose, and unfastened her from the chair while keeping her wrists still tied together. He did the same to Jacko.

'Car ready?' he snapped.

'It's outside the door,' Rogers muttered pathetically. 'All the security lights are off. I'll go and check for passers-by at the top of the drive.' He hurried out, happy to be in the fresh air, away from it all.

'Good of you to leave the keys so conveniently accessible,' Toller said smarmily as the two of them lay in the hallway. Nice car too, pity to have to write it off.'

Toller waited for the all clear signal from Rogers then dragged Jennie out, hoisted her against the car, and called Rogers down. Together they bundled her into the back seat, then did the same with Jacko and shut the doors. Both men were out of breath.

'First, clear up any mess,' Toller ordered and waited while Rogers made to go inside. 'Use bleach if there's any blood,' he hissed after him, 'I need to get this device secured to the car. And don't piss about, we haven't got long.' He was about to enter the garage to fetch some tools when Jacko's phone rang from inside the car.

'I thought I told you to take the phones off both of them!' Toller shouted angrily to Rogers. He opened the rear door and searched through Jacko's clothes until he found the phone and threw it to Rogers. 'Take out the SIM and the batteries,' he ordered, 'then destroy the whole lot completely so they can't be used for tracking.'

* * *

Flett was in a darkened police HQ looking at a room full of files, boxes and empty chairs. Jennie still hadn't rung in. Could just be she forgot, he thought, but that wasn't like her, and this new information on Toller was worrying. Jacko should have been waiting in the car, even if she'd met a problem. He'd rung him too but got no reply. MacBrayne should soon be up from London, Roberts was supposedly on his way in, and the armed officers were kitting themselves out downstairs. He didn't require Roberts' authorisation for firearms, but he needed to cover his back by keeping him in the picture. And he wanted Roberts operationally involved for once. He'd just unfolded a large-scale map of the area around Toller's house when MacBrayne emerged out of the darkened corridor.

'Came as soon as I could, boss.'

'Good. Get in touch with command centre,' Flett said with urgency in his voice, 'and see if they can track mobile phones – Jacko's and Jennie's, you've got their numbers.'

MacBrayne vanished into the outer office and, after a series of calls, shouted across, still holding the phone to his ear. 'They can, but not precisely, they're on the job now.' There was a pause. 'Sounds like Jacko's is off, but Jennie's is giving out a GPS signal.' Another pause. 'They've placed it in the Middle Belford area – it's stationary.'

'Right,' said Flett decisively, 'Let's get the circus out there fast, but discretely. Dunc, you maintain contact with comms on your radio, I'll co-ordinate with armed response and get as much back-up as we can. My car, pronto.'

The hastily gathered convoy of five vehicles led by Flett was about to leave HQ when Roberts' shiny Range Rover Evoque slid into the car park and Roberts emerged, in a measured and authoritative manner gesturing the vehicles to stop.

'Shit,' was Flett's immediate response before winding down his driver's window. 'Get in the back, quick, sir.'

Roberts bent down to speak to Flett through the opened window and MacBrayne, seeing a potential problem unfolding, leapt out of the car, opened the rear door and assisted the Superintendent's entry assertively into the back seat.

'Sorry about that, sir,' MacBrayne muttered, almost lying on top of him as Flett roared off, 'bit of a hurry here, I'm afraid.'

'This is unforgivable, Alastair,' Roberts complained loudly after pushing MacBrayne away and dusting down his suit. 'You better have a good explanation for all this nonsense. You're acting like cowboys.'

MacBrayne's radio crackled before Roberts could continue. 'Car's on the move, sir. It's going north-east, country roads by the sound of it,' he said, looking at the map which he unfolded, partly covering the Superintendent. 'It's just countryside. If it was going towards the motorway or to any of the towns it wouldn't take that route.'

Roberts' peered over the map, his eyes following MacBrayne's finger. 'Ah, the escarpment road,' he said, 'you get fine views from there – it's the highest point around here – a splendid panorama of the countryside. I used to walk up there, you know.'

'Roughly how far are we away?' Flett asked, his brain whirring.

'Mmm, about ten minutes,' MacBrayne suggested.

'Why, if they were in the car and not going to a town or to a major motorway, would Jennie be driving into the middle of nowhere instead of going home?'

'Maybe she wasn't driving, boss.'

'But let's say Toller was driving, then why would he take the car off into the countryside?' There was an uneasy silence.

'Disposal,' they both said almost simultaneously.

Roberts was lost in this exchange and was about to say something when MacBrayne's radio bleeped again. 'Car's stopped,' he said. 'As far as they can tell it's still on a road but can't give us a precise location.'

'Okay, sir,' Flett said, turning to Roberts. 'You seem to know this escarpment, what's up there?' he asked. 'Is it a beauty spot or what?'

'Well since you ask, it's really no more than a pleasant drive along through the woods. There's nowhere to stop really other than a couple of lay-bys for the view. One's on a sharp bend. Damn silly place to put one if you ask me. There's a sheer drop of about fifty metres right on the edge. Splendid views though.' He pointed to it on the map.

'What d'you reckon, Dunc?' Flett asked.

'No other obvious option. Looks like there's another lay-by before we get there, but it's fairly open. No trees on this map. Has to be the one with the sheer drop then.'

* * *

Henry Toller pulled his dark blue BMW into a lay-by in the darkness. Rogers had followed him up the steep hill in the Focus and stopped behind him. He had little idea where he was other than being high up. The wind was blowing hard.

Toller got out and came over. 'This is the place,' he said as he looked at Rogers through the open window. 'There's bugger all traffic this time of night. But the danger of the bend is for cars coming the other way – not this way.' He went over to the rickety wooden fence at the edge of the lay-by, kicked part of it down and went back to the car to the anguished Rogers. 'Ha, it's almost a sheer drop,' he said, pleased with himself. 'We'll drive on, turn around, then you steer back towards the gap. And don't forget to stop at the edge,' he joked. 'I'll activate the device once you're there, we'll push the car through the gap, then get the hell out of here. There'll have been a terrible accident.' He smiled at an uncomfortable Rogers and genuflected sarcastically. 'Too late to wimp out now, my friend. Better start praying for a bit of salvation.'

* * *

MacBrayne's radio bleeped again. 'Car's moved off, boss, north-east still, probably on the same road. Not much more than five minutes away.

'Okay, alert the armed unit behind us. Tell 'em to get on stand-by for a starburst as soon as we stop.'

'What in God's name's a starburst?' asked Roberts feeling completely superfluous.

They ignored him as the convoy passed an empty lay-by. 'Not this, it's the next one,' MacBrayne said. 'Can't be far off now.'

His radio crackled. 'Car's turned boss. It's coming back towards us.'

'Shit, shit. Keep in contact. Where's the lay-by? How far?'

'Couple of minutes.' MacBrayne had his radio to his ear waiting for any news. 'Car's stopped again, boss. Must be facing this way.'

Flett screeched to a halt, much to the consternation of the following vehicles, leapt out and gave revised instructions to the drivers.

* * *

Rogers had turned the car around, returned to the lay-by and parked with the nose pointing to the broken fence. Toller's BMW was nearby.

'Right,' he shouted across to Rogers, 'we need to get the woman into the driver's seat and the bloke into the passenger seat, we'll cable tie her to the steering wheel, him to the inside door handle. The plastic ties won't survive the explosion and the fire that follows, nor will the gaffer tape. To any accident investigator, she'll have been driving too fast, didn't take the corner properly, went through the fence and the car exploded on impact at the bottom. Terrible tragedy, but these things happen.' He smiled at Rogers' ashen face. 'Not getting cold feet, are we?'

Between them they hoisted Jennie, now conscious and wriggling, into the driver's seat, and Jacko into the passenger seat, still desperately trying to free himself. Rogers fastened them in, fumbling with the pack of cable ties and dropping several on the floor, while Toller activated a small device attached to the front grill of the Focus.

'Nearly done,' Toller shouted. 'It's timed to detonate in three minutes, ideally when the car hits the bottom. Get round the back and start to push, I'll take off the handbrake and steer it through the gap over the edge.'

Rogers reluctantly went to the back of the car and started to push but with minimal impact.

'Harder for fuck's sake,' shouted Toller. 'Come on, put your back into it, it's barely moving.' He looked at his watch anxiously.

Jacko's and Jennie's eyes were wild. Wriggling was doing no good, but they both struggled rather than let the end come peacefully.

'Harder, for Christ's sake!' Toller yelled.

Rogers was red-faced with effort. 'I don't think I've the strength,' he moaned. 'Can't push any harder.'

Toller pulled the handbrake on and rushed around to the back, 'Grab the wheel, take the brake off and steer, for Christ's sake. I'll push.' He was becoming frantic. 'We're running out of time.'

Rogers put one foot on the brake pedal through the open driver's door, trying to avoid Jennie's fiercely kicking feet and shouting with pain as she landed kick after kick on his shin.

'Now,' yelled Toller as he heaved his weight against the car's hatchback, 'take the handbrake off,' but just as he did so there was a roar of engines, the lay-by was lit up by searchlights, and a group of weapon-carrying officers wearing body armour sprang from a minibus scattering in a starburst in all directions, taking up positions surrounding the Focus.

JOHN HUNTER

'Police. We're armed,' shouted a voice through a loudspeaker. 'Put your hands above your heads and move away from the car.'

Rogers froze. Toller shielded his eyes from the glare. He couldn't see how many were out there, or even if they were armed. Could have been a trick. 'Take the fucking handbrake off,' he shouted at Rogers again, 'there's less than a minute left.'

'Move away from the car,' the voice shouted once more. Toller pulled out his handgun and rushed round to the driver's door, pushed a petrified Rogers out of the way, then leaned in and released the handbrake. The car began to roll forwards.

'Hold fire,' Flett shouted to the armed officers as, almost from nowhere, MacBrayne appeared and dashed towards the other side of the car, using it as a shield from Toller. He grabbed the door pillar with one arm to slow the car down, saw the cable ties and instantly fumbled in his pocket for the pen knife that he always carried. Distracted, Toller lashed out at him across the two frightened occupants, giving the opportunity for Flett to emerge out of the darkness on the other side and fling himself on to Toller's back, jamming them both against the open driver's door.

'Can't hold it, boss,' shouted MacBrayne as he slid alongside the moving vehicle, penknife in hand, sawing away at the tie holding Jacko to the door. Finally it gave, Jacko was free and MacBrayne pulled him out to the ground, feet still bound as the car began to pick up speed. He dived in to do the same for Jennie. Toller was wrestling with Flett, the pair of them half in, half out of the vehicle, Jennie kicking

329

out for all she was worth until MacBrayne, lying almost horizontally with his feet waving from the passenger door, cut her free and dragged her across and out of the passenger side as the car accelerated. 'Leave him, boss, get out,' he yelled as the car approached the edge. The armed officers were now running to try and hold it back, 'Get the hell out.'

Flett had Toller underneath him as they both struggled to get the upper hand. His rough Scottish upbringing served him well and a head butt into Toller's face sprayed the windscreen with drops of blood as Toller groaned and went limp underneath him.

'I'm taking you police bastards with me,' he said, with the best he could muster of a smirk.

'Oh no you're fucking not,' said Flett, noticing the cable ties that Rogers had dropped in the footwell.

'Get out boss!' shrieked MacBrayne. The armed officers had arrived and were doing their best to hold the car back, but the momentum was too great and the front wheels were inches off the edge.

Flett grabbed a cable tie and, with the deftness, precision and care of an experienced model-maker, fastened Toller's left wrist to the steering wheel, jerking it tight.

'Got you, you bastard,' he snarled, staring hard into Toller's face, gaining some satisfaction from the look of fear and terror in the man's eyes. A split second later Flett's feet were grabbed by fellow officers, dragging him out and face down to the ground as the car plunged over the edge. There was an uneasy silence which seemed to last an eternity followed by a fireball, a series of secondary explosions, then a hush broken only by the crackling of flames far below them.

CHAPTER 31

Flett, accompanied by Superintendent Roberts, sat in the hurriedly opened canteen at HQ mulling over the night's events. They were alone at the table: MacBrayne was busy elsewhere co-ordinating the day's paperwork, while Jacko and Jennie were being treated at the hospital at Banbury where they'd been taken from the scene by ambulance, but neither had serious injuries. Jennie was the worse of the two with a broken nose. Both were being checked over and patched up but they were insisting on returning as soon as possible to see the case through. The media had clocked that something big had happened but the story put out by the police media co-ordinator was that there'd been a serious traffic accident, which was why the road was closed temporarily. Toller was assumed dead and would no doubt be identified from his body parts later in the morning, but the Rev Rogers was in custody, feeling very sorry for himself and refusing to talk until a solicitor could be found.

Flett was tired, both physically and mentally, as well as bruised from being pulled from the car. He'd refused ambulance attention and now sat leaning on the plastic-topped table, his mind drifting into thoughts of packing the whole business in, mindlessly stirring his tea and fiddling with an undercooked bacon sandwich. He looked down at himself – his suit jacket was ripped and blood-stained, there were soil marks on his shirt and gravel tears on his trousers. By contrast, Roberts, sitting opposite, was unruffled, still immaculate in his suit, and droning on about reports and action logs.

'I have to say, Alastair, the bravery of both you and young MacBrayne was outstanding tonight. The manner in which you both selflessly risked your lives to rescue our colleagues was exemplary. What's more, your own personal efforts to pull Toller out of the car at the last minute, albeit unsuccessfully, and even though he was a criminal, was well above the call of duty.'

Flett looked at him curiously. If that's what Roberts wanted to believe, he thought, then he might as well keep it that way. The last thing he wanted was for Toller to survive – it was a better kind of justice than the courts or the liberal whitewash that Roberts could serve up. MacBrayne probably agreed with him but would never dare say so in today's climate of political correctness. He'd almost certainly seen what went on in the car, but he knew better than to say so.

'All in a day's work, sir,' Flett said, feigning brightness. 'But we do need to keep this under wraps, sir, even within the force, certainly until this manor job's done. I can't stress that enough. Can't afford even the tiniest leak outside this group. Information's been getting out somehow.'

'Oh absolutely,' Roberts agreed, half-distracted. He wasn't allowed bacon sandwiches at home and was enjoying wiping every last drop of bacon grease off his plate with his finger. 'That's clear. Have you any idea how the leaks are happening?'

'Toller, maybe? What with his background in electronics as well as explosives, he'd have the necessary know-how in phone tapping, computer hacking and so forth. Don't forget, he was waiting when Jacko and Jennie went to his house, and only a limited number of people knew the arrangements.' Flett pulled his chair closer. 'What's more, the security people now think that explosion at the Pear Tree had Toller's hallmark.'

'Goodness me. Well at least he's dead now.'

'He might be dead, sir, but I wouldn't like to draw a line under him just yet.' He fumbled in his briefcase and shoved a file across the table. 'I've just had these printed out – you should see them.'

Roberts spent a few minutes looking at the text, flicking through some pages, taking his time over others, then shut the file and stared at Flett with worry etched on his face. 'Good God,' he said, 'I see what you mean. This man's an animal. He's got an entire CV of latent booby traps and killing or maiming people.'

'Seems he got out of hand in the military and they gave him the boot. Oh yes, the bastard may be dead, but we've no idea what tricks he's left behind for us to find, do we?'

'Not quite sure what you mean, Alastair? What sort of tricks?'

'Booby traps, delayed explosives, you name it – he's done them all. He may have planted latent devices in his house timed to explode in days or even months, or triggered by movement when we search it – same in the manor, his car, even your car, sir, for that matter.'

Roberts took on the frightened rabbit look again, 'But I didn't even know the man.'

'I'm just making the point, sir,' Flett added, enjoying the Superintendent's discomfort. 'He's an utter bastard even when he's dead. We don't know what traps he's laid. Maybe when we interview Rogers we might learn a bit more.'

* * *

'But I have no solicitor,' Rogers squeaked.

'Listen,' MacBrayne said across the bare table in the equally bare interview room. 'This isn't about you, and the conversation's not being recorded. It's about other people and trying to be helpful. I can't make promises, but if you co-operate now it might be beneficial to you later.'

'I didn't do anything,' Rogers said pathetically. 'I've been a reluctant party in all of this. You have to believe me.'

MacBrayne ignored him. 'Tell me about Henry Toller.'

'He made me go along with it,' Rogers wittered, visibly shaking, 'I'd no choice. I'm not saying anything without my solicitor.'

MacBrayne sighed. 'This conversation isn't about you,' he repeated quietly, 'it's about Toller. We know you got dragged into it. Right now, we're not interested in what you did or didn't do. Tell me about Toller.'

There were a few moments silence. 'He killed old Seth Hetherington.' Rogers said bluntly, causing MacBrayne to sit up in his chair, and to startle Flett who was watching behind the one-way glass. 'I didn't know until afterwards. Hetherington wasn't a good man by any means, but he didn't deserve that.'

'Why did he kill him then?' asked MacBrayne.

'He saw too much of what was going on at the manor. Murdered him in the old stables.'

'What exactly was going on at the manor?'

Flett's ears pricked up behind the glass.

'I need my solicitor,' was the only response.

MacBrayne let it pass. 'We think Toller's going to kill other people too, probably with explosives and booby traps planted before he died.' Rogers looked up at the suggestion.

'They don't deserve to die either, do they?' MacBrayne pointed out and leaned back in his chair. 'Today,' he said sternly, 'officers will be searching the manor, its outhouses, sheds and its grounds. They're just doing their job. They're trying to make our community a better place. Many of them will have families, young children or aged parents. Think about it. If you can tell us something, in fact anything, about the danger they might be in, don't you think you have a duty to help prevent further tragedies?'

Rogers clasped his hands together on the table, not so much through prayer as through nervous tension. 'Henry was very risk-averse,' he said with a shaking voice, 'and very suspicious of people, even paranoid. Every time he had a "mission" as he called it, he'd set up a series of devices, usually in the workplace, houses or cars of whoever had commissioned him. No-one knew about them. You see he just didn't trust anyone. If the mission was successful he'd diffuse them afterwards. It was a sort of insurance in case he was double-crossed.' He paused, 'Or got killed,' he added.

'Any idea where he might have put devices in the manor?' MacBrayne asked him.

Rogers shook his head. 'I've given you all I know. I want my solicitor present now.'

MacBrayne decided he'd get no more out of him. 'You'll get him as soon as he arrives. Thank you for being helpful.' He signalled to the waiting uniformed officer that Rogers should be taken back to his cell.

CHAPTER 32

The teams were accustomed to lengthy waits and were in position around the manor at 5 am, settling down and suitably kitted out. Flett had men stationed around the perimeter, some inside the grounds out of CCTV range. Cars were positioned at discrete points in the village to follow any suspect vehicles, and both the force helicopter and the armed response unit were on stand-by. The weather was cold, although it wasn't raining, but there was little in the way of leaf cover and the gusting wind was gradually blowing off any leftovers in the branches. The manor was still in darkness.

They were told to expect anything, and to keep their eyes and communications open. Around 6.30 am they were rewarded. It was becoming light and the imposing splendour of the manor could be made out as a watery autumn sun slid up above the trees. A long wheelbase white transit van moved quietly up the drive, or as quietly as it could on the gravel surface. It turned around near the side door and reversed against the small porch where MacBrayne and others had encountered the obstreperous housekeeper. The driver opened both back doors to some half-hearted barking from the kennels, and lights appeared in the adjacent downstairs windows. There were the indecipherable sounds of voices, and some female shouting before the van doors were closed and the vehicle wound its way down the drive and towards the M40. As it passed through the village of Middle Belford it was picked up and followed by an unmarked police vehicle which kept its distance until the motorway. There the van turned south towards London and was picked up by another unmarked car.

Flett and MacBrayne sat in a Mondeo which was backed into a field track not far from the manor. At about 8 am MacBrayne received a message that the van had turned off the M40 and was heading for north London. So far so good. There were still no signs of life at the manor and the curtains remained drawn. A newspaper boy on a bike rode up the drive, deposited a *Daily Telegraph* in the letter box, and rode away again. The Wainwrights would soon be reading its main headline, *Shortest Ministerial Appointment on Record*, before throwing it in the bin. The headline in the *Guardian* would be more lascivious. At 8.25 am MacBrayne took a call to say that the van was safely inside 27 Pennsylvania Gardens with its rear doors open against the side door of the house. Just as he was about to motion to Flett to give the signal there was a commotion at the other end of the phone. 'Christ,' MacBrayne uttered in astonishment. 'Good God.' Flett looked at him. 'The arrogant bastards,' MacBrayne went on. 'Why didn't they tell us? Yes, I'll let the boss know.

We're going in now.' He switched the phone off and thrust it back on the dashboard with a loud, 'Shit.'

'What the hell's all that about?

'It's the DI running the Met operation in Pennsylvania Gardens, boss. Seems the intelligence services and the immigration bods knew the van was coming, lay in wait then jumped it inside the gates. A couple of dozen of them came over the wall at the back dressed as builders – place in lockdown. Shit, I can't believe it.'

Flett thumped the dashboard in frustration. 'Why didn't they bloody tell us, the tossers?'

MacBrayne went quiet. It dawned on him they must have been the so-called builders he and Jacko had met. No wonder the windows were boarded up at the back, they were probably filming through small holes they'd made. Must have thought he and Jacko were utter plonkers.

Flett grabbed his radio. 'We're going in,' he bellowed. The various units were all in place and responded instantly. MacBrayne started the car and swung the Mondeo out of the field gateway, its wheels spinning in the soil, and screeched down the road to the manor's driveway where the police blockade was moved to one side to let them through. They tore up the drive and skidded to a halt in the courtyard next to the Wainwrights' dark green Bentley parked in the corner. By that time the house was surrounded by officers. Flett, warrant in hand, strode up the steps and pounded with one gloved fist on the door, ringing the bell with the other. He repeated the operation twice more, on each occasion shouting, 'This is the police, open the door.' There was no response from inside. He nodded to the OSU officers behind him who, seconds later, took great delight in battering down the door with a steel ram to the loud splitting of timbers. The OSU team burst in with strict instructions to maintain control of the corridors and go no further.

'In here, in here,' came a stressed female voice from the inner depths of the building, and a door opened at the far end of the corridor revealing the outline of a well-dressed middle-aged woman clearly in a state of anxiety.

'It's Sir James,' she said with a mixture of anger and despair in seeing a line of officers dressed in body armour lined up along her polished parquet flooring. 'I think he's had a stroke.'

Flett strode down the corridor towards her. This was all he bloody well needed. If it was a ploy, it was an outrageous one; if it was genuine, the timing was monumentally ironic, so monumentally ironic in fact that it was verging on the comic. That said, the woman seemed genuinely upset and, from the haughtiness of her voice, he assumed her to be Mrs Charles Wainwright. Conscious of a potential trap and not trusting any of them an inch, he took the two nearest burly officers with him and followed her into the room. Sir James was lying across the sofa, clearly in a bad way. His face was ashen grey and he seemed unable of movement other than with his eyes. Charles Wainwright, obviously distressed, was leaning over him, trying to get a response. He turned to Flett.

'You caused this, you bastards. It's all your doing. I'll have you for this. You'll be directing traffic for the rest of your miserable career.'

Flett ignored him and quickly took stock of the situation. 'When did this happen?' he asked, feeling for Sir James' pulse.

'About five minutes ago with all that din and shouting outside.' Wainwright shouted. 'Are you bloody surprised – he's an old man.'

Flett phoned directly for the air ambulance – it was the quickest way of getting the paramedics out and there was plenty of space for the helicopter to land in the grounds. He put the phone down.

'I'm sorry, sir,' he said, 'but no matter how inconvenient this is, I have to serve this warrant to search the property.' He held out the paper to Wainwright who ignored it. Flett placed it on the table.

'Can't it bloody well wait?' Wainwright shouted. 'Can't you come another time? I thought you were coming tomorrow.' He checked himself quickly. 'Can't you see the situation we're in here?'

'Sorry, sir,' Flett said, noting the slip. 'We have to go ahead. I'd be grateful if the three of you could remain in this room.' He pointed to a large officer whose human features were mostly obscured by body armour, 'This officer will contact me if you need anything, and when the helicopter arrives.' He looked over at Sir James, whose features had now become drawn and his eye movement less rapid, then he left the room and drew his search officers together outside.

'Okay,' he said when they were all gathered, 'a man on every landing – MacBrayne's team can start searching the top floor, the OSU's the first floor, explosive dogs in first on both. Do a quick general search for now, we can do a more detailed one later. Don't open, lift or move anything without a dog sniffing it beforehand – not even the toilet flush – got it?' They all nodded enthusiastically, sick of hanging around.

'When you've done, do the ground floor together, its more complex. Let me know when you've finished. I don't want to start on the cellars until we've a copy of Jackson's ground plan to follow.'

He stood outside for a few minutes, hands in pockets, hoping to hear the sounds of a helicopter. Instead an old VW scrunched along the gravel towards him and pulled up. Jacko and Jennie climbed out, both patched up and looking slightly the worse for wear, Jennie with a large bandage across her nose, but both intent on joining in. Jacko handed the rolled-up ground plans of the cellar over as Flett put them in the picture.

'Could be a ruse, couldn't it?' Jennie asked when she'd been brought up to speed, also suspicious of the timing of Sir James's collapse.

'Don't think so,' shrugged Flett, 'had a close look at him – looks to me like he's about to peg out. Bloody good play acting if he isn't.'

Jacko was looking at the Bentley, wondering why anyone who splashed out that kind of money would leave it out in the open to get covered in leaves and bird shit.

Any further thoughts were interrupted by MacBrayne's voice crackling on Flett's two-way radio, 'General search on both upper floors done, boss – attic rooms at top, mostly empty, just a few bits of junk and a load of cobwebs. Nothing to report on the first floor either, though we've not taken the bath side panels off yet. Floorboards solid everywhere, drawers and wardrobes as you'd expect. We're starting the ground floor now.'

As he spoke the throbbing of a helicopter started to make itself heard flying in from the east, becoming louder until it hovered over the manor, drowning out any conversation in the yard. It circled for a while then settled down on the flattened area of lawn by the swimming pool. Two paramedics dressed in green leapt out while the rotors were still spinning and ran crouching to the house. Flett, ever wary, checked their credentials, directed them in and left them to it. He had no option other than to wait.

Eventually, one of the paramedics emerged. They'd done all they could on a temporary basis, the old chap wasn't really fit to travel but they'd no option and needed to fly him out straight to intensive care. Flett nodded. It was what he'd expected. What he hadn't expected – in fact it hadn't occurred to him – was that the Wainwrights might want to go to the hospital with him. That placed him in a quandary – he didn't want Wainwright out of his sight while the search was ongoing. He knew full well that if he found evidence while Wainwright was off the premises he'd be accused of planting it there. But he had no grounds for keeping him at the manor – he didn't have anything to charge Wainwright with, and it would have looked bad preventing a son being with his dying father.

The paramedics appeared at the door carrying Sir James securely strapped to a stretcher, an oxygen mask around his face with bits of moustache projecting from out of the sides. The two other Wainwrights followed, Charles expressing a mixture of anxiety and anger, his wife following in comely manner wringing her hands as though performing in some Shakespearian drama.

'Can't take you in the chopper, I'm afraid,' one of the paramedics said as Wainwright followed the stretcher across the lawn. 'No room. You'll have to follow by car.'

'We'll take you, sir,' offered Flett immediately, wanting to ensure they were under observation at all times. 'A driver and out-rider will get you there in no time.'

'Nonsense, I'll bloody well drive myself,' Wainwright shouted, then rudely instructed his wife to gather them both some overnight things in a case. The helicopter rotors began to turn slowly. 'Get a bloody move on, woman,' he yelled at her as the engine noise began to build, leaves and dust swirling around the garden in the downdraught.

'No, we'll take you, sir,' Flett insisted once the noise had died down and the helicopter climbed away.

'I'm damned if you will,' Wainwright spat. 'Don't you think you've done enough already?' He caught sight of Jacko by the cars, 'All of you, especially him,' he said, pointing to Jacko.

Flett backed off, having no other option. 'In which case we'll provide you with an escort, sir. A blue light will help, and I can radio ahead to make sure the road's clear.'

'Not necessary,' Wainwright snapped. 'Just get out of my bloody way.' He went inside the house, slamming the door behind him.

Flett walked over to the others. 'He's up to something,' he said, and rang the hospital to make sure there would be an officer present for when Sir James was admitted, then arranged an escort to be put in place from the bottom of the drive, whether Wainwright wanted one or not.

A few minutes later the Wainwrights reappeared carrying armfuls of hastily packed luggage.

'Surely they can't be thinking of making a run for it?' MacBrayne said, looking at the amount of baggage they were hauling down the steps. 'They can't be that stupid?'

Just then Flett's phone rang. He answered it, moving away into a quieter part of the yard, before returning with a sly smile. He stood in Wainwright's path blocking his route to the car.

'Before you depart, sir, I have to tell you some information that I've just received,' he said calmly. 'We now have a positive DNA match between your missing worker Seth Hetherington, the blood in the old stables, the human remains found in domestic rubbish bags which we believe came from here, and the human teeth in the faeces of your dogs,' he gestured towards the kennels. 'Would you like to comment on that, sir?'

'No I bloody well wouldn't,' came the sharp reply. 'Now get out of my way.'

'Well, do bear in mind, sir,' Flett said, moving to one side, 'that I'll be asking you the same question when you get back.' He paused, 'That and other questions, to you both,' and he looked at Mrs Wainwright, who was visibly shaken at the possibility of being interrogated. 'It might be an idea,' he went on in a patronising way, 'if you could give the matter some serious thought.'

Wainwright moved up to him. 'Off the record,' he said in a sneering way into Flett's face, 'I'll give it no thought whatsoever. But what I will give thought to is how to get you demoted, and how I can completely fuck what's left of your miserable career through my friend the chief constable.'

'And off the record, sir,' whispered Flett, 'I think you'll find that the chief constable won't care a shit about you anymore – you're damaged goods now.' He walked back to the house as Wainwright, seething, threw cases and coats into the back seat of the Bentley.

Jennie took some pity on the woman as she struggled to heave a large suitcase into the back while her husband climbed into the driver's seat ignoring her requests for help.

'Here,' she said, 'let me give you a hand. Wouldn't it be easier to put it in the boot?'

'Leave it, it's locked,' Wainwright snapped. Flett turned around instantly, his mind alert. Wainwright got out of the car again, pushed Jennie to one side and threw the case on the back seat. Jennie walked back to Jacko in disgust. 'Arrogant bastard,' she muttered.

'Wait a minute,' Flett shouted across from the steps. 'Has that car been searched yet?'

'No, boss, it's down to be done with the outbuildings,' came the voice of one of the search team.

Wainwright climbed back into the car as Flett walked more quickly towards him, 'I'd like you to open the boot for us, please, sir.'

'No I bloody well won't,' he shouted back, now reddening in the face, his wife a contrastingly white colour in the passenger seat. The electronic window slid shut and they began to fasten their seat belts, followed by the loud 'click' of the internal door locking system.

Jacko looked at the Bentley and a thought struck him. Something wasn't quite right. It was covered in leaves so hadn't been driven for a while. Why leave it outside when there were so many covered places to park it in the courtyard? And why was it parked up facing a corner, meaning it had to be reversed out, when the courtyard was amply wide enough to sweep round in a complete circle? Wainwright switched on the ignition and the engine purred into life. Jacko then remembered, through a half-haze, Toller doing something to the front of the Focus while he and Jennie were trussed up in the back. It was a misty recollection but it fired a warning shot somewhere deep in his sub-conscious. A sense of danger washed over him. He started to move towards the Bentley yelling, 'Don't reverse,' then louder still 'don't reverse. Stop!' Hearing the desperation of Jacko's voice from up by the house Flett turned in horror and Jennie felt herself shiver, but Wainwright, if he'd heard him at all, ignored him and thrust the automatic into reverse. Jacko threw himself at Jennie and they hit the ground together as an explosion blew off the doors and roof of the Bentley. A split second later the petrol tank ignited and a huge ball of fire engulfed what was left. Even at a distance, Flett was bowled over by the blast, the manor windows blew in and for several seconds pieces of metal and fabric rained down into the gravel. Lying on the ground all Jacko could see was the dark silhouette of a metal chassis inside the blaze.

It took several minutes for them all to get to their feet and regroup by the back door. Apart from bruises and shock, none of the search team appeared to have been injured. Two squad cars came screaming up the drive to see what had happened. The fire brigade was called but there was nothing it could do other than prevent the blaze from spreading to the house and outbuildings.

Such was the extent of the debris, the stink of burning flesh and the emotional impact of the blast on the search officers that work in the cellars was put off until the following day. Neither Flett's car nor Jacko's battered VW were ever likely to run again – both looked like they'd been hit by a missile, in fact the manor courtyard had all the appearance of a war zone. They picked up squad cars to get them home, Flett, MacBrayne and Jacko all jammed together in the back of a Volvo Estate with Jennie in the front. It was a silent journey, the end to a tumultuous twenty-four hours. They were all deep in thought, the explosion triggering different mental responses in each: Flett wondering if he was still suited to the job, his mind continually returning to his roots along the western shores of Scotland; Jacko thinking about his relationship with Lucy and the safer realities of sticking to normal archaeology; Jennie, wondering about Jacko and suddenly realising the dangers she'd been placing herself in without thinking, and MacBrayne looking aimlessly out of the window wondering what tomorrow might bring.

The silence was broken by Flett's phone.

'Yes?' There was a pause. 'I see,' he said slowly then, 'thank you.' He switched the phone off and put it back in his jacket pocket.

'Sir James,' he said to the others quietly, 'got to the hospital – pronounced dead on arrival.'

They all fell silent again. No-one felt like saying much, or if they did the words became lost or muddled in other thoughts. Ironic, Jacko mused, that in substantially less than twenty-four hours the Wainwright political dynasty had been humiliated, defrocked and obliterated. Unwittingly, they'd all played a part in it.

CHAPTER 33

It was a sombre team that arrived at the manor the following morning, to be greeted by a scene out of some doomsday scenario. The fire fighters had long since gone, but the courtyard had been cordoned off and Barty Webb's team was standing with Zanbar the pathologist working out how best to approach the debris. Given Wainwright's importance and his dramatic fall from grace as a minister it was breaking news at a national level: satellite vans had been parked up in the road; at the gate TV cameras stood on tripods with their reporters awaiting press statements, and curious onlookers queued up to see if they could catch a glimpse of anything remotely gory. Rumours were rife both locally and nationally as to what had happened, and Flett had prepared a clarification statement for the media that Roberts would present at 11 am. It was hard to reconcile the hubbub and intensity of activity outside with the grim stillness that hung over the courtyard. Few would recognise the pile of black twisted metal lying grotesquely amid scattered pieces of debris as once being a vehicle, never mind a Bentley. Only those who knew what they were looking at could make out the partial torsos of two people blackened and fused to their seats. There was an acrid smell in the air, and an uncanny silence.

* * *

'Dogs first,' Flett ordered as the teams assembled outside the cellars. 'We've copies of Jacko's ground plans for you. It's a bit of a labyrinth in there, use torches and search the place room by room, ticking each one off on the map on completion. Any questions?'

There weren't any, and the teams moved into position using the two outside entrances that Jacko and Alex had inadvertently blundered into, as well as the staircase that led down from the kitchen inside. Jennie and Flett each accompanied one of the teams from the outside, while Jacko and MacBrayne followed the group through the kitchen where they spent some time poking around. There were a few cupboards, a tall fridge-freezer, a dishwasher and an elderly washing machine all lining the wall opposite a huge Raeburn stove. The room looked out through mullioned lattice windows over what was once a vegetable garden.

In one of the cupboards Jacko drew MacBrayne's attention to a collection of well used large aluminium cooking trays and pans – the sort typically found in places where communal cooking took place like youth hostels or schools.

'Suppose it's what you might expect in a big place like this,' MacBrayne pointed out, 'large dinner parties, presumably, catering for a load of people.'

'Doesn't seem to match the crockery much does it?' He pointed to a sideboard on which were neatly stacked expensive dinner plates, Royal Doulton or something similar, with matching sets of bowls, cups and saucers. 'It's like there's two levels of catering, a sort of upstairs, downstairs thing. But they've only got a single housekeeper, haven't they?' MacBrayne shrugged, not really interested in the social nuances of country houses.

'Wonder what's in the fridge?' Jacko mused, turning his attention to the adjacent wall. 'What were the Wainwrights intending to have for dinner last night, I wonder?' He called over to the dog handler whose spaniel duly obliged and, after much resigned sniffing, proclaimed the fridge-freezer safe for opening. The fridge part was on the top and Jacko opened the door to be greeted by a tub of Flora, milk, an open pack of bacon, some eggs, salad-like things in a bowl, some cold meats and two bottles of Chilean Sauvignon Blanc. Hardly a reflection of affluence, he thought. 'Let's see what's in the freezer – probably frozen chips, peas and ice-cream on this performance.' He pulled open the door.

* * *

Down in the cellars Flett and Jennie's team, led by an enthusiastic dog, found themselves in a wide room full of boxes and crates. The dog was unimpressed by the junk and the team equally unimpressed by the vaulted ceiling that had excited Jacko so much previously. The small flight of steps leading into the chamber where the body had been found led off in the dark to the left. Flett told them to stay and ventured down the steps himself, flashing his torch, sensing a light whiff of death as he went. He stopped at the bottom – the room was exactly as Jacko had described it, flanked by slabs at waist height on three sides, some form of pantry probably. But it was empty apart from some sacking on the floor. He went back up to be greeted by a line of expectant faces looking nervous and ghoulish in the torchlight.

'Bugger all,' he said in answer to their unspoken questions. 'Have we got a cadaver dog anywhere?'

The handler gave Jennie the lead of the explosives dog while he went to get the body dog from the van.

'What am I supposed to do with this?' she said.

'Nothing, unless he holds his front right paw off the ground and freezes.'

'What do I do then?' she asked, looking at him suspiciously.

'Run like buggery,' he chuckled, 'he's scented explosives,' and he went back down the passageway.

A few minutes later he returned leading a chocolate Labrador which gave the impression of being either drugged, half asleep or a combination of both.

'Is it alive?' asked Flett sarcastically, watching it drag itself along.

The handler ignored him. 'Come on, Frisky,' he said, 'Good boy, find, find,' and set him off down the steps.

Frisky stood at the top step, stretched, yawned and carefully made his way down, step by step, sniffing each one half-heartedly as he went. Once down, he pottered around the floor systematically working the room from one end to the other as he'd been trained to do, until he came across the sacking. At that point his lumbering apathy turned into demonic frenzy – he tore at the sacking, barking loudly, and tried to dig into it with his front paws, growling between barks and wagging his tail simultaneously. The handler called him off, patted him and gave him a treat.

'What the hell was all that about?' Flett asked.

'That's his response signal, boss. There's been a body there alright.'

* * *

MacBrayne was being sick in the kitchen sink. Jacko was standing aghast, looking at the open freezer door. Inside, resting coyly on one of the wire shelves and staring directly at him, was the head of the bearded man whose body he'd seen on the slab in the cellars, and whom he'd first met in the woodland high above the Pear Tree all that time ago. The exit wound on the forehead glistened with frost and the man's beard had become solid with congealed blood and ice. Jacko felt himself sweating uncomfortably and could only make involuntary gurgling noises to match MacBrayne's gagging in the sink. He kicked the door shut and sat on the floor. MacBrayne poured them water in some glasses he'd found and they slumped next to each other, leaning against the cupboards.

'Oh lord…' MacBrayne gasped, out of breath from heaving into the sink. 'Wasn't expecting that.'

'It's the bloke who was in the cellar,' Jacko told him. 'Wonder where the rest of him is, or whether he went in the cooking pot too?'

At that moment the rest of their team returned from clearing the way ahead with the sniffer dog and were surprised to find them both sitting on the floor together.

'Sorry, gents,' the dog handler joked. 'Not disturbing anything consensual are we?'

'Nah,' MacBrayne said sarcastically, 'just looking for evidence under the table. I've bruised my arm badly. Maybe you could see if there's some ice in the freezer, could you?'

'Sure thing, boss.' He bent down, pulled open the freezer door and let out a scream before shutting it again quickly. 'What the fuck's that?' he squealed. 'Jesus, did you know that was there?'

'It's a human head,' Jacko reassured him. 'And yes, we'd just found it. Let us know if you find the rest of him, will you? It'll be around here somewhere.'

They both pulled themselves to their feet, MacBrayne sealed the freezer with tape, and they moved down the short flight of steps that led into the butler's pantry where Jacko had eavesdropped before. The table was in the same place, and the rug remained neatly over the drain cover. He turned to the sink and pulled out several dirty plates and bowls, all chipped and cracked, quite different from the upmarket crockery in the main kitchen.

'Funny, this. Wonder why the bowls are all down here and the large-scale catering goes on up there?'

'And why is there a lockable door in between?' added MacBrayne.

At that point Flett's group emerged from the maze of cellars at the other end of the room, where Jacko had crept a few nights previously, Jennie still with the explosives dog on a lead.

'All done then,' Flett said with disappointment, 'body's been taken, nothing to show for it all. Bit of a damp squib, unless we've missed something.'

'You've searched all of it?' Jacko asked in surprise.

'Walked every passageway, been through every door,' Jennie answered cheerily. 'See, we've ticked them off on your plan. Nothing there.'

Jacko put Jennie's crumpled ground plan on the table and made them gather round. 'You must have missed something. There's effectively a secure area down here, accessed only by those steps from the locked kitchen and those two doors that lead out into the grounds. Remember, they've been altered so they can only be opened from the outside.' He drew a circle around a set of passages and rooms. 'Don't you see?' Flett gave him one of his impatient looks. Jacko ignored it. 'If you're looking for an area where people can be contained, fed and watered for a short period of time, this is it.' He paused while they started to orientate themselves. 'You cook for them in the main kitchen, serve it up in cheap bowls down in the butler's pantry, where incidentally they're made to wash up afterwards, and they live and sleep somewhere down in the labyrinth between here and the outer doors.'

'Come on Jacko, we've searched all the rooms – there's just nothing there.'

'You can't have done. What about these two rooms on the plan for a start?' He pointed to the plan with his pencil. 'Why haven't they been ticked off then?'

355

The others glanced at each other uncomfortably. 'Well, we didn't come across those,' Jennie admitted. 'We assumed there must have been a mistake with the plan.'

'A mistake with the plan?' Jacko squeaked barely able to get the words out in disbelief. 'A mistake? Give me some professional credibility. I drew this fucking plan for the local authority,' he shouted, 'and I didn't add in rooms just to make it look nice.' He snatched it off the table and strode off into the labyrinth, checking as he went, moving backwards and forwards through the passageways, then came to a halt, frowning. 'Something's not right,' he said, deep down wondering if he'd made a blunder himself. He looked at the plan again then looked at the stonework and followed it from one room to the next. The others followed, more out of politeness than with enthusiasm. Flett hung at the rear, periodically glancing at his watch.

'More torches please,' Jacko said, and the stone walling was lit up as he fingered it, trying to examine the mortar.

'Over here,' he said with some excitement in his voice as he walked round a pile of junk and boxes stacked up against one side. 'Mortar change, different mix in the nineteenth century structures. It's coming back to me now. Behind here,' he said, gesturing to the junk, 'has to be the doorway through to two more chambers.'

'But this crap's only covering the bottom half of the wall,' Jennie said. 'There isn't enough room for a door.'

'There can be if there are steps in a sunken stairwell. Bet that's why all the junk's been stacked here.' He pulled one of the boxes away at the front, then another, followed by a large piece of plywood sheeting and exposed a step leading down towards the wall. 'There we are,' he said, delighted. 'All we've to do is move the rest now.'

Jennie interrupted him. 'Jacko', she said with a note of fear in her voice, 'the dog.'

'What about the dog?' They all looked at it. It was standing frozen still against the junk with one paw raised in the air.

'Shit,' said Flett. 'Where's the handler?'

'Putting the other dog back in the car, boss,' MacBrayne answered, moving slowly away. 'Should be back any minute.'

'Right, let's evacuate the place quietly and carefully,' Flett instructed, his voice not entirely confident. 'Don't touch or move anything on the way out. Let's go.'

Once outside they all breathed a sigh of relief, and they waited in the fresh air on a raised terrace overlooking the rear garden while the explosives people were called in. The OSU team had been brewing up near the burnt out car and brought tea across in plastic cups. Flett's team were sitting together on the cold ironstone steps, mostly in silence, waiting until they could get access to the chambers again, when Zanbar the pathologist appeared from around the corner and sat himself down among them, pouring hot coffee from a flask.

'Morning all,' he said brightly, plopping an artificial sweetener into his flask top. 'Bit of a mess, all this. Your CSI team's a cheery lot though, good to work with. Not like the explosives person – he's a military bod – miserable as sin. Should get through it all by tomorrow at this rate.'

'Anything we should know at this stage?' Flett asked him.

'Nope, don't think so. All pretty straight forward.' He took a long drink from his flask. 'Ah, but there's one thing

I'd like to ask you, though,' he said as he wiped his lips. 'The two victims in the Bentley, did they have any visible peculiarities, perhaps?'

They all looked at each other. 'Not that we noticed,' Flett replied on behalf of them all. 'Anything in particular?'

'Hmm, pity. It's a small detail really,' Zanbar continued in his dead pan voice, 'it's just that so far we've recovered five human legs.' There was stunned silence. Zanbar stood up and screwed the top back on his flask. 'I was wondering if you could apply your combined detection skills in helping me out on this one? Mind you,' he added, 'I've only identified two heads, so that's reassuring, isn't it?'

He was walking off when Jacko called after him, 'By the way, there's a third head in the fridge-freezer in the kitchen – it may help with the arithmetic.'

Zanbar turned, 'Ah thank you, that's most helpful – it starts to make more sense now. I'll get Barty's people to do the usual with it before I take it away.'

Flett and Jennie appeared to be in shock. 'Sorry,' Jacko said quickly. 'Forgot to tell you. It's the head of the bearded spook – the corpse that used to be in the cellars. The rest of him must have been in the boot of the Bentley. I suppose that was why Wainwright didn't want us to open it up.'

* * *

When they eventually received the green light to return to the cellars, the CSIs had moved the junk and exposed a small flight of stone steps leading down to a doorway. Ominously, it was a new door, made of solid oak and heavily padlocked; it survived three attempts with the steel ram before it splintered. MacBrayne pushed aside the broken timbers and, with a small sea of curious faces peering over his shoulder, shone his torch inside. It showed pretty much what Jacko had anticipated – a whole series of low beds or mattresses, maybe fifteen in all, crammed together with little in the way of walkway between. Bedding, such as it was, consisted of old rugs and horse blankets. The place was cold and filthy, with a chilly blast coming through air vents set well above the ground level outside; the floors were damp and the walls dripped. Jacko found a light switch near the door and flicked it on. The place looked no better fully illuminated. They stood in the doorway in horrified silence taking it all in. MacBrayne put tape across the entrance, sealing off the room for Barty's attentions, and they moved outside, regrouping again on the steps in the fresh air.

Flett spent some time on his mobile getting a fuller picture of events from his equivalent in the Met who'd found himself stranded outside 27 Pennsylvania Gardens. It turned out that the van was full of frightened women, and that both the driver and front passenger were of east European origin who immediately claimed diplomatic immunity. By the time the mess had been resolved higher up the food chain, the hubbub had died down, and the spooks were undertaking their own enquiry in harness with staff from immigration. 'Between you and me,' Flett explained when the phone call was over and he joined them sitting on the steps, 'it seems we got most of it pretty much right. The scam that the Wainwrights were into involved importing women illegally. They used the manor not just for food preparation, but as an initial safe house to keep the women secure and hidden once they'd arrived. Then they sold them on to work in the sex trade in London via the Pennsylvania Gardens address. The women were held in the cellar there in much the same way as here. They came in through Newcastle I'm told – seems there was a loophole in the immigration system there. They were smuggled in on cargo ships about ten at a time every few weeks, on the promise of hotel work and a new life, and then traded on to gang-masters. Middle Belford seems to have been a convenient staging post on route to London, courtesy of the Wainwrights. On the Met's calculations the Wainwrights were netting over a million a year from it.'

'But why the hell would they want to risk all their political clout and elevated social status with a shabby venture like that?' Jennie asked. 'It doesn't add up. They don't seem short of a bob or two – just look at the place.' She waved her hand at the manor, the grounds, horses and the charred pieces of the Bentley that littered the lawn.

'It's a familiar story, Jennie. Dunc's been looking at their finances. Bit of a mess, aren't they, Dunc?'

'Certainly are, boss. The Wainwrights have been running a family business making cutlery for years, but not very well, it seems. It's on its last legs, probably due to competition from far eastern imports. The annual accounts show that the company's debts are larger than their assets and what's more, it turns out too that the manor has a second mortgage on it. The Wainwrights have taken out various loans, which now don't look like being repaid either. In a nutshell the family's broke and trying to keep up appearances – fast cars, riding, golf, posh restaurants, usual shite, all on tick.'

'And is that where the Pear Tree fits in?' Jennie asked, 'Using their posh friends to provide the food? The supply chain must have been pretty crucial to the overall operation if they needed to kill the bearded spook for getting wind of it, not to mention booby-trapping Judy and Jacko's food trolley.'

'That's where Toller gets involved,' Flett pointed out. 'There's no doubt that the booby-trapping has to be his initiative – no-one else has the skills – and it puts him firmly in the frame as hatchet man. He had old Seth killed too, according to the vicar. The old boy saw too much or nosed round in the wrong place, probably while he was gardening. I suppose the same applied to the spook with the beard – he just got too close for comfort and gets cut into bits for his troubles, probably by that wizened old housekeeper woman – the Butcher of Belford. Not sure what happened to her. She probably did a runner as soon as her butchery and cooking duties were done. There's no evidence of her here, or in the Pennsylvania Gardens house, and she wasn't one of the nine women that the Met told me were in the van.'

'Nine?' queried Jacko, 'That's odd. There were supposed to be ten when I overheard them.'

Flett shrugged, 'Nine, I checked. Like you I was expecting ten.'

'That reminds me, what about that other, younger woman?' MacBrayne asked thinking back, 'The one we saw with the old bag in the garden at Pennsylvania Gardens. Who's she? Was she part of Wainwright's crew too?'

'She's one of the vicar's adopted twin daughters,' Jacko said, slightly embarrassed. 'I don't know which one though from a distance. In fact, it doesn't really matter which because it looks like both twins were involved, though not as part of Wainwright's outfit. You have to thank the boss for finding all this out. Both twins were recruited by intelligence services. Among other things it explains why they spent time learning east European languages, especially Russian, and why one's based in Newcastle keeping an eye on where the women were smuggled in. The other one must have been placed undercover in London as an assistant for the old housekeeper there. They probably changed places every so often – no-one would ever notice anyway. It also explains why one of them was so keen to talk to me in London, probably to find out first-hand what I knew. And I have a funny feeling that she engineered my hotel room change into one that had been bugged.'

'But what about her old man, the vicar?' Jennie asked. 'Where does he fit in, or doesn't he? I'm a bit confused. He went to college with Toller, and it looks like he made old Tommy redundant from winding the clock. I mean, I don't see how the pieces fit together. He's in custody, but what are you going to charge him with, boss?

'Plenty. We'll do him for blackmail, for conspiracy to murder Tommy, conspiracy to murder Jacko and Jennie here, and for first degree murder.' He stood grinning at them. The Crown Prosecution Service's happy with all of it. They think there's a strong case on each count.'

There was a stunned silence.

'First degree murder?' asked Jennie, not quite understanding what was going on. 'Who is he supposed to have murdered?'

'His wife, Mrs Rogers,' Jacko said.

CHAPTER 34

This time the Rev Rogers was accompanied by his solicitor in the same dismal interview room. Flett sat on the opposite side of the same bare table. Rogers had been told that he'd be charged with conspiracy to murder on the basis of his connection with Toller and his attested involvement, witnessed by Jennie and Jacko, in their attempted murder. Rogers couldn't deny being involved – in fact he had no option – but his solicitor, a smartly dressed thirty-something with a slick suit and greased back hair, was endeavouring to have Rogers' actions ameliorated on the grounds of coercion by Toller. On the charges of blackmail, conspiracy to murder old Tommy and the murder of his wife, Elizabeth Ann Toller – they rejected them out of hand, indeed found them laughable.

Flett sat and stared at them. Rogers, back against the wall, came across as a weak, unlikeable individual, and Flett settled himself down for a long afternoon. He leaned over and switched on the tape recorder with a loud click, then introduced the persons in the room to its dull whirring.

'I'd like to know the whereabouts of your wife Elizabeth Ann Rogers,' asked Flett directly.

'No idea,' Rogers replied dourly, 'we split up about fifteen years ago. I've not seen her since.'

'I'd like to know why you split up.'

Rogers shrugged, 'We just grew apart when we lived in Cheshire. Different interests, I suppose. She liked town life, you know, shops, theatre, dinner parties, things like that. I'm afraid I'm not much of a social animal.' He gave a weak smile. 'Maybe I was too obsessed with the Church and with my ministry. She certainly wasn't interested in anything I did, nor I with her social interests. When I was moved to Middle Belford we decided it would be a suitable time to split. Simple as that. I came up here and brought the girls with me, as you know.'

'Where did she go? Did she stay near Chester?'

'No idea, and to be honest I don't care.'

'Her friends in Chester told us she'd come up here with you,' Flett pushed some papers across the table. 'These are statements from her closest friends in Chester. They've never seen her since, and she's never contacted them. Don't you think that's odd? They certainly do.'

'I can't comment on her relationships. That's between them and her.'

'But no-one up here's ever seen her either. In fact, they all assumed she'd stayed in Chester. So what happened? Did she vanish into thin air?' Rogers remained silent, avoiding eye contact with Flett, 'Did she ever contact you after you split up then?' Letter, email, telephone, anything like that?'

Rogers shook his head

'What about the girls? Didn't she contact them – Christmas, birthdays, things like that? Didn't she want to know how they were getting on at school?'

He shook his head again. 'She may have done. Ask them,' he said bluntly.

'Mr Rogers,' Flett said, giving an impatient sigh. 'You're not doing yourself any favours here. Aren't you at all concerned about her well-being?'

'Look here,' Rogers raised his voice, 'I'm not remotely interested in her well-being. I don't know what happened to her, I don't care what happened to her. Maybe she ran off. She had other interests. If you must know, she wasn't particularly faithful as a wife. She could be anywhere, with anyone – changed her name perhaps, gone abroad. I told you, I don't know and I don't care. I've brought up the girls on my own, and I've done the best I could with them.'

'Just look at it from our point of view,' Flett said slowly, 'and we've done our checks. At roughly the same time as you come up to Middle Belford, your wife disappears off the face of the earth. People in Chester think she's up here, people up here think she's in Chester, so no-one reports her missing. During all the years you've been here, she's not contacted anyone, not even her two adopted daughters. She's never used her passport or cashed her investments, never used the NHS or had a prescription, never borrowed money on credit, never used her store cards, and never had a bank account in her own name. What am I supposed to think?'

At this point Rogers' solicitor leaned across the table and suggested to Flett that this line of questioning had been exhausted. A break perhaps?

* * *

'Let me tell you what I think,' Flett said to him when they'd returned. 'I think you killed your wife up here almost as soon as you arrived. Perhaps you didn't mean to, perhaps an argument got out of hand, but either way you killed her, and you buried her in a concealed part of the vicarage grounds.' He was giving Rogers an escape route. 'What d'you say to that?'

'I am advising my client not to answer that question,' interrupted the solicitor.

'Killed her? That's nonsense,' Rogers snapped, ignoring his brief's advice. 'Buried her? Where could I have done that around the vicarage?' 'In the walled garden would be my bet,' Flett suggested slyly.

'Ha, nonsense!' Was Rogers' immediate retort. 'The archaeologists have ripped it to bits. If she was there, she'd have been found. You're just being ridiculous – they found a Viking cemetery, and some medieval bits and pieces.'

'But they *did* find her, didn't they,' said Flett, pushing Rogers' curiosity further. 'Grave 13, I think it was – a female burial – the last one to have been interred.'

'I don't know what you're trying to do, but this is laughable,' Rogers snapped. 'You've been watching too much television, it's clouded your judgement. You know as well as I do that they were Viking burials with a vicarage nineteenth century garden sitting on top of them. Come on, archaeologists know all about layers and things – ask that Dr Jackson – this is a nonsensical assertion.' He looked for support across to his solicitor, who nodded.

'What do you know about archaeology?' Flett asked bluntly.

'Very little, other than some general material relating to the holy land. It's not something I'm particularly interested in.'

Flett sighed again and sat back in his chair, giving Rogers a tiresome look. 'You're being very silly, Mr Rogers,' he said, and he pushed another piece of paper across the table. 'We're not stupid you know. This is a copy of your degree certificate from Cambridge. According to this, you took a degree in archaeology and anthropology before you took holy orders. So, my assumption is that you know a damn sight more about archaeology than you want me to think. Now why would that be, I wonder?'

The solicitor leant over to Rogers, 'I do think you should refrain from answering more questions until I've been briefed further,' he said, with urgency in his voice.

Rogers ignored him. 'This is ridiculous. What difference would knowing about archaeology make?'

'Well, to an old philistine like me not much, but to someone with Dr Jackson's experience and understanding, quite a lot. I have to take my hat off to you both – you for trying such a bold and ambitious subterfuge, and him for seeing through it. You know, I think you made the wrong enemy there. Shall I tell you what you did, or would you rather tell me yourself first?'

The solicitor suddenly became more assertive, and increasingly irritated, as he saw his client slowly digging a hole for himself. He leaned over to him, 'Mr Rogers, I implore you not to say anything else at this stage. It may detract from your defence. Mr Flett, I insist on having an adjournment to be briefed by my client.'

Rogers pushed his solicitor away. 'You're flying bloody kites,' he shouted at Flett. 'Just trying to trick me.'

'No tricks, Mr Rogers,' Flett said calmly. 'Just facts. The facts are straightforward. When you tried to dig a grave to bury your late wife in the walled garden you didn't expect to come across an old Victorian flagged surface under the topsoil, did you? You realised that if you dug a hole through it, it'd be pretty obvious to the forensic world if they ever came to look for her. So you carefully took up the broken slabs where you wanted to bury her, dug the grave, and then replaced them as carefully as possible afterwards in the same order. Am I warm? What's more, you tried hard to keep any bits of mortar around the flags from falling in the grave – it would have shown that the grave was dug after the flags had been laid, not before. You see, Dr Jackson has trained me in these dark arts.'

Rogers had gone silent and sat staring at Flett's expressionless features. 'Unfortunately for you,' Flett went on, 'Jackson excavated that grave very carefully, made sure it was sieved, and found lots of bits of modern mortar in it, and even bits of flagging that you didn't notice. And what's more,' he said, keeping his eyes on Rogers' rapidly deflating self-confidence, 'the plans of all the layers that the archaeologists made, including the plan of the broken slabs, are a complete give-way. It's even obvious to me – and I know virtually nothing about archaeology – that you dug a hole right through the flags. Nice attempt, I grant you, Mr Rogers, but lamentable application.'

Rogers gave a disgruntled snort, 'You're bluffing. You've no scale drawings, plans or records to show that, have you?' Rogers pointed out with a smirk, 'they were all destroyed in the fire.' He smiled smugly at his brief, who continued to look uncomfortable.

'Unfortunately for you they weren't.' Flett told him calmly. Rogers looked up in genuine astonishment. 'Jackson was already suspicious. He took the plans and records home for safety that night. They'll be used as evidence. And as for the fire, well you knew from your archaeological training that those plans would be the determining proof, so you had the shed torched. Didn't do it yourself of course, that would have been beneath your dignity.' Flett raised his hand to acknowledge the solicitor's imminent objection and called a halt. 'Tea break, I think,' he said cheerily.

* * *

'Mr Flett, my client believes your accusations rely on a combination of circumstantial evidence and vindictiveness,' the solicitor announced as they returned to the interview room.

'We'll let the court decide that one. Anything else your client would like to say?'

Before he could answer, Rogers decided to take the offensive himself. 'You're going to look pretty silly in court,' he said breezily, 'when it's shown that grave 13 had an attested bronze Viking brooch found with the body. Trying to accuse me of a Viking murder, are you?' He grinned at his solicitor, who gave him a half-smile in return.

'I don't think so,' Flett answered confidently, 'You're the one who'll look rather silly. You see Dr Jackson has good friends in the British Museum, in fact one's a leading authority on bronze Viking brooches – bit esoteric for me, but whatever floats your boat, I suppose. He tells us that one just like it was reported stolen from a museum in Cheshire around fifteen years ago. Isn't that a coincidence?' He looked hard at Rogers, whose face had visibly paled at this. 'Of course, all museum objects usually have inventory numbers painted on in small letters, somewhere out of sight for when they're put on display. The number on this one had been carefully erased, well visually anyway, but unfortunately for you it's still visible under ultra-violet light. Again, nice try, Mr Rogers, but poor application.'

'My client,' insisted the solicitor, moving in, 'maintains that this evidence is still wholly circumstantial and that you have no tangible evidence to associate this Viking burial with the body of Mrs Rogers, or any other person for that matter.'

'Good God, what more do you need?' asked Flett sarcastically.

'Dental records are the usual way of supporting identification,' suggested the solicitor. 'My client tells me his wife attended a dentist in Chester, her records will still be there. I'm sure that will clarify this misunderstanding.'

'You know, I thought you might follow that avenue. That's probably why your client pulled all her teeth out after he'd killed her – a bit obvious and a bit amateur really. No, I'm afraid that's not an option anymore.'

'That's a wholly unfounded accusation,' the solicitor said with an air of disbelief in his voice. 'I suggest you release my client as a matter of immediacy,' he demanded, gathering his papers and preparing to leave.

'Sorry, can't do that,' Flett pointed out, 'because of the DNA evidence.'

'But you haven't got any,' Rogers said, looking worried and beginning to sound uncertain. 'She had no relatives, the twins were adopted, so there's nothing to compare the DNA of the body in grave 13 with.'

'Well, sadly for you there is, I'm afraid.' Flett pointed out. 'She left a lock of hair for the twins. Remember? They told us about it. It seems they're more interested in finding out what happened to her than you are. They kept it safe, they'll vouch for its authenticity, and that's what's been used. I can assure you that the body in grave 13 and the lock of hair from your wife belong to the same person.' He paused, looked at the solicitor, then at the subdued figure of the vicar sitting opposite him. 'Yes, you killed her, Mr Rogers, there's no doubt whatsoever about that, and if it wasn't for Dr Jackson working out what little tricks you were up to, you might well have got away with it. Is there anything else you'd like to say before I formally charge you?'

Rogers appeared to begin to sob, elbows on the table, his head in his hands. 'We kept having arguments,' he mumbled, 'one after another. We had one when I'd just taken up the incumbency at Middle Belford.' He stopped to take out a handkerchief and dry his eyes. 'She didn't want to come,' he continued, sniffing, 'she was having another of her affairs. We had a shouting match upstairs in the vicarage there and she slapped me, called me names. I tried not to retaliate. I tried, but it got too much, I went for her and she slipped, fell down the stairs. You have to believe me,' his voice rose, 'in God's name, it was a complete accident. I had a panic attack, didn't know what I was doing, and then I buried her wherever I could, out of shame.'

'This must stop,' the solicitor demanded, 'my client is distraught, he doesn't fully realise what he's saying.'

But Rogers carried on, impervious to advice. 'I've felt guilty ever since,' he said quietly, 'it's come between me and my sleep – I've been taking comfort in my work for God, done my best to make amends.

'You're a liar as well as a murderer, Rogers,' Flett said disdainfully, 'and give me a break on the theatrics. You'd already stolen the Viking brooch by that time, because you'd already planned her death. Now stop pissing me about, stop pretending to be remorseful, and let's hear the rest of it.'

'There's no more,' Rogers wimped, looking up. 'Look, I've told you all there is.'

'As I said earlier, Mr Rogers, we're not stupid.' Flett was getting angry. 'Don't you think it's about time you told us about Tommy Johnson's part in all this? Tell us what happened that night you buried your wife, and where he fits in? Or shall I tell you what I think?'

Rogers said nothing. Flett got up and strode around the room, making Rogers feel nervous. 'There you were,' he said, glaring at the vicar, 'busy digging a hole to bury your murdered wife, or maybe you were filling it in, when old Tommy appears to see the new vicar. No answer at the door so he pops round the back. He wanted to make sure you knew he was the clock winder – that was his life – and he wanted to make contact with his new incumbent, a social call. Bad timing for you really, wasn't it?' Rogers still said nothing. 'How did you explain what you were doing? That you were doing God's will, or something else theologically appropriate? That she was a bad woman? Maybe you even got him to help – he was a bit of a rural simpleton, so you thought you'd get away with it.' He stopped. 'Am I along the right lines, Mr Rogers, or have I missed anything out? Then of course, in time, Tommy started to blackmail you, didn't he? Not the simpleton you thought, maybe? So you paid him off, week by week, in cash. Pretty reluctant to, weren't you? Nothing went through the books. And you'll be pleased to know he used the money sensibly – helped out his friends and neighbours when they needed it, and enjoyed a bit of high living himself at restaurants. But after a while, something happened, didn't it? Did he get greedy and want more money? Did he threaten to spill the beans when the clock was going to be motorised? Whatever it was, you had to get rid of him, and you had to plot a way of doing it.' Flett sat back in his chair and waited. 'Would you like to say anything now, Mr Rogers?'

Rogers looked at his solicitor, 'Don't know what to say,' he whispered quietly, the defiance in his voice gone, 'but I didn't kill him. One death's enough on my conscience.'

'Oh, it's true, you didn't *personally* kill him,' Flett agreed. 'You got Seth Hetherington to do that for you, didn't you?

One octogenarian to kill another – are you proud of that, Mr Rogers?' He paused for a few moments to see if Rogers would respond, but his head had fallen into his hands again in shame. 'There's no point in trying to deny it. Dr Jackson worked out how it was done – quite clever really, I suppose. A bit risky and a bit of luck involved though.'

'I think you're making a big mistake here,' Rogers mumbled, 'it's entirely supposition – there's no way you can implicate me in Tommy Johnson's death.'

'You can hear me out, anyway,' Flett snapped, 'then you can come up with a better story – if you can think of one.'

The solicitor interrupted again, 'I do think we need a tea break so that I can talk to my client in confidence. You've made a number of assertions here that we need to discuss.'

'Fine,' Flett retorted. 'We'll have one in five minutes when I've finished, then you can have your Earl Grey with slice of lemon. I think establishing how an old man was brutally murdered takes priority right now. You can confer as much as you bloody well like afterwards.'

'In that case I advise my client not to say anything,' the solicitor said gruffly. Rogers slumped back into his chair, staring at the table.

Flett went on, 'Stroke of luck really, that the window cleaner's round was roughly on the same day of the week and at the same time as Tommy Johnson wound up the clock, wasn't it? All you had to do was delay the window cleaners at the vicarage – give them tea and engage them in conversation – just long enough for Seth to whip that long ladder off their van and get up on the church roof, do the business, and get back again afterwards. The window cleaners thought it was a bit unusual you kept them talking for so long, but I'm pleased to say they enjoyed Mrs Jefferson's scones. Perhaps you'd like to see their statements?' He waved some sheets of paper in front of him. 'You see, Seth hid in the belfry then slipped down to the clock chamber during the noise of the 5.45 chimes. Do you know we timed them? He had a full twelve seconds – plenty of time. Then he waited quietly, came up behind Tommy Johnson as he peeked over the parapet to see where the weights were, then held him there with one hand, releasing the weights over his head with a long pole specifically used to nudge the ratchet if it got jammed. Jackson showed me how it was done – clever, but risky, I thought. Poor old Tommy struggled, the mineral grains under the nails of his right hand show where he clawed at the wall on that side, and the contusions on the body were from Hetherington, pushing him against the wooden parapet.'

'You have a fine imagination,' Rogers said, looking up defiantly. 'You can't prove any of that.'

'For once, you're absolutely right, I can't,' Flett agreed. 'Both Seth and Tommy are dead, but believe me, there's enough there for a jury to work on. Old Seth made a few blunders too that our friend Jackson spotted – you really shouldn't rely on old men to do jobs like this for you, Mr Rogers. Seth said he left the manor that evening when he heard the clock chime the hour, but oddly enough, as Jackson discovered, you can't hear the clock from the manor. He left earlier than that to make sure he could borrow the ladder and get on the roof in time. And then there's the end date that Seth added to the list of winders on the door of the mechanism – a sort of apologetic epitaph in his own handwriting – then denied doing it. But his biggest mistake was in telling Jackson that he didn't know how to use the pole for un-jamming the clock mechanism. That's what he used to release the weights to kill Tommy, and he was taught how to do it by the engineers from the company that serviced the clock. Again, Dr Jackson sorted that for us,' he pushed two papers across the table, 'These are the statements from the engineers. You see, old Seth, bless him, was lying through his teeth for you, wasn't he? Wonder why?'

'I don't have to listen to any more of this,' Rogers mumbled. 'There's no evidence for anything.'

Flett ignored him and continued to hammer home the points. He was on a high. 'Seth was a useful ally to you, wasn't he? You got him to set fire to the archaeologist's site office when you thought the plans were there, you got him to murder an old man who was blackmailing you, and then, when you realised the bat trust had cameras in the belfry, you had him torch their offices too. Couldn't risk anyone being recorded up there – might have been a bit suspicious? Well you were too late, Jackson had those images safely stored at home. So why did Seth do all that for you? You know, I really think you must have had some hold over the old boy.'

'You're clutching straws,' Rogers argued with a quaking voice. 'Fanciful.'

'No, I don't think so,' Flett retorted. 'My guess would be that it had something to do with the arson attack on the house in Frampton – the one where two people died years ago. We don't know the ins and outs of what went on but we think Seth Hetherington was involved. Perhaps you saw him round there, recognised his description when it was broadcast, and gave him an alibi. Thought it might come in useful as a lever later? Indeed it did. Did he confess to you, pour out his soul for his sins and seek forgiveness while you rubbed your hands knowing you might use him one day? And so, when the time came for you to say "jump" Seth Hetherington had no option, did he? Can't see any other reason why he'd kill his old school friend Tommy. Must have been some hold you had on him.'

'I think we should terminate the interview now,' insisted the solicitor. 'My client and I have many things to discuss.' Rogers nodded slowly in agreement, now staring glumly at the table.

Flett switched off the recorder, stood up smiling and collected his papers. 'Fine by me, sort yourselves out and let me have a statement,' he said, satisfied with the afternoon's work. 'Mr Rogers, you'll be taken back to your cell to enjoy the delights of a custody suite dinner, one of many I think, stretching far off into the future.'

CHAPTER 35

Jacko's contract only had a few days left to run before he could go back to a more normal life in the less exciting but safer world of historic landscapes where explosions, cannibalism and decapitation were replaced by the more seemly practices of field survey, geophysics and trial trenching. But before then there was a public presentation to face – this had been instigated by the chief constable to award the team commendations for their work. Superintendent Roberts said it would be a wonderful boost for public relations, Flett said it would be a pain in the arse, and Jacko was inclined to agree. The only brightness on the horizon during this period of anti-climax was that Lucy was coming to stay. She'd insisted on going to the presentations with him.

* * *

Lucy arrived at Jacko's late and by the time they reached police HQ they only had an hour to spare before the presentation. None of the team wanted to attend, but they'd made the reluctant pact that they'd each go if the others went and had arranged to meet up in the cafeteria. DC Lazenby was the only absentee – he was finally enjoying the delights of paternity leave. The cafeteria was still serving food and Jacko and MacBrayne commandeered a table in a quiet corner, while Lucy and Jennie wandered off to freshen up.

'What's the CC up to then with this presentation, Dunc?' Jacko asked. 'Just a PR exercise?'

'Pretty much. Can't see what else he gets out of it. A mixture of that and giving a public demonstration of what a brilliant leader he is – all crap anyway.'

'Once the vicar gets done, he'll probably call another one just to keep his force in the limelight.'

'Talking about the vicar,' Jacko said, 'I still don't understand how he fits in with all the goings-on at the manor, and with Toller.'

'Don't think we ever will. The boss has a hunch other fish have escaped the net and might make sense of it all, but right now he thinks there were two separate crimes running, one from the vicarage, and one from the manor, and they dovetailed at two points. Weird I grant you, but dear old Seth did the business for the vicar and then got his comeuppance at the hands of mad axe-man Toller for poking his nose in at the manor – that's one connection. The other's that the vicar and Toller were old college chums – coincidence they should end up in the same village though. Maybe Toller knew that Rogers had done his wife in and made him help in trying to get rid of you and Jennie? I don't know. Rogers didn't seem to be a willing partner. I suppose we may find out a bit more once he stands in the dock.'

Jacko shrugged. It wasn't his business any more, his job was done. What's more, any nagging doubts he had were instantly dismissed from his mind as Jennie and Lucy returned from freshening up, both looking unbelievably attractive and demur, and both fully aware of it. Even MacBrayne noticed.

'There's something about scrubbed up women,' he said. 'You both look stunning.' He crouched down on one knee. 'Jennie, will you marry me?' he asked with feigned humility.

The reply was an instant, 'Piss off.'

Lucy came and sat next to Jacko, put her arm round him and gave his ear a quick nibble. 'How do I look, Sherlock?' she asked.

'Bloody terrific,' Jacko said with genuine feeling. 'You make me feel scruffy, I'd better go straighten up.'

Lucy looked at her watch, 'No time. Anyway I'd rather have you scruffy, it makes me look even more glamorous when I'm sitting next to you.'

* * *

The group took their seats near the front of the lecture theatre used for the presentations. Flett was already seated. Jacko sat next to him with Lucy by his side. Jennie squeezed up next to Lucy and the pair of them chatted away as the auditorium began to fill. The TV people had set up lights and cameras and, other than the trial and sentencing of the vicar, this particular ceremony was generally viewed as being the swan song of the whole exercise. Before long the platform party appeared through a side door, conversation died away and everyone stood up.

'Why are we standing up for this lot?' Lucy whispered, 'It offends my egalitarian nature.'

'Mine too,' Jacko replied in a low voice, 'but it's what police do when senior officers come in.'

'Huh,' came the nonplussed response.

Jacko was trying to make out who all these important people in suits were – there were six of them, two clearly more important than the others, one of whom he remembered seeing holding a balloon outside the Pear Tree. He grinned to himself remembering how Judy wished she'd taken a photo of him so she could sell it to the newspapers. He'd hoped she might have joined them for the presentations, but she said she had better things to do. Of the four lesser beings on the stage, one was Superintendent Roberts who was seated at the back of the group as befitted his low status, the others he assumed were ACCs or council members.

'What's Roberts doing up there?' he whispered to Flett.

'Probably been on an "Essential Arse-licking" course.' His voice was louder than intended, heads turned. 'Didn't see him go up on the stage, must have gone up on all fours,' he added more quietly, smirking.

The second important person stood up and introduced himself as Police Commissioner Herbert Longstaff, giving a brief outline on policy, law enforcement strategies in the county and crime statistics – a monologue tinged with more than a little political colouring. It was a 'haven't-I-done-a-lot-and-don't-you-think-it's-time-I-got-a-knighthood' type of speech, ineptly delivered and soporific. He then gave an over-dramatic précis of the investigation and its success, naming all those officers involved, and then Jacko. To the team's disgust he gave pride of place to the 'dedication and hard work of Superintendent Roberts' who could be seen with a sickly smile on his chubby face in the back row. Jacko could hear Flett making obscene guttural noises from the adjacent seat. The commissioner then invited the chief constable to award the commendations and returned to his seat amid tepid applause.

The chief constable took the podium, a tall greying man who oozed authority, and smiled benignly at the assembled masses. 'Thank you, Mr Commissioner,' he said, and continued to shower praise on his subordinates, but his address suddenly became inaudible to those sitting around Jacko, who appeared to be suffering from an apoplectic choking fit. Lucy slapped him hard on the back twice and he regained something approaching his normal breathing. His eyes had watered and the chief constable was a distant blur in the background.

'You alright?' Lucy whispered, concerned. 'Want some water?'

'That's it,' Jacko whispered hoarsely, looking at Flett. 'That's the voice.'

'What voice?'

'The one in the cellar in the manor, the voice of the man I couldn't see when I hid there with Alex, talking to Sir James and the east Europeans. It's him.'

'You sure?'

'Yes,' Jacko croaked, 'thought it was Toller originally, but it's him. I can't receive an award from that man. I'm leaving,' he started to stand up, but Flett tugged him down.

'No, no, go through with it – can't let on we even have an inkling at this stage.'

Jacko's mind was turning cartwheels. 'It explains how they were always one step ahead,' he whispered, 'every bloody step of the way, all that access to communications he has, Roberts innocently telling him everything, access to spook intel – it all fits – he's involved up to his neck.'

'Keep quiet for God's sake, Jacko. For now, go with the flow.'

'What are you two whispering about?' Lucy butted in, 'Can't hear what he's saying.'

They leaned back in their seats while the chief constable droned on. Flett lowered his head across to Jacko, 'It's a waiting game, a long one. Patience, laddie.'

The chief constable concluded his diatribe and invited members of the team to receive their certificates. They went up one by one to the accompaniment of flashlights and applause from the audience. Jacko's turn came. Lucy kissed him on the cheek as he left his seat and climbed the platform. He took his certificate from the chief constable who shook his hand.

'Congratulations, Dr Jackson. Well done,' he said in an educated voice. 'I've heard a great deal about you from Superintendent Roberts, but I don't think we've come across each other before, have we?'

'I think perhaps we may have done,' Jacko said quietly.

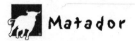

For exclusive discounts on Matador titles,
sign up to our occasional newsletter at
troubador.co.uk/bookshop